"Rea..."
—Kerrelyn Sp..., ...bestselling author of
Sexiest Vampire Alive

Praise for

Real Vampires Don't Wear Size Six

"This is an amazing series! It flies by, and the levels of action, compassion and humor are all well-balanced. Read the entire series, right now!"
—*Fresh Fiction*

"I have said it before and will say it again; this is a great laugh-out-loud series. This series is a keeper."
—*Night Owl Reviews*

Real Vampires Have More to Love

"A book that you can reread again and again. I have been with Glory from the start and can't wait to see what happens next. Each book is like coming home and catching up with old friends. These books are keepers . . . I will keep reading this series as long as Ms. Bartlett keeps them coming."
—*Night Owl Reviews*

"Fans will learn new and interesting tidbits about familiar characters and meet some fascinating new ones, making this addition to Bartlett's vampire series an entertaining read."
—*RT Book Reviews*

Real Vampires Hate Their Thighs

"Laugh-out-loud fun . . . the story that sets up several interesting prospects for future Glory adventures. *Real Vampires Hate Their Thighs* has a reserved spot on my keeper shelf!"
—*Fresh Fiction*

continued . . .

Real Vampires Live Large

"Gerry Bartlett has created a laugh-out-loud book that I couldn't put down. *Real Vampires Live Large* is a winner."
—*The Romance Readers Connection*

"Glory gives girl power a whole new meaning, especially in the undead way. What a fun read!"   —*All About Romance*

"The return of ancient vampiress Glory surviving in a modern world is fun to follow as she struggles with her lover, a wannabe lover, vampire killers and Energy Vampires; all want a piece of her in differing ways. Fans of lighthearted paranormal romps will enjoy Gerry Bartlett's fun tale starring a heroine who has never forgiven Blade for biting her when she was bloated."   —*Midwest Book Review*

Real Vampires Have Curves

"A sharp, sassy, sexy read. Gerry Bartlett creates a vampire to die for in this sizzling new series."
—Kimberly Raye, *USA Today* bestselling author of *Sucker for Love*

"Hot and hilarious. Glory is Everywoman with fangs."
—Nina Bangs, *USA Today* bestselling author of *Wicked Edge*

"Full-figured vampire Glory bursts from the page in this lively, fun and engaging spin on the vampire mythology."
—Julie Kenner, *USA Today* bestselling author of *Aphrodite's Kiss*

"Hilariously delightful . . . Ms. Bartlett has a winner."
—*Fresh Fiction*

"Nina Bangs, Katie MacAlister, MaryJanice Davidson and Lynsay Sands, make room for the newest member of the vamp sisterhood, because Gerry Bartlett has arrived."
—ParaNormal Romance.org

Titles by Gerry Bartlett

REAL VAMPIRES HAVE CURVES
REAL VAMPIRES LIVE LARGE
REAL VAMPIRES GET LUCKY
REAL VAMPIRES DON'T DIET
REAL VAMPIRES HATE THEIR THIGHS
REAL VAMPIRES HAVE MORE TO LOVE
REAL VAMPIRES DON'T WEAR SIZE SIX
REAL VAMPIRES HATE SKINNY JEANS

Real Vampires Hate Skinny Jeans

GERRY BARTLETT

BERKLEY BOOKS, NEW YORK

THE BERKLEY PUBLISHING GROUP
Published by the Penguin Group
Penguin Group (USA) Inc.
375 Hudson Street, New York, New York 10014, USA
Penguin Group (Canada), 90 Eglinton Avenue East, Suite 700, Toronto, Ontario M4P 2Y3, Canada
(a division of Pearson Penguin Canada Inc.) • Penguin Books Ltd., 80 Strand, London WC2R 0RL,
England • Penguin Group Ireland, 25 St. Stephen's Green, Dublin 2, Ireland (a division of Penguin
Books Ltd.) • Penguin Group (Australia), 250 Camberwell Road, Camberwell, Victoria 3124, Australia
(a division of Pearson Australia Group Pty. Ltd.) • Penguin Books India Pvt. Ltd., 11 Community
Centre, Panchsheel Park, New Delhi—110 017, India • Penguin Group (NZ), 67 Apollo Drive,
Rosedale, Auckland 0632, New Zealand (a division of Pearson New Zealand Ltd.) • Penguin Books
(South Africa) (Pty.) Ltd., 24 Sturdee Avenue, Rosebank, Johannesburg 2196, South Africa

Penguin Books Ltd., Registered Offices: 80 Strand, London WC2R 0RL, England

This is an original publication of The Berkley Publishing Group.

PUBLISHING HISTORY
Berkley trade paperback edition / April 2012

Library of Congress Cataloging-in-Publication Data

Bartlett, Gerry.
Real vampires hate skinny jeans / Gerry Bartlett.
p.   cm.
ISBN 978-0-425-24562-0 (pbk.)
1. Saint Clair, Glory (Fictitious character)—Fiction.   2. Vampires—Fiction.   I. Title.
PS3602.A83945R427   2012
813'.6—dc23
2011045196

PRINTED IN THE UNITED STATES OF AMERICA

10   9   8   7   6   5   4   3   2   1

ALWAYS LEARNING   PEARSON

To all of my fans,
especially my street team members,
who are always willing to spread the good word.
Thanks so much!

Acknowledgments

This book is possible because of the many people who support me. I had a very tough year with the loss of my mother to cancer. As always, my critique partners, Nina Bangs and Donna Maloy, were by my side. My great agent, Kimberly Whalen, was my first reader and steered this book down the right path. And, of course, I am grateful to the fantastic team at Berkley, headed by my editor, Kate Seaver, who has remarkable patience. I also have a copy editor with an eagle eye and an art department that always gets the cover just right. Thanks to them, Glory and her pals get to you in good order and on time despite my best efforts to make it otherwise. All of you help make this series one of the favorite things I've ever done.

One

"*Knock. Knock.*"

"Who's there?" I said it without thinking, then realized there was someone inside my head, playing the old joke on me. I jumped up just as the dead bolts flipped and the door to my apartment crashed open.

"Your favorite nightmare, Glory St. Clair." Alesa, a demon who could look gorgeous when she wasn't showing her true nature, leaned against the doorjamb, a grin on her hellish face. Tonight she wasn't bothering to hide a thing and I shuddered.

"You're not my favorite anything. Go back to hell, where you belong." I frantically glanced around for a weapon. I was at a serious disadvantage with wet polish on my toenails and a deep conditioner on my hair under a towel turban.

"I wouldn't toss that polish remover if I were you. It won't hurt me and it'll do a real number on your hardwood floor." Alesa sauntered into the room, morphing into her human form, which was a huge relief. Not that it meant she'd *act* human, but at least I didn't have to stare at razor-sharp fangs or scaly snout and skin anymore. Total freak-out.

"What do you want?" I grabbed a nail file with a sharp

pointy end. At least I could make her bleed. Oh, wait. Demon blood, black and oily. Infectious. Not a good idea. I'd learned that the hard way.

"That's right, sugar plum. Don't want to get my blood in you again, do you?" She smiled, reminding me that she could read my thoughts without breaking a sweat. She was still sporting those evil teeth. "Last time I got inside you, we did some serious partying." She glanced down and patted her tummy. "Guess what? I got what I wanted out of it."

I gawked. Oh, no. It couldn't be. "Is that what I think it is? Say it isn't—"

"A baby bump?" Alesa came closer and I could smell her sickeningly sweet scent, the burned sugar candy smell of hell gone terribly wrong. "Oh, yes. When you and Rafe made it, Gloriana, you *made* it, if you get my drift."

"No, that's impossible. I'm a vampire. I can't have children. My equipment died when I died. When Jerry turned me." I sank down on the couch, my hand over my own stomach. It had been one of those unforeseen consequences I hadn't thought through at the time. I'd been young and so hopelessly in love with Jeremiah Campbell back in 1604 I hadn't cared what I'd lose as long as I could live forever with him. Only later, when the lust had burned off a little had I realized my hope for children had disappeared along with my mortality. Tears blurred the room.

"Aw, dry up, kiddo. This is great news. In a way, this baby is part yours, you know. You were my hostess with the mostess while I got Rafe to give me what I wanted. I told him when I arrived here in Austin that I wanted his baby." Alesa sank down on the couch next to me and I gagged at the smell this close. "And I got it." She looked at me critically. "Quit breathing, dumbass. Vamps don't have to inhale, you know. Geez, who has morning sickness here, anyway?"

"Sorry, I guess it was just . . ." I took a last shuddery breath. What was Rafe going to do? He hated Alesa and sure didn't want a child by her. A demon child. Sure, he had some demon blood, but he didn't want to perpetuate that. "I've got to call Rafe."

"Sure you do. Call the man and give him the good news." Alesa leaned back and rubbed her swollen stomach again. "Get him to bring in some food. I know better than to expect you to have anything here. Burgers, fries"—she glanced down—"chocolate milk shakes for the little nipper."

I began doing some mental calculations. It had been a tense spring, but a peaceful summer since I'd rid myself of Alesa. That bump was significant. "How far along are you?"

"Do the math, Glory. Six months. And I'm planning to stay right here until the little demon pops out. Won't that be fun? We can be roomies." She looked around, spotting my current roommate's computer on the kitchen table. "You are living alone, aren't you?"

"No, I'm not. This won't work, Alesa. I have a fledgling vampire living here with me. And I really don't want her around you. She's already met two of your cohorts from hell. That was two too many." I grabbed my cell phone. I did need to call Rafe but I dreaded it. He was doing well with his new club. We'd settled into a nice friendship, though it was still a bit tense since I'd gone back to Jerry, my sire, my always lover. Oh, God, what would Jerry think of this situation? Nothing like reminding him that I'd slept with Rafe while Alesa possessed me.

I stopped with the phone in my hand and gave Alesa a narrow-eyed look. "Are you sure that's how you got pregnant? While you were inside me? That really doesn't make sense."

"Sense? What world are you living in, vampire?" Alesa put her feet on my beautiful black lacquered coffee table. Nobody put their feet on that, especially not while wearing high heels, even if they were this season's Prada.

I stalked over and lifted them off and pushed them over to my tired thrift store sofa. I had a few pieces of nice, new furniture, courtesy of a fight Jerry and Rafe had had in my living room. They'd replaced the stuff they'd demolished and I was trying to keep the quality pieces in good shape. The sofa? I was saving up for a new one. Prada was actually an upgrade.

"Look. I'm not buying your story. I think you got yourself knocked up by someone else. Either after you left Austin or before you got here. Now head out. Take your tale to the real daddy. Or let Lucifer take care of you."

Her lips trembled and her eyes filled with dark tears. "Lucifer? Are you kidding me? He won't help. He's furious with me. Because I came back to hell pregnant. He didn't want me to ruin my figure. Doesn't want brats running around down there either. It's an adult playground, he says. Babies spoil the mood." She wiped her wet cheeks. "Bastard. He could care less about *my* needs."

"Yes, well, he's the Devil, Alesa. What do you expect?" I almost felt sorry for her. Except she was such an evil person herself. What kind of mother would she be? And what kind of mother would want to bring up a child in hell anyway? I shuddered. "Who's the real father, Alesa?"

"I told you, it's Rafael. I'm thrilled. He'll be a wonderful father." She sighed and leaned back on throw pillows. "This is a miracle. A dream come true."

"No, it's not. But I'm calling him anyway. He can help me get the truth out of you." I hit speed dial for him. When he answered, I was suddenly speechless.

"Glory? What's up?" His voice was calm and I could hear music in the background. I glanced at the clock. It was still early and the club wouldn't be too busy yet.

"Can you come over, Rafe? I have sort of an emergency here." I turned my back on Alesa's grin. Oh, but she was loving this, that she'd get Rafe involved with her again and that I was the one putting them together.

"Food," she whispered.

"Sure. Can you give me a hint? What kind of emergency? Life and death? Or just one of your mini-crises. If it's one of those, call Blade." Rafe was all business. Which was the way he'd been treating me lately. It broke my heart.

"Work with me, please. This isn't something Blade can help with. I need you. I have company. Someone who wants to see you. Could you stop and pick up a sack of burgers and fries on your way? Oh, and a chocolate shake?" I was getting mental messages for dessert but ignored them. The baby was probably already going to be born reeking of sugar. Who knew what pouring more inside it would do. Bad enough that it had Alesa for its mother.

"You sure you didn't take one of those drugs again? That lets you eat? You remember what happened last time."

"No, I learned my lesson." I put my hand on my tummy that could have passed for a minor baby bump itself. "Please hurry. This is someone you need to see."

"From the amount of food, sounds like you have more than one person there." The noise around Rafe stopped, so he must have stepped into his office. "You okay?"

"For now, but I'll feel better when you get here. See you soon?" I gripped the phone tightly, wishing we were back to our old easy friendship.

"On my way." He ended the call.

I turned to Alesa. "I swear." I cleared my throat. "I swear that if you hurt my friend I will make sure there aren't enough pieces of you left to go back to hell for Lucifer to fry. Are we clear?"

"Wow, Glory, get radical, why don't you?" Alesa widened her eyes. "And, remember, I'm going to be a mommy. Think of my baby."

"I am. The biggest favor I could do that child is to make sure he or she never sets eyes on you." I stomped into the kitchen and plucked a bottle of supercharged synthetic blood out of the refrigerator. I twisted off the top and took a gulp. It wasn't as good as fresh, but took the edge off. Then I hit speed dial and called my fledgling.

"Penny, are you working all night?" I'd seen her off to her job at a lab just an hour before Alesa had arrived.

"Supposed to. Though Ian's talking about letting me off early. Trey and I may hook up later."

"Great. Can you stay with him? I've got some company. An old, uh, friend." I hated calling Alesa that, but didn't want Penny to worry. My fledgling had a relationship with Trey, the shifter who worked for Rafe at his club, and had been spending a lot of time with him lately. I wasn't going to feel guilty now suggesting she stay with him for her death sleep. She'd done it before and was basically an adult. We'd recently celebrated her twentieth birthday.

"No problem. You sound funny. You sure you're okay?"

I sighed. Penny Patterson is a genius. No kidding. A prodigy with a doctorate and a bunch of other degrees at her young age. Of course she'd picked up on my stress.

"Not okay, but Rafe is on his way over to help me with this person who isn't actually a friend. We'll manage but thanks for asking. Just stick with Trey so I don't have to worry about you too, okay? I don't want you to meet this character. We have a bad history." So much for not worrying Penny. But I really didn't want her popping in, not even for a change of clothes. "Seriously, don't drop by. I mean it."

"Whatever you want, Glory." Penny sighed. "But I could help, you know. Don't underestimate me in a fight. Ian's been working with me. He's got some amazing weapons here."

"I just bet he does. Thanks, but not this time." I hung up. Penny worked for Ian MacDonald. The vampire was another genius and had probably come up with some stuff I could use against a demon. But a pregnant one? That had to give me pause.

"Glory, you know I can read your thoughts and hear your conversations, don't you?" Alesa stood in the doorway. "Come back to the living room and tell me what you've been up to lately. Who is this Penny?"

"Like I'd confide in you? Forget Penny. Sit on the sofa and wait for your food." I finished my synthetic and rinsed out the bottle for the recycle bin. Good thing I didn't need to inhale, because the sweet stench of hell would have put me off my drink completely. When I heard the knock on the door, I realized I still had a turban on my head and no makeup. Swell. The only upside of this is that Alesa's news was bound to take my looks completely off Rafe's radar. At least my jeans were clean and hugged my butt and my T-shirt was a flattering red color.

I walked to the door, aware of Alesa's eyes following me. She had a smirk on her face that made me want to slap her. My stomach knotted as I threw the dead bolts.

"I could smell demon from the bottom of the stairs, Gloriana. What the hell is going on here?" Jeremy Blade, my lover and my maker, strode into the room. He stopped at the foot of the couch and stared at Alesa, who stretched as if to show off her plump breasts in her low-cut violet sweater. He didn't seem to notice, busy pulling one of his knives out of his boot.

"Jerry, stop. You know you can't kill a demon with a knife." I put my hand on his arm. I wasn't sure what it took to kill a demon. Everything we'd tried had failed. They seemed indestructible. The most you could hope to do in a fight was to send them back to hell and it took a priest or other type of holy man and some other powerful stuff for that.

"Maybe not, but I could enjoy trying." Jerry wasn't about to put his knife away. "What's this bitch doing here?"

"Causing trouble, what else?" I pulled Jerry toward the kitchen. "Alesa, don't say a word. Please. Let me handle this." I gave her a look that she actually heeded. She just sat back with a smile and a wave.

"Handle what? Me?" Jerry looked down at my hand on his arm. "I thought we were finally done with demons."

"So did I." I sighed and leaned against him once I had him in the kitchen. Jerry and I had been through some really rough times. He'd managed to forgive me for betraying him with Rafe, who was part demon. I'd blamed my infidelity on Alesa being inside me. Demon tricks. Then other demons had come back and made more mischief in our lives. Through it all, Jerry had been there for me.

I held on to him. He'd positively hate this latest development, but he'd see it as nothing to do with us. Rafe had a problem, end of story. I was going to have a fight on my hands if I wanted to help see my friend through this. And I was determined to do just that.

"She's pregnant, Jer." I looked up when I said this. To gauge Jerry's reaction.

"The hell you say." He slid his knife back into his boot. "Why'd she show up here?"

"She claims it's Rafe's child. Made while she was inside me."

"That's a cock-and-bull story if I ever heard one." Jerry shook his head. "She wasn't corporeal. And you . . ." He hugged me. "Sorry, lass, but you've got to know you can't conceive a child."

"I know that. I said the same thing to her. But here she is, stomach swollen, claiming Lucifer kicked her out for being pregnant and saying it's Rafe's." I pushed back. "He's on his way."

"Let them hash this out, demon to demon." Jerry watched me with narrowed eyes.

"You know I can't do that." I sighed. Now it started. Jerry would never understand the depth of my attachment to Rafe, the man who had guarded me for five long years. He'd risked his life for me and shared secrets that I'd told no one else. I loved Rafe. Just as I loved Jerry. Well, maybe not just as. Jerry and I had a long and turbulent history, four hundred years' worth. Rafe and I were friends, briefly lovers and equals in a way Jer and I could never be.

"You *could* leave them to it, but you won't." Jerry turned to stare into the living room. "I see no way for this to be resolved without you getting hurt." He faced me again and shook his head. "Demons play dirty, you know that. Alesa will make sure you have naught to do with Rafael if she wants him for her babe's father."

"You're right. Yet here she is. At my home, asking for my help." I bit my lip. Was I being set up? Alesa hated me. I'd humiliated her in her world, keeping her trapped in my body far longer than most hosts would have managed, according to the other demons I'd met. And Lucifer wasn't crazy about me either. Had he sent her here to get even with me? I'd managed to best him the last time we'd met. I knew he'd been pissed off about that. And when you pissed off the Devil . . .

"Tell her to leave. To take her brat and deal with Valdez elsewhere." Jerry grabbed my shoulders. "It's the only way you'll be safe."

We both turned at the knock on the door. I really needed to breathe. I'd missed the smell warning of Jerry's arrival and now Rafe had managed to sneak up on me.

"Well, he's here now. Let's see how this plays out." I touched Jerry's cheek. "No matter what, please don't pull out a knife again. That will only make things worse."

"You've got two demons in your home and another one on the way. How could things get worse, Gloriana?" Jerry strode toward the door.

He just had to ask, didn't he?

Two

"What the hell is a demon doing here?" Rafe asked as soon as I got the door open.

"That's exactly what I said." Jerry grabbed the sacks of fast food and took them into the living room. "I can guess who these are for. Don't breathe, Gloriana, you know this food is torturing you."

"Tell me about it." I followed him, helpless as I inhaled salt and fat anyway. I couldn't keep back a moan. "I swear I would kill for a french fry."

"I'm not sharing, even if you could eat real food." Alesa smirked. "I'm starved."

"You're lucky anyone bothered to get that for you, demon. Glory never should have let you in the door." Jerry dropped the sacks on my coffee table.

"I didn't tell Rafe who it was for. And I had to let her in. She threatened me and I know she can follow through, Jerry." I snatched the large chocolate shake from Rafe to get a whiff of chocolate and ice cream. Too bad someone who didn't deserve it was getting this pleasure.

"I don't believe it." Rafe had just spotted Alesa, who still lay stretched out on the sofa. "Call a priest."

"Believe it, lover boy. And you won't want a priest once you see the gift I brought you." Alesa patted her tummy. Demon magic. She now wore a pink maternity top with silver letters and an arrow that said "Baby," in case there was any confusion about why her stomach was the size of a soccer ball.

Rafe looked at me, then Blade. "Are you kidding me?"

"No, I'm not." Alesa got to her feet, suddenly flashing red eyes and fangs. "I'm pregnant, Rafael. With your child. You're going to be a daddy. Deal with it."

"No, hell no. You're lying." Rafe put up his hands and backed away from her. "I never slept with you. Not in hundreds of years anyway. We've had this conversation. You couldn't pay me to fuck you this century, demon, and that's a fact."

Alesa's eyes brimmed with tears. "No reason to be mean about it. And get a clue. You did sleep with me. When I was inside Glory here. You two went at it like sex-starved teenagers. See it all the time down there in hell. It's one of Lucifer's favorite shows—*Nymphos Gone Wild*." Alesa rolled her eyes. "Quantity not quality, if you ask me. But no one ever does." She glanced at Jerry and back to Rafe. Both men looked ready to blow.

"Shut up, Alesa." I didn't have to read Jerry's mind to know she'd painted a picture for him that I'd never be able to erase with words. In moments she'd undone months of work to get our relationship back on track. I itched to strangle her until she couldn't wheeze out one more incriminating word. But among her nasty powers was the ability to freeze me where I stood. Her gaze flicked over me and a jolt of her power hit me like a lash.

"What Glory and I did had absolutely nothing to do with you, demon. And the idea that you somehow witnessed our lovemaking sickens me." Rafe just had to say that. I didn't dare look at Jerry.

Alesa smirked at me. "Sorry. Lovemaking. Guess bunnies in heat call it that too." She poked Rafe in the middle of his black and red N-V T-shirt. "And your swimmers obviously still have what it takes to make a baby." She waved a hand down to her stomach. "Exhibit A."

"Shit. I don't have to listen to this." Jerry headed for the door.

"Jerry, wait." I grabbed his arm. "You knew what happened. Alesa's exaggerating. It wasn't like that."

"Spare me the excuses, Gloriana. I don't want to hear them." Jerry looked down to where I held his arm. His muscles flexed under his short-sleeve shirt. I could see them tighten in his jaw too. He avoided looking at Rafe. That was progress. In the past, he'd have lunged for my friend and pounded him again for what we'd done. Thank God he'd never lay a finger on a woman, but I could see in his eyes that he wanted to flatten Alesa for reminding him.

"Jerry, please. You know I love *you*. I thought we'd gotten past this." I tried to pull him into the kitchen for a little privacy. He let me take him as far as the dining area.

"Unless you're going to tell Valdez to take this elsewhere, we're obviously not past this. Am I wrong?" Jerry looked me in the eyes, daring me to tell Rafe to take his demon and go somewhere, anywhere but here, to thrash this out.

"I can't just turn my back on this. I was there, involved. Can't you see that?" I let go of his arm. Honestly, I was the one who'd made love with Rafe. If that somehow got him tied to Alesa, didn't that make me an accomplice or something?

"Gloriana, obviously the demon manipulated things. Is still determined to manipulate all of us. Don't let her." Jerry put his hand on my chin and made me look at him again. "I'm calm now. I'm here for you. Actually feeling sorry for the poor bastard." He jerked his head toward Rafe.

I heard a grumble from Rafe in the living room.

"Thanks, Jerry." I smiled with relief to hear him being so sensible. Before he'd made me look into his eyes, I'd been staring at his chest, at the white cotton shirt that was unbuttoned just enough to make me want to finish the job. I doubt if he'd done that deliberately, Jerry didn't think that way. But it worked just the same. He looked sexy to me, always had. But that wasn't why I was determined to salvage our relationship.

"It's Valdez's problem, not yours." Jerry pulled me close. "Stay out of it."

"Give me a few minutes to think. This was big news." I felt Alesa and Rafe waiting and tugged Jerry back into the living room. Rafe clearly wanted me to let Jerry take off. Alesa wanted Rafe to herself. I wasn't about to go with either of those options.

"Think about *this*. It sounds like from what I heard just now that you were a victim. That when Alesa possessed you it was part of the demon's plan to use Valdez as a sperm donor. Everything is clear to me now. Obviously you never really wanted Valdez; the demon worked her wiles to attract you to him. So she could have his baby." Jerry grabbed onto this theory like a life raft that could save our relationship. And it was tempting to go with it. But not the truth. I knew the attraction had been alive and well without Alesa along for the ride.

Rafe had a wry look on his face when I glanced at him. "You going to say you never wanted me, Glory? Go ahead. Let Blade finally feel less threatened by the shifter he hired as your bodyguard."

"Threatened? By God, the day a shifter makes me shake in my boots is the day I walk into the sun." Jerry's look was pure Highland arrogance.

"Settle down, both of you." I sighed. "Look, I can't lie about it, even if it would make my life much less complicated." I rested my hand on Jerry's sleeve. "I'm sorry, but I was drawn to Rafe long before Alesa came on the scene. I hate to hurt you like this, Jerry, but that's the God's honest truth. Yes, Rafe and I are friends, but there were sparks between us, chemistry, that Alesa had nothing to do with." It felt good to get that off my chest. Stupid maybe, but good. Jerry could usually see through my lies anyway.

"Chemistry? Well, you can just forget scratching that itch, Glory St. Clair. Rafe is off limits now. He's mine." Alesa growled and pushed into our circle, resting a claw on Rafe's shoulder. "We're starting a family."

Rafe was on the other side of the room before any of us could blink. "Yours?" He couldn't have looked more disgusted. "I don't know what kind of kinky scenario you've worked up in your warped brain, but I'm not and never will be yours, Alesa. Get it?" He shook his head. "Damn, I'm sorry, Glory. Blade's right about one thing. I need to get her out of here. You don't deserve to have her polluting your atmosphere."

"And do what with her, Rafe?" I stayed out of claw range. "Alesa, have some pride. He doesn't want you. Give it up, girl. Take this mythical baby bump and peddle your story somewhere else. You have to know we're not buying it."

Alesa's eyes filled with tears that oozed, dark and slimy, down her face. "It's not mythical. This baby's real. And I have nowhere else to go. Rafael *is* the father." She glared at him where he stood rigid against the door out to the hall. "Obviously he plans to be a deadbeat dad. No surprise there. Demons are notorious. What was I thinking?" She sniffed and wiped her nose on the back of her hand. "Maybe I should go to your grandfather, Rafael. What will he say when I lay this story on him?"

"You leave my family out of this." Rafe shoved away from the door. He looked as scary as I'd ever seen him.

"Calm down, Rafe. I think we need more information." I jumped between them. I didn't like the idea of a fight with a pregnant woman involved no matter how I despised her.

"She's right. Demon or not, you need to step up if the babe is yours." Jerry stared at Alesa's stomach. "Though I can't credit how it could be possible."

"Exactly. It's a damned fairy tale." Rafe hit his leg with his fist.

"Think what you like. Food's getting cold." Alesa huffed and pulled open a sack to unwrap one of the hamburgers.

"I'm starved and all this drama's not good for the baby. Sit down, everyone. I need to eat. I'm getting woozy."

I looked from Jerry to Rafe. To my surprise, they both seemed inclined to follow Alesa's suggestion. They each took a chair, staring hard at the demon as she wolfed down two burgers and a large order of fries. By the time she slurped down her chocolate shake, I was ready to scream.

"I don't believe a word you've said since you walked in that door." I'd pulled Penny's computer chair over to the living room while Alesa ate. Now when I jumped up it rolled back until it slammed against a bookshelf. I stomped over to stand next to the couch.

"Tough. I'm telling the truth. Deal with it." Alesa licked chocolate off her lips.

I reached down and jerked up her shirt. Well damn. Her stomach really was swollen, looking like pictures of pregnant women I'd seen in magazines, the ones who'd worn bikinis to proudly show off their tummies.

"Satisfied?" Alesa grinned and pulled down her stretchy maternity pants so we could see her stomach all the way to the edge of her tiny panties and her Brazilian wax job. "Little Rafael here is growing every day. Kicking and everything. I've been reading up on it. He's right on schedule."

Little Rafael. I might throw up. No way had this really happened. I shook my head and must have looked as bad as I felt because Blade was suddenly on one side of me and Rafe on the other, both of them carefully easing me toward my bedroom.

"Get a cool cloth for her face. I think she's going to pass out," Rafe ordered.

"You get it. I'm taking off her shoes and unsnapping her jeans. She always wears them too tight. And what the hell is this on her head?" Jerry reached for my turban.

"She's conditioning her hair. Does it about twice a year. Don't mess with it." Rafe obviously had gone for the washcloth because the next thing I knew I was on the bed, shoes off, pants unzipped and something wet on my face.

"Are you all right, sweetheart?" Jerry held my hand.

"Did I pass out?" I blinked up at him after I pulled off the washcloth.

"Yes, you did." Rafe stood right behind Jerry. "Alesa's still on your sofa. I'll get her out of here if I have to carry her. I figure this is my mess, I'll deal with it."

"Glad to hear it. When she originally came to Austin to find you, she was spouting nonsense about an anniversary. That's how she got inside Gloriana in the first place. This all started with you and an ill-advised alliance with the demon." Jerry squeezed my hand.

"I know. I married her when I was young and stupid. Got the thing annulled as fast as I could." Rafe glanced toward the living room. "Alesa's just stubborn enough to refuse to accept that. But she'll have to accept that Glory's no part of this latest scam of hers. Somehow I'll make this go away."

"Excellent." Jerry nodded. "You have to admit Valdez is doing the right thing, Gloriana."

"Rafe, you know you can't just send her away, not without the truth. If it could be your child . . . Well, scam or not, I'm helping you sort this out." I held my other hand out to Rafe. "What we need is a DNA test. Call Ian MacDonald. He should know if there's a way to do it before the baby's born."

"Great idea. I'll get on it." Rafe took my hand and kissed my palm, ignoring Jerry's growl. "You really don't have to be involved, Glory. For now, I'll put Alesa up in a hotel. Don't worry about her. How much longer has she got?"

"She says three more months. If demons take the usual nine like humans do." I sighed. That sounded like an eternity.

"Yes, they do." Rafe frowned. "She's sure not staying with you and Penny, I don't care what she says."

"Thanks." I closed my eyes. Fainting wasn't my thing, but it had come in handy this time. The guys were at least moving forward together. Well, not together, but Rafe was getting Alesa out of the apartment—I knew the exact moment when the hall door closed behind them both—and that made Jerry happy. Now I just hoped that a DNA test would prove her claim was a ridiculous lie. Had to be. How could she conceive in my dead womb? Didn't make sense.

"She and Valdez are gone. Now quit playing possum and open your eyes, Gloriana. Talk to me about this chemistry between you and the shifter."

My eyes popped open. "Over. Done with. An experiment that failed. We decided we're better as just friends, nothing more." I sat up and touched his cheek. "Did you feel that? The zing we get every time we touch? Now *that's* chemistry." I pulled his head down to mine. "Kiss me. Remind me why I keep coming back to you century after century."

"Could it be you just like my . . . broadsword?" Jerry chuckled as he jerked the towel off my head. "Valdez was right. I shouldn't have disturbed your 'conditioning.' Do you need to jump in the shower and wash this mess off?"

I smiled against his mouth as I kissed him. Oh, but I loved the taste of him. "Yes, I believe I do. Why don't you join me? We can play conquering the castle. You can use your . . . sword." I gasped as he pulled me up and into his arms to carry me to the bathroom. I had learned over the years how to distract Jerry when I needed to. Of course he was still smarting from Alesa's vivid reminder that Rafe and I had had hot monkey sex six months ago. So I'd show Jerry the best way I knew how that I still loved my sire and that my time with Rafe was ancient history, hadn't changed a thing in my relationship with Jerry.

But something I couldn't quite put my finger on *had* changed. Yes, I loved Jerry, but I realized I'd become more critical when we were together. Not of his lovemaking. Are you kidding? Jerry could please me in ways no other man ever could.

But try as he might to move with the times, Jerry's attitudes still had that eau de ancient male that could drive me crazy. Which was ridiculous. Rafe was even more ancient, according to a calendar. So why . . . ? Maybe it was because Rafe hadn't known me back in the day. He'd only met me five years ago. So he treated me differently. Like the new Glory.

Who could run her own business, balance her checkbook and shape-shift now without freaking out. Jerry's knee-jerk reaction still was always to try to save the helpless Glory he'd first met. So not cool.

Well, I couldn't think about that stuff now. Not when Jerry was soaping my body and taking a fine long time with it.

"Oh, no, my lord! How did you enter the castle?" I backed against the tile wall as the water sprayed our bodies. I took a moment to appreciate his in all its masculine beauty. Sigh.

"Some careless soldier left the postern gate unguarded, madam. Now you must surrender your body or I will kill all within these walls." Jerry growled and held my hands together over my head. He brushed my soapy nipples with his fangs and I shivered.

"No! Whatever will my husband say when he comes back from war and finds that I have been with another?" I gasped when Jerry turned me and slid one hand along my side to stroke my hip. He pressed a knee against me to widen my legs.

"You must tell him, madam, that you did what you were forced to do to save the castle. Now open for me." His voice was harsh as he slid two fingers inside, teasing a response from me that made me shudder. I tried to free my hands, to touch him, but he wouldn't have it. I felt his hardness press against my backside and the slide of the soap up and down my ass. Oh, yes, he was playing this game the way he liked.

"Please, sire, may I not touch you?" I didn't have to pretend the quaver in my voice or the gasp as he jerked me closer to probe my buttocks with his cock. For a moment I froze, reminded of a time when my shower had been invaded by the devil himself. "Jerry?"

"'Tis I, Sir Jeremiah, leader of the fierce band who has come to ravish you." He leaned down to whisper a soft word of encouragement. "Relax, lass. I'm here, no other."

"Then I must let you have your way with me. Pray, be kind, sir." I shuddered as his fangs trailed over my jugular.

"Nay. Gentle is for losers. I've got you where I want you, wench." He grasped one of my breasts, his thumb and one finger pinching hard as he slid inside me, filling me until I moaned and bucked against him.

"Yes, I'm yours, my lord. Use me as you wish. I will do anything, anything to save my home." I let my head fall forward, my wet hair trailing to my chest. When he released my hands to wrap his arm around my waist and tug me closer, I couldn't hold back the scream of pleasure/pain as he surged deeper, pressing hard thighs against mine. He began to move, his arm tight as he kept us together, one hand toying with my breast.

"Say you surrender, woman. Say it." He growled and leaned over me, his fangs scratching my shoulder, the sharp scent of my blood filling the air.

"I am ravished, completely and totally at your mercy." I reached back and grasped a handful of his hair, pulling his head to my neck. "Drink me, devour me. I want to be everything to you."

"You are, my lady. Always." He roared his satisfaction just before he plunged his fangs into my neck, taking my vein and pulling my life force into him with a mighty draw. The water had cooled, but it didn't matter. We fell against the tiles and held each other, my back to his front, together in the most elemental ways possible until he finally slid away from me with a kiss and a sigh.

"You will be the death of me, lass."

"*I'll* be the death of *you*?" I turned and ran my hands up his magnificent body. Then I reached around him and turned off the water. "Who shoved into me so hard I almost made dents in the tile? I have a security deposit here, you know." I managed a smile that widened when he picked me up and carried me out of the tub before he set me on my feet to begin gently drying me.

"Did I hurt you? Go too far? I think I took the warrior role to heart that time." Jerry slid a bath towel around me to pat my back dry. "I'm sorry, Gloriana."

"Don't be. I am well loved and could have called quits at any time. I know that." I reached up and swiped a towel across his wet hair. I did love him so. Even though I had to admit his warrior had been fiercer than usual. Residual anger? Probably. But he needed to work out his feelings and his smile now was easy and confident.

"Let me make it up to you." In my bedroom Jerry pulled me into his lap and gently combed out the tangles then blew my hair dry.

"Well now. I never expected you to act the lady's maid, my love." I grinned as I admired my reflection. Yes, I can see myself in a mirror, a gift from Lucifer that I expected him to take away at any time. He only gave it to me out of spite, so I could see my figure flaws. That's why there are no full-length mirrors in my apartment.

"Did I earn points for pampering you?" Jerry's grin was wicked.

"More than points." I slid to my knees and gave him attention that soon had him calling my name. Oh, but I loved to make him lose his mind like that.

By the time sunrise was close, we were both more than ready to crawl into my bed and rest in each other's arms.

"Wonder if that baby could possibly be Rafe's," I murmured against Jerry's chest.

"If it is, it's because the two of them got together somewhere before or after she possessed you. Surely you don't believe this nonsense she's spouting, do you?" Jerry brushed my hair back from my face. "You aren't having fantasies that somehow this child could be part of you, are you?"

"No, don't be silly. I know that ship sailed hundreds of years ago. I wish I could have given you a child, but, since I couldn't, I decided a vampire's life would be no life for a child anyway. Am I right?" I drew a heart on the smooth skin over his barely beating heart with my fingernail. I never had finished my manicure and had stopped with a basecoat.

"There are born vampire females who bear children. They seem to make it work. With trusted shifters and such who watch the babes during the day." Jerry captured my hand and pulled it to his lips. "You would have been a wonderful mother. I don't doubt that."

"Thanks, Jerry. But how sad. To never get to play with your child in the sun." I sighed. "It's better this way. I chose my life and I'm satisfied with that choice. Alesa is obviously pulling some sort of scam. For all we know another demon got her with child. For some reason she's fixated on Rafe as the father she wants for the baby but we can't let her get away with it."

"Stupid female. The man obviously has no interest in her. She should move on." Jerry yawned. "I almost feel sorry for Valdez."

"Yes, you should. Rafe has told me how important family is to him. But his demon blood made him something of an outcast in the shape-shifter community. He'd never want to be responsible for bringing another child with mixed blood into that. If Alesa, by some weird trick, did manage to have his child . . ." I tightened my arms around Jerry, suddenly very glad he was the man I held. "Well, Rafe will never forgive her. Or let her keep the baby to raise." I felt the day dragging at me.

"You don't want to be in the middle of a demon fight, Gloriana." Jerry patted my shoulder. "Dawn's coming. Sleep well."

I sighed. "No, everyone loses when demons fight."

Three

"So, Gloriana, what's this about a DNA test?" Ian MacDonald strolled into my shop the next night. He turned more than a few heads. He was a handsome man with a strong build and the bright blue eyes of a genius who missed nothing. He'd always reminded me more of a Viking than a Highlander with his long blond hair and hawklike features. As usual, he had two surfer types along as bodyguards.

"I guess Rafe called you. How much did he tell you?" I gestured Ian toward my back room. I needed privacy for this meeting and sent a mental message to my clerk to take over the front. Bonnie was a new hire, a local vampire recommended by the owner of the muffin shop next door who was also a vamp.

"I've got it, Glory. Take your time." Bonnie zeroed in on the guards, clearly into blond guys with deep tans. Fortunately there were few customers in the shop at the moment. They'd have a hard time getting her attention away from these two guys who positioned themselves near the storeroom door.

I closed that door when Ian and I were in the room where I priced items and stored extra stock. It also held a bathroom and a refrigerator for my synthetic blood. I offered Ian a drink but he shook his head.

"I've developed a new synthetic you should try. I'll send you a case. Tastes like tea with milk and sugar. Like I drank when I was a lad, before I was turned. Does that sound good to you?" Ian grinned, some of his Scottish roots showing in his voice.

"Are you kidding? I used to love my tea that way when I was alive." I frowned. "But keep it. Your inventions tend to give me bad aftershocks. That's why you were analyzing my blood. Any luck with that?" I'd had a horrible reaction to one of Ian's better efforts, a drug that allowed vampires to eat solid food. It had worked great on Penny. Me? I'd had horrible pain after the meal and still had a slightly swollen tummy as a souvenir. Death sleep should have gotten rid of it but for some reason it lingered. Too bad the food hadn't even been that great.

I'd let Ian take a blood sample after that to see what was up with me. This hadn't been the first drug of his that had given me bad side effects. The scientist in Ian had been eager to explore the reasons why I was the only vampire to react the way I did.

"Your blood sample is why I came over. The DNA thing is secondary." Ian settled into a chair while I sat on the large table I used when I worked on merchandise.

I'd worn a short black skirt and bright blue blouse that matched my eyes. I hadn't tucked in the blouse of course. I never tuck, especially not after the tummy thing, but I still felt like I was doing a pretty good job with the figure I had. Ian seemed to appreciate the view of my legs in high heels and the fact that the blouse had a deep vee neckline. His eyes gleamed as he looked me over. I didn't mind a little admiration from a hot guy.

"So tell me, Ian. What did you find out? Was there something in my blood that explains why my reactions to your drugs are always so weird?" I unscrewed the top of my bottle of synthetic and took a swallow.

"Yes, there was. You were never human."

I spewed. Yep. Blood went everywhere, hitting Ian right in his handsome face to drip on his black knit shirt. I coughed and choked and set the bottle down beside me. I have to admit, Ian took it well. He jumped up and found a roll of paper towels in the bathroom, wiping his face and hair then handing me several to clear up the damage to myself.

I blotted my face where tears rolled down my cheeks. Swell, mascara leaks. I jumped off the table and walked into the bathroom. I hadn't heard right. Or this was Ian's idea of a sick joke. He and Jerry were ancient enemies. This was a MacDonald's way of getting even with a Campbell. Ian knew Jerry and I were tight. I finished repairing my makeup then stormed out to face the doctor.

"Okay, Dr. Death, now tell me the truth. What was in my blood? And don't give that bull about not being human. I know when I'm being jerked around." I put my hands on my hips.

Ian stood and faced me. He was a good foot taller than my five foot five but I had on heels. Still, it was a long way up to give him a hard look. I managed.

"I'm not kidding, Glory. I wish I was. I ran every test I knew of. Compared your sample to literally hundreds of others from different vampires and humans. I've had your blood for months now, you know." Ian put his hands on my shoulders. He tried to look sympathetic but was more intrigued than anything else. I didn't like that. It made me think he was telling the truth.

"Yes, it's been months. I figured I was low on your priority list. Penny told me you have lots of experiments going. And then there was your move from California in the middle of that. I didn't expect . . ." I stepped back from him. His gaze was too intense. He was reading my mind so I threw up a block. Of course any probe of *his* mind hit a blank wall, solid as steel.

"This isn't about a MacDonald versus Campbell feud, Glory. I swear it. I don't give a damn about the Campbells.

I told Blade that. We've avoided each other since I moved here and we both like it that way." Ian gestured to the chair and I sank into it.

"If I'm not, uh, never was human, what the hell does that mean?" Of course I'd been born to humans. My parents had lived in London. I'd married young to get away from their strictly religious household and, in just a few years, been widowed. Jerry had taken my mortality away when he'd turned me vampire. Before then, I'd been an ordinary female. One hundred percent. "You're wrong. Run more tests."

"I've run dozens. A hundred or more." Ian leaned against the table. "Like I said, I compared your blood to humans first. I got samples by mesmerizing some on the street, different ages, sexes, even nationalities. When that didn't give me a match, I went to other vampires. I even found a blond, blue-eyed English-origin female vampire, similar age. There was an anomaly. You simply don't fit. So I started on other paranormals—the fae, shape-shifters, weres—to see if that's what you could have been before you were turned. So far, no luck."

"I don't believe you. I have fangs. I drink blood. I fall asleep at dawn. I'm a perfectly normal vampire, right?" I heard my own defensiveness but it kept me from throwing up all over Ian's expensive Italian loafers.

"Are you? There's that tummy bulge you keep complaining about. Penny told me you gripe about it endlessly. Yes, don't bother trying to hide it. That was just the latest in your weird reactions to my formulas." Ian caught my hand in the act of jerking down my blouse where it was supposed to do the camouflage thing.

"I don't believe you. Jerry would say you're poisoning me. And now you're playing mind games. Not ever human? Don't make me laugh." I shot out of the chair, unable to just sit still when he was trying to make everything I knew into a lie.

"You don't believe me? Ask Penny. I had her rerun every test, just in case you copped this attitude." Ian held my shoulders and met my eyes so I could look into his mind and see the truth there.

"Oh, shit." The next thing I knew Ian had me back in the chair, my head between my knees. Great. I was turning into one of those females who fainted at the drop of a hat. Well, maybe this was a bit more than a hat drop. More like an ocean liner hitting an iceberg. Okay, I'd always been a drama queen. But this news deserved a three-act play, was Billy Shakespeare worthy. I sighed and pushed his hands off me before I sat up.

"Seriously, Ian. I have memories of my human life. I had parents, a husband, worked at the Globe for crying out loud." I saw my hands shaking. There. Human hands, no weird claws or . . . My mind froze. Ian took them, holding them tight. He was on his knees in front of me, staring into my eyes like he could will me to his way of thinking. I looked away, not about to be whammied into something.

"We both know how false memories can be planted, Glory. It's possible those things never happened to you. That your life before you met Blade wasn't what you think." Ian sighed and stood. "I'm sorry if you don't like what you hear, but I'm just reporting what I found."

"Don't you think Jerry would have noticed when he met me if I was something other than . . . ?" I swallowed. "You know."

"You'd think so." Ian stared down at me, studying me like I was a really interesting lab rat. "Penny has told me the story about how you met Campbell. Some romantic nonsense." Ian smiled. "Seems he was struck by Cupid's arrow."

"Don't mock what you obviously don't understand." I pressed my hands to my eyes. What did this mean? How could it possibly be true?

"You're right. Love that could last for centuries sounds like a magic spell or an obsession." Ian snapped his fingers. "Maybe I should try to find a druid. Legend has it that they're extinct, but I know better. Ireland. That's where—"

"Stop it! I don't believe you." I held my hand to my stomach, still not sure I wasn't going to hurl as I faced him on rubbery legs.

"It's science, Glory. Believe that. Now I want to take a new blood sample from you. Compare it to more entities. I know what you're not, but I'm determined to figure out what you *are*. Or rather were." The bastard actually looked intrigued, still studying me with a clinical detachment that made me squirm. He stepped closer and sniffed me.

"What? I don't smell like a demon, I know that. I'm way too familiar with their reek." I put a hand in the middle of his firm stomach and pushed.

"You're right. Not demon. I already compared your blood to a demon anyway. Well, to Valdez, who is part demon as you know. He didn't want to give me his blood until I told him it was to help you. Interesting relationship you two have." Ian tapped his chin and looked at me. I wasn't about to share so he went on. "Anyway, I've never had such a challenge. I'm determined to solve this puzzle."

"Swell. Glad to be entertaining." I collapsed on the chair again, not up to standing. "What other paranormals haven't you tested besides a druid?"

"Penny says you know a Siren. Is she still around?" Ian pulled a small notebook and pen out of his jeans pocket. Of course he was going to take notes. Penny had stacks of similar notebooks in the apartment. Now I really was a glorified lab rat. Glory-fied. I bit back a hysterical giggle.

"Aggie. Yes, sure. Why not a god while you're at it? Maybe I'm Zeus's girlfriend, on break from Olympus. Sometimes Aggie's boss, the Storm God, hangs around the lakes here. Bet he'd love to give you a blood sample." I did laugh then and earned a sharp look from Ian.

"You need one of my vampire tranquilizers, Glory?" He reached into his pocket.

"No, thank you. With my luck, it would do the opposite. Send me into a frenzy and then make my thighs explode into massive drumsticks." I leaned back and closed my eyes. "God, Ian, this is crazy." I felt his hand on my shoulder and looked up at him. Sympathy. It made me want to lean against him and sob. Nope. If I started, I might not be able to stop.

"I'm just trying to cover all avenues of investigation, Glory." Ian squeezed my shoulder then stepped back, pen in hand. "You want to give me the Siren's number?"

"I'll call her." I sighed, my mind whirling. "Anyone else? I still think you're wrong. I remember my mother and father. Too many details to be faked. Dad was a baker. My mother . . ." I cleared my throat. Details. Were there really so many? I tried to concentrate. "She read the Bible out loud every night after supper. Does that sound nonhuman to you?" But could I quote any verses? Other than the ones I'd learned myself going to church in recent years?

Ian smiled. "Powerful entities can erase your memory and change it completely, you know that. This background you think you have may be entirely fabricated. If we do discover what species you belong to and it's not human as I suspect . . ." Ian patted my shoulder again. "Sorry, Glory, but you may have to come to terms with the fact that everything you thought about yourself is a lie."

"Species? A lie?" I swallowed. "Even my name?"

"Probably." Ian put his notebook away. "Now about the DNA test Valdez mentioned. I can do one while the woman is pregnant, but it might endanger the fetus. The fact that she's a demon makes this even more complicated, though intriguing, of course. I assume she's a pure demon so I'll definitely want a blood sample from her." Ian had the nerve to wink at me. Like we were coconspirators or something. "As for the DNA test, is the woman willing to undergo the procedure?"

I felt whiplash from the subject change. "Alesa probably won't allow anything that might hurt the baby. She wants it and wants Rafe. The longer she can string this out, the better in her mind. What you said about endangering the fetus just gave her an out. And I'll have to tell her the truth about the risks. I'd never lie about something like that. She can read my mind through my blocks, anyway." I sighed. "I'll let Rafe know. Can you examine her? Be her OB for this?"

"Since I seem to be the only paranormal doctor in Austin, I guess I'll have to be. I've never worked with a demon before." Ian frowned. "I want to examine her right away, of course, and I'll definitely want to do an ultrasound. I'll have to order a machine but that's no problem. I wonder if demons ever have multiples."

"Twins? Triplets? A litter of demons? Life could not be that cruel." I closed my eyes, sending a prayer straight to the Man Upstairs. Then I made myself look at Ian again. He was studying me, like he was looking for weird symptoms.

"While you're at it, see if you can pinpoint exactly when this baby was conceived. Alesa's saying she got preggers when she was inside me." I stood, felt the room wobble, then got it under control. "Is that possible? She was just a spirit or something, inhabiting my body, when Rafe and I did the deed. I don't see how she could conceive that way."

"When you're dealing with nonhumans, I've learned anything's possible." Ian pulled a small black leather case out of his jeans pocket. "Can I take that fresh blood sample now?"

"Came prepared, didn't you?"

"I've been carrying this around in case I run across an unusual type of nonhuman. But I want a new sample of your blood to see if anything's changed since I took the first one. Do you mind?" Ian opened the case and pulled out a syringe and an extra vial.

"No, have at it. I want answers too. But I do take blood from Jerry on a regular basis. Drank some just last night." I unbuttoned my sleeve and pulled it up then held out my left arm.

"I'm sure you also drink synthetics. Doesn't matter. Your core type should remain unchanged." Ian wrapped a tourniquet around my upper arm. "Just like mortals eat rare beef but their blood doesn't become like that of a cow's."

"Nice comparison, Ian." I winced when he tapped a vein with a finger then stuck me with a needle.

"Of course ingesting any substance can temporarily alter our blood, like the drugs I sell. Uppers, downers, the daylight thing. But it doesn't last." Ian didn't look at me, just released the tourniquet and watched my blood fill a vial, as if interested in the color.

"Maybe you got my sample mixed up with someone or something else's."

"Not possible. I keep meticulous records. Crosscheck everything. And I think you know how I am about security." Ian filled several vials efficiently.

Yes, Ian had an army of guards. Whether they were to keep Campbells out or to guard the secret to his various drugs, which were very expensive, I didn't know or care. After he slipped the needle out of my arm, he wiped a drop of blood from the spot with his finger and tasted it.

"You know, I've discovered something else interesting about your blood, Gloriana."

"What?" The way Ian was staring at my jugular made me wish I'd worn a turtleneck.

"It contains special properties." He moved closer until I was almost lying back on the table. "Don't suppose you'd let me have a real taste."

"Don't suppose. Back off." I used a vamp move to get away from him and onto the other side of the room. "Now what do you mean? What special properties?"

Ian smiled. "I concentrated one of the vials I took from you before into a few tablets, then ran a little experiment." He sat on the edge of the table, his eyes suddenly sparkling with the excitement of a scientist who'd discovered something great. "Imagine, Glory, your blood actually enhanced my vision, gave me strength and"—his smile turned wicked—"did great things for my libido." He flashed his fangs at me. "I don't know what in the hell you are but, woman, your blood is very, um, compelling."

"Hold it. You took some of my blood?" I kept my distance as he stared at me like I was the hottest thing since Vampire Viagra.

"I did. In the interest of science. It was a small dose but the benefits! No wonder Campbell wants you all to himself." He tapped his pen against his notebook. "I didn't give the bastard credit. But then he can hardly help himself. You're bound to be addictive."

"Don't play mind games with me, Ian. Jerry loves me. He stays with me because he wants to." I stomped over to face him. "What is so hot about my blood again? Spell it out."

"I told you. It enhanced all of my senses. I could see things more clearly, hear what was being said a block away, much farther than before." Ian flexed his hands. "And strength. I think I could have ripped that steel door off its hinges without breaking a sweat."

My mind was racing. Jerry had never said a word about my blood being special. And my other vampires lovers? They'd been few and far between. Because I'd been selective and drawn more to mortals when Jerry and I had been apart. Men I could easily control and who certainly never drank my blood.

"We could make a fortune with your blood, Gloriana. Imagine. Vampires will pay big bucks for the chance at that kind of boost. And all you'd have to do is donate a pint every once in a while. I'd do all the rest." Ian carefully stowed my blood vials in a padded container and slipped it into his pocket along with his black case. His eyes were bright and he scribbled something in one of his damned notebooks. "Who knows what else we may find it can do as I investigate further?"

"I've listened to Jerry rant about your family for years. Now you think I'd go into business with you? Get real." My needle prick had already healed so I rolled down my sleeve and buttoned it.

"Just think about it. You're always in need of funds to hear Penny tell it and I have even come up with a name: Clarity. Brilliant if I do say so myself. A play on your name, though we'd have to keep you anonymous. Wouldn't want some nefarious characters like those Energy Vampires to get hold of you and drain you for their own profit."

"Hold it. Stop. I'm having a moment of clarity myself. This is a crock. I don't believe a word of it." I shook my head. And even if it was true, I'd had enough run-ins with the EVs to know I wasn't about to do anything that made me attractive to them.

"I thought you'd say that." He picked up his phone. "Send her in." He smiled. "I have someone in the car who I think you will believe."

"What?" I heard a sharp knock then the door from the shop swung open and Penny walked in. "Please don't tell me Ian has let you try one of his drugs."

Penny looked down at her black flats. She was in the jeans I'd picked out for her and a nice black jacket with a green shell underneath. The girl who'd arrived at my door months ago looking like a Goth reject had come a long way. Now she cleared her throat.

"We are scientists, Glory. Sometimes we . . ."

"Experiment on yourselves? I don't think so." I stalked up to Ian. "What did you make her do? You know Penny needs this job. Tell me you didn't threaten her to make her try some of your weirdo drugs."

"I didn't force the girl to do anything. Did I, Penny?" Ian relaxed against one wall.

"No, Glory. I wanted to try Clarity. Ian kept raving about the effects and we'd been doing all these experiments on your blood." She moved closer and put her hand on my arm. "I guess he told you the bad news."

"That I'm not human? You seriously believe that?" I sat down in the chair, my legs suddenly useless again.

"The evidence is there, irrefutable. I'm sorry, Glory. I wish we could tell you something different. But the good news is your blood is the bomb!" Penny laughed. "I took a small dose and, my gosh, the things I could see, smell, hear. And then I went home and just jumped Trey's bones. The poor guy didn't know what hit him. Though he was happy enough to want more of the same."

"Too much info, Penny." I leaned back. It was easy to see that Penny was telling the truth. My blood could actually do those things. "Clarity. Clever. And, what, I'd just put a spigot in my arm or neck so you both could siphon off what you need?" I waved my hands in a shooing motion. "You're both crazy if you think I'm going for this."

"Don't dramatize, Gloriana. It would be a simple blood draw, a pint at a time." Ian frowned and it looked like Penny was about to burst into tears.

"Seriously? You'd let this opportunity pass you by? Think of the implications. For science." Penny sighed.

"No, it would be to make money. Right, Ian? I see no great value to science. It's nothing but another kind of Vamp Viagra. I don't think so, no matter how much I'd like to be rich."

"It's more than just a sexual tool. I'm sure Mr. Blade fills up before he goes into battle, doesn't he?" Penny was flushed, but determined.

"You did not just go there." I jumped to my feet. But then I wondered. Had he? Used me for a jumpstart when he had a tough situation to face? No, surely not.

"Maybe we can work around you. I know you wouldn't turn my twin sister, but you did turn someone vampire once, didn't you?" Penny faced Ian. "What about using a vampire she made? Would that work?"

"Not sure. It's possible, I suppose, but a long shot. If that theory held true, Campbell's blood would be the source, since he made Gloriana vampire. But then we know she was never human so all bets are off on how that affected her blood." Ian was scribbling in his notebook.

"Who was she, Glory? Who did you turn vampire?" Penny grabbed my hand. "I realize now you were right not to turn my sister Jenny when I begged you. She's enjoying her cheerleading, wouldn't want to miss out on all her sorority activities and normal college life. Being a vampire would definitely screw that up. And if she knew I'd been turned . . . Well, I am glad you talked me out of telling her."

"Exactly. So trust my instincts now, both of you." I patted her shoulder then glanced at Ian, who had his pen poised over his notebook. "You don't want anything to do with the one vampire I did make. It was an emergency or I never would have done it. I found Lucky Carver bleeding out in the alley back here. After I made her, Lucky turned Ray vampire. A little act of revenge that ruined his life. That's why Ray's so crazy to get your sunlight drug, Ian. Yep, the one and only vampire I ever sired killed the famous rock star Israel Caine, then turned him vampire. How's that for cruel fate?"

"Don't know about fate, but it's interesting." Ian scribbled in his notebook. "So Ray's got some of your blood in him too."

"More than a little. I've had to feed him a few times since then." I sighed, my brain on sensory overload.

Ian winked. "Relax, Gloriana, I don't want to cut you out. You're the source, the best option. Keep an open mind and we'll meet again. When I examine this demon for you. See? I'm doing you a favor, so you'll owe me."

"I may need your help with Alesa, but that doesn't mean I'm willing to become your blood donor." I stalked over, ready to wrench open the door. "Good-bye, Ian. Penny, maybe you need to start looking for another job. This one has some requirements that you need to think about. Like becoming one of Ian's guinea pigs."

"There are no other jobs for paranormal scientists in Austin, Glory. Besides, I'm learning a lot from Ian. I'd never quit." Penny smiled at her boss. "Think about his proposition. We've got a Web site ready to launch. Brochures set to print. Clarity could bring you millions. And make vampires all over the world happy."

I hated to see my fledgling sucked into Ian's world where money was king. Next thing I'd see Penny trying his weight-loss drug. Which would be a shame when she'd just learned to dress right for her size fourteen petite figure.

"Stop this runaway train. I will not help you make this drug." I saw Penny's smile fade. "I really don't believe it will work anyway. Jerry's certainly never mentioned any effects from it."

"Back to Campbell, are we? Yes, he would be unhappy to hear we're working together. But don't let his attitude stop you, Gloriana. There's plenty of money in this, you know." He glanced around my cluttered workroom. "Think what that could mean. But if you're afraid to go against your lover's wishes . . . Are you?" Ian shoved the notebook in his back pocket and held the door while Penny scooted out of the room.

"Of course not. I please myself." I lifted my chin. Not human. And I had weird blood that Jerry had never mentioned yet drank every chance he could. I couldn't stop thinking about it. I cleared my throat.

"Right." Ian smiled and leaned against the door.

"About Lucky." I met Ian's amused gaze. He thought I was just changing an uncomfortable subject. "Pay attention, Ian. Don't look her up. Lucky Carver, real name Luciana Carvarelli, is bad news. She's a loan shark for paranormals. Last I heard she had the Eastern European territory working collections for her father. Trust me, she's just tough enough to be able to handle the Transylvanian vampires and squeeze payment of bad debts over there."

"Interesting." Ian pulled out that damned notebook again. I was surprised he hadn't switched to electronic note-taking, but guessed he was still old-school in this one way. "Interesting" seemed to be his favorite word. "Maybe I can send one of my guys over to get a blood sample, ask a few questions. What could it hurt to just reach out to her?"

Hah! Easy for him to say. I was sorry I'd ever given Ian Lucky's name. But at least her father had forbidden her to come back to the States. So we were safe from her.

"Just listen to me for once, Ian. The woman is not worth the heartburn." I practically shoved Ian out of the back room. He passed a sputtering Flo with a nod, collecting his bodyguards on the way out of the shop.

"What was going on back here, *amica*?" Flo followed me into the room and shut the door again. "You look strange. Did he do something to you?" She grabbed my arm and made me face her. "*Mio Dio*, you look like you have been given bad news. That man. He and Jeremiah hate each other. What did he say?"

"Uh, nothing." I was tempted to cry on Flo's shoulder, let it all out. But then what? Dump the whole "I'm not human" story on her? I couldn't do that.

"Did he come over here to get even with Jeremiah about something?" Flo led me to the chair and forced me into it. "Was he trying to get you to take one of his drugs again? Pah! Who needs drugs? I am high on life, I say."

I just shook my head, still overwhelmed by the last half hour. "Forget it, Flo. He's helping me with something. For Rafe. No big deal."

"Well. I hope it is worth it. You know Jeremiah won't approve." Flo glanced at the closed door. "He hates the doctor."

"I know." I wanted to scream, cry, break something. "Let's drop it. I see you have on new shoes. Tell me where you got them. Was there a sale?"

I had asked the right question and Flo was happy to chatter away about her recent discovery of an Internet site with designer shoes at a discount.

"It is not as much fun as sitting down and trying on. Smelling the leather, touching the suede and walking around the shop, but I adapt. It is so easy, I click on the mouse thing and the shoes are on their way." Flo slipped off the suede pump and handed it to me to inspect. "Almost too easy though. I find six boxes at my front door tonight. Six! And I don't remember ordering but three." Flo sighed.

"I have to stay away from that online shopping. For me it's as addictive as the gambling." I didn't have much of a credit card limit either. I rubbed the place at my inner arm where Ian had taken my blood. It would be simple enough to solve my cash flow problem. No, not getting into the drug business, especially not with a MacDonald. I hadn't listened to Jerry all these years without learning a few things about that devious clan.

"I can see how it can be. But Ricardo is so modern, I must try to be too."

"Right. We should be aware of what makes our men happy." I handed her back her shoe. And just what made Jerry happy? My blood that tasted like some kind of fine champagne and gave him super powers? I had to talk to him, get the truth out of him. Was he addicted to my blood? Did I really want to know?

Four

"No friggin' way I'm going to some vampire doctor." Alesa crossed her arms over her chest and plopped into a chair. "You fangers stick together. Next thing you know he'll suck my baby right out of me."

"He would not!" I was horrified. But leave it to a hell-spawn to think of that. "Ian's interested in your pregnancy. He's brilliant and he'll make sure whatever you're having arrives safely."

"Listen to you. Whatever? I'm having a *child*, Glory. Not a thing." Alesa blinked back tears. "Damn, I'm so emotional these days. Bring me some of that chocolate ice cream Rafael put in the freezer."

I stomped into the kitchen. Yes, Rafe had reluctantly dumped Alesa and five bags of groceries on me right after sunset. I'd insisted he rush back to the club. It was Friday night and he had an important band scheduled to play. Ian was supposed to meet us here for his first examination of Alesa. He was really getting into this and had even ordered an ultrasound machine but it hadn't arrived yet.

Now Alesa was playing hard to get. So we were having a meet and greet. Somehow I was going to get her to go along with this. I thrust the pint of ice cream and a spoon at Alesa when I heard a knock on the door.

I made myself take a breath. I'd quit breathing as soon as Alesa had arrived. Now I could smell who was outside the door. No, not tonight. I thought I'd made it clear when I'd called her earlier to ask a favor that we'd get together later. But, just like all paranormals, this one worked on her own schedule.

I grabbed the remote and turned on the TV. "Look, there's Home Shopping. Baby stuff." I pumped up the volume then tossed the remote to Alesa before I opened the door and slid out to the hallway.

"Not a good time, Aggie. Seriously. I have company."

Aggie wiggled her perfect nose. When the Siren was in human form, she had perfect everything—from her size six figure, tonight poured into a pair of skinny jeans and a teal sweater, up to her long blond hair and sea green eyes.

"Yuck. Are you kidding me? More demon trouble? What now?" She grabbed my arm with nails done in a ruby red. "I thought you sent them all back to hell."

"I did. But it's that demon Alesa. She claims she's pregnant. With Rafe's child. I know you don't want to see her, do you?" I remembered the last time the two had met. Aggie has this great power where she can turn people to stone. It's her pride and joy. Well, Alesa can do it too. Oh, yeah. She'd stuck Aggie in her place and taunted her. It was not a happy moment.

"No way. *You* called *me*, you know. Tell me what you want me to do and I'll meet you somewhere else when that bitch isn't around. No demon ever again." Aggie tossed her hair and gave my door a glare that should have sent it up in flames. If it had been Alesa throwing the look, it would have. "Man, I bet Rafe is beyond freaked. But what was he thinking? Sleeping with that skank?"

"He didn't sleep with her. It's a long story. Baby's probably not even his. Who takes Alesa's word for anything?"

"Oh, I hear that." Aggie waved her hand in front of her

face. "I'm out of here. The reek of that demon is getting to me. What did you say you wanted?"

"I need a blood sample from you. For an experiment. Do you mind?" I eased her toward the stairs. I knew Alesa had batlike hearing and she didn't need to be in on this. Luckily I could hear an ad for a wonder diaper that was sure to have her riveted. One change a day? Who wouldn't be glued to the tube?

I pulled Aggie to the top of the stairs. "The doctor is on his way to see Alesa. He's a vampire, the same one doing this experiment. Would you let him take some of your blood? Just a bit?"

"Fangs or a needle?" Aggie gave me a narrow-eyed look.

"Needle, of course. If he bit you, he'd swallow. It's what we do, you know. And I bet you'd be delicious." I hid my smile as Aggie paled. "Come on now, I know you're not afraid of vampires. You sure showed Ray and me who was boss when we met you." Aggie had trapped Ray and me in an Austin lake and put us through our paces once when she'd been cursed by an angry goddess. It was a miracle that we were on speaking terms.

"No, I can handle vamps as you know. But I really, really hate needles, Glory." Aggie shook her head. "And why are you helping this guy?"

"This from a powerful Siren who can make men quiver with terror? Or fall at her feet with lust?" I couldn't help it. I grinned. "He's my fledgling's boss. Come on, girlfriend. One little stick. Do it as a favor to me. This will help Penny's career. Cooperate and I'll talk to Flo. The three of us can go shoe shopping together."

"At the mall?" Aggie's eyes lit up. There was nothing she wanted more than to have girlfriends. Seems she missed her Siren sisters since she was stuck way over here in an Austin lake most of the time. The rest of the girls were in the Mediterranean, Siren Central apparently. Aggie was being punished and Austin was considered a serious downgrade in Siren terms.

Flo had invited her to be a bridesmaid in her wedding but hadn't spoken to her since. Aggie isn't exactly good company, always threatening to turn you to stone if you don't do things her way. We were going to have to work on her social skills.

I felt guilty, playing on her feelings that way. But she'd done some really dirty tricks to me and to Ray, so I pushed down the guilt and went with the plan. And, hey, I *would* arrange the shopping trip. She'd love it. It would be a nice evening for her, and Flo owed Aggie. The Siren had done a decent job throwing a wild bridal shower when Flo had scraped the bottom of the bridesmaid barrel. My bud Flo doesn't exactly make girlfriends either. Obviously I have interesting friends.

"Yes, we'll hit the mall and every shoe store there. Cute boots. Suede platforms. What do you say? Isn't a little needle stick worth it for some female bonding? Maybe we'll stop by Rafe's club after and you can pick up someone to dance with." I got her to the bottom of the stairs and punched in the security code to open the door on . . . hello, Ian.

"Who's this?" He smiled and gestured for his guards to move on up the stairs. Aggie watched them go, appreciating the way they filled their tight jeans before focusing on Ian. Her eyes widened and she batted her long lashes. The woman didn't believe in easy on the mascara.

"Aglaophonos, but call me Aggie. I'm a friend of Glory's," She held out her hand. "And you are?"

"Ian MacDonald. I'm the doctor she may have told you about." Ian raised a brow at me. "I sense that you are a Siren. Fascinating."

"Yes, Sirens are that. If you haven't tried one . . ." Aggie did a hair toss and pulled back her shoulders so that her impressive boobs, showcased in cashmere knit, couldn't be missed. Not that Ian had missed them. "Well, let me say this." She licked her lips. "We have a certain reputation for seduction. And we've earned it. Google us." Her smile was an invitation for more than an Internet search and I fanned

myself while the two sent each other scorching mental messages. Whew.

"Dial it down, Aggie. Ian's here to see Alesa. The pregnant
demon upstairs?" I tugged on Aggie's elbow. "I just asked
Aggie about the blood sample, Ian. Well? Are you willing to
let Ian stick you? With a needle?" I wanted to laugh at the
look on her face. She was torn. Fear of needles versus hot doctor. The battle didn't last long.

"Sure, why not? You won't hurt me, will you, Doctor?"
She leaned in. "But then if it's for a good cause . . ." She
smiled and ran a fingernail down his bicep. "I never did get
to play doctor as a, um, child." Aggie as a child? My mind
boggled.

"I promise to make it painless." Ian grinned, clearly interested. He put his card into her hand. "If I didn't have a
patient waiting, I'd definitely be all yours right now. For any
games you wished to play." Ian winked at me.

I rolled my eyes. "Why don't you two set a date? I'm
going upstairs before Alesa takes off. She's reluctant to let
you examine her, Ian. She's going to take some convincing."
I headed up the stairs. I could hear more flirting going on
behind me. Seriously? Did Aggie not care that she sounded
like a slut? Oh, wait, that was in the Siren job description.
Along with luring sailors to their deaths. Of course that was
old-school. Aggie had confided that new technology had
made the Siren business more difficult. So her boss, the
Storm God, was working on a new game plan. I shuddered
to imagine what it could be. A Siren app?

Ian caught up with me. He was chuckling as he reached
around me to open my door. His bodyguards took up posts
on either side of it. He ordered them to stay outside unless
he called for them.

"Aggie's quite a character."

"Yes, she is. Be careful around her. She can turn you to
stone if you displease her."

"So can I, Doc." Alesa had moved to the sofa, her shoes

off, her empty ice cream carton and spoon making a puddle on my lacquered table.

"Then I'll have to be careful, won't I, Miss Alesa?" Ian set his black bag down on the table then handed me the carton and spoon.

"Who says I'm going to let you anywhere near me?" Alesa gave me a dirty look when I grabbed a cloth and quickly wiped up her spill. I gave her the same look back. "Glory and Rafe think they can get rid of me and my baby. They can think again." She used the remote to turn off the TV.

"*Is* there a baby?" Ian sat in a chair across from her. "Perhaps proving that should be your first step. That would be a fine slap in the face to Glory here and Valdez. That is who you claim is the father."

"I don't just claim that. He is my baby's daddy." Alesa swung her feet to the floor and sat up. "You doubting me?"

"Don't get huffy. I'm offering you a way to prove some things. That puts me on your side, I would think." Ian smiled. "Watch the anger. It's not good for the baby. If there is one."

Alesa put her hand on her swollen belly. "There is one. Feel." She gestured for Ian to join her on the couch.

I sat in a chair, afraid to say anything as Ian walked over and sat beside her. He let Alesa take his hand and put it over her tummy.

"Well, I do feel something. Let me use my stethoscope to listen for a fetal heartbeat." He frowned as he moved his hand over her brown knit maternity top.

"Guess listening couldn't hurt." Alesa watched him carefully as he opened his bag and pulled out his stethoscope. He fixed it around his neck, put the ends in his ears and began to listen. When he pulled up her shirt, Alesa didn't object, just let him move the stethoscope around on her taut skin.

She finally couldn't stand his silence or the look of concentration on his face. "Well, what do you hear?"

"There's a lot of echo. I'm not sure what I hear. Could be

gas, could be heartbeats." Ian pulled down her top. "I need a blood sample. Increased hormones in the blood are a great indicator of pregnancy."

"Wait. Heartbeats. Like more than one?" I just couldn't keep quiet. This was, like, my worst fear. Multidemons.

"I said I couldn't really tell, Glory." Ian pulled out a syringe like the one he'd used on me a few days ago. "I need more information. Blood first, then an ultrasound."

"Whoa, whoa. I never said I'd let you stick me with a needle. Or look up my hoo-ha either." Alesa obviously wasn't keen on giving blood. "And what's an ultrasound?"

"Relax. I'm just going to take a little blood. All you'll feel is a tiny prick. And the ultrasound is painless, not invasive at all. It will give us a picture of what's going on in your womb." Ian pushed up Alesa's sleeve and stuck her as if she'd given permission. I had to give him credit for guts. I wouldn't have poked a demon like that. Of course I wondered if he'd ever seen one in action like I had.

"Don't be ridiculous. I'm not scared for myself. But I've got a baby on board." Alesa watched black blood fill a vial. "Pretty, isn't it?"

"Careful with that blood, Ian. That's how she got inside me. Her blood seeped into my open wound." I glared at her. "Having her in my body was hell and that's no exaggeration."

"Wimp." Alesa smirked.

"Explain to me how you could get pregnant when you weren't physically present." Ian pulled out the needle, wiped off the puncture wound with a sterile pad, then watched as the spot healed. He nodded then carefully put away the blood-gathering gear and this time actually pulled an electronic pad out of his doctor's bag and fired it up.

"Well . . ." Alesa smiled and sat back. "This is where I got really clever. I was nearing the end of my fertile time. Demons only have a certain number of years to get pregnant, you know."

"No, I didn't. How many would you say?" Ian began typing rapidly.

I tuned them out as they talked about demons and life in hell. I didn't care, didn't want to know. Because what if that was what I'd been before Jerry had turned me? No, I wouldn't believe it. I didn't have that sweet smell for one thing. And my blood wasn't black sludge. Of course Rafe was part demon and he didn't have either of those attributes. Oh, God.

A demon taint might explain why Lucifer had taken a strange fancy to me, though. No. Since I'd been turned, I'd gone to church, handled holy water, done lots of things that my buddy Rafe, kind soul that he was, wouldn't dare. And Ian had compared my blood to Rafe's without finding a match. Okay then. Not demon.

"I'll do it." Alesa shook Ian's hand. "When?"

"Tomorrow night if the equipment gets here as promised. Penny can tell Glory where I live and work." Ian put his pad away and turned to me. "Can you bring Alesa to my house?"

"She's going to do the ultrasound?" I really had spaced out.

"That's what I said. Are you driving me or do I need to get Rafael, on a busy Saturday night, to abandon his club and take me?" Alesa sighed. "He's going to have to support a family now. I really think he should tend to his business."

"I have a business too, you know." I didn't like the way my own interests were being dismissed. "Saturday is a big night for us in the shop."

"I would have Penny bring her, but it's her night off. She's going to the UT football game, to see her sister on the cheerleading squad." Ian shook his head. "Your fledgling is positively wholesome, isn't she, Glory?"

"Gag me." Alesa got up and walked into the kitchen. "I want chips and salsa. Sorry you two can't join me."

"I just bet you are. Do your eating in the kitchen." I turned to Ian. "I'm glad Penny is going to the game. She needs to do some normal college things instead of spending her whole life hunched over a microscope." I rubbed the back of my neck, tight with strain. This whole thing—Alesa here, worrying about Rafe, not to mention thinking about how Jerry was going to take my working with Ian—was giving me another headache. "I'll arrange things so I can take Alesa."

"Great. You obviously are feeling the stress of this and your other situation." Ian nodded toward the kitchen. "I won't mention it here but with Aggie's sample and now Alesa's, I feel I'm close to the truth about you." He opened his black bag. "Don't suppose I can interest you in a pain reliever for that headache." He held out a packet with a pill inside.

"No, no drugs." I rolled my neck. "And I'm still not interested in Clarity either." There was a noise outside the door. Thumps, groans, then the door crashed open.

"What the hell is going on here?" Jerry strode over, not waiting for Ian to move. He knocked the packet out of Ian's hand then shoved him against the wall. A picture I'd really liked fell to the floor, the frame cracking. "Trying to drug her again, MacDonald?"

"Jerry, stop!" I jumped up and landed behind him, wrapping my arms around his waist. "Ian's here as a doctor. Stop acting like a Campbell and listen to me."

Ian threw Jerry's hands off of him. "Listen to you? That's too reasonable for a man like Jeremiah Campbell. No, I forget. Jeremy *Blade*. That's the asinine name you gave yourself a century ago." Ian laughed. "Can't say I blame you. Who wouldn't want to be shed of the Campbell curse?"

"Why you—" Jerry lunged, but I got between them.

"I said stop. You're in my home. My rules. Remember?" I looked up and touched his face. "Both of you. No feuds here. If you wish to kill each other, take it outside. But I need you both, so do me a favor and shelve this ancient animosity."

"Gloriana, you heard him insult me and my family. Am I

to just allow that?" Jerry showed all his teeth and fangs. "The man is asking for a beat-down."

"Seems like you took care of your aggressions on his guards. That was not well done of you, Jerry." I turned my back on him.

"Ian, it was not well done of *you* to taunt him that way. And there's no Campbell curse that I know of. Jerry's always been proud of his family and his name. We all change our names from time to time. It's what an immortal has to do." I saw Ian's jaw flex. He glanced over to where his guards had pulled themselves together and waited in the doorway, obviously for a signal to attack Jerry. Three to one. The odds were terrible.

"He never told you of the curse? I'll leave it to him to explain. And ask him about your blood. See what he says. Should be interesting." Ian gave Jerry a smile that made Jerry growl Gaelic obscenities I'd heard before. "Until to-morrow night, Gloriana. Come around ten and don't bring Campbell with you." Ian pushed past us, picked up his bag and headed out the door.

"Wow. The testosterone level in here is off the charts and the yelling's not good for the baby." Alesa yawned. "I'm going to lie down for a while. Rafe is picking me up after the club closes. About three he said. So can I collapse in the fledgling's bed till then?" Alesa headed down the hall. "Why am I asking? I'm doing it anyway. You two obviously need to talk. A curse? How ridiculous." Alesa laughed.

"Is it? Ridiculous?" I walked into the kitchen and pulled out a bottle of synthetic. Jerry was right behind me. He shook his head when I offered him one. Right. He still preferred a live donor. Obviously he'd had a drink on his way over.

"Of course it's ridiculous. The MacDonalds hired an old witch centuries ago to lay a curse on my family. It caused some of my kin to do things out of character." Jerry ran a hand through his hair. "Power of suggestion. Obviously. It was about that time that my parents began having trouble in their marriage, went their separate ways for almost a century. Then one of my brothers was killed in a skirmish with the MacDonalds. Sheep died. A well went dry. Of course everyone with a superstitious bent blamed the curse. Taken individually, these things happen. Put together, the MacDonalds took credit, claiming their curse had done its job."

"Well, I guess one more coincidence was that you changed your name." I took my drink to the living room and sat on the couch. I quickly jumped up again and opened the windows, letting the cool fall air get rid of the demon stench.

"It *was* a coincidence. I had used the same identity too long." Jerry sat beside me and took my hand. "I've never been ashamed of my family or afraid of some stupid hag's curse."

"No, it doesn't sound like you." I took a drink.

"I also went to London and met you. That certainly turned out better than all right. No curse there." Jerry smiled and kissed my knuckles.

"Of course not." I was putting off asking him the big question. "That was quite a scene with Ian. I have a headache, but I wasn't about to take the pill he offered me for it."

"MacDonald's guards tried to keep me out. Were going to toss me down the stairs." Jerry frowned. "You didn't think I was going to meekly accept that, did you?"

"No!" I dropped my bottle on a coaster and grabbed Jerry's thigh. "I'm sorry, Jer. That was not well done of Ian. He has to know you are always welcome here."

He put his hand over mine. "I'll always distrust a MacDonald, there's too much history there. But I wouldn't want you upset, Gloriana."

"Thanks, Jerry. But . . ." I had so much to tell him and he had plenty to tell me. "I need to know something. Tell me all about how it was when you first saw me. Back in London. What attracted you to me? How did I appear?"

"This is an odd subject. Trying to keep me from getting on you about having that demon here?" Jerry lifted my hand to his lips and nibbled the sensitive skin between my thumb and my forefinger.

"No. I offered to handle this for Rafe. My choice. Now humor me. Refresh my memory." I smiled at him and leaned against his arm. He had on a soft black sweater and it suited him. His jeans were worn and hugged his strong legs. Even his boots were masculine, a rough brown suede probably scuffed when he'd kicked Ian's guards out of his way.

"I noticed you at the Globe backstage helping with costumes. I'd come to see a play and went to pay my compliments to Shakespeare."

"I remember seeing you there." Who wouldn't have noticed the man in a kilt? He was so handsome in a dark, slightly dangerous way. He'd shed much of his Scottish accent since, but back then he'd spoken with a burr that had enchanted me.

"And I saw you, always busy. I liked the golden color of your hair and the generous shape of your body. Will said you'd been trying to talk him into putting you on the stage in a minor part. Against the law, of course, but bribes in the right quarter took care of that and audiences loved to see an occasional female on the stage." Jerry had his finger wound around one of my curls. I'd let my hair grow long again and he liked it that way.

"Yes and it paid a bit more if you could get your chance at it." I knew most of the women who'd had a turn on stage had wound up mistresses of rich men. I'd been terrified, but desperate enough to risk it by the time I'd asked for my chance.

"Will told me that your husband had died in an accident and he'd let you stay on so you wouldn't starve. Looked to me like you weren't eating like you should. Your face was gaunt."

"Yes, I had cheekbones back then." I sighed. Unfortunately Jerry had fattened me up before he'd turned me vampire. He liked a buxom lass.

"I may have given Will a push to let you have your chance." Jerry ran his hand down my arm and pulled me closer.

"So I have you to thank for my big break!" I reached up and kissed his cheek. "Can't say I did much but wear a shockingly low-cut dress and carry a milk pail, but I got heaps of roses backstage after that."

"I couldn't take my eyes off you. I wasn't the only one who liked your milk pail either. You had a crowd lingering by the stage door that night." Jerry leaned down to kiss me. He put some energy into it and I almost let the interrogation go. No, I needed some answers.

"But you soon cleared them all out. They thought I was a strumpet. You treated me like a lady." I sighed. "You had to know I hadn't been raised as one."

"I didn't know that. You were well spoken and had an air about you." Jerry slipped open buttons on my blouse until he could see my lacy bra.

"Did I ever do anything to make you suspect that I was other than what I appeared?" I eased away, not about to be distracted by his clever hands when I had finally gotten to the reason for this trip down memory lane.

"What do you mean?" Jerry stopped with his hand on the clasp of my bra.

"Could I have been something other than a simple human female? Daughter of a baker and raised in Cheapside?" I stayed frozen, afraid of his answer.

"Where is this coming from, Gloriana?" Jerry jerked his hand away. "Did Ian put this idea in your head? By God—"

"Jerry, why would you think that? And why would it get you excited? If there's nothing to it, no worries." I wiggled over to sit in his lap. "Seriously, you remember when Ian took some blood from me? After I had that adverse reaction to one of his drugs?"

"Poison! Honestly, Gloriana. I hope you will finally listen to me. He has attempted to poison you on more than one occasion. Why can't you see that? This is all about our feud. MacDonald misdeeds wrapped up to look like a damned curse. I tell you, you can't trust him." Jerry stared into my eyes, willing me to wake up and smell the peat smoke.

"No, stop blaming the stupid feud. He tested my blood. He found out something strange. That I, I wasn't human before I was turned vampire." Tears filled my eyes and I couldn't blink them back.

"By God! The balls on that man! To drag you into our quarrel. Is no weapon beneath him?" Jerry pulled my face to his chest. "Don't cry, Gloriana. He's lying. He obviously wants to hurt you to get to me. I knew you then. I drank your blood before you were turned. It was human blood. Warm, delicious. It was like honey on my tongue." He kissed the top of my head. "Damn that man to hell. What was he thinking telling you something like that?"

"Is that all, Jerry? What about when you drink my blood now? Is it just delicious vampire blood or does it give you something more?" I eased away from him, determined to see his face when he answered me.

"What do you mean?" Jerry's face was blank. I knew that look, the look of a man who had secrets or was searching for an answer.

"Spill, Jerry. This 'honey on your tongue.' Did it also give you special powers? Does it still? And is it why you always come back to me, century after century?" My nails dug into my palms.

"Gloriana, what did Ian say to you? What lies is he filling your head with now?" Jerry reached for me but I was across the room before he could touch me again.

"Don't start with the feud again. I won't listen to that. My blood isn't human, Jerry." Tears spilled down my cheeks and I angrily dashed them away. "And, don't worry, I wouldn't take Ian's word for something that important. Penny can verify everything he told me."

"The hell you say. He's accusing me of using you for some kind of drug? Is that what he's saying?" Jerry was on his feet too, his eyes blazing.

"Isn't that the truth? That after we have our sweet nights together and you drink your fill, you are stronger, your senses enhanced and your libido . . ." I laughed and wanted to slap myself back to sanity. "Well, I'm here to tell you, it's certainly five star."

"Stop this. I won't deny you have a wonderful taste and that you fill me with a certain"—he ran his hand through his hair—"I don't know, feeling of well-being, I guess, call it euphoria. But I'm damned if it's more than just great vintage vampire blood. And that feeling is happiness, by God. Because I've been with the woman I love."

"Either you are fooling yourself or you're a damned liar." I collapsed on the sofa.

"If you were a man, I'd kill you for saying that." Jerry stared at me until I looked away.

"I'm tired. I can't think about this anymore tonight." It was the simple truth. The only truth I could grasp right now. "I'm sorry if I've said things . . . I know you're an honorable man. Maybe you don't even realize . . ." I shut up, not sure what I could say at this point that wouldn't destroy our relationship.

"MacDonald filled your head with these doubts." Jerry's eyes were dark with hatred for Ian as he sat beside me. "I'm thinking I have a broadsword with Ian MacDonald's name on it. This time you won't be stopping me, Gloriana. He's gone too far. I will meet him and settle this. Our reckoning is overdue."

"You will not touch him. Not if you claim to love me." I put my hands on his cheeks and made him look into my eyes. His jaw was rigid with his fury.

"Of course I love you. That's what brings me back to you again and again, not some blasted blood. And you were human, no matter what that bastard told you."

"Just . . . listen." I took a shaky breath, summoning up the evidence. I'd had time to think about it since Ian had first dropped his bombshell. Not human. Jerry pulled me tight against him.

"Whatever it is, lass. I'm here. I'm not going anywhere, you ken?" He murmured the soothing words in my ear and ran a hand up my back. "Spit it out and let me call it non-sense, there's a girl."

"If only it were that simple, Jerry." I wanted nothing more than to lay my head on his broad chest and forget it all. But I was ever practical. That much of me I could see as a human quirk. "There's something off with me. Even you have to admit I've never been a normal vampire. I don't have the killer instinct. And look how long it took me to shape-shift. Hundreds of years!"

"I admit that was frustrating. But only for your own safety." Jerry shook his head. "Still, Gloriana, you had your reasons. You were just sensitive. Afraid you'd be stuck in another skin. I understood."

"Yes, well, it seemed logical at the time." Seriously, I'd had terrors that I would shift into a bat or something equally ugly and be stuck. Now, I was comfortable that I could get back to Glory as usual, no problem. "Maybe the fact that you came to London and found me then is just more of the Campbell curse."

"There *is* no curse. And what I found was an uncommon woman, Gloriana. Warm, generous, with a good heart. Thank God you don't have the killer instinct." Jerry smoothed my hair. "Why did I fall in love with you? I don't think it was because you were some kind of strange paranormal creature. I think it was because you made me feel like a human man again, not a freak. That's your gift, Gloriana. A human gift. Don't let MacDonald convince you otherwise."

"Jerry." I was determined not to cry again. "This isn't about Ian trying to convince me of anything. With him it's all science."

"Well, know this: I don't give a good damn what you were, I know what you *are*. Mine. My beautiful girl." Jerry lifted me into his arms and carried me into the bedroom. He slowly peeled away my clothes, worshipping me with his mouth and hands until he had me naked. Then he stripped and fell on me, seeming determined to claim me once more.

There was desperation in him that I hadn't seen in a long time. Was this about besting Ian in their feud? Distracting me from the blood issue? I didn't care. I stroked his hair, explored his body and whispered love words as his hands traveled well-worn paths. Yet the paths always felt new and left me trembling. His lips followed, hungry, tender, then ravenous again.

I never tired of exploring his hard body, tracing the ancient scars there, tasting the special flavor of male that I knew so well and yet never tired of. I nipped at his firm chest, dragged my hair down his muscular stomach to trace the veins in that rampant sex that he could control for as long as I needed him to. I smiled up at him before I squeezed his sacs and took him into my mouth.

"Perhaps *you* are the witch who cursed my family. You seem to have cast a spell on me. Why can't I ever get enough of you?" Jerry groaned and reached for me. "Come here, Gloriana. Quit your torture and sit astride."

I sat up and threw my hair back over my shoulders. "Crying uncle so soon, Jeremiah?" I grinned and crawled up his body. "So you've discovered my secret. I've got you in my power." Even as I said the words playfully, ran my hands up his sides and tweaked his nipples, I felt a frisson of something, a warning. Silly superstitious nonsense.

He growled as he kissed me hungrily, then pushed me back to study me. "You are all woman, Gloriana. Never doubt it. You slay me." He lifted me and set me on his cock, filling me. "Take me and prove to yourself that this is how we are meant to be. And I won't drink from you. I'll show you that your blood is not why I want you." He began to move, the pleasure of being so filled pulling a sigh from me.

"Jerry, I love you. Please believe that." I moved with him, running my hands through his hair before touching his cheek. "No matter what I might be." Stupid to bring that up now.

"I believe you. I also believe that you can love more than one man, Gloriana. That's why that damned demon is down the hall. Don't think I haven't figured that out." His eyes burned as he rose to press deep inside me again. He was still angry. Old wounds, not healed.

I had no answer for him so I just held his shoulders as his hands gripped me. He surged into me harder, faster, pushing us both to fulfillment. He was right. Perhaps it was my failing, my fatal flaw. I loved Rafe, more than I should. And even Ray if I let myself look deep into my heart.

But Jerry. He was here, now, and still my forever lover. I let him see that as I leaned down and pierced him with my fangs, taking his blood to unite us in the way of vampires. It felt warm and right and tasted better than anything. My orgasm roared through me as he called my name.

Yes, he loved me and I owned him, body and soul. He would die for me if I asked it of him. Those hard thoughts shocked me. Where had they come from? And why did the very fact that he was so desperate to hold me give me such bone-deep satisfaction? What was I? Did I really want to know?

Five

"She really agreed to it all? Unbelievable." Rafe paced the living room. He looked tired and worried.

I wanted to pull him down beside me on the couch and say something to make him feel better, smooth those worry lines between his dark brows. Problem was, even with his jaw set and his body fairly humming with frustration, he was one hundred percent yummy male. I couldn't forget how we'd been together, how he'd wanted me. I kept my hands twisted together in my lap, determined to keep this friend-ship platonic where it belonged. I was happy with Jerry and that was enough for me. I was one sick puppy if I couldn't be satisfied with the incredible man I had. My stomach churned at the truth of that.

"Well, we didn't actually get into the DNA test question yet. Jerry dropped by and all hell broke loose."

"Oh, yeah?" Rafe managed a smile. "I bet it did. The feud still goin'?"

"I'm trying to keep a lid on it. For now, we're just about confirming the pregnancy and, I hope, proving that the tim-ing's off for this baby to be yours."

Rafe put his hand on my shoulder. "It's a start. Where's the demon anyway?"

"She's asleep on Penny's bed." I'd peeked in on her just before Rafe had arrived. Jerry had taken off to deal with some business after he'd promised to leave Ian alone. It had been tough to squeeze that promise out of him, but Jerry could be a reasonable man when approached with logic. Plus he was Mr. Accommodation right now, probably trying to prove he wasn't addicted to my blood. I was reserving judgment.

"Why'd she agree to go along with using Ian as her doctor?" Rafe started pacing again. His restless energy was wearing on me.

"She wants to prove she's got a baby on board. I take it as a bad sign that she's willing to let Ian examine her." I patted the couch next to me. "Sit. Try to relax."

"Relax, right." Rafe darted into the kitchen and came out with a package of Twinkies. He ripped it open and stuffed one in his mouth before he collapsed next to me, chewed and swallowed.

"You've done enough, Glory. Alesa doesn't need to be hanging out here." Rafe went for another Twinkie. "This is my problem."

"Is it? You really believe a word that demon says?" My heart ached for him. I laid my hand on his firm thigh. I felt the muscles tense as he made quick work of the other Twinkie.

"No, but I'd never forgive myself if by some weird trick she did have my child and she took it down to hell with her."

"Well, the DNA test should take care of that." I sighed and leaned into my corner of the couch. Not telling Rafe my latest problem. He had enough on his plate already.

"DNA? I don't think so." Alesa's voice shattered the moment like a bullet hitting glass.

"Relax, Alesa. Ian can't do a test until the baby's born. You've got a few more months to pretend this baby's Rafe's. Enjoy your nap?" I ignored her one-finger salute.

"Not really. There were about six air fresheners back there. What are you trying to hide?" Alesa sat in a chair.

"We used to keep lab rats in Penny's room. Don't suppose you found any leftovers in the bed." I smiled. "I have a cat too. Boogie's been under my bed since you came on the scene. Seems you can't even charm a kitty."

Alesa gave me a toothy grin. "Like I'd want to. I tossed the lavender shit out the window. Rats? No wonder I'm hungry. Rafael, bring me a snack. And keep the cat out of my sight. Unless it's big enough to make a pair of slippers, if I see it, I'm turning it into a toad."

"You harm my cat and I'll rip every hair from your over-sized scaly-snout head." I ran to shut my bedroom door. I'd already left Boogie's food and water in there when I realized how freaked-out he was.

"Ooo. I'm terrified." Alesa laughed and shook her hands in the air. "And my head is in perfect proportion, thank you. Cheap shot."

"Can the attitude, Alesa. I'm through waiting on you." Rafe stayed put. "Get your own damned snack. And you can pick up the tab at the hotel too." Rafe smiled at me and put his feet on my coffee table. When I gave him a look, he eased them back off but kept his smile. "This is your last visit to Glory too. Until we get positive DNA, I don't see any proof that I'm the father here."

"Glory put you up to that rebellion?" Alesa stood and stalked into the kitchen. We heard the refrigerator door slam, then cabinets open and close. Finally she came back into the living room with a block of cheddar cheese and a box of crackers. She also carried a knife. I didn't like seeing Alesa holding a knife.

"Don't blame Glory for my attitude. I just got tired of being jerked around." Rafe stood and grabbed the knife and cheese from her. "Use a paper plate and don't be a pig. You're not eating all the cheese."

I scooted over when Alesa took his seat on the couch. "Rafe's right. He doesn't have to do anything for you. Neither do I. All we've got is your word that this baby has any-thing to do with either of us. And the word of a demon isn't worth spit. Your whole façade is put on. So the baby bump could be part of your human fakery. Until Ian confirms that you're expecting and that Rafe is the father, you're on your own."

Uh-oh. Suddenly I was staring at the fangs, scaly snout and claws of Alesa in all her demon glory. Her red eyes sent flames licking at my face, singing my eyebrows. Not again. It had taken me weeks to grow back my eyelashes after a previous demon encounter. Alesa did have a tummy bulge, not that it was obvious with all the other gross stuff going on. She growled and snagged my sweater with one claw.

"On my own? I don't think so. Did you forget how I can make your life here an outpost of hell? Want to play stat-ues?" She drew me up, claws clamped around my arms, until my toes wouldn't touch the ground. In her demon form she was over six feet tall.

"No. Down, girl. Want me to start singing church songs?" Maybe I wasn't being humble enough, but I'd had it with demon dirty tricks. I saw Rafe come out of the kitchen with a plate full of cheddar slices.

She winced. "I can take it. And you can't sing if your mouth is sealed shut."

"Put her down, Alesa. You're melting the cheese." He sauntered over to the coffee table and put down the plate. "Damn, I could have made myself some nachos while I was in there. We've got tortilla chips. Glory, any jalapeños left?" He had the nerve to wink at me.

"Quit torturing me, Rafe. You've got to know I've never tasted a jalapeño in my life." I knew there was going to be more than one hole in my sweater, not to mention red marks on my arms. Rafe was obviously trying to keep things calm and to distract Alesa but, suspended in the air by my arm-pits, I was having a hard time playing along.

Alesa wasn't going to kill me. I knew that. It wouldn't gain her anything and would ruin her plans for the so-called baby.

Who else could she go to if she let her temper get the best of her and took me out? She could, however, make the next few months around here miserable. We needed some rules and regs. So this was the time to lay them down. I sent Rafe a mental message to jump in on this.

"Alesa, think this through. Mistreating the hostess isn't the way to get her to help you. And showing her your ugly mug? Dumb move. I say get human or get out." Rafe walked back to the kitchen and came out with a beer and a bag of tortilla chips. "Glory's been pretty nice to you, arranging a doctor and all." He twisted off the beer cap and took a drink. "You shouldn't be losing your temper like that, Mama."

Alesa dropped me with a thump. "It's these hormones. Damn it, I would love some nachos. Jalapeños? Now you're talking." She got back into human form and sat down to scoop up the melted cheese with a cracker. "Will you make me some, Rafael? I promise to behave." A dark, slimy tear trickled down her cheek. "I know you can kick me to the curb, both of you. But where else can I go? I'm desperate, don't you see? Hell was my home. Luc doesn't want me so I've come to the only friends I've got."

I choked and Rafe took a gulp of his beer. We were her *friends*? How pathetic. I had no words. I glanced at Rafe and he shrugged then went back into the kitchen. To make nachos. He had a soft heart though he'd never admit it. I examined my sweater for holes. Yep, it was ruined. My wardrobe wouldn't be able to withstand too many of these hormonal meltdowns.

"Alesa, if this is how you treat your friends, I'd sure as hell hate to see how you treat your enemies." I threw myself into a chair, as far away from her as I could get.

She looked up and gave me a smile full of fangs. "Trust me, my enemies pray for death long before I'm through with them. You want me to be grateful? Fine. Help me with this situation and I'll take out anyone you say. Your enemy is my enemy. How does that sound?"

I shuddered and shook my head. A deal with a demon? It

sounded like a fast ride down to her former playground. And one I wasn't having any part of.

"You can't live here, end of story."

"But what if I like it here? Think about this, Glory. Your friends aren't my friends. If I want something, I will get it, one way or another. Even if it means stalking every one of your little friends and making their lives hell on earth until you see the light." Alesa laughed then slurped down more cheese. She threw me a look that made me wish for a shower and lots of soap.

Ian called and said the ultrasound hadn't come in yet. But the blood test showed that Alesa was definitely pregnant. Oh, joy. We rescheduled for Monday night. I decided to head down to the shop like I always did on a Saturday evening. I needed to be there—we were usually busy—and Rafe and I stayed firm that Alesa could fend for herself. Of course that left me wondering what she'd do next. I didn't figure her for idle threats.

She hadn't given me a cell phone number or any way to reach her but I knew she'd find me, unfortunately.

I hadn't been in the store ten minutes when my cell rang. My best friend Flo was trying to get a group together to go dancing at Rafe's club.

"Not really in the mood, pal. Another night." I smiled at a customer who was carrying a skirt to the counter.

"But, *amica*, you love to dance. What is this mood? Tell me." Flo didn't like taking no for an answer. "You close at midnight. Call Jeremiah and meet us then. Rafael will reserve a big table for us on the balcony."

I was tempted. I'd love to cry on Flo's tiny shoulder. But doubted I'd be able to escape from Alesa to do it and no way was I letting the demon within scenting distance of my best bud. Flo's husband, a former priest, would go ballistic if I got near his wife with another demon. She'd had a close call with hell the last time I'd involved her in one of my freakfests and I sure didn't want to remind Alesa who my friends were.

"Tell her yes. I love to dance." Alesa was suddenly in front of me. "Unless we'll still be at Ian's."

"I'll call you back, Flo." I ended the call. "Not going to Ian's tonight. That special machine didn't arrive." I grabbed Alesa's arm, but carefully. After all, she *was* pregnant. "Back room. Now." I did a quick check. Erin could handle the sparse crowd.

"Since you asked so nicely and all." Alesa jerked her arm out of my grasp and flounced toward the back room. As she did, an expensive sweater fell out of the back of her skirt. I scooped it up off the floor.

"What the hell? Were you shoplifting? In *my* store?" I barely suppressed the urge to throw the demon against the table before I started to shut the door to the shop. It took everything in me not to slam it.

"Hold it, Glory. Is that demon with you?" Diana Marchand, owner of Mugs and Muffins, the coffee shop next door, stuck her foot in the door.

"Yes." I glanced at Alesa, who just smiled and studied her fingernails like she was looking for a chip in the black polish. "What has she done now?"

"She just left my shop without paying for the half dozen muffins she scarfed down." Diana pushed her way inside my back room and waited until I had us closed inside. Diana, a vampire and a friend, didn't hesitate to get in Alesa's face. "I don't tolerate deadbeats."

"Pay her, Glory." Alesa brushed crumbs off her shirt front. "Great muffins, by the way. Though not very filling. I could have eaten a few more."

"Stay out of my store. I don't want a demon in there. You hear me?" Diana turned to me. "What the blazes are you doing hanging out with such as this?"

"Not my choice, believe me." I started to argue about the bill with Alesa but didn't want to do it in front of Diana.

"Tell Erin up front what you're owed and she'll take care of it." I glared at Alesa. "This won't happen again. I'm doing my best to get rid of the problem."

Diana looked from me to Alesa and back again. "Honey, I figure you must be over a barrel to tolerate this, um, critter." She patted my shoulder. "Let me know if you need my help." She clasped the cross at her neck. "Though what I could do . . ."

"I appreciate the thought anyway."

"Run along, little vampire. We're just fine. And, seriously? Your coffee is weak and I've had better service in hell." Alesa sniffed.

"Well, glad you mentioned it. Coffee. I'll add that to your bill." Diana jerked open the door and looked at me one more time. "I'll say some prayers for you, Glory."

"Thanks, I need all of those I can get."

"Gag me." Alesa shot the finger at Diana's back before I shut the door again.

"See what happens when you cut me off without a penny? I'm reduced to walking without paying the check, shoplifting when I need a nice cardigan to wear. The evenings are cold here." Alesa pretended to shiver. "I'm used to a much warmer climate, you know."

I counted to ten, twenty. "Why are you even here in the shop?"

"Looking for you, obviously. We had an appointment. You weren't in the apartment so this is the second place I looked." Alesa smirked. "Your clerk never noticed when I stuffed that sweater down my skirt. Hell, I could have taken half the blouse rack and she'd have missed my smooth moves."

"Erin's a good clerk. She was ringing up a sale. I can't believe I didn't smell you the minute you hit the door." I'd been talking on the phone. No wonder we were losing inventory.

"That chick's shop next door had just taken a batch of

cookies out of the oven. Great disguise for me. Sneaked right up on you." Alesa wrinkled her nose. "So when are we going dancing?"

"Never. You can't be around my friends. Not Flo and Richard. You remember what happened the last time you were around them?" I rubbed my forehead. Headache. Too much stress. And between the reek of Alesa and those cookies next door, I really couldn't breathe. It was taking a toll.

"Oh, yeah. That Italian shoe freak married to that religious zealot managed to orchestrate the love-in that got me sent back to hell when I was stuck in your body." Alesa sighed. "I wanted to go back, you know. Seriously. Your body wasn't exactly a demon's playground, even if there's plenty of room in the hip area." She gave me a look I recognized, the skinny girl superior smirk. I wanted to slap it off her face. Couldn't even breathe through the urge. I just shrugged.

"You can only imagine the tears of joy shed that night when I finally felt you pop out of me." I gave her my own condescending once-over. "Good triumphs over evil. There were trumpets in Heaven playing the 'Hallelujah' chorus."

Alesa shuddered. "As if anyone up there noticed your fat ass." She sniffed. "Lucifer was certainly glad to see me. At first anyway. Then he noticed I had this little bun in the oven and ordered me to get rid of it." She shook her head. "No way in hell or in any other dimension, baby. I told him that, right to his beautiful face. I'd worked too hard to get knocked up." She let me see the tears glittering in her eyes. "So we had it out. Of course I lost that battle. Luc rules down there." Big watery sigh.

"So you can never go back?" My heart fell to my feet. No way was I going to be stuck forever with this hellspawn and her offspring.

"Not saying that." Alesa managed a smile. "I have some leverage. A few secrets I can use to bring Luc around. But I have to have the baby first."

"And you'd raise him or her in hell? Is that even possible?" I couldn't wrap my mind around the image of a nursery down below. I'd heard stories of torture, sex and perversion there. Even a demon baby deserved love and a peaceful upbringing.

"Yes, it's possible, Glory. I was raised in hell and look at how I turned out." Alesa ran her hand proudly down her body.

"No thanks, I value my eyesight." I sat on my only chair.

"Contrary to what you think, Glory, I was a favored demoness in the inner circle." Alesa tossed her long black hair over her shoulder and posed like she was ready for her close-up as "Demon of the Year." Then she deflated. "Which is why Lucifer went so ballistic when he realized I'd been unfaithful to him with another entity. He might have handled it if I'd done the deed with another demon." Big sigh. "But he knew with one sniff that this baby wasn't going to be pure. Rafe has that shifter side, you know. Unacceptable in Luc's world. The Devil doesn't mind growing his flock but he's got these rules about it. You see Luc himself can't procreate."

"Thank God," I murmured.

Alesa sniffed. "Whatever. This is a minor setback. I'll win the big guy over again. Especially in about ten years when the little sprig here is fully grown." She touched her tummy. "Then I'll take him back downstairs and Luc will see how truly awesome he is, even if he's not a pureblood."

"Ten years?" I felt sick. A decade of Alesa? No way.

"Don't look so freaked. Rafael and I won't have to stay here, you know. Must I remind you that you were just the vessel?" Alesa picked up the cardigan she'd appropriated, a nice green one, and slipped it on. "What was I thinking? Green is way too festive. Black is my color."

"Give me that. You pay for anything you get here." I snatched the sweater and folded it with shaking hands. "That's it, Alesa. As soon as you admit this pregnancy has nothing to do with Rafe either, you're moving on. Stay away from my shop unless I bring you here." I dropped the sweater on a shelf. "And no more shoplifting. From anywhere."

"Give me a break. Rafe's cut off my money and Luc certainly didn't send me off with a credit card." Alesa's smile chilled me. "Of course I could always knock over a liquor store, snatch a purse or two. It's easy when you can turn people to stone."

"Absolutely not!" My headache was turning into the vampire equivalent of a migraine. "Here's a challenge. See if you can get your money honestly. You figure out how to do that and I'll take you dancing with me."

"Honestly?" Alesa spat the word. "You've got to be kidding me. Demons don't do honest." She looked down at herself. Tonight she had on a long black knit skirt and a black and silver top that said "Baby on Board" in rhinestones. She also wore black tights and black and silver demiboots. "Though I do know fashion. You've got customers out there who could use some help."

"You can't work here." The very thought had me up and out of my chair. I put myself between Alesa and the door into the shop.

"Kidding. Demons don't work either unless it's to garner a soul for Lucifer." Alesa batted her ridiculously long dark lashes at me. "Come over to the dark side, Glory, and we'll have a ball. A little petty crime is barely a blip on the sin scale and Mugs and Muffins seems to be raking in the cash. I could take out that vamp behind the counter while you empty the register. Then I'd have money for a new hotel room."

"A blip? Stealing is so much more than that. Even if the owner Diana and I weren't friends, I'd never do that." I shuddered at the way her mind worked. "And a new room? What's wrong with the old one?" I thought Rafe had her settled in a hotel, one fairly cheap and far enough away to keep her out of my thoughts.

"Never mind. You've challenged me. So I'll give it a try. Honesty. Maybe it'll be fun for a change." She smiled that creepy smile of hers.

"Yes, it might even grow on you." And it certainly would

be a better role model for her baby. Unfortunately I really didn't think she could do anything honestly. But if she did somehow manage it, I'd make sure we went dancing on a night when Flo wasn't going.

"Oh, no, you don't. Not putting me off. We'll go tonight. I can avoid your saintly friends. In fact, wouldn't be caught dead with them." For some reason that made her laugh. "Or undead. Gee, Glory, where's your sense of humor?"

"I lost it when a pregnant demon knocked on my door." I knew I was being backed into a corner.

"What time?" Alesa had a gleam in her eyes I didn't trust. She'd been reading my mind of course.

"You expect to make money tonight?" I wanted nothing more than to go upstairs and lie down with a cold cloth on my aching head.

"Oh, I guarantee it. And I won't rob or kill anyone to get it. Now what time, Glory?" Alesa walked to the back door, the one that opened into the alley.

"We close at midnight on Saturdays. Meet me here then." I sighed. "And no one gets hurt, Alesa."

"Right. Got it." She smiled. "See you before midnight, cash in hand. Oh, this is going to be fun."

"Glory, there's something going on across the street you need to see." Erin had just come in from her dinner break and slid behind the cash register where I was finishing a sale.

"What do you mean?" I handed the customer her bag then turned to my clerk.

"Go see for yourself." Erin laughed. "No, not funny. Sorry."

Somehow I knew this was Alesa's doing. I pushed open the door and looked toward the corner. There were several people standing in front of a woman who held a hand-lettered sign. No rhinestones now. Alesa, barefoot and dirty, wore a sad-looking and very faded knit maternity dress. Her sign said "Pregnant, Hungry and Homeless" and a paper grocery sack sat on the ground in front of her. While I watched, a man dropped a few bills into the bag. I heard Alesa say, "Bless you."

Bless you? From a demon? I ran across the street.

"She's not homeless!"

"Yes, I am. They kicked me out of the hotel this afternoon. Something about a little fire and Rafael canceling his credit card." Alesa sniffed and wiped her eyes. Dark smudges, which humans watching would assume were mascara, made her look haggard. "And of course you told me I couldn't stay in your apartment."

"Why are you hassling her, lady?" Another man dropped a twenty in her bag. "Haven't you ever fallen on hard times?"

"Yeah. And where's this baby's father, honey?" A woman handed Alesa a pamphlet and a ten-dollar bill. "There's a shelter where you can sleep just a few blocks from here. Be sure to eat first. They lock the doors at ten."

"Bless you both. The father's denying everything. He's insisting on a DNA test. Can you believe it? And he knows I was true to him." Alesa sniffled. "Some people are so kind. Some"—she shook her head at me—"aren't."

Just then a police car pulled up to the curb.

"Move along. No panhandling or I'll have to take you in." The policeman said through his open window.

Alesa waved her pamphlet at him. "No worries, Officer. I'm on my way to the shelter." She picked up her bag, which I could see was full of cash, and started down the sidewalk.

I hurried to catch up with her. "'Bless you'? I'm surprised Lucifer didn't singe your tail for talking like that."

"I didn't say the 'G' word." Alesa winced when she stepped on a stone. "This outfit did the job, but I can't stand looking poor and pitiful one more minute!" She blinked and now stood clean and changed into black leather, maternity style. It was a hip look and I wished I had an outfit like that to sell in my shop. With the metal studs and thigh-high boots, she could have been a motorcycle gang's Madonna.

"What are you thinking? Doing magic in public and on

the street?" I frantically checked for shocked or bewildered bystanders. Luckily it was dark and we had the park on one side and an abandoned building across the street. The police car had disappeared around the corner.

"Relax. For a vampire you are way too uptight. Anybody ever tell you that, Glory?" Alesa stopped and looked me over. "I read your thoughts. So Ian told you something about being a super freak. Never human. I know he's right. You're a weird combo. When I was inside you, I did a little poking around. You've got powers you've never even tried to tap, girlfriend."

Okay, I'd never trusted this demon but she did literally know me inside out. I had to ask.

"What do you mean?"

"Come here." She dragged me into the deserted park. The only occupant was a man asleep on a bench. Someone really homeless. She poked him on his shoulder. "Get up."

"What are you doing, Alesa?"

"An experiment. Here's someone who needs a shelter and shower. And you say *I* reek, Glory?" She dragged him off the bench.

"What the hell? This is my bench. Get yer own!" He hit at her and lunged back toward his home sweet home. Alesa just laughed and danced away from his filthy hands.

"Puh-lease. You can keep your precious bed." She reached into her bag which she'd turned into a black leather tote. "Five bucks if you walk to that tree and back."

The man stopped and licked his lips. "What's yer game?"

"No game. Easy money. Now walkee, walkee." Alesa fluttered the bill in front of his bloodshot eyes then gave him a shove.

"Damned students and their stupid 'speriments." But he did start to stagger down the dirt path.

"What are you up to, Alesa?" I'd stayed downwind of both of them. Not that I was breathing, but I didn't want the stench clinging to my hair or clothes.

"Giving you a chance to strut your stuff, vamp girl."
Alesa gave me a toothy grin. "Now concentrate. Stare at this
stink weed and turn him to stone." Alesa waved at him.

"Are you nuts? I'm not a demon." I gaped at her. "I could
never . . ." Turn someone to stone? If only I could. It was an
awesome power. The best defense possible. I did stare at the
man. Easy target, barely moving, obviously under the influence of something. Was it possible . . . ?

"Didn't say you were a demon. Know you aren't. You
should be so lucky. But while I was stuck in you, I did a
Glory gut check." Alesa shuddered. "And I thought hell
could be a pit. Amidst all your gooey goodness I found some
interesting tidbits, hints of some stuff just lying around,
waiting to be used." Alesa's fangs appeared. "How dumb can
you get? Honey, you want your guys to respect you, you need
to pull up a little of your inner badass from time to time."
She nodded toward the man who'd decided he'd done five
bucks' worth and was headed back to his bench. "This statue
thing is a perfect way to show you can kick butt."

"I don't believe . . . Surely if I could . . ." I shook my head.
Alesa just stared at me, daring me to give it a go. What did
I have to lose? This was probably a trick. Alesa would watch
me try it then laugh her ass off. But I whirled around, glared
at the poor man who'd made it halfway home and thought,
"Freeze!"

He stalled in mid stumble. I held my breath, then ran up
to him.

"Hello? Can you hear me?" He still didn't move. I poked
him in his filthy jacket sleeve but he lost position abruptly
and staggered a few steps, collapsing against me.

"Eww, yuck." I pushed him away. "Well, that was an epic
fail."

"Not really. More like a five-second freeze. You lost focus.
Try again." Alesa stood behind me, her hands on my shoulders. "Keep your mind on your business. Don't get distracted
by his stench."

"'Less yer buyin' me some booze or passin' me the moolah, take yer 'speriments somewheres else." The man patted his pockets. "If someone hadn't stole my knife, I'd show ya what happens when ya mess with Jimmy Flint." He coughed and sputtered, obviously about to spit right at me.

"Freeze!" I yelled out loud this time, staring at him hard. His mouth froze before he could cut loose. *"Freeze, freeze, freeze,"* I thought furiously as I stepped closer and moved my hand in front of his eyes. He never blinked.

"I did it!" I couldn't believe it. Had I really had this power all these years? Even Jerry couldn't freeze people. And this guy was solid. I poked him gingerly. Yep, as solid as I'd been the times people, most of them higher on the paranormal pecking order than I'd ever hoped to be, had turned me into a statue. This was freaking amazing.

"Yep. You've got the power. Now step out of range. He's going to spit when you thaw him, no doubt about it. Let me go ahead and take him out and hell can have him. According to my demonic rolodex, Jimmy Flint was one bad dude before he pickled his think tank." Alesa rubbed her hands together, obviously more than happy to put this man down like a rabid dog or something. "Sending him below to his just reward could win me some points with Luc."

The idea made me sick to my stomach. Or was that the stink in the air? Bad dude or not, I wasn't allowing murder and Alesa knew it. She made a face and stepped back, muttering about "gooey goodness" again.

"I think living on a bench in his condition is a pretty good punishment for the here and now. And you know I'm not going to let you take out anyone. Not if you want my help with that pregnancy." I had to say it, just to make things crystal clear.

"Yeah, yeah. Why do I even bother?" Alesa leaned against a tree. "You want to know how to thaw him out, agree to take me dancing with you tonight. No last-minute excuses."

Blackmail. Of course it was in the demon repertoire. And

I *had* been trying to figure out how to stall her until another night. "You said all I have to do is lose focus." I turned my back on the guy. "That should do it."

"Not when he's in full statue mode, vamp girl." Alesa smiled. "Look at him. Before, he wasn't concrete yet. Now it takes a special technique to thaw him. You want it? Let's make a deal." She put her hands on her hips and hummed a popular dance tune.

I checked back to be sure. Too bad but she was right. My "'speriment" was still solid. "Fine. I'll take you to the club. I'm sure you can find some poor sap to dance with you." Yes, I had an attitude, but being saddled with a demon again, new power or not, was working on my last nerve. "You look like a pregnant dominatrix. I bet that works as some perv's fantasy."

"Why, Glory, you do say the sweetest things." Alesa actually did look pleased and even added chains to her boots and a spike through one eyebrow.

I turned to the project at hand. I had a statue, his nasty three layers of coats blowing in the chilly breeze. How was this possible? I couldn't resist. I raised the man's arm, testing to see if it fell. It didn't.

"Any idea what I could be? Why I can do this?" I didn't look at Alesa, still fascinated by what I'd done. Raise his foot, it stayed. In control, he would have fallen over.

"Damned if I know. Come on, quit playing with him. Just stare into his eyes and think 'Thaw.'" Alesa stomped over and poked my back. "Hurry. I should've used more of your hairspray. This night air's doing a number on my hair, making it go flat. In Texas, I think I should have big hair. Am I right?"

I couldn't argue with that. Loved big hair myself. Playing with him. That finally got through to me and I thawed him before we got out of there quickly. I did make sure Alesa dropped the five dollars she owed him in his lap.

"Waste of money. You erased his memory," Alesa whined as we headed to the shop.

"Are you honest about anything? Never mind." Of course

she wasn't. But she had been right about this power that could turn people to stone. "Seriously, any idea what I could be, Alesa? If I'm not a demon?" This really worried me.

"I've known lots of creatures with the freeze trick, even some ancient vamps. No telling what other untapped powers you've got." Alesa glanced at her wrist and was suddenly sporting a Cartier tank watch. "Eleven o'clock. Is that what you're wearing?" She grinned. "Hey, I just had a thought. Pawn shops. I can pawn stuff like this." She held up her wrist. "And I can create an endless supply. It's a demon thing. We have a treasure trove. Stuff we've stripped off the losers who end up down there when their tickets are finally punched. You know how they say you can't take it with you? You wouldn't believe how many people think they can." She laughed merrily, but, trust me, a demon's merry laugh will make your hair stand on end. Big hair, but think Franken-stein's girlfriend.

Finally she gasped and wiped her eyes again. "Problem solved. As long as Luc doesn't cut me off, I'm good to go for funds here." She sighed. "Best head to your place and fix my makeup. I left my luggage there."

I wanted to scream. "Made yourself right at home, didn't you? I don't recall giving you a key."

"Demons don't need keys. Or invites. We do as we please. And I want us to be pals." Alesa gave me her best smile, full fanged. I'm sure in hell it played well. Me? I wanted to puke. "This was a good time, Glory. Playing statues with you. I think there are more powers I could teach you. We'll be like sisters, you and me. Money or not, I'm moving in. I don't mind sleeping on your couch. Compared to the rack I've got downstairs with Luc, it's pretty cozy." She slipped her arm through mine.

"You've lost your mind." I was still freaked by the fact that I could, yes, turn people into stone. She thought I had more untapped powers? What could they be? I was desperate to know. But not so desperate that I was willing to act like her sister.

"Try to keep me out. Need proof I can do what I want? Just wait." Alesa clung to me and I couldn't get away from her. Demonic power pushed us back to the shop where Erin assured me she could close by herself. Then we headed upstairs.

"Stop this, Alesa. Let me go."

"Fine. Just call your little friends and get this evening going." Alesa plopped on the couch, listening in while I did call Flo, then Jerry. Somehow I would enjoy being with my friends and keep them away from Alesa. I knew it wasn't going to be easy. But I couldn't wait to tell everyone about my new power, maybe even show it off.

Wait a minute. That was demon thinking. A power like that was better reserved for an emergency. Hopefully, I'd never even need it. Yeah, right. With *my* life?

Six

N-V was packed, the usual situation on a Saturday night. Trey, Penny's boyfriend, let us in and directed Alesa and me toward the balcony where Flo and her party waited.

"Alesa, you know I'm not taking you up there." I smoothed down my black dress which was short to show off my legs and cut low to show off my cleavage. I know how to make the most of what I've got. Alesa still had on her black leather and got some admiring looks despite being obviously pregnant.

"Like I'd want to hang with *your* friends. The action's down here anyway." She smiled at Trey. "Can you set me up at the bar?"

"Sure." Trey didn't smile. He knew exactly what Alesa was by smell. He was a shifter and he gave me a look, like what was Penny's roommate doing running around with a demon? "Jack, the bartender, will take care of you. Enjoy the band."

"Maybe you could dance with me on your break." Alesa made it sound like a command as she snagged a sharp finger-nail on his black N-V T-shirt.

"And maybe not." Trey nodded toward the door. "My girl will be here any minute. She gets my dances."

"Right. Penny is at the football game with her parents." I tugged Alesa away from Trey. "Hands off this guy, Alesa. Trey, tell her where I am, but, if her parents are with her"— I made a face—"good luck with that." Penny's mortal folks had no idea their daughter had been turned vampire the previous spring. We'd been doing a lot of lying and juggling ever since. Nothing new there. It's called blending. We were surrounded by mortals now and I'd downed a bottle of synthetic at the apartment before we'd come so I could keep my fangs under control surrounded by all the warm, rich blood I could smell everywhere. It was working so far, but I was ordering more synthetic as soon as I got to the bar.

"Having a little thirst issue, Glory? Come with me to the bar and we'll get you that drink. They have the stuff with alcohol for you fangers?" Alesa had her arm hooked through mine again. It was driving me crazy that she thought she could actually act like my friend.

"Hush. Remember where you are, Alesa." I glanced at the mortals around us. "And of course they have stuff that I like. It's Rafe's club. He caters to us." I jerked away from the demon, risking the kind of scene she'd relish. I felt eyes on me and looked up at the balcony. Yes, Jerry was up there and he'd already headed for the stairs. I sensed another presence and turned. Rafe was working his way around the edge of the large room toward us. He gave me a nod, frowning when he noticed Alesa's hold on me. Thank God for friendly faces.

"What the hell are you doing here? And still bugging Glory? I told you to leave her alone." Rafe dragged Alesa away from me.

"Like I listen to you." She waved at the vampire bartender and ordered a shot of tequila.

"Not happening. No alcohol with a baby on board." I signaled the bartender for my usual blood with alcohol.

"Doesn't hurt my kind." Alesa smirked. "Take the stick out of your butt, Glo."

"You claim what you carry is part shifter." Rafe's hand came down on the bar. "Play by the rules while you're here. We don't serve alcohol to pregnant women." He gave his bartender a look. "Give her a bottled water."

"Well, you're no fun. For that, you have to dance with me." Alesa put on a pouty face.

"Not in this lifetime." Rafe turned his back on her. "Glory, Blade and I want to talk to you. Come to my office."

Jerry was right behind him. "Yes, we've got something for you there."

"What is this, an intervention?" I was familiar with those, but not for myself. Well, not recently anyway. In Las Vegas, I'd needed one for my gambling problem. Back then Rafe had been in dog form as my bodyguard. He and a few vamp girlfriends had done the deed making me cut up my credit cards and sending me to a program when I'd lost control at the poker tables. I'd be forever grateful.

"Do you *need* an intervention? Why are you still running around with that creature?" Jerry glanced from me to Alesa, who smirked like she knew a secret. "And what have you two been up to? Gambling?" He leaned close to whisper in my ear. "Ripping out throats in dark alleys?"

"Jerry! No and hell no!" I put my hand on his chest then glanced at Rafe. Both of them looked so good to me. Safe havens. I was grateful for their strength, not to mention loyalty. And then there was the obvious . . . If I ever needed another twelve-step program it would probably be for a sexual addiction. These men were just about irresistible, each in his own way. Jerry had that rugged, battle-worn look that always made me want to soothe his hurts while he soothed mine. Then there was Rafe, who was 100 percent Latin lover.

I indulged in a little fantasy about what could happen in Rafe's office if these men really had reached some kind of truce. Oh, yeah. And I'd be in the middle. My cheeks felt warm, my thoughts well blocked, as we eased through the crowd to the door behind the stage.

"She's attached herself to me like a leech. Threatening my

friends. I don't know how to get rid of her. Any suggestions?" I saw the men exchange glances, for once in accord about something but silent until we got past the stage. The famous band on tap for the night had questions for Rafe about the venue. Then one of the guys recognized me from a party I'd attended with Ray. It would have been rude to just brush him off so I gave the man a Ray update. I was glad I could say Israel Caine was on the wagon and writing music again.

Finally Jerry just grabbed my hand, pulled me into Rafe's office, and slammed the door once Rafe slipped in behind me. The soundproofing there was impressive and we soaked in the sudden silence. It took me a minute to realize we weren't alone.

"Here's our suggestion, Gloriana." Jerry gestured at the woman who sat on the corner of Rafe's desk. Gorgeous. And a lot of her. When she stood, she hit over six feet in her platform tennis shoes. She had glorious golden red hair streaked with black and the iciest blue eyes I'd ever seen. Right now they examined me until I squirmed and wanted to check to see if a black bra strap was showing. Instead, I took a breath. Shifter.

"Hello. Are you here to get Alesa off my back?" I smiled. "I'd be forever grateful."

"No kidding." She didn't smile back. Hmm. "Demons are after only one thing, Glory St. Clair. No matter what they tell you they want. You dumb enough to give one of them your soul?"

That wiped the smile off my face. "No."

"Ease up, Laurie." Rafe put his hand on my shoulder. Jerry had already laid his hand on my other one.

"She's got to get this straight right now. I can't protect her if she's running around with a demon sidekick like they're friends or something." Laurie, since apparently that was her name, crossed her arms over her chest. It wasn't a big bosom, but decent. The kind I'd like to have. So I could wear a blouse that buttoned up the front and I wouldn't have to worry about it gapping open. You know what I mean?

"Who the hell is this? It's not like I have a choice, guys. Of course I don't want to be near Alesa. But what can I do? She's been making threats. How is this person supposed to protect me from a demon?" I knew what this was now. They'd hired another bodyguard for me. Hah! And Jerry wasn't taking chances this time. A female bodyguard. He and Rafe had actually agreed to work together. I liked that, but not that they'd sneaked around and arranged this without consulting me.

"Laurie Mehta. She's a were-cat. Shifts into a Bengal tiger." Rafe grinned. "You should see it, Glory. Absolutely awesome. Nothing bigger on the cat grid. She can take out whatever comes after you."

"Even a demon? Isn't that why you're hiring her?" I tapped my foot. "What can a were-cat do against a demon?"

"More than you think." Laurie aimed those glacial eyes at me and I had to steel myself not to squirm. She had some real intensity going there. "I've trained with some of the best spiritualists in the business. Believe it or not I can shut your demoness down when she tries some of her crap." She smiled and polished her pale pink nails on her brown T-shirt. She wore a no-nonsense outfit of that plain T-shirt with drawstring khakis. I hated to tell her but, if she was going to run around with me, she was going to have to upgrade her look.

"Sounds like bragging to me. I've never seen anyone have any effect on Alesa except for an ex-priest. And even he couldn't do it alone." I shook my head. "Come on, guys. Why are you wasting your money?"

"First, it's not a waste. You're determined to have business with MacDonald, Gloriana, and Laurie can be present for every minute of your visits with him." Jerry smiled his approval of the were-cat. "Second, if she can control Alesa, then I will definitely feel better about your being around her. I stopped by your shop earlier and Erin said you'd disappeared with the demon. I sure as hell couldn't find you."

"Yes, I'll tell you about that later. Something really cool happened." I heard the excitement in my voice. Uh-oh. Cool and Alesa together? Was I being pulled over to the dark side? No, it was the power I was excited about. Alesa had just called it to my attention.

I saw Laurie whispering with Rafe. They would make a nice couple. If nothing else I should encourage that. Let Rafe go and he could move on to someone he could be happy with. He smiled at something she said. Yes, a were-cat would be a good mate for him. I wanted to slap myself in the head. Mate? When Alesa was supposedly carrying his child?

"Glory?" Rafe stood in front of me. "You can't be alone with Alesa all the time. She's dangerous. We both know that." He looked over his shoulder to where Jerry was giving me a "Do this, Gloriana" stare.

"Yes, though the apartment is getting pretty crowded." I took Rafe's hand. "I know you mean well and I *am* freaked-out by having Alesa around. She's been kicked out of the hotel. Apparently she started a fire there today. Probably on purpose. So I'm going to let her sleep on the couch. Where will Laurie sack out?"

"Don't worry about me. I'm used to the bodyguard gig. Won't be the first time I've bedded down on the floor." Laurie nodded at Jerry. "Now the demon's living with her. Seems I hired on just in time."

"No kidding. Gloriana, why are you allowing that?" Jerry put his arm around me.

"I didn't feel like I had a choice. For some reason Alesa is determined to stay with me. She can hurt my friends, hurt me. Shit, she's literally hell on wheels. And we need to keep an eye on her until we know if she's carrying Rafe's child." I looked at Laurie. "Seriously? You think you can handle her? And squeeze into an overcrowded apartment?"

"It's what I'm paid to do. And as long as you have plenty of meat and a bathtub, I'll be fine. I do like my soaks. Which I can do during the day while you sleep."

"Uh, yeah. I can manage that." I didn't want to picture a Bengal tiger tearing into sides of beef then soaking in a tub to get the blood off. Weird. But then my life was one long episode of "Weird Gloriana."

"I've got the meat deliveries all arranged, Gloriana. They'll happen during your death sleep. Won't disturb you at all." Jerry dragged me toward the door. "Now let's go upstairs and explain to our friends why you came into the club with a demon."

"Aw, Jer, did they all smell Alesa?" I dreaded the scene.

"Of course. Richard was on his feet with a crucifix as soon as you hit the door." Jerry sighed. "Coming, Laurie?"

"On the clock right now, Jerry." Laurie smiled. "Relax, Glory. I've got your back. This demon will no longer be a problem. Guaranteed."

I smiled back. Guaranteed? Either Laurie had serious skills or she was terrifyingly overconfident. Either way, Alesa versus the tiger? I wanted a front-row seat for that party.

"Glory, Aggie called me tonight. About shoe shopping. You promised her we'd go together?" Flo made a little face. "Why didn't you warn me?"

"I'm sorry. Too much on my mind." I looked over the railing and saw Alesa dancing with a man who had also embraced the black leather philosophy. She threw back her head and laughed as they shook their butts to the beat. The band was kicking it into high gear and the floor was packed. I felt ancient, sitting up there watching. But the mood for dancing like a wild thing had left me as soon as I'd seen Richard's frowning disapproval.

"I can see that you're upset." Flo put her hand on mine. "It's all right, *mia amica*. We will go shopping with the Siren. Whatever you want. I hate this demon thing. And don't mind Ricardo. He is worried about me. But I promised him not to get near the she-devil. You won't bring her to the mall, will you?" Flo clutched my hand. "Swear it!"

"Relax, Flo. I won't. Cross my heart." I knew Flo was

scared of what would happen if Alesa tried to persuade her to sell her soul to Lucifer. Flo had almost caved once. Because she wanted to see her own reflection. It drove her nuts that I could see mine and she couldn't see hers. She'd gotten a glimpse of her reflection when a pair of demons had made a run at her soul. Then they'd snatched the mirror trick away. Only Flo's absolute devotion to her very devout husband had helped her resist hell's diabolical promises. Hey, she figured she was going to live forever anyway.

"I am so, um, weak when it comes to resisting what I want. You know?" Flo glanced at Richard, who was talking to Jerry and Damian on the other side of the table.

"No, you're strong. But I wouldn't want either of us put to the test again." I squeezed her hand. "Thanks for helping me with Aggie. I needed for her to give Ian a blood sample. For some tests he's running. So I had to bribe her with shoe shopping. She still wants to be pals with us."

"And who wouldn't want to be our friends, I ask?" Flo grinned. "But what's this about blood samples? For Ian Mac-Donald? Does Jeremiah know?"

"Yes. That's one reason I have a new bodyguard. Because I'm going to be seeing Ian not only for Alesa but for myself. To figure out why I always have those weird reactions to Ian's drugs." I pulled Flo's hand to my stomach. "Feel. I have a lumpy stomach now, Flo. Because I took a new drug and had a strange reaction to it."

"Why did you take it? Will you never learn?" Flo poked my tummy. "This is strange. You never had this before. I remember how you looked—not thin, more like a Rubens painting, round and pretty and very smooth. What was the drug for?"

"It was a wonder drug. Penny took it too. It let us eat real food." I sighed. "You see why I had to try it?"

"You and your craving for such things. Cheetos! Chocolate!" Flo shook her head. "Me? I never wish for Nonna's pasta. Though it could make you weep, I tell you. *Delizio!*"

She kissed her fingertips in typical Italian fashion. "It was too long ago, I have moved on." She grabbed my arm. "But, Glory, you know you always have bad things happen to you with Ian's drugs!"

"So I'm stupid." I was getting irritated, more with myself than with Flo. "I get that. But these blood tests helped Ian find out something important." My eyes suddenly filled with tears.

"What? *Amica*, what is this?" Flo gestured for Richard. "Ricardo, come here."

"No, I shouldn't . . ." Then I was sobbing on her shoulder.

"Life of the party, isn't she?" Laurie stood behind Flo.

"What's going on?" Jerry sat in the chair beside me.

I couldn't quit crying while Flo patted my back and murmured soothing Italian words in my ear. Finally I seemed to run dry and sat up.

"Sorry about that." I sniffed and looked around for a tissue.

Laurie patted her pockets. "Guess this gig's going to have different requirements from guarding a blood importer for the Transylvanian mob. He never cried. At least not until I told him I was leaving." She sighed when she came up empty.

"Yeah, start carrying tissues, an extra lipstick in my favorite color and sunglasses, in case I have swollen eyes from all the weeping and wailing I'm going to do." I gratefully took the tissue Flo dug out of her designer clutch. "And if that mobster had the issues I've had lately, I bet he would have had a meltdown too." I mopped at my eyes.

"I get a bonus for these crying jags, Jerry?" Laurie raised her eyebrows at him. He was right beside me now, as usual speechless when I fall apart.

"Don't promise her that, Jer, you'd go broke." I dredged up a smile and looked around the table. "Sorry, guys. Guess I needed to unload and Flo has the best shoulder for that." I glanced at Jerry. "I know. Yours is great, but you always want to fix things."

"I could fix if I knew what in the hell you are crying about, *mia amica*." Flo handed me another tissue. "We can go to the ladies room. Do something about your makeup."

"Too crowded. Employee break room. Rafe won't mind." I stood. "Guess Laurie comes with us."

"Lucky me. Yes, I do." She was right on our heels.

I heard Jerry whispering excuses to Damian and Richard. I stopped and turned around. "Tell them my problem. Maybe they can help me figure this thing out."

"You're sure?" Jerry was on his feet and by my side in an instant.

"If it won't get me kicked out of town by the council. First make Damian promise this won't go to them." I sighed. "That's all I need, a town eviction notice."

"My brother will not dare." Flo clearly shot Damian a hot mental message and he jumped to his feet. They exchanged glares and a few hissed words in Italian, not bothering to use mental messages. Finally they both gestured and Damian sat again.

"Relax, Gloriana. I am your friend first of all, council member second, as my sister reminds me." He gave me a charming smile, obviously able to turn his mood around on a dime.

"Thanks, Damian." My voice cracked and I felt the urge to sob again.

"See? It's settled. Now let's go." Flo pulled me toward the stairs.

With the band playing, the employee break room was empty as I knew it would be. I used the mirror and supplies from my purse to erase all signs of my crying jag. Enough waterworks. Not even when I told Flo the whole story. And I was going to have to. She paced the room while she waited for me to finish with lipstick and mascara. Her frowning glances at me in front of the mirror made me realize I was torturing her with this so I hurried.

"Sorry, pal. Now about the blood samples. Ian discovered from the first one he took that when Jerry turned me vampire I wasn't . . ." I sucked in a breath. Not crying. No, no, no. "Human."

"Excuse me?" Laurie said this first. She actually stepped close to me, picked up my hand and sniffed my skin. "I don't get it. Vampire, that's all I'm reading. And the various cosmetics, hairspray and that demon you've been consorting with."

"Not human?" Flo's eyes were wide. "*Ridicolo!* You know what you were before. You told me about your life in London. Your first husband. How you met Jeremiah. Is this some trick to hurt your lover? Part of the feud between these Scots? In Italia there were forever these vendettas. Pah! Why can't these men let them go?"

"No vendetta, Flo. I wish it was just a trick to hurt Jerry. He still believes that's Ian's agenda." I sat on the couch and patted the seat beside me. "But Ian's convinced me it's true. He's been comparing my blood sample to other paranormals, trying to figure out what else I could have been. When he heard I knew a Siren, he wanted Aggie's blood sample, for comparison to mine. She's scared of needles so the only way to get her to cooperate was to promise the shoe-shopping trip."

"I never thought I would say it, but I can't think of shoes with you in such a fix!" Flo collapsed against the sofa cushions. "This is *insensato!* Here." She grabbed my arm and pulled it to her nose as Laurie had done. She inhaled. "*La tigre* is right. Nothing but vampire. Good, clean vampire with a hint of that lavender bodywash you like. If you had something else in you, wouldn't you reek of it?"

"That's what I thought. Maybe Ian *was* messing with me. That stupid feud behind it. Until something else happened tonight, Flo." I glanced at Laurie. "Something that convinced me this might be true."

"What? Is the demon filling your head with stories? She crouched inside you like a creepy disease for a while. Maybe she infected you and that's what Ian found. What is going on?" Flo leaned forward and took my hands. "Tell us, Glory."

"Not sure I'd believe anything a creature from hell spews." Laurie walked over and turned the lock on the door then plopped down in a chair across from us. "But if she managed to prove something to you, spill."

"She showed me that I can turn people to stone!" I winced when Flo's grip tightened and she gasped. Clearly she was impressed. Laurie? I would have to make the earth spin backward to impress her.

"Oh, yeah? Let's see it." Laurie jumped up, opened the door and dragged a girl in from the hall. She locked the door again, did her tiger magic on the puzzled girl which got her to smile, suddenly happy to see us.

"Hi, y'all. Laurie here said you wanted to see me? Buy me a drink? I'm Amber." The blue-eyed blonde blinked. She'd obviously already enjoyed a few drinks at the bar.

Since Laurie had never spoken out loud to her, I had new respect for my tiger's powers. "Sure, Amber, I'll buy you a drink." I got up to face her, looked in her eyes, concentrated and did my freeze thing.

"Glory! Look at her. You did it! She can't move." Flo jumped to her feet, prodding the girl with a bronze-tipped nail. "This is *fantastico*." She raised the girl's arm and it stayed. Waved her hand in front of her eyes and Amber never blinked. "Can you teach me?"

"No, she can't. This is a power, Florence. Glory's got it. You can't buy it or learn it." Laurie nodded approvingly. "Will make my job easier. Good going, Glo. Guess I can put up with your girly crying thing if you can kick butt like that."

"Gee, thanks. Now I just have to thaw her. Can you get her out of here, Laurie?" I dug a ten-dollar bill out of my purse. "Give her this for that drink."

"She's had enough. I'm going to suggest she switch to bottled water. That man she's with thinks he's got a sure thing. This woman needs to learn some self-respect." Laurie waited for me to thaw Amber then did some mental messaging that got Amber out the door and on her way with no memory of us.

"Glory, you *must* be something else," Flo said quietly. "Something . . . Well, I never thought . . ." She studied me like she'd never seen me before. "Could you be demon now?"

"Flo, honey, I'm the same as I was five minutes ago!" I touched her shoulder. To my horror, she flinched. "Seriously. No matter what I used to be, I'm all vampire now. You said so yourself. No taint of that hellish sweetness. Right?"

"Of course, what am I thinking?" Flo stood and brushed down her skirt. As usual, she looked great in a red leather miniskirt and red and black sweater that hugged her figure. "I'm just sorry that Ricardo and I are going to Paris at the end of the week. We won't be here to support you with this demon problem. Or this other . . . thing."

"Leaving? This is the first I've heard of it." And I bet it would be the first Richard heard of it too. Flo was getting out of town because of me. I wanted to bawl again. My best friend was afraid of me. No, surely not. She just needed time to process this. And I was sure Richard would be glad for them to leave because of Alesa anyway.

"About the mall. Monday night?" She smiled, obviously determined to act like nothing had happened.

"No can do. That's when I take Alesa to see Ian. He's going to be her doctor. Tuesday?" I wanted to nail this down.

"You're sure Alesa won't try to trail along?" Flo wouldn't meet my eyes, straightening the silver and gold bangles on her wrist.

"I won't let her, Florence." Laurie walked to the door, opened it and checked the hallway. "You can rest easy on that score."

"Well then. Tuesday night. We'll shoe shop with Aggie." Flo linked arms with me. "Too bad you can't come to Paris with me, Glory. Now *there's* some shoe shopping." She chattered about European shopping as we headed upstairs. I had no doubt she'd tell Richard what had just happened in the break room. Which meant I'd have to tell Jerry. What would he think? Only one way to find out.

"Glory, my parents are downstairs. Can you bring Mr. Blade down so they can meet him?" Penny had found us at our table a few minutes after Flo and I had rejoined the men.

"Of course." Just what I needed, faking my way through a meeting with Penny's mortal parents. I didn't have a problem introducing Jerry to them, of course. In his business world he worked with mortals every night and had easily convinced them he was absolutely like them.

Jerry and I followed Penny to a table away from the dance floor. Her parents were talking to Trey. It wasn't the first time they'd met me or Penny's boyfriend. We got along fine because I'd set Penny up in a clean apartment. You should have seen the mess she'd lived in before. I knew they liked Trey too. He was gainfully employed and actually attended classes at the nearby university during the day. He also clearly adored their brilliant daughter.

"Glory! Good to see you. This must be your young man." Penny's mother rushed up to me and gave me a hug.

"Yes, this is Jeremy Blade. Jerry, Mr. and Mrs. Patterson." My "young" man happened to be over five hundred years old but looked thirty. I just tuned out the introductions as I scanned the room for Alesa. I did not want her anywhere near this. "And this is my friend Laurie Mehta. Penny, Laurie's going to be staying on our couch for a while. Just lost her lease." I smiled at Penny's expression and sent her a one-word mental message: *"Bodyguard."*

"Cool. Hey, Laurie. Nice to meet you." Penny introduced her to Trey and her parents then turned. Her twin sister, the cheerleader, and her date walked up, flushed and laughing, from the dance floor. "My twin, Jenny and her date, Darren." They exchanged nods with Laurie. Darren was a little awestruck at Laurie's unusual height and look and it took an elbow from Jenny to get his attention back on his date.

"How was the game, Jenny?" I had just spotted Alesa trying to work her way over with a wicked gleam in her eyes. I glanced at Laurie and she got the message.

"Awesome. We did a pyramid. I was near the top. Totally rocked it." Jenny chattered on. She grabbed a Coke off the table, took a sip and never stopped talking. The parents gazed at her adoringly. Even Penny smiled indulgently.

I wanted to put in a few words about the valuable research Penny did every night but realized it wouldn't matter. Normal life versus our weird vampire subculture? Forget it. Penny worked on things that these mortals would and could never know about, never care about. If a vampire got to see daylight or eat a taco? So what?

In fact they'd freak if they knew they had a vampire daughter. So they'd stay in blissful ignorance. But it wasn't so blissful for the daughter who couldn't brag about her life to them. Or let them know that her boyfriend was really a shape-shifter who could, damn it, become just about anything he could visualize. And how cool was that? Much cooler than Darren getting set to play varsity basketball next month.

I saw Laurie and Alesa exchange a few words on the other side of the room before I made a lame excuse and dragged Jerry away from the party. Rafe walked up just then, Trey not far behind him.

"I just heard from the bartender that Alesa's been bragging that she's moving in with you again. Is that right, Glory?" Rafe looked ready to blow.

"She's broke. Needs a place to stay. Where else can she go? At least till we know about this baby." I had three pairs of eyes on me. "Trey? You need something?" He really wasn't supposed to be in on this.

"I don't want Penny living with a demon." He kept his voice low and I was sure the high volume of the music kept us from being overheard.

"Neither do I. But what choice do I have? Penny's my fledgling to mentor." I glanced up at the balcony. Damian was still there. He hadn't brought a date but had danced with several mortal women who'd apparently come to the club single. One of them was draped over him now, probably destined to become his late-night snack.

"I see where you're looking. I already asked him. As head of the vampire council, Damian can decide if Penny still needs a mentor or not. He says with her steady job, relationship with Ian, who many on the council respect, and her months of successful blending, he's willing to let her live on her own now." Trey nodded, like he had a mental checklist. Done and done.

"Really? You just took it upon yourself to jump into our business?" I heard my voice rise but, come on, this was my fledgling we were talking about. I'd taken her from pathetic and angry child wearing black lipstick and horizontal stripes to a self-assured woman who looked good and could blend anywhere. Not only that, she could walk among these delicious mortals surrounding us right now and not show a hint of fang. There were some older vamps who couldn't manage that.

"I love her, Glory. I'm only thinking of what's best for her." Trey made serious eye contact, begging me to understand.

"Okay, okay. I get it. I love Penny too. And she's so smart, she'd think she could handle whatever Alesa dishes out. Am I right?" I worked up a smile. Nice that Trey had proclaimed his love like that. Penny had snagged a keeper. I realized Rafe and Jerry were both tense, not pleased with the way Trey had challenged me. I didn't see anything wrong with Trey's attitude. We were on the same page—worrying about Penny and wanting her away from Alesa. I let him see that in my eyes.

"Then she's going. I'll take care of it." Trey turned on his heel and marched toward the family table where Penny still chatted with her parents. Jenny and date were back on the dance floor.

"The shifter could have shown more respect." Jerry eased his hand around my waist.

"I'll talk to him. He shouldn't be pushing into vamp business. It can get him in trouble." Rafe glanced at me. "He's letting his emotions cloud his judgment."

"It happens. I think it's sweet. Penny's a lucky girl." I nodded to where Trey had pulled Penny out to dance with him. The song was slow and romantic. It was the kind I liked to dance to, but I knew better than to pick from the two men next to me.

"Laurie's managing Alesa pretty well." Rafe had his hands in his pockets. "She's kept her away from Penny's table and, more important, away from you. There's no way she should have bulldozed you into having her in your home though. I'm going to try to get her to move in with me. I'd hate it but it's my mess, not yours."

Rafe looked like he'd just been sentenced to life without parole as he trudged over to where Alesa leaned against the bar watching us as she sipped water. It didn't take vamp hearing to see that she wasn't interested in his proposition. Which made me wonder exactly what she was up to.

Alesa stomped up to me. "Have you seen his digs, Glory? I made a little trip over there when I first got to town. Not that he invited me." She sniffed when Rafe growled. "Bachelor shithouse. I wouldn't take a shower in that place on a bet." She looped her arm through mine. "Sorry, pal, but you're stuck with me."

"I'll hire a cleaning crew. Redecorate. Just leave Glory the hell alone." Rafe looked around as he started to jerk Alesa's hand off of me. Apparently he thought better of it with the crowd of mortals around us. "I thought this is what you wanted, for us to be a family."

Alesa sneered. "Maybe I'm thinking your whole attitude since I've got here reeks. A family doesn't have to be a mommy and daddy. It can be Auntie Glory and Mommy. If you're lucky, maybe I'll grant you some visitation after the little devil gets here."

Rafe gave Laurie a look over my head. "Meet Laurie, another member of the family. She'll be staying with Glory now. Maybe you'll change your mind about where you want to live after you get better acquainted."

Alesa turned and scoped Laurie out. Her hiss was pure displeasure. "This just proves how unfit you are to be a father figure. Bringing in one of *these*." She turned to me. "Glory, are you really on board with having this creature in your home?"

"If she makes you unhappy? Bring her on." I smiled at Laurie then Rafe. "Thanks for trying, Rafe. And, Alesa, since you've figured out how to get money now, maybe you would be happier in a hotel."

"Oh, no, you're not getting rid of me that easily." And with that Alesa flounced off to the edge of the dance floor where she gestured and soon had a man pulling her into a dance.

"I'd like to know why she's so intent on sticking with you, Gloriana, but right now you look like you could use a dance too." Jerry clasped my hand. "And I'm sure Valdez has business to tend to." Jerry didn't bother to ask, he knew me too well. He just pulled me out to the dance floor.

I melted into his arms, glad to let the stress of the night go. I felt several pairs of eyes on me again, not all of them kind. Figuring out Alesa was beyond me for now. At least I was safe for the moment, and anyone who tried to take me out could damn well expect to become a statue on the spot.

I closed my eyes. Oh, yeah. Just try to mess with Glory St. Clair. I was powerful, whatever the hell I was. Overconfidence. Of course I was riding for a fall.

Seven

The apartment door opened before I could get my key out.

"So this is your guest." Penny smiled. "Wow. Dig the outfit. I'm Penny Patterson, Glory's fledgling and roommate."

"Alesa." The demon breezed by me without even a nod for Penny. "I'm starving. Hitting the fridge."

"Well, what did we do to deserve this?" Penny made a face, obviously remembering her last encounter with demons.

"Don't ask. And now she's bent out of shape because she didn't pick up any souls tonight for the big guy downstairs." I waited for a reaction and wasn't disappointed. Alesa stuck her head out from the kitchen.

"Not bent. Didn't give it a real shot. Not that I need to explain myself but I figured why should I go to any trouble for a man who tossed me out in the cold, literally, when I needed him the most?" She made a rude gesture at the floor, sniffed then disappeared into the kitchen again.

"Good news for the souls in Austin anyway." I smiled at Penny and settled into a chair. "Now why aren't you with Trey?" Laurie prowled the apartment while keeping an eye on Alesa. If Laurie were in her cat form, her tail would be twitching.

"He's still at work, helping with closing. He wanted me to stay, hang out, but where's the fun in that? Besides, I thought I should touch base with you without a crowd around." Penny sat in the other chair. We could hear Alesa rummaging in the kitchen. "Guess I could ask *you*—where's Mr. Blade?"

"Business call. He owns casinos in several states. Which is ironic considering I'm a recovering gambler."

"Good thing Texas doesn't—" Penny jumped when she heard a noise from the kitchen. Clearly Alesa was making her nervous. "Tomorrow's Sunday, Glory. You up for church? I figured it would be a demon-free zone."

"I heard that too." Alesa sang from the kitchen. She stopped in the doorway to pry the lid off a pint of Ben & Jerry's. "Seriously, you girls need to embrace your dark side. It's fun over here."

"Church without demons sounds like a bit of Heaven to me." I grinned at Penny. "Wouldn't miss it." We usually did attend the Sunday evening services at the Moonlight Church of Eternal Life and Joy. No way a demon could get past the giant crosses flanking the doorway. Not unless she was trapped inside a really good person. I sent Alesa a mental reminder of that little incident. She popped me back with a comment too ugly to repeat.

Penny frowned when Alesa dropped onto the couch and dug a spoon into the ice cream.

"Where did that come from? And do you have to eat it in front of us?" Penny sighed. "That's just cruel and unusual."

"Aw, vamp girl. Having trouble adjusting? Rafael bought it for me." Alesa scooped up a big spoonful of Chunky Monkey, waved it in front of us and then stuffed it in her mouth. "Mmmm."

"Demon bitch," Penny muttered.

"Thanks, sweet thing. Words like those are music to my ears." Alesa smiled and licked her lips.

"Okay, enough. Now, Penny, how was the football game?

You handle the crowd all right?" I turned my shoulder to Alesa.

"No problem. Jenny was in her element of course. And the home team won. It was fun being in the crowd. I could pretend for a few hours that I was, you know, normal." Penny sighed. "Anyway, I loaded up on the synthetic blood first, of course, just like you taught me. Didn't flash my fangs once." She seemed to shake off her regrets and suddenly grinned. "I really came by because I have big news! Trey's asked me to move in with him."

"Wow! Are you ready for that step?" I kept my thoughts blocked. So Trey's solution to getting Penny out of here was to have her with him. Nice of him, but was Penny really ready to live with the shifter? If he was only doing this to keep her safe—

"You know I can read through your puny vampire mind blocks, Glory. Are you really going to bring the kid down with a bunch of objections? She's in *looove*." The way Alesa said the "l" word made it sound like a disease that had to run its course. She had stretched out on the couch, the ice cream carton empty on the table, the spoon inside it. "Let the girl enjoy her hot stud while the fire's still burning. You know what I mean?" The demon grinned. "Hah! Sure you do. You should poke around in Nickel's mind. The girl gets some good lovin'. Don't you—what does he call you?—love bunny?"

"Penny, not Nickel. And excuse me? You, you're reading through my block?" Penny jumped up, clearly outraged. "How, how rude!"

"Another compliment. Quit kissing up, will ya?" Alesa yawned. "Glad to hear you're going. I can move right into your little bedroom. Love the rat perfume you've got going on. Makes me hungry, but then just about everything does these days." She patted her tummy.

I shuddered at the thought of Alesa right down the hall. Obviously she'd never be civilized. I saw Penny's horrified expression and knew the sooner my fledgling got away from her, the better.

"I hate to admit it, but Alesa's right about one thing. Follow your heart, Penny. You and Trey have been going together for months. If you want to take the next step toward commitment, go for it. Just don't feel like you have to rush into something because this *thing* is camping out here. I've got Laurie for protection now. We should be perfectly safe with her watching over us." I felt the heat of Alesa's eyes flaming my way. "I know living with a demon isn't exactly on your top ten list."

"You'll be as safe as if you were in church, Penny. Count on it. So stay if you're not ready to shack up with your boyfriend. I'll keep Ms. Alesa in line." Laurie began to pull things out of the duffle bag she'd brought up from her car she'd left parked outside N-V. "Burning some cleansing incense right now. Suggest you move your butt down the hall, demon. This is going to sting. Though we'd purely enjoy watching you crying and reaching for a tissue. Am I right, ladies?" Laurie grinned as she waved a branch of what looked like weeds and clicked a lighter to set them aflame.

"I'm going. That shit is nasty!" Alesa hurried down the hall toward Penny's old room. "Don't be surprised if I start emptying drawers and tossing stuff into the hallway."

"Will she?" Penny sniffed. "I think this incense or whatever smells nice. Beats the hell out of the rat poop stench I've been sleeping with."

"Yes, she'll probably throw out your stuff, but if you're moving . . ." I stood and waited while Penny got up too. "Are you?"

"Yes. I love Trey. And I want to be with him. Maybe this hurried our relationship along a little, but I'm okay with that. I'm sure you'd like some of your space back." She glanced at her big computer set up on my kitchen table. She'd used it when she'd still been doing research at the University of Texas. Now she did most of her work on Ian's state-of-the-art equipment in his lab. But I was sure it would go with her. She'd even named it. She'd also brought her cat. I'd grown really attached to Boogie and if she wanted to leave him here, I was fine with it.

"I loved having you here. Don't leave on my account." I hugged her. "I just want you to be happy. But getting away from Alesa is probably a good idea." Penny and I grinned when Laurie started chanting and circling the room with her smoking weeds. "Even with Laurie here, there's still danger. I don't want you anywhere near the demon."

"I'm sure that's why Trey asked me this tonight. He's sweet, wanting to look after me. Kind of like how Mr. Blade always wants to protect you." Penny peered down the hall and frowned. "She just dumped my underwear drawer. Can you believe it?"

"Nothing Alesa does surprises me." Did I dare warn Penny about protective men? Should I? They meant well. Too bad they sometimes went too far, didn't know when protection became control. Some lessons we needed to learn for ourselves. And Trey wasn't Jerry. Maybe he knew not to cross that line with Penny.

"I'll take care of this." Laurie's growl, when half of Penny's closet landed just feet from the bathroom, made the hair on my arms stand on end. She stormed down the hall and we heard Penny's bedroom door slam.

"What is she?" Penny clutched my hand.

"Were-cat. Turns into a Bengal tiger. I don't think there's enough space in your crowded room for her to shift, but she says she's also got some kind of mystical mojo going, besides the incense, that can handle a demon." I sighed and sat back in a chair again. "I hope she's right."

"Cool. And the energy in here already feels better. Bet Mr. Blade brought her in. Did he?" Penny began dumping papers into a cardboard box.

"He and Rafe got together on it." I glanced down the hall, expecting noise of some kind, but it was eerily quiet. "Where demons are concerned, I let my independent woman thing go and allow them to pay the freight."

"Good. I'm glad." Penny started unplugging wires. "Trey wants me out of here tonight and I'm glad about that too. He's bringing a truck after he finishes closing."

"Fine." I watched her for a moment then closed my eyes, life without a headache a dim memory. "I know it's for the best." Penny had come to mean a lot to me and I really would miss her.

"You know how I was raised, Glory. With Gramps a preacher, we practically lived at the church. I can't handle all this evil in my face all the time." I felt a hand on my knee and saw Penny squatting in front of me. "Why are you putting up with it, Glory? Why is she here?"

Alesa stood in the doorway, a frowning Laurie right behind her. "Because Glory wants to know if this baby is Rafe's, don't you?"

"I know it can't be Rafe's." I gave her a hard look. I was sick of this particular lie.

Penny's mouth dropped open. "This is Rafe's baby?"

"No, it's not. Alesa *claims* she got pregnant while her spirit or whatever inhabited me. Isn't that insane?" I shuddered and appealed to Penny. My fledgling was smart and logical, a scientist. Like Ian, she would surely back me up that this couldn't be true.

"Well . . ." She frowned, obviously thinking it over. "Come on, Glory. The whole idea of vampires and demons even existing is insane. After I woke up with my own pair of fangs, I learned not to discount the possibility of anything."

"I simply refuse to buy into it." I felt Laurie's hand drop onto my shoulder, a warm weight that comforted me.

"Didn't say I was buying it. But I know Ian came over here this week about that other thing." She patted my hand. Penny turned to Alesa, who'd strolled over to stretch out on the couch again. To say that the demon cared less what we thought was an understatement. "Is he working with you too? As a doctor, he wouldn't discuss a case with me. I swear he never mentioned your name, Alesa."

"Yes, he's my obstetrician. Good to know he's sticking to the doctor/patient privilege thing." Alesa smiled. "But, hey, you seem pretty smart. For a vampire." She flicked me with a dismissive glance. "And I like your open mind. So tell him I want you on my case too. He can fill you in. We have an appointment Monday night. He's going to do an ultrasound so we can get a sneak peek at my little bundle of joy. You can be there for it."

"Wow. Oh, just wow." Penny's eyes were wide.

"That is if you're all moved out by dawn today." Alesa examined her fingernails. "Oh, and I didn't have time to steal much from that cheesy hotel Rafael took me to. You could leave me a few essentials. Some hair product. A manicure set." She eyed Penny's size fourteen figure. "No clothes, obviously. But I have magic fingers. I make my own." She laughed. "I can do the rest too. But sometimes it's fun to play human, you know?"

"Uh, no, I don't." Penny glanced at me, then down at her feet, thinking.

"Oh, give it up, Penny." I put my fledgling out of her misery, obviously she was torn between loyalty to me and her thirst for knowledge. "I know what a chance to study a demon would mean to you. Ian was all over it too. I'm sure God and Gramps would understand. I do." This time I hit Alesa with my own look. "How often do you get to play doctor with a real freak?"

Alesa hissed but Laurie was right there, between us, before the demon could do more than mutter a few choice words. I was so loving my new bodyguard.

I got up and patted Penny on the back. "Go, be happy with Trey. And tell Ian to let you assist him on this."

"Seriously? I won't be abandoning you?" Penny hugged me hard when I shook my head. "This is so cool of you. You're right about this rare scientific opportunity. A pregnant demon. Radical." Penny let me go and approached Alesa. "Can I, uh, feel your stomach?"

"Knock yourself out. Nice to see someone appreciates me." Alesa lay back, her hands behind her head. "Little devil loved the ice cream. He's kicking up a storm."

Penny cautiously laid a palm on Alesa's rounded tummy, on top of the black leather. "This isn't any good. Leather's too thick. Can I pull up your top?"

"Yeah, why not? I'm not modest." Alesa grinned at me. "And I've got nothing to be ashamed of. Even pregnant, my stomach's flatter than *somebody's* on their best day. Right, Glory?"

I wanted to slap the smug smile off her face. Of course Alesa had given herself a beautiful human package. Penny pulled up the demon's top and laid her hand on porcelain skin. Then my fledgling jumped and squealed.

"What?" I ran around the coffee table to her side.

"It moved." Penny looked at me then back down at Alesa's stomach. Sure enough, you could see something undulating under there, like a serpent trying to escape. I shivered. Penny cautiously laid her hand on the skin again.

"You can feel it, right?" Alesa laughed. "Try it, Glory. You're a witness. You can tell Rafael that there really is something inside me. My baby. *Our* baby."

I was fascinated and not a little creeped out but I put my hand beside Penny's. Sure enough, I felt something stir under Alesa's warm, silky skin. I don't know what I expected, but it actually wasn't creepy. Instead, I felt sorry for whatever was growing inside her. Because that tiny creature was doomed. Rafe was right. Alesa for a mother. What a future.

"What about me? Can I join the party?" Laurie peered over the back of the sofa.

"No! You think I don't see your intentions, tiger? You'd like nothing better than to rid the world of a demon before it had a chance to see daylight." Alesa glared at Laurie. "Stay away from me. I mean it."

The were-cat just smiled and nodded. Penny and I backed away. Alesa had actually seemed—dare I say it?—afraid of Laurie. I nodded at my bodyguard approvingly then followed Penny down the hall to help her pack. What do you know? My headache was actually gone. Seemed a little positive energy and a fierce were-cat were better than Excedrin.

Too bad I had another headache in my future. I'd never gotten around to telling Jerry about my new statue skill. He'd had an urgent business call while we were at the club. Yes, at 1:30 in the morning. That's a vampire's life for you.

"Finally, we're away from that demon's reek. Insane that you're actually letting her live with you." Jerry dragged me out into the hall and up the stairs to the roof.

"I really don't want to argue about it, Jer." I jerked my hand from his. "Insane"? His word choice hit me wrong, that was for sure. "Where are we going? If you don't mind my asking."

"Somewhere we can talk without all those people around." He opened the door to the rooftop and cool air hit my warm cheeks.

"All those people? Penny and Trey were trying to move her stuff. You could have offered to help." I strode to the edge of the roof and looked down at the alley. Trey had borrowed a pickup truck and I could see half of it already filled with boxes. Penny's precious computer was going last, in the backseat of her car. She'd asked if her cat could stay with me for a while and I'd been happy to agree.

"The shifter can handle things by himself and you and I need to get this settled between us." Jerry stood next to me, his temper fairly vibrating the air between us.

"Settled? Doubt it. Because in your mind that means I'll stand back and let Laurie do whatever it is she does to run Alesa out of there. It's tempting. I admit it." I could see in his face that I'd hit the target. "But I don't want to stir the pot, Jer. An angry demon is a dangerous demon. So I'm just going to let Alesa park in Penny's bedroom and then I'll go with her to Ian's Monday night. Where's the harm?" I smiled at him, but I knew my fangs were showing. I was pissed at the way he'd rudely dragged me out of there. I'd wanted to help Penny with the move.

"I'm afraid you're in over your head, Gloriana. There's only so much protection Laurie can offer." Jerry actually tried to take me into his arms. I wasn't having it.

"My female, less than equal to the task, head." I threw myself across the roof. Yeah, I was definitely in a snit. "God, Jerry, when will you get me? You may think I'm dumb as dirt. Or naïve. But would you at least *pretend* to respect my decisions?" I swear, if I were a demon, my eyes would be flamethrowers. Lucky for Jerry, I just had my fangs to show how truly furious I was. Too bad he'd see a move by me to rip out his throat as foreplay.

Four hundred years and it came to this. Block-headed Scotsman. Why did I still love him? I swept my eyes over him. Sure, he had a hot body but lust only went so far. And, yes, he protected me and cared about me, but that felt more and more like a suffocating blanket and less and less like the warm fuzzy comfort it had in the beginning.

"Gloriana, you've made many excellent decisions. But you tend to trust people who simply aren't trustworthy." Jerry didn't come close, staying on his side of the roof. Okay, at least he realized that trying to win me over with a sexual move right now would send me screaming into the sky.

"Rafe? Ian? Or both, Jerry?" I leaned against the metal door to the roof. I had no intention of letting anyone interrupt this long overdue showdown. "Never mind. Don't bother. I know the answer. Once a person hits your shit list, that's it. No second chances."

"Some things are simply unforgivable, Gloriana. I don't know why you can't understand that." Jerry was stony-faced. Not promising.

"No, I'll never understand that." I wasn't about to bring up the most obvious problem Jerry had with Rafe—my affair with the shifter. Unforgivable? Jerry had seemed to give me a pass while putting all the blame on Rafe. Obviously Gloriana was easily manipulated, putty in a bad man's hands.

"And *I'll* never understand why you persist in your dealings with MacDonald. What are you trying to prove?" Jerry's fists hit his hard thighs.

"Prove?" I heard my voice rise and took a breath. "This isn't about you. Get it? So Ian made the mistake of having the last name MacDonald. Big freakin' deal. He's a doctor. We need a doctor. That's all there is to it. He's not done one thing to warrant your continued suspicion of him."

"He's done nothing? What's this then?" Jerry stood in front of me in an instant, lifting my shirt to poke at my swollen stomach with a blunt fingertip.

I gasped. "Really? Is it so offensive? Don't look at it then." I jerked down my top. I'd changed into low-riding jeans and a green tank to help Penny pack. Bad choice since the knit clung in all the wrong places.

"It's not offensive except as a reminder of what Mac-Donald's drug did to you." Jerry actually tried to drag the top up again. "You are always beautiful to me, no matter how strange your stomach looks."

"Keep talking, Jerry, and you will never see me naked again." I darted to the opposite side of the roof.

"That didn't come out right. Besides, that's minor compared to this latest nonsense he's filling your head with— blood with powers, making you out to be some kind of paranormal entity. It's insane!" He held both hands up, obviously still unsure how to make his unwieldy tongue push out the right words. "On some subjects, such as your loyalty to Valdez, you've lost all perspective. There's no reason to risk your immortal soul to protect the man's by-blow." He gave me a narrow-eyed look. "Unless there's more between you two than I know."

"You know there's not anything going on now except friendship. And my immortal soul?" I clenched my fists. "You're assuming I ever had one. News flash, Jer. Whatever I am may not be in the running for a nice hereafter."

"Of course you have a soul. You're good, Gloriana. Too good for Valdez with his demon taint. You've got to know that Alesa's story of conceiving while inside you is bullshit. If that baby is his, then it's clear he bedded the she-demon before or after she inhabited your body. He did marry her once. What does that say about his standards?"

"Lay off, Jerry. Even you were young and foolish once. Does the name Mara ring a bell?" I had him there. His ex made Alesa look positively angelic. Mara had a history of lying that included keeping the truth about who her daughter's father was for hundreds of years. That's why Jerry had only recently learned he had a daughter, made before he was turned vampire.

"Don't try to change the subject." Jerry had crossed the roof, close now. "We're talking about Valdez."

"Rafe denies sleeping with the demon and that's good enough for me." I was so tired of Jerry always taking the wrong side of these arguments.

"Valdez has demon blood. Lying is like breathing to those creatures. Why are you forgetting that?" Jerry tried to approach me again. "You're letting your fondness for him overcome your common sense. Think, Gloriana. The man is not who you thought he was. He played a part with you for five years. Now he's finally showing his true colors."

"He played a part because you paid him to do it, Jerry!" I felt my temper explode. I wanted to hurt him for not seeing my side of things. Damn him for being so blind and stubborn.

"Calm down. See reason, Gloriana." Jerry reached for me. That did it. Rafe bashing, discounting my own instincts, I'd had it. I concentrated and he froze where he stood.

Yep, I turned Jerry, the love of my life, to stone. He couldn't even blink but his eyes burned as he realized what I'd done to him. I backed away. For a moment I actually gloated. Hah! Look what Glory could do. Then I came crashing down to earth.

Oh, God. What now? A quick thaw? Or should I explain this while I had a captive audience? Because he sure as hell wouldn't listen to a thing I had to say once he was mobile again.

"Uh, sorry about that. Meant to tell you. While I was with Alesa earlier, she said she discovered I had some untapped powers when she was inside me. Part of my non-human thing, I guess. She taught me the statue trick. I take it as proof that Ian didn't lie about that at least. That I started out as some kind of paranormal." I gulped and tears stung my eyes. "Jerry?" This was bad, very bad. I could read his thoughts and they weren't words he usually used around me. Jerry hated feeling or being helpless. As a warrior it was his worst nightmare.

"You see? This could be a clue about what I am, er, was." I was babbling, stalling. This wasn't going to be pretty when I released Jerry from the freeze. Had to do it. I stared at him, wisely put a dozen feet between us first, then did the deed.

He whirled as if testing his freedom, then glared at me. "What the *fuck* was that?"

"I told you. A new skill." I took a shaky breath. He was stalking me, bearing down like he was intent on shaking me until my fangs rattled. I deserved it.

"And you used it on me," Jerry ground out, mere inches from me now.

"S-s-sorry about that. Really. But you made me lose my temper." I backed up until I hit that door to the stairs.

Jerry slapped his hands against the steel on either side of my head. He leaned down until his breath touched my cheek. "Sorry? Sorry that you made me look foolish, standing there unable to so much as twitch?" He wound my hair around his hand, his voice so menacing I felt my knees go weak.

He wasn't hurting me, but I could feel the pressure and see the urge to kill in his set jaw.

"Jerry, please. I didn't mean—"

"To make me helpless? To shut me up so you could win your argument?" He watched as I licked my dry lips and I saw heat flare in his eyes.

Oh, no. Arguing had fired his blood, made him want to punish me. Show me that he was stronger than I was, as long as I didn't cheat with powers that came from God knew where. His gaze roamed over my body where my top clung to nipples suddenly alert to his nearness. Stupid knee-jerk response. He pressed closer, obviously aroused, and I reacted shamelessly before I could stop myself. *Down, Glory.* I'd be damned if I'd let this end in bed.

"Bed? Of course I'm reading your thoughts. Why don't I just drag you down to this concrete and take you there?" He gave my hair a sharp tug. "But I'd never make it, would I? You'd turn me to stone before my thought became deed. What else has the demon bitch taught you? Can you read through my blocked thoughts now?"

"Don't know. Haven't, um, tried. But I wouldn't—" I slid my hands across his chest. "I will never, ever do that to you again, Jerry. It was a mistake. Unfair. No, *mean.* And I love you too much to do that to you." I did press against him, deliberately this time, and reveled in the taut proof of his lust. It would be so easy to settle this that way and so wrong. "I hated seeing you like that. Helpless." *Shut up, Glory.*

"No more than I hated feeling that way." He hadn't released my hair but he did ease the pressure. "I want to hear you swear it, Gloriana. With your mind open. That you will never use that power against me again." His lips were within a breath of mine.

"Yes, I promise, Jerry. I wasn't thinking clearly. I'll never do it again." I leaned the inch it took to touch my lips to his. "Please forgive me. My temper got the best of me."

"You never used to have a temper." He released my curls and ran his hand down my throat, stroking my pounding pulse there.

"It's living with a demon. I won't deny it's working on my last nerve. I could really use some sympathy here instead of another lecture." I stretched my neck when he followed his hand with his lips.

"Yet you're allowing her to teach you tricks such as this

statue maneuver." He raised his head and stared down at me. "It's a valuable defense. I'm glad you have it. Though it raises questions."

"Yes!" I slid my hands up to twine in his hair. "What can I be that I have this power? Thank God Alesa assures me that I'm not demon. Not that I ever thought I could be. I do attend church, hold crosses, talk to God. All things a demon can't do."

"Exactly. And I'll say again that, except when you're in a temper, you're a fine and decent person, Gloriana." Jerry finally smiled.

"I owe you some serious groveling to make this up to you." I ran a fingertip around his ear then traced a scar just visible in the open collar of his shirt. "Perhaps ending up in bed isn't such a bad idea."

"That sounds like an interesting proposition. But it won't be in that apartment of yours. It smells like Willy Wonka's candy factory down there." Jerry frowned. "And knowing the demon is down the hall is a real joy killer."

"Willy Wonka?" I laughed. "What do you know of such things?"

"My daughter decided we needed to catch up on some of the things parents did with their children when they are growing up. She rented a pile of children's movies and made me watch a marathon of DVDs. That was one of them." Jerry laughed. "It was a nice evening. The kind a mortal family would share. Beat the hell out of Lily bringing home another undesirable male."

"Movie night sounds like fun. Next time I'd like in on it." I leaned against him. "I'd be happy to go home with you and grovel. But not tonight. It's late and I wouldn't have time to do a proper job. Maybe tomorrow after church? What do you say?"

"I say that if I can't change your mind about your current situation, I'll take what I can get." He rubbed my back and we just held each other for a long moment. "Church, eh? I bet your demon didn't like the sound of that."

"Exactly. So of course Penny and I wouldn't miss it." I kept my arms around Jerry's waist, appreciating how solid he felt.

"Tell me, are there any more powers lurking inside you that the demon knows of? Anything else she can teach you?" Jerry looked into my eyes. "You know I'm all about defense. And if you can use the creature while she's camped in your apartment, I say you should take full advantage." He brushed my hair back from my face. "As long as it doesn't cost you your soul."

"No worries. My soul stays where it is." I sighed. "Alesa did mention there might be more untapped powers, but to learn them I'll have to go along with her notion that we can be like sisters." I shuddered. "Can you imagine? With a family like that, I'd fall on the first available stake."

Jerry started to speak, then shut his mouth. Restraint. Because I knew exactly what he'd started to say. If it bothered me so much I could forget Rafe's involvement and kick Alesa to the curb. No secret power was worth putting up with her. I patted his cheek then traced the curve of his firm lips.

"Nice job. Can we move on to the kiss-and-make-up portion of the evening now?" I smiled at him and looped my arms around his neck.

Jerry glanced around at the plain concrete rooftop, then up at the clear night sky. "We have an hour until dawn and a bit of privacy. I think there's time for full-on make-up sex."

"On this hard concrete?" I sighed when he slipped his hand under my top. I pulled his head down for a deep and satisfying kiss. At least we'd moved on from the statue thing and the endless fight about Ian, Rafe and the demon. And I was happy to put off going downstairs. My home was no refuge, that was for sure.

Jerry sent me a mental message and we were soon shifting to fly to a deserted area of a nearby park. There was a stream glittering in the moonlight and a cushion of leaves on the ground for a bed.

"Am I allowed to see you naked, lass?" His eyes gleamed as we shifted to our human forms beneath a large oak tree. "Or did my unruly tongue get me into too much trouble for that?"

"Your tongue can be unruly. Or very talented." I sauntered up to Jerry and toyed with the collar of his shirt. "Naughty as well." I made quick work of his buttons and tossed the shirt away. "I think I shall make you work for a glimpse of my hideous stomach."

"Gloriana." Jerry groaned when I bent my head to lick a path along the muscles of his chest. I sucked one brown nipple into my mouth, then the other, enjoying the way his hands clutched my back as I gave him pleasure. I did so love to have him in my power.

"Now it's your turn." I lay back on the bed of leaves and held out my hands. "Whatever I do to you, do to me."

"With pleasure." He fell on top of me, making quick work of my top and then my bra. He gazed down at my breasts, his eyes bright with lust. "You are beautiful. I never tire of this sight." He bent his head to swirl his tongue around each peak, causing me to gasp. If he never tired, the wonder of it was that I never failed to feel that new bite of ecstasy when he touched me. You'd think the feelings would wane, grow stale after hundreds of years. And yet each time was as thrilling as the first. As if a magic spell had been cast on us.

"Jerry." I gripped his hair and pulled him closer as he suckled me, the draw of his mouth and the scrape of his fangs making my womb throb with longing. Finally I gently pushed him away. "My turn."

"What now?" His eyes were drowsy as he lay back and slid his hand across my waist. "What's your pleasure?"

"Take off your jeans, your shoes. Well, hell, just strip off." I grinned. "I'm feeling much too lazy to do the job myself."

"Wonder why." He grinned and went to work on his belt, the sound of his zipper sending a thrill through me that made me reach for my own. We raced to see who could get naked first. He won, of course. My jeans never came off easily. I struggled with spandex.

"Did I ever tell you how beautiful you are?" I gazed down at him, spread out for my taking. He had a rough masculine beauty that made me sigh. His sex stood tall and ready, the hair dark and curling around it. His legs were long and well muscled and his scars from long-ago battles just made him even more desirable in my eyes. I leaned over him to trail my hair over his body, across his cock, up over his stomach and then back down again.

"A man is not beautiful." He slid his hands over my ass and tried to hold me still above him. "This, this is beauty. These full breasts that taste like heaven. This sweet, wet crease that is the gate to paradise." He nudged my legs apart with his knee. "And then there's this ass, so round and soft that I could write poetry to it if I had the words for such."

"I think you just did." I sighed as he explored me, our game deteriorating into a sensual slide of skin on skin, lips to skin and then lips to lips. He pulled me up to probe me with his tongue until I bucked and could stand it no longer. I cried out and grabbed his ears, twisting until he shoved me down hard on his cock. It filled me as another orgasm surged through me and I heard him shout my name. We breathed together, an old habit from our human days.

No, I'd not had human days. But I must have known how humans made love. Jerry and I had spent nights together before he'd turned me. He'd become my lover, teaching me things my husband had never dared. Or had I had a husband at all? My mind whirled, suddenly full of doubts about what was real and what were mere fantasies planted by some unknown entity. Why? Who? How had I really come to be in Jerry's life?

As I lay across his chest, still connected to him thigh to thigh, heart to heart, I struggled with these questions and more. If I had never been human, what had I been before? And could Jerry love that, that *thing* as he loved Gloriana St.

Clair? Hah! Even the name was undoubtedly a fiction. I could lose this man, lose everything with the truth. I shuddered and tightened my hold on him. Once again I'd denied him my blood, Ian's claims about it making me withhold that pleasure. And Jerry had gone along with it. Could Ian have made up all of this? Fooled Penny somehow with his test results? I helped Jerry into his clothes, then he helped me into mine just before dawn and he left me at my door with a sweet kiss. Laurie grinned at me from the couch.

"The demon's made herself at home in Penny's room. You can relax. She won't bother you during the day."

"God, that never occurred to me. Thanks, Laurie." I took a shower, scrubbing myself clean quickly then falling into bed as I felt the dawn hit me. Demons didn't seem to ever sleep, which left them plenty of time for mischief. I didn't like that idea one bit.

Eight

"I thought Rafael was going to be here." Alesa threw herself out of my car Monday night, ignoring the guards who'd stepped forward as I'd pulled to a stop in front of Ian's house. "I don't see his car. Which is probably a good thing. I'm not sure I like his attitude."

"Maybe he flew in." I'd listened to her gripe all the way out here. She didn't want the top down on the convertible. Her tummy was upset. No surprise there. I'd watched her down a frozen bean burrito which she hadn't bothered nuking, a quart of Ben & Jerry's, and two packs of Rafe's Twinkies. Oh, and that was after the nachos she'd become addicted to. My apartment smelled like a mall food court.

"Wouldn't blame him if he skipped this. You gave him an out. I'd jump on it if I were him." Laurie had managed to pretzel herself into my tiny backseat.

"Who asked you? And quit breathing down my neck." Alesa glared at Laurie. "What did you have for dinner? A whole cow?"

"At least I don't look like one." The were-cat smirked as she climbed out of the car.

My stomach heaved. I'd rather whatever Laurie ate during

the day remain a mystery. "Alesa, you are going overboard with your eating. I swear you're bigger tonight than you were when you first arrived a few days ago."

"It's all baby. And I'm sick of all this negativity." Alesa slammed the car door, barely missing Laurie's foot. "It can't be good for the little one."

"I'd bet demon babies thrive on it, devil woman." Laurie grinned. "Didn't you like the surprise under your pillow?"

Alesa's screams when she'd discovered an ancient prayer book and crucifix tucked into her bed could have been heard down on Sixth Street. She'd broken land speed records getting away from them and ended up taking Laurie's spot on the couch, muttering about her room being "defiled."

"Keep it up, tiger. Your day is coming. When Luc snaps to the fact that he wants me back, he'll be glad to get even with anyone who caused me pain." Alesa sniffed.

"Obviously your evening with Laurie wasn't a success." I'd gone to church with Penny, then spent the rest of the evening at Jerry's, leaving Laurie to demon-sit.

"She kept chanting, burning her shitty leaves and leaving religious things where I'd trip over them." Alesa gestured at her with a middle finger. "Leave me with her again and you'll regret it, Glory." She shot me a red-eyed look.

"I'm quaking in my boots." I glanced down. These were pretty cute but years old. Tomorrow night I'd try to find some new ones. I was actually looking forward to my shopping trip with Aggie and Flo. Another night away from any demon influences. I hated to do it to him but, if necessary, I'd get Rafe to ride herd on Alesa just to keep her safely occupied.

"Seriously, Glory, you're starting to look like the reason for all those dumb-blond jokes." Alesa sniffed and tossed her dark hair back over her shoulders. "If you're not scared of me, you're too stupid to live."

"Not living, haven't lived for hundreds of years." I smiled as Penny opened Ian's front door. "We're here. Please tell me the ultrasound machine arrived and is ready to go."

"Yep. Got here during the day. One of the shifters set it

up." Penny gestured for us to come in. "We've been playing with it, making sure we know how it works." She leaned closer and glanced at the silent bodyguards who'd followed us inside. "Shifters have the most interesting internal organs."

"Fascinating." Alesa breezed past us. "Where's the doc?"

"Here I am. Valdez and I were conferring. I took a DNA sample from him. To compare with your baby when the time comes." Ian smiled at me then got serious when he met Alesa's gaze. The moment he noticed Laurie behind her, he stiffened. "I see you've got a new bodyguard. Gloriana? Is she yours?"

"You can speak to me directly, Ian. And don't pretend we haven't met." Laurie smiled tightly. "And more." She shrugged when my eyes widened. "Blade knows about my history with MacDonald. It was a selling feature in my resume. Let's just say if Ian becomes a target? I won't hesitate."

"Fierce. Tiger, you have finally said something I can admire." Alesa looked like she'd enjoy watching a showdown.

Ian slapped on a smile again. "Lauren and I had a bad breakup. I got over it."

"Obviously." I looked from Laurie to Ian. The air practically shimmered between them. Heat? Anger? Unresolved issues. Alesa laughed.

"Who cares? Tonight is all about me. Where's Rafael now?" She glanced around the large room that reminded me of Ian's Malibu digs. He favored contemporary furnishings, heavy on the white leather, modern art and lots of glass with a water view. I had to say I liked his style.

"He's out on the terrace, getting some air. As soon as he got a whiff of demon, his temper got the best of him." Ian smiled at me. "Says you've got him in a twelve-step program for anger management, Gloriana. He's working right now to calm down before he comes inside to join us."

"Yes, this is hard for him. And I'm glad he's gaining some self-control." Now that I knew where to look, I could see his dark shape outside where he leaned against the stone wall surrounding the large terrace.

"This is hard for *him?*" Alesa started across the large room. "Give me a break. He's not carrying around the Karate Kid kickboxing his kidneys. I'll make it hard for him."

Laurie blocked her path. "Let's go take this test. Where's the ultrasound?"

"Yes. Why don't you show Alesa the dressing room, Penny?" Ian gestured for my fledgling to escort Alesa down a hall. "I know you don't want to be examined, Alesa, but I'm going to have to do it anyway. Penny will assist me. Undress completely and put on a smock." Ian was suddenly the doctor at work. "Lauren, are you sticking with the demon or staying with Gloriana?"

"Please, Laurie, just stay with Alesa." I could see my bodyguard was clearly torn. "You know she's the threat here. And Blade wants you to watch Ian too. So go with them, I'll be there in a minute. I want to talk to Rafe." I stopped next to the French doors. "You know I'll be okay with him."

"If you say so. Demon watch. Fine. But be careful." She followed Ian down the hall, stopping once to glance over her shoulder. "I'll wait outside while you examine the demon, Ian. No way do I want to see her naked."

"She doesn't want me to examine her. I may call for help. I'm sure you can handle her." Ian winked at Laurie and she actually flushed. Hmm. Interesting.

I headed outside. "Rafe, got a handle on your anger yet?"

"What do you think?" He turned and leaned back against the wall. "I can't have the woman I want, my worst nightmare has come back to haunt me, and I'm supposed to act *civilized* about it?"

"Gee, when you put it like that . . ." I stood beside him, careful not to touch him. I wasn't about to encourage him to get closer now. "Anything I can do?"

"Get Alesa to admit this is a hoax?" Rafe laughed. "Right. Like that's going to happen. Damn, I'm sorry you're having to put up with her. I don't know why she's fixated on you. How's Laurie working out?"

"Great. She's actually got Alesa on the defensive." I gave

in and touched his shoulder. "Relax, Rafe. You know this has got to be a big lie. Time will tell us the truth."

"Well, that's the problem. The longer I'm around her, the more insane this makes me. How can you stand having her in your apartment? I would have killed her by now. If I could figure out how."

"Yes, that's a problem. How do you kill a demon?"

"Good question. And about time you thought to ask it." The voice came out of the darkness. Rafe and I both turned. He suddenly had a knife in his hand and I clutched my car keys like a weapon.

"Who's there?" Rafe jumped up on the low stone wall, ready to rumble.

"Oh, get over yourself, shifter. I'm much tougher to kill than a mere demon. Lucky for you I'm not the one with the beef here." Aggie strolled up a side path that had been carved into the cliff from the lake below. She was wrapped toga-style in a big white towel. Clearly she'd been skinny-dipping in the cold water, her wet hair slicked back behind her ears.

"Then why sneak up on us? You could have identified yourself sooner." I reached up for Rafe's hand as he jumped back to the terrace. "And what's with the eavesdropping?"

"It's how I learn the most interesting stuff." Aggie grinned. "Though you two weren't exactly spilling your guts. And talk about clueless!" She strolled over to a wrought iron chair and plopped down, crossing one bare leg over the other.

"What does that mean?" I swear she was flashing Rafe and enjoying his reaction. "Don't you need to go find some clothes? It's chilly tonight."

"Doesn't bother me. I'm a Siren. Water is my element. After a swim like I just had, I'm stoked." She did rearrange her towel so she wasn't giving Rafe such an excellent view. "Better, Glory?" She winked at me. "Now back to demons. The grapevine tells me you two, along with Blade and my dreamboat Israel Caine, took out Honoria not so long ago. Is that true?"

"The goddess the EVs worshipped." Rafe glanced at me,

finally able to tear his gaze from Aggie's peep show. "Yeah, we managed to take her down. What of it?"

"That bitch called herself a goddess, but she was nothing more than a three-headed demon. Lots of power, a great line of bullshit, but so not in the hierarchy according to my boss man." Aggie looked skyward. "And he should know."

"The Storm God." I shuddered. My encounters with him had proved he was way too powerful to be taken out with a sword. "Come to think of it, you're right, Aggie." I clutched Rafe's arm. "We know how to kill a demon. Whack off her head or heads as the case may be. Alesa has just one, even in demon form."

"Finally she gets it." Aggie smiled and stood. "A stab through the heart will do it too, but that can be tough. They don't always have one where you'd expect it. And sometimes they have more than one, to go along with the head thing. Maybe Ian's machine will help you find this chick's thumper."

"Good idea. I'll have to mention it to him." It was great to have hope, maybe a strategy to get rid of Alesa. But as long as she was pregnant . . .

Aggie stretched and her towel slipped to reveal one perfect breast. "Oops. I'd better get dressed now. Ian and I are going out after he gets through with your little problem." She wiggled her fingers and headed for the door then stopped and turned. "Watch." Suddenly her hair was dry, a golden tumble down her back, and she had on a stunning red dress, cut to show her curves. Her elegant designer shoes made my mouth water. As usual everything was expensive and fit her perfectly. "Siren magic."

"Nice. So you sat around here naked just to toy with us." I glanced at Rafe. It hadn't been me she'd been playing with.

"Why not? I get my fun where I can." She grinned at Rafe, her hand on the doorknob. "By the way, I gave Ian that blood sample yesterday, Glory. And you know how I hate needles. So you owe me." She smiled and I shivered. "See ya tomorrow. Shoe shopping. I like to buy as well as make with magic. It's a girl thing. I'm sure you understand, Glory."

Understand? A Siren? Never in a million years. But she was right, I owed her for that blood draw.

"She's sure a piece of work." Rafe slung his arm around my shoulders as soon as she disappeared inside. "What's this about blood?"

"A little experiment. I can't imagine I could possibly . . . Tell you later." I eased away from him. "Alesa. She's the immediate problem. At least now we do know how to kill a demon, but we're obviously not going to do it. Not while she's carrying a baby."

"Not everyone would have such qualms." Rafe paced the terrace. "Granddad's affair with a woman from the dark side was frowned on by both shifters and demons, especially when it had consequences. Apparently Lucifer didn't want the baby since he was only half demon. And when Granddad made the mistake of bringing home my father? Hell, some members of my own family were all for making sure 'tainted shifters' never survived to adulthood. I'd have never been born if the purists had had their way." Rafe's voice was soft, but it was laced with a pain I'd never heard from him before.

"But any child, raised in a loving home . . ." I looked into his eyes.

"That's what I have to think. I've never let my demon side dominate. And if Alesa has my child, I'll make sure the baby becomes a solid citizen, no matter what I have to do." Rafe ran his hand through his hair.

"I know you will, Rafe." I hugged him, hoping it didn't come to that.

"Ian's ready for the ultrasound. Alesa wants Rafe in there. You can come too, Glory. As a witness, she says." Penny stood in the doorway. She had put on scrubs and looked very much like the doctor she hoped to become one day. "The physical exam just confirmed what we already knew—that she's pregnant and a grade A bitch." Penny made a face then turned on her heel. "Follow me."

Oh, God, but I wanted to shift out of there and avoid this

whole thing. I had no desire to see whatever was growing inside the demon. But I followed Rafe into the house and we both trailed Penny down the hall and into a bedroom that had been outfitted like an examining room.

"Here he is. My baby's daddy, the worthless sod." Alesa was gowned and draped so that only her stomach was exposed. Ian, who looked a little harried, stood next to her. A monitor was nearby and he was adjusting some knobs while he held a tool that he was apparently going to run across her tummy. Laurie had parked in a corner and she nodded as I walked into the room.

"Give it a rest, Alesa. Lie still and do what the doctor says." Rafe sounded furious. I guess the stress was finally getting to be too much for him.

"Look. I don't appreciate the attitude." Alesa turned big eyes to Ian. "Tell him, Doctor. Stress upsets the baby and can cause premature delivery. I read it on the Internet."

"I have no way of knowing what your normal vital signs should be, Alesa. Whether you're under stress or not. For all I know, you're getting off to this attention." Ian glanced at Rafe, then me. "Penny and I have been trying to figure out how far along she is, as you requested. Maybe the ultrasound will give us a better idea."

"Are you people *listening* to me?" Alesa raised up on her elbows. Her eyes were red and we could feel the heat. "I don't have to submit to this. I can get the hell out of here right now."

"You bolt and we'll know for a fact that this was all one of your cons. Yeah, do us a favor and take off." Rafe opened the hall door. "What's the matter, Alesa, afraid of what the machine will show? I know you're wearing a façade right now. That human coating is pretty thin. Can't you put one around your baby? Or is it too ugly for us to see?"

"Shut up, just shut up." She sniffed and a dark tear trickled down her cheek.

"Rafe, take it easy." I moved to his side. "Let's just do this and get it over with." Laurie had stepped closer and was obviously ready to jump in if Alesa tried anything toward me.

"Yes, that's the plan. Lie back, Alesa. This gel is cold but will let the machine pick up the image of what's inside you." Ian squirted the substance on her stomach, then began to slide what looked like a long-handled computer mouse over her skin.

"*What?* There you go again. It's a baby." Alesa shuddered. "That *is* cold. Hurry this along. I hate all of you. Even hell wouldn't have you."

"There it is." Penny adjusted the screen on the computer monitor. "We can take photos and print them out, you know. So you can have some to take home."

"Swell. You can send out announcements, Alesa. We're having a . . . What the hell is that thing?" Rafe leaned closer. "Two-headed hydra?"

"No, I think it's more than one baby." I glanced at Ian, who was very intent as he manipulated the mouse and watched the screen.

"She's right. Just as I suspected. You're carrying more than one child. Twins, Alesa." Ian frowned. "Penny, turn the screen so that she can see."

"Sure. What was I thinking?" Penny adjusted the screen so Alesa also had a view.

"Two babies?" Alesa's voice wobbled. "It's a miracle. A rare and wonderful thing. Luc will be . . ." She glanced around at us. "Never mind."

"No, I want to hear what you were going to say. What about Lucifer? I thought he didn't want you to have a baby. That this had nothing to do with him." Rafe moved closer to the computer monitor and poked it with his finger. "Look at that screen, demon. It's pretty murky in there, but I swear I see snouts, claws, demon markings. Not a sign of shifter whose babies look human in the womb or so I've heard. Tell me the truth, Alesa. Are those babies mine or not?" He grabbed her shoulders, pressing her down to the examining table. His own eyes were red now.

"Get your hands off her!" Suddenly Rafe flew through the air until he hit the wall and crumpled to the floor.

A glowing light filled the room with a pulsing heat. I heard a moan. Oh, that was me. Because I recognized that light and was instantly pulled back in time to a night that had almost been the end of me. I turned and gagged, grabbing an empty trash can as the last bottle of synthetic I'd chugged came roaring up and out. Ian dropped his probe and Penny screeched and crouched behind him, holding on to his legs as a man materialized next to the examination table.

Rafe, never one to be intimidated, scrambled to his feet with a shout but was knocked back against the wall again. A dark whirlwind roared through the room, tossing papers and twisting wires. Equipment fell with a crash and Ian cursed as he dove for his precious ultrasound machine.

"Luc! What are you doing here?" Alesa reached for him and he took her hands. He speared Ian with a glance that sent him sliding across the floor to land in a heap next to Rafe. Penny crawled under a desk and cowered there, her arms over her head as she muttered prayers and asked God to save her.

"Silence!" Lucifer was as scary as the hell he came from. No one dared disobey him and Penny shut her mouth with a snap. Smart girl. I could see her shivering and tears leaking from her eyes, wide with terror.

I'd always thought Luc was the most beautiful man I'd ever seen. Not that Lucifer was really a man. He was the Devil, made irresistible so he could tempt anyone over to the dark side. He used his looks just like he used his minions, his blond hair, turquoise eyes and perfect body tools of his trade. I'd never seen him in what was probably his true form. Did he have a snout and scales like his demons? The stereotypical horns and a tail like a cartoon character, all in scarlet? If he did, he was careful to never let that side of himself show.

Tonight he wore a white silk shirt, open over his sculpted chest and close-fitting cream tailored trousers that ensured Penny and I noticed he was well-endowed behind the zipper.

He swept his disdainful gaze over us then focused on Alesa. If he'd been capable of it, I'd say it was actually with some affection.

"I've had enough of this play of yours, Alesa. Come home. Have my children there, where you belong." He pulled her up to a sitting position. "Twins. Not for millennia have there been twins born from one of my mates." He wiped away the gel with a cloth, then smoothed his hand over her stomach. "Give me the photo, Doctor." He glanced from the computer screen to Ian. "Now."

Ian scrambled to his feet and righted the rolling cart with the keyboard on it. He started to say something, probably a complaint about the way Luc had knocked things over, but obviously thought better of it. Instead, he punched buttons and wiggled cords until a printer in the corner suddenly came to life. I sagged with relief and saw Ian do the same when he grabbed the printout and handed it to Luc.

"Here. You can see—"

"You've done your part." Luc swept Ian aside with a nod and the doctor slammed against the wall again. I stayed absolutely still, trying not to call attention to myself.

"Is it really . . . ?" Penny whispered.

"Lucifer. Yep." I managed to find my voice and dropped the trash can with a clang. Fury suddenly wiped away my nausea and probably my common sense. "Lucifer! You mean this was all one of your tricks, a setup just to make me miserable? Oh, and Rafe, of course."

"Tricks? Like anything I do is so trivial." Lucifer raked me with a look that made me feel stripped and violated all over again. Oh, God. "I didn't appreciate the way we parted the last time we met, Gloriana. But this game was all Alesa's doing. I certainly can't be bothered with 'tricks.' I indulged her out of fondness for her. You were not important enough to warrant my attention again."

My fury dissolved under his steady gaze and I wanted to cower under the desk with Penny. But then I saw Alesa grin as she adjusted her gown. Grin. Like all she'd put us through had been a fun little diversion for her.

"I don't see how you can deny that you and Alesa were in on this together. I doubt she can go anywhere without your permission, especially in this condition." I glanced at Rafe, who was apparently stuck in stone, mute. "Why torture Rafe?"

"He rejected her. Alesa has her pride." Lucifer ran a fond hand down her cheek. "She could not allow his rejection to go unpunished. It was amusing to watch him sweat, wasn't it, my dear?"

"Sure was." She took his hand and jumped off the table. We all got flashed as her gown opened in the back. "But this whole thing quit being fun about two days ago. I'm more than ready to come home, Luc. Not to say this hasn't had its moments, but I missed you, lover." She put her arms around him and gave him a kiss that made me wish I was anywhere but here. Of course I'd already been wishing that since the bad guy had arrived.

"Alesa claimed you couldn't procreate, Lucifer." I just couldn't keep my big mouth shut. My reward was a blast of heat that knocked me back against the door.

"And you believed that?" Alesa laughed. "Honey, this man is the stud who created ninety percent of the demons in existence. Good thing incest is a virtue down there. Am I right, baby?"

"Don't waste your time talking to these inferior creatures, Alesa. I'm not entirely happy with your behavior on this assignment. If you weren't carrying my children, I'd be punishing you right now."

"But, honey pot, I only—"

"Save it." With a touch of his hand, Luc made Alesa vanish. "Now that she's gone, I have one more thing to say, then I'm done with you. Gloriana, you did me a favor by taking out Honoria. That and this little trick that I allowed Alesa to play makes us even. I never want to have dealings with you again. Are we clear?"

"You think I *want* to deal with demons?" I picked myself up and stalked over to stand across the gurney from Lucifer. Everyone else in the room had been turned into statues. I was the only one there, besides Lucifer, who could move. I'd have felt better about that if I wasn't worried about the way he was staring at me. His eyes threw out heat that sizzled against my skin, reminding me that he was still pissed that I'd basically rejected him the last time we'd been alone together. I wondered if I'd look like a boiled lobster if I lived through this.

"Want, need, whatever, we seem to be crossing paths way too often." Luc finally quit staring and examined his nails. "I, for one, am bored with it."

"Then let Rafe off the hook for good. No more tricks, debts or any other calls from the dark side. Pretend that dab of demon in him doesn't exist. Because I swear, if you mess with him, you mess with me. What do you say? Do we have a deal?" I didn't bother to hold out my hand. I wasn't ever shaking hands with him. I had a feeling he could suck out my soul on contact.

"Fine. I lost interest in him long ago. Why Alesa . . . Never mind. This is over. Be glad that I am letting you carry on with your so-called lives." He shimmered and was gone.

Rafe was suddenly up and across the room to throw his arms around me. "I can't believe you actually stood up to Lucifer and dictated terms, Glory. Are you nuts?"

"Suicidal maybe." I sighed and leaned against him. "Are you okay?"

"Just a few cracked ribs. I'll heal." Rafe looked around. "He did a number on this room."

"True. But I've got a picture of two demons in the womb." Ian jumped to his feet and directed Penny as they straightened the equipment. Rafe and I gathered up papers and piled them on the gurney. Then Ian strode to the door.

"Very brave of you facing Lucifer that way, Gloriana. Hope you're still feeling that adrenaline rush, because I have news for you and you may not like it." He pulled open a drawer and grabbed a fat file. "Come into my office."

"Test results?" I glanced at Rafe, then Penny. "Penny knows but I haven't told Rafe about this." That sick feeling was back in the pit of my stomach and I wanted Rafe, my best friend, to be there by my side when I heard the news.

"Told me what?" Rafe stared into my eyes, trying to read my mind. As if I'd let him.

"Just come with me. Ian can explain." I tugged him after the doctor.

Laurie stopped us out in the hallway. "You okay, Glory?"

"Laurie! I'm fine. How about you?" Honestly? I'd forgotten all about her. She'd been a statue in the corner from Lucifer's first appearance.

"So much for my special skills. Obviously I'm not worth shit when it comes to the head bad guy." She stuck her hands in her pockets. "You can fire me, wouldn't blame you."

"No, I understand about Lucifer and his powers. At least he and Alesa are gone." Saying it out loud helped me actually believe it. "I'm almost finished working with Ian anyway. I won't fire you, but I may not need you after tonight."

"I understand. Rafe's right. You were awesome going up against the Devil himself. I'd like to know how you found the nerve." Laurie moved closer.

I shrugged. What could I say? Was I a walking dumb-blond joke risking my life like that? No. Hair color didn't define me and neither would whatever Ian had found out about my blood. I took a deep fortifying breath.

"Adrenaline, a momentary lapse of judgment. Who knows? Right now I've got to see Ian in his office about something personal. You can wait, but Rafe will be with me." I sighed, dreading it.

"Fine. I'll camp here in the hall, just in case you need me. Jerry doesn't trust Ian and neither do I. He starts something you don't like, call me in." Laurie looked like she hoped that happened.

Rafe and I stepped into the office and shut the door. Ian dropped that fat folder on his desk.

"You sure you want Valdez to hear this too?"

"Yes." I looked around. "Penny?"

"No, I have her cleaning up the ultrasound equipment and checking it for damage. It's a rental and goes back tomorrow. You can tell her later if you wish."

"Fine." We settled into seats in front of Ian's desk. By the time Ian sat behind the beautiful antique piece, I wanted to scream. Every move the doctor made seemed in slow motion, deliberate and precise. I swear if he started straightening the pens on his blotter I was plunging one into his throat.

"Gloriana, you know I compared your blood sample to literally hundreds of paranormals and mortals."

"Yes, you told me that before, Ian." I heard the edge in my voice and told myself to take a chill pill. "Thank you. This is way beyond the call of duty."

"I did it for myself as well. I needed to know why you had an adverse reaction to my drugs. In case this happened again with another patient." Ian smiled and pulled out a sheet of paper. "The last blood sample I took was a winner." He started to pass the paper across the desk then shook his head. "I guess these numbers wouldn't mean anything to you, so I'll interpret."

"Rafe, I didn't tell you this, but Ian claims I wasn't human before Jerry turned me vampire."

"You're shitting me." Rafe was on his feet. "What kind of scam are you pulling here, MacDonald?"

"No scam. I've run hundreds of tests. Penny ran them too. Now I know what Gloriana was before she was turned. Found out just last night."

"Rafe, I believe him. Sit down and let him speak." I tugged on his hand until he sat again.

"Glory, does Blade know what's been going down here?"

"Yes, and he's not believing it either. But I do, so just listen."

Ian cleared his throat and rustled his papers. "Can I proceed now?"

"Spit it out, Ian. I can take it." I hoped I was wrong, but I was very afraid I knew what Ian was going to tell me. Rafe was practically vibrating with nerves and I put my hand on his knee.

"You were a Siren, Glory. You and Aggie were almost a perfect match."

Nine

"A Siren? That's impossible." I jumped up and looked around. What for, I didn't know. Escape maybe. From the truth. Somewhere inside me this fact resonated, even though it made no sense whatsoever.

"She's right. Glory hates the water. Can't swim worth a damn." Rafe was up beside me now, keeping pace as I walked the perimeter of the room. I'm sure I looked as wild-eyed as I felt.

"Whoever did this to her obviously erased not only her memories but did a number on her previous abilities as well." Ian was standing, ever the Highland gentleman.

"Sit, Ian. I want you to run the test again. I just can't believe this is right." I stalked over to my chair and hit the seat hard as I sat again.

"I ran it a dozen times and more. Took another sample from Aggie and, boy, did that cost me." Ian grinned ruefully. "You know she hates needles. Not sharing details, but let's just say the woman's insatiable."

"Oh, God." I put my head in my hands. "And that's what I'm supposed to be? A sex addict with a fish tail?" Rafe's arm went around me, his warm breath near my ear.

"Glory, there are worse things you know. Sirens are beautiful. Men adore them."

"Right." I looked up and met his dark gaze. "And follow a Siren's song to a watery grave. I've heard the legends." I turned to Ian. "Tell me what *you* know about Sirens, Ian. I'm sure you did an in-depth study once you figured out what you think I used to be."

He nodded and opened the folder again. "You're right, of course. I interviewed Aggie, did some research online, though that was a dead end. The Internet is full of ridiculous nonsense and wild speculation. I doubt true scholars post their findings for the uneducated to read there." He pulled out a sheet of paper. "Aggie tells me her boss is Achelous, the Storm God."

"Right. I've met him." I grabbed Rafe's leg. "See? I can't be a Siren. He would have said something when we were face-to-face. Right?"

"Would he, Glory?" Rafe had been there when we'd confronted Achelous. "If you escaped from him or he kicked you out of the club, he obviously wouldn't be all that thrilled with you." Rafe settled his hand on the back of my neck. "I don't know what all this means, but he's a freakin' god. Who knows how they think? He scared the pee out of me. I remember that."

"Yeah. Me too." I sighed. "Achelous didn't let on but he must have recognized me." I shook my head. "If Ian's right, I'm dead to the Storm God. I don't know what I did but it must have been so bad that he tossed me out of his harem." Harem. I'd heard Aggie talk about serving that god. The thought made my stomach heave. "I think I'm going to be sick."

Ian gave an alarmed look at his expensive Oriental rug then jumped up and shoved a trash can between my legs. "Stay here. I've got something for nausea. Be right back." He muttered something about how I'd already defiled one of his trash cans then disappeared into the hall, shutting the door behind him.

"Put your head between your knees. Breathe through your nose." Rafe still held on to me.

"What? Put my head in the trash can?" I heard hysteria in my voice and made an effort to shove it down along with the sick feeling in my stomach. "I'm okay. Unless I faint." I dropped the can to the floor and tried to process this news. What the hell did it mean? "A Siren? Seriously? They're kind of like mermaids. You know, Rafe. We saw Aggie swim, morph into a thing with a fish tail on her bottom half." I looked down at my legs in black slacks, trying to imagine it and just couldn't. Amnesia? Or a trick? This time by Ian. I'd heard Jerry's warnings about the MacDonalds for too many years not to be wary of them and their "results."

"I can't believe this." I said it out loud again.

"There are worse things, Glory. Seriously. You could have demon blood." Rafe sounded bitter.

"Stop. This is my moment. Focus on me, Rafe." I knew how that sounded but really. I was sick of the whole demon issue. This *was* all about me, damn it. Rafe had known about his demon blood all his life. I'd had about a minute to deal with this idea of a previous life sitting on a rock singing for sailors. *So I could kill them.* The very thought made me want to heave again. I held my hand over my mouth and breathed through my nose.

"You're right. Sorry. Sirens. Yeah, they lured sailors to their deaths. Can't quite see you doing that, Glory." Rafe picked up the paper Ian had left on his desk. "'Sexual beings, able to ensnare men with their powers. Irresistible to males who become helpless once they hear the Siren's call.' Okay, I'm buying that one. You had me the first time you patted me on my furry head." He had the nerve to grin at me.

"You think this is *funny*?" I was up again. Rafe had been shifted into a dog body when I'd met him. I'd even rubbed his tummy. Yeah, I just bet he'd got off to that. I stomped around the room, avoiding his hands when he reached for me.

"This Siren deal explains everything. How I got Jerry in the first place. Why you won't forget me and move on. Hell, why Ray, a world-famous rock star, still makes passes at me even after I've turned him down more than once. You've got to know that's not his normal behavior with women." I stopped, blinked away stupid tears, and met Rafe's gaze. "I'm a damned Siren, Rafe. You guys are in thrall to me. You can't freakin' help yourselves."

"Don't be ridiculous, Glory. I'm in thrall to nobody. I have free will. I can walk away at any time. So can Blade. Ray never even got a real chance at you. Still, I don't see him camped on your doorstep, begging for your favors, do you?" Rafe tried to pull me into his arms but I knocked away his hands. I just couldn't be distracted right now or comforted. I had to figure this out.

"Go back for a second. Can you? Can you really walk away, Rafe?" I thought about how I used our friendship, how I leaned on him. Rafe deserved a life of his own. A love of his own. Not my crumbs. I knew I wasn't ever going to give him my whole heart. Or at least not that I could imagine anytime in the near future. "Then let's test it. Go. Date other women. Screw your brains out. Have a relationship, a *real* relationship with another woman and forget me. I dare you."

"What's that going to prove? I love *you*, Glory. Would it be fair to another woman to use her to get my rocks off while I'm still in love with you?" Rafe's mouth was tight with pain. "My feelings for you won't go away just because you tell them to."

"Get a clue. You're under a damned spell, Rafe." Tears filled my eyes and ran down my cheeks. "I've ruined your life." I sobbed and fell into the chair again.

"No, baby, you haven't. Let me be with you. We can have a life together. A great life. If anybody's in thrall, it's you. That damned Blade bit you, drained you and sired you. Made you *his* vampire and you've been under his spell ever since."

I raised my head at that. There was something to what Rafe said. The sire/fledgling bond was strong, some said unbreakable. I'd never seriously tried to sever it. Oh, what was I thinking? Jerry had never given me a chance. He was so crazy about me, he'd never let me go, even paying for a bodyguard when I'd actually given independence a shot over the years. Under my spell? I took a shuddering breath.

"You don't know the half of it. Ian says there's something in my blood that is addictive to vampires. You can't imagine it, but he's even thinking he can make a drug out of it. Like the Energy Vampires have their Vampire Viagra."

"Now you've convinced me this really is a scam. That doesn't make sense. You and Blade have taken breaks. We were in Las Vegas for almost five years when he didn't see you. Are you telling me he was able to just give up your 'addictive' blood for all that time?" Rafe stomped over and grabbed the file. He glanced at it then threw it down in disgust. "This is a bunch of scientific mumbo jumbo. But it's bound to be a ploy to get to Blade."

"Don't be ridiculous. Why would he bother using me? Ian has an army at his disposal. Besides, he swears the feud between their clans is old news." I did see Rafe's point. Jerry and I had taken breaks. Was he able to walk away from my blood because he was just that strong? Or could this be a lie and Clarity was all a scam?

"You're exhausted." Rafe smoothed my hair back from my forehead. "Let me take you home. Your emotions are all over the place right now."

"Home. Yes." I felt strangely lethargic.

Ian stepped into the room with a syringe. "Will you let me give you a tranquilizer? It will also help your nausea. You can lie down in one of my spare bedrooms. You've had a shock. And you probably should have a talk with Aggie later. To get more information. What do you say? A little nap now. Talk later? So you can process all this new information." Ian moved closer.

"Are you nuts? You know what happens when I take your drugs." I waved him away. "But I do need to talk to Aggie." My stomach heaved again and I did take the bottle of synthetic Ian held out to me. "I need to stay here, Rafe. I'll just lie down for a while. I'm feeling a little off-kilter. Confrontations with Lucifer always leave me drained."

"Fine. I think you're actually in shock, Glory." Rafe watched me drink every drop in the bottle.

"Now who's the doctor? But Valdez is actually spot on. Shock. You sure you won't let me . . . ?" Ian waved the syringe then put it on the desk. "Fine. Distrust me till the end. But you're welcome to a bedroom. Second room down the hall." He studied me. "I think she's on the verge of passing out, Valdez. Carry her."

I did feel strange and didn't object when Rafe picked me up and lugged me down the hall. He laid me on a soft bed, peeled off my boots, then covered me with a blanket. I closed my eyes and let myself drift away. This wasn't my death sleep so I had dreams. Of fish and fins and boats with men screaming for me to kill them.

I jerked awake but was quickly sucked under again. To a beautiful sea. I lay in warm water, floated in the sun and played with dolphins and starfish. I chased sharks into caves where strange creatures lived in the darkest parts of the ocean that I knew I'd never seen before. I rolled over on the bed and came up against a hard body. Warm arms held me tight. I inhaled and knew I was safe. I finally slept peacefully, dreamlessly.

"You say she's a Siren? That's ridiculous." Jerry's voice. Impossible. Here in Ian's house?

"No, it's not. I can show you the scientific proof if you're not too dense to understand it." Ian obviously didn't care that he was throwing down a gauntlet.

"Aye, I'm sure you've managed to create evidence that seems to back up your claim, MacDonald. Now you've drugged her again. What's to keep me from cutting out your heart right here and now?"

"The dozen guards surrounding you? And I didn't drug

her. She's sleeping off the effects of the horrific night she's had." Ian's voice grated, the tone less of threat and more of amusement. It was bound to goad Jerry into doing something foolish. I struggled to wake up.

"Stop, both of you." I rolled toward the door and threw off a blanket as I sat up. Not drugged? I wondered. Could Ian have put something in that bottle of synthetic he'd had so handy? The room spun and I wiped at my blurry eyes. There they were in the doorway, facing off. It was almost a surprise to see Ian and Jerry in jeans and knit shirts instead of plaid and battle gear.

"Gloriana! Thank God you're awake." Jerry pushed Ian aside to stride to the bed. "How are you feeling? You look like—" He obviously decided "hell" wasn't the right word. "You've had a shock."

"Yes, I have." I took Jerry's hand and let him pull me out of bed. My legs felt a little rubbery but I managed to stay upright with his arm around me for support. I looked around for Rafe but saw no sign of him. I knew this was a busy night for him in the club, maybe he'd gone to check on things. "Ian's been nothing but helpful. Quit trying to start something with him."

"Helpful? Filling your head with nonsense about Sirens?" Jerry glared at Ian. "You have to know that's impossible. No one here knows you better than I do. You hate the water. I love you, but even you admit you can't sing worth a damn. I've known you these four hundred years and more and seen no signs of a Siren in you. This entire idea is madness."

"Obviously she was deprived of her Siren powers before you met her, Campbell. So of course you never heard her sing, saw her swim or kill with her call as Aggie can." Ian shrugged. "Gloriana needs to find out what happened. Why she seemed an ordinary mortal when you met her. I think the Storm God will have the answers."

"You want her to meet with him?" Jerry pulled me into his arms and I went, a rag doll, flopping where he put me. I fought off the effects of what I was pretty sure Ian had slipped me. "If he is the one who did this to her, that could well be suicide."

"Slow down, both of you. I want to talk to Aggie first. If I *am* a former Siren, I want to find out more about my, uh, profession." I sighed as Jerry's strength surrounded me and I absorbed it. I didn't know myself. Or what was real.

And God knew what would happen when Jerry snapped to the fact that he'd never stood a chance with a Siren luring him to turn her vampire. Of course I wouldn't have wanted to be mortal. I might not remember my Siren days, but obviously I'd have been desperate for the immortality a vampire had to offer. And Jerry had been in thrall to me for over four hundred years! Crazy. For a strong man like him, could he live with that knowledge?

But when I'd tried to reason with Rafe, he hadn't been able to hear me. Was the spell I'd cast so strong? Did either man really love me at all? I realized Ian had left and Jerry was staring down at me.

"You honestly think you could have been a Siren once?" He brushed my hair back behind my ears and eased me down onto the bed again. Then he sat beside me. "You're certainly beautiful enough. And you had me bewitched from the moment I saw you."

"First, thank you. But I'm not nearly as pretty as Aggie. Or her perfect size either. And second?" I sniffled as tears filled my eyes. I hated all this crying but couldn't seem to dry up. "Do you think that would make me proud? That I might have tricked you into loving me?"

"No. I didn't mean . . . Hell. I can't seem to say anything right lately. You are the love of my life. No matter what MacDonald claims, that will never change." He buried his face in my hair, his arms tightening around me. I felt him inhale, taking in my scent.

"Jerry." Tears spilled down my cheeks and clogged my throat. "Your words are just fine."

He raised his head and gazed into my eyes. "Believe me then. When I met you, all I saw was a full-blooded, delicious *human* woman with the kind of curves a man could lose himself in. A woman who stirred me like no other. Never forget that, Gloriana. No matter what nonsense MacDonald or that Siren fills your head with. And it wasn't your damned blood either."

"Thanks, Jerry." I kissed him then, tasting him and loving him as much as I ever had. No matter how I'd gotten him, I wanted to keep him. But I couldn't do it unfairly. Damn.

He pulled back, looking serious. "Yes, I had to have you. But I didn't want anyone else to have you either. Remember, Gloriana, that I selfishly made you mine. I killed *you*, not the other way around."

I shuddered when he ran his thumb over my jugular, making it clear that he meant every word he said. I reached for him, needing to taste him again as I did remember how it had been, the urgency between us. It was still and always there, the need that kept us together. His fangs scraped my tongue as we kissed, our blood mingling as my own pierced his lip. I could have kissed him forever, pouring my love for him into that simple joining of mouths, our bodies straining together.

Only when I heard the tapping of high heels coming down the hall's hardwood floor did I finally ease away from him.

"I love you, Jeremiah. But I need some time to figure out what to do with this news. Please?" I stroked his cheek. He hadn't shaved, obviously coming here as soon as Rafe or Laurie had called him. I was betting on Laurie.

"Just keep in mind who told you this news. No matter what 'proof' MacDonald may have offered. And the Siren has not been a friend to you either. Will you?" He caught up my hand and kissed the back of it.

"Yes." My mind whirled. Paranoia on Jerry's part? Or could I hope . . . ? "I want to hear what Aggie has to say."

"As you wish. I'll be waiting for you." He smiled slightly as he stood and looked down at me. "And I won't get into it with MacDonald. Laurie is standing guard between us. Valdez is still here too. They seem to think you want the doctor alive for now."

"Yes, I do." I saw Aggie in the doorway. "Come in. Jerry is just leaving."

"So I heard. Yes, keep the doctor alive. I still have a few uses for him." She winked as Jerry strode from the room. "Ian told me the blood test showed we're a match. You were once a Siren." She pulled up a chair and sat, then just stared at me. "Hmm. Not sure I'm buying it. Never saw one of the sisters with an ass like yours."

"Do you always have to be such a bitch?" I adjusted the pillows at my back as I got settled in the bed.

"Sure. It's in the job description." Aggie laughed and tossed back her hair. Now that I really looked at it, I could see that the color was very similar to mine, though hers had more highlights. Guess she actually could go out in the sun. My few streaks were courtesy of a clever beautician when I had time and money to visit her.

"Tell me more about your job description. I know legend says you sing to lure sailors and their ships onto the rocks." I swallowed. "To their deaths."

"Yeah, well. That was old-school. Too much technology today to let us get away with random shipwrecks. Achelous—that's the Storm God, you know—he's working on some new things. He can bring up the bad weather but we have to stick to certain areas for our luring. We use the Bermuda Triangle and a few other areas where ships and even planes disappear on a regular basis." She laughed. "Can you believe aliens get the credit?"

"Why?" I couldn't imagine how anyone could justify killing as a sport which is what this sounded like.

"Why kill people? Destroy ships and planes?" Aggie shrugged. "Beats me. Gods and goddesses are greedy and bloodthirsty. There are spoils, money, of course. I'm just a worker bee, do what I'm told. And there are perks." She tossed her hair again, obviously a habit with her. "We have a tremendous sex drive and you get lots of action before you, well, I can see you don't like the fact that we dispose of our lovers after we're done, but that's Achy's policy. They bite it with a smile on their faces when I'm through with them." She actually looked proud of that.

"Seriously? You love 'em and lose 'em. Just like that?" I couldn't believe how completely unemotional Aggie was about the whole thing.

"Honey, you don't have a choice. I learned long ago just to keep my nose to the grindstone, so to speak. You don't follow the rules . . ." She shuddered. "Well, bad things happen. I've heard that some Sirens have disappeared. Guess that's what Ian's sayin' happened to you."

"So you think maybe I didn't follow some of Achy's rules and he kicked me out of the ocean? Stripped me of my powers first, of course. Then I guess that's when Jerry found me." I tried to reconstruct my meeting with Jerry. "But I had memories of a family, a human family, and a first husband."

"Sure. You know paranormals can plant stuff like that. Sirens get vacations on land from time to time. We're not allowed to knock off our lovers then, might get unwanted attention. So I once told a guy I got tired of that he'd left a wife and five kids for me. He's probably still looking for them." Aggie laughed, then pulled a purse off her shoulder and extracted a nail file. "Mind control is a simple trick and I know you use it yourself when a mortal sees something he shouldn't."

"Yes." I'd whammied plenty of mortals in my shop when they'd seen fangs or overheard incriminating conversations between two paranormals. It was self-preservation. Now I was beginning to see it as a dirty trick.

"Hey, I'd love to know what you did to piss Achy off, Glory." Aggie began smoothing out her thumbnail. "For future reference."

"You and me both." I reached out and grabbed her file. "Look at me. Seriously. Do you really think it's possible I could be like you? A Siren? Forget blood tests. Look at other evidence." I made myself hold the eye contact when Aggie gave me her full attention. "Alesa, that demon we just got rid of, taught me to turn people to stone. Like you can."

"No shit?" Aggie grinned. "Cool beans. And, yeah, that's one of our tricks. Not many paranormals can manage it." She jerked back the nail file. "Give me your hand. I'm going to deep dive into your psyche. It'll hurt but if you want to know more? It'll be worth it."

I put my hands behind my back. "Wait a minute. How bad will this hurt? How deep a dive?"

"Good questions." Aggie stuffed the file back into her bag. "It'll hurt like I was jerking out your fangs with a pair of pliers, but won't last long. And I'm diving from head to toe. To see if there are some other clues there. I know Ian's all about the blood, 'cause he's a doctor and a vampire. But I'm all about the powers and the memories. The statue thing *is* part of our repertoire, but there are a few other paranormals who have the same skill set, ya know?"

"Yes, I do." I cautiously offered her one hand. I needed to know this. The pain thing was a worry, but I was a badass vampire, I could take it. "You promise you're not going to just hurt me for kicks and then refuse to tell me anything?"

"Damn, you may be a sister Siren after all, Glory. You're seeming smarter all the time." Aggie popped me on the shoulder. "Love doing stuff like that—playing tricks, fooling the ignorant." She smiled as if remembering some of her better ones. "But this will get us good info. We both need it and you'll be awake, able to see what I see. I can pick up any memories Achy didn't sandblast right out of you. See if you truly were a Siren once."

"You'll just read me? Won't try to make me do your bidding?" I didn't exactly trust Aggie. We'd had a serious run-in not all that long ago.

"Hey. Ian says your blood is Siren blood. So I'm taking his word for it until proven otherwise. The sisters stick together."

She leaned in to whisper. "Even against Achy when he's in one of his moods." She sat up and held out her hand. "You ready?"

"Guess so." I swallowed, not a little scared.

"Then lay your hand in mine."

"Okay, let's do it." I put my palm on hers and she gripped it. Oh, yeah, there was pain all right. It shot up my arm and seemed to take a bullet train to the top of my skull where it did a three-sixty about five times before starting a journey through the rest of my body. Among the jolts of searing agony, I saw stars, rain, some people falling to their knees and a few statues. I also saw the ocean, so beautiful and deadly.

I gasped for air, drowning in that sea when the pain hit my lungs. I bent over, unable to breathe. Stupid since I didn't need . . . Forget logic. I craved air and knew what it was like to die in that moment. Aggie held on to my hand, refusing to let go when I desperately tried to jerk free.

The torture continued down through my middle and I retched, clutching my stomach, my head on my knees. The room went dark and I heard men scream and beg for mercy. Boats broke apart and a body washed overboard in the roiling waters. The wind blew and waves crashed upon the rocks where I sat proudly, head back and naked. I was on the pinnacle, singing and crying out for the men to come to me. I would save them and give them pleasure.

Then the pain rolled on, lower. I wanted these men inside me, laughing as I made love to them. I held them until they drove into me, their screams as they used their last breath pushing us both to the ultimate fulfillment. Then I threw their spent bodies into the surf, jerking yet another sailor into place. Satisfaction. Why could I never be satisfied?

I shrieked as the pain ripped downward, toward my toes. Only there were no toes, just beautiful fins that gleamed with iridescent green and turquoise scales. I raced through the water to the castle beneath the sea where my lord waited. He would be proud of me, want my tally of this night's work.

I lay with my head on his feet, panting as his displeasure

roared over my head. Not enough. Never enough. I had no passion for the work. No skill at the taking. I'd failed, my kills weren't true and the men lived. I was unworthy, a wretched creature who could not serve this god with any honor.

I kept my eyes closed as a hand stroked my hair. I heard the murmur of soothing words when the pain finally vanished, leaving a blessed calm and . . . emptiness. Slowly I came back to the world. This world. Where I sat across from a true Siren. One who did the job and reveled in it. Who killed and didn't sob later for the lost souls she'd taken.

"Sister." Aggie paused with her hand on my head. "I'm so sorry."

"Sorry?" I shoved back from her. "I guess I got what I deserved. I was a disgrace. The Storm God threw me away. I couldn't serve him." I wiped away my tears. Why had I been crying? Surely not because I hadn't had the killer instinct. I had never wanted it. The fact that I had once done Achelous's bidding sickened me.

"I've heard stories about lost sisters, Gloriana. Yes, I remember now. Your name. It is written in the archives. I can't believe he let you keep it." Aggie's face was wet with her own tears. She shook her head, blinked her sea green eyes, then firmed her lips. "Well, that was quite a trip down your memory lane. No doubt about it. You were an epic fail as a Siren. You're lucky Achy didn't fry you with a lightning bolt instead of letting you go."

"Yeah." I didn't know what else to say. Aggie obviously felt sorry for me. But I was beginning to realize being kicked out of the Siren sisterhood was actually a pretty good thing. Couldn't be a stone-cold killer? I was so out of there.

Aggie pulled out her compact. "Look at me. I'm a mess and I have a date with Ian later." She reapplied her lipstick. "I'm going to have to tell Achy about this, you know. Of course he saw you not too long ago, didn't he? Wily bastard. Never said a word. No wonder he stuck me here in Austin. Bet he wanted to check up on you." She arched a brow and looked over at me. "Think he's having second thoughts? Might want you back?"

"God, don't even go there." I jumped up, then fell back onto the bed. I felt reamed out, weak. The pain tour had done me in. Of course the Storm God didn't have designs on me. He'd seen me and let me go. If he wanted me back I'd be floating in an Austin lake right now with a rock for a bed. I dismissed the idea. Simply couldn't wrap my brain around it.

"You're right. Coincidence." She laughed like she knew something I didn't and went back to fixing her face.

I let it go, something else on my mind. "What powers did you see, Aggie? I was so caught up in the k-killing, I didn't . . ."

"Good question. Well, there are a few things I can teach you. Amazing that Achy left you anything to work with. But the very fact that he let you keep your name is proof that he had a soft spot for you. Either that or he's slipping. And, girlfriend, that man just doesn't slip." Aggie paused with her lipstick in her hand. "Powers. The statue thing, of course, you've got that. And I'll bet you can read minds through blocks when dealing with vampires, shifters, the lesser be-ings. Try it. You'll love it." Aggie pulled out lip liner. "Can't read mine, of course, so don't even try."

"I will. Try with others, I mean." I fell back on the pillows, still horrified that I'd been like Aggie. She just sat there, calmly touching up her makeup after watching what amounted to a video of me doing the Siren thing like it was nothing. Yeah, another day at the beach. Literally. Swim out, kill a few sailors after some slamming sex. Business as usual. I wondered if I dared ask for one of Ian's tranquilizers. Oblivion looked really good right now.

Aggie smiled as she put away her beauty tools. "No won-der you look shell-shocked and strangely flushed. Ian said you faced off with Lucifer tonight too. Not bad, sister."

"I'm lucky he let me get away with it." I put my hands to my cheeks. They did feel hot. Probably caused by that weird trip Aggie had done or maybe still singed from Luc's blast of heat in my face.

"I'm sorry, hon, that Achy did a number on anything to do with water and you." She shuddered. "I can't imagine my life without being able to swim in the sea. For a Siren, that's worse than death."

"Yes, well, until tonight I didn't remember it was ever important to me. I avoided anything deeper than a Jacuzzi tub." I pulled the covers up to my chin when Aggie stood and walked to the door. "Tell the men I'm resting, will you? I need to think. I really don't want to deal with any of them now."

"Fine. I'll tell them. But I doubt they'll listen to me. If your Jerry or Rafe heard those screams they're probably already crowded around the door. I'm surprised they didn't burst in here. Ian's guards probably kept them out." Aggie stared at me for a long sixty seconds. "A Siren. Un-freakin'-believable. Wait till we tell Flo tomorrow night. She's going to go nuts."

"No, you can't tell her." I was across the room in an instant, even though it left me with a bad case of the shakes. "She's leaving for Paris at the end of the week. Let her take off in blissful ignorance. I'll tell her when she gets back."

Aggie narrowed her gaze. "Why? You ashamed of your Siren heritage?"

"I don't know how I feel or what I believe. But I do know I don't want to deal with Flo's reaction to the news right now." I put my hand on Aggie's arm. She was dressed for her date in a winter white sweater and bronze leather pants. Her leather heels were cute but not quite right for the outfit or the season. "You need new suede pumps. Right?"

Aggie looked down and frowned. "Maybe. Well, yes. These really aren't working, are they?"

"You get Flo stirred up about the Siren thing and we can kiss shoe shopping good-bye." For myself, I couldn't imagine dredging up any shopping enthusiasm. Or even crawling out of bed anytime soon. I was already feeling wobbly again. I staggered back to bed.

"You're right. Tell her later." Aggie grinned. "Shoes are a Siren weakness. Because in the old days we so rarely got to walk on land. Thank God times have changed."

"Um, it's okay for you to say 'God' like that?" I sank down on the bed again. There was so much I didn't know about Sirens. Not sure why I bothered to ask this question. With their history, there was no way a true follower of the Storm God had a Heavenly future. The thought made my stomach turn.

"Sure. Thank God, the Storm God, whoever." Aggie rolled her eyes. "Lighten up, Gloriana. You are way too serious. Sirens are immortal. We don't worry about Heaven or hell. Lucky for you, you're a vampire now so you've got the immortality thing covered again. Otherwise, you'd be dust." She tapped her perfect chin. "When did you meet your vampire?"

"1604." I fell back on the bed, thinking about it.

"Yep. You are one lucky gal. If your guy hadn't sunk his fangs into you back then, you'd be long gone, sister. I'm sure Achy never wanted you to live forever and he was really surprised to see you were still around when he did run into you." Aggie stopped in the doorway. "By the way. That memory thing didn't have to hurt. Call it payback for you and Flo ignoring me since the wedding." She tossed her hair. "Hope you learned your lesson. I'm going for cute brown suede pumps tomorrow night. See ya." She took off.

"Bitch!" But forget her and her evil tricks. Oh, yes. Achelous and I *had* met before and not that long ago. Yet he'd said nothing. Had he arranged for me to become immortal or had that been a happy accident? And, if he really hated me, why hadn't he acknowledged me when we'd met? Dread built up inside me so strong that I wanted to run somewhere where there was no water whatsoever. A desert maybe. West Texas was supposed to have vast stretches of open range with little water. I could be there in a few hours.

I heard a commotion at the door and figured Jerry and Rafe were thrashing out who was going to get to see me first.

I heard Aggie tell them to chill and settled back just as my phone chimed that I had a text. I looked around and saw my purse on the floor next to the bed. When I read the text, I realized it had been too much to hope that Alesa could have just vanished down to hell without a final word.

Left gift 4 U N $ at apt☺ A.

I sent a quick text to Penny to meet me outside, then slipped out through the window. Of course I ran into one of Ian's guards, but I just smiled and waved when Penny came running to meet me.

"What is it? Your text sounded urgent." She still had on her lab coat.

"Alesa left us a little present at the apartment. I don't know about you, but I figure it can't be a good thing." The ground seemed to shift under me, but I sucked it up and kept going. I had to do this. I couldn't give in to weakness.

Penny grabbed my arm. "God, no. She mentioned me specifically?"

"If you translate into a dollar sign." I dragged Penny around the house toward her car.

"Of course. She never called me by my correct name." She dug her car keys out of her pocket. "Let's go." She stopped next to one of the guards. "If Ian looks for us, tell him I took Glory home and we need some alone time. Got it?" The guard just nodded as we climbed into Penny's beat up economy car.

"Maybe we should have shifted. It would have been faster." She glanced at me as she drove through the hills from Ian's isolated place toward town.

"Couldn't have managed it." I rolled down the window and let the cool air hit my face. My cheeks were still hot. "I think Ian put something in the bottle of synthetic he gave me. I'm still shaky."

"I didn't say anything but you look like you've been wind-burned or were too liberal with blush, which I know you wouldn't be." Penny stopped at a red light. "Another weird side effect?" I could tell she was itching for a notebook. "Ian shouldn't have done that."

"News flash, Penny. Your boss does what he pleases. In this case, he probably thought I needed the tranquilizer. But my Siren blood obviously doesn't react well to his stuff." I glanced down. "Good news though. I think my stomach is finally going down."

"Wow. So eventually the side effects do wear off."

"I can only hope." We were getting near Sixth Street. What had Alesa done to our apartment? Penny had moved out, yet the demon had included her in the surprise. I had a sick feeling in the pit of my stomach that I knew what or who was waiting for us upstairs as Penny parked in the alley and we sprinted for the stairs. The door to our place wasn't locked and we both stopped and did a gut check before I carefully shoved it open.

Ten

Staring at us from a seat on the couch was Penny's twin Jenny. She was frozen in place with a wild look in her eyes.

"Oh, tell me she didn't—" Penny sank down on the couch next to her sister.

"Read her mind, Pen. She's freaking out, sure you're going to bite her on the neck any minute." I headed to the kitchen for a fortifying bottle of synthetic I knew wasn't doped. I took my time opening it. When I got back to the living room I heard Penny telling her sister how sorry she was about all this.

"The first thing we've got to figure out is if I can thaw her." I took a swallow then set the bottle on the kitchen table, out of the way in case I was successful and Jenny made a break for it. I was going to stop her, of course.

"Look at me, Jenny." I sat on her other side. "I'm going to try to fix it so you can move and talk again. But here's the deal: you can't scream or run out of here. You and Penny need to talk. And I'm Penny's mentor in this so I'll be here too. To help her explain things."

"Whoa. Did you read her mind then, Glory?" Penny's

eyes were tearing. "She hates me. I think I'm going to have to just erase this whole night from her memory."

"It would probably be for the best." I took Jenny's hand. "Thaw first. Decisions later. Now no screaming, Jenny. Penny, lock the door and stand in front of it in case she bolts." I stared into the girl's eyes and thought hard about thawing her. To my relief she jerked her hand from mine and glared at me.

"Don't you dare think you're gonna erase my thoughts, you two blood suckers. That demon—oh, Jesus save me!—warned me you'd try it. She said she'd come right back up here and do terrible nasty *hellish* things if you did such a dirty trick."

"Well, that's not good." Penny abandoned her post at the door.

"Get back!" Jenny darted across the room when Penny reached for her. "My sister's a vampire! Oh, my blessed Lord. I can't believe it. Show me your fangs but stay waaay over there."

Penny sniffled but did produce a fang-filled grimace. "Satisfied? You think I wanted to become one of these nightmares? It was the most horrifying night of my life." She wiped her eyes. "I wanted to tell you, Jen. But look at how you're reacting." Penny glanced at me. "You were right, Glory. I was crazy to think she'd get it."

"Get that you're an even bigger freak now than you've always been?" Jenny was shaking so badly she had to lean against the wall. "How did this happen?"

"That's not important. It's done. I can't go back." Penny tried to approach her sister but Jenny squealed and tossed a book from the shelf at her.

"Stay away from me. I mean it." Jenny frantically searched for escape but quickly figured out we had the only avenue blocked.

"I won't bite you. Ever." Penny held up her hands.

"Pinky swear?" Jenny started to hold out her little finger then seemed to think better of it.

"Jeez. Are we in third grade? Quit looking at me like that. I repeat: I won't bite you." Penny slouched over to the couch. "Yeah, I'm a certified freak now. It was bad enough being a brainiac. Never having a date in high school that Daddy didn't pay for."

"Oh, that was just for prom and Daddy didn't exactly pay Cousin Jimmy, just offered to gas up his truck once a week until he graduated from vocational school." Jenny felt her way across the wall to a chair and collapsed into it. Then she jerked up the neckline of her sweater until it was at her lower lip. "Glory, that d-d-demon said you were a real old vampire, hundreds of years old. Is that right?"

I got my bottle of blood off the table and took a drink. "Yes, that's right. So kind of Alesa to fill you in. And, quit worrying about your neck. This is a bottle of synthetic blood. I drink it instead of people."

"What about you, Pen? Are you into the bottled stuff too? Or"—Jenny swallowed—"draining people dry and leaving their dead bodies in alleys."

"Quit sounding like a grade B movie, Jen. I drink the bottled stuff or hit my boyfriend's vein during sex." Penny flushed. "At least as a vampire I don't have trouble getting dates. Trey's actually an ancient shape-shifter. He appreciates a woman with a full figure. And his blood is awesome."

"My God in Heaven!" Jenny shrank back in the chair. "You people are insane. That demon—Jesus save me!—she proved to me that she's real with some horrible tricks. So I know you're not lying, but Pen! This world, what you are . . ." Suddenly Jenny's eyes rolled and she fainted dead away.

"That was fun." I stomped the hardwood floor. "Thanks a heap for the parting gift, Alesa." I glared at Penny. "And did you have to brag about taking Trey's vein? That was the final straw, you know?"

"I couldn't help it. She's a cheerleader. And all that in her sorority. This vampire thing is my one bragging right." Penny flushed then knelt in front of Jenny and patted her cheeks. "What are we going to do, Glory?"

"I'll get a cool cloth for her cheeks. Why don't you move her to the couch?" I finished off my synthetic then headed for the kitchen where I ran water over a dish towel. I carried it into the living room while I went through all the potential Jenny complications in my mind. I understood where Penny was coming from, and wasn't about to fuss at her again.

"She's coming around. I know you don't want me to do it, but I have to make the offer." Penny gave me a hard look.

"I get it, she's your twin. Now that she knows the truth about you, make it and see what she says." I settled into a chair to watch the show.

"Jenny . . ." Penny wiped her sister's face with the cloth. "Wake up and talk to me."

"What?" Jenny sat upright with a wild look on her face. I was familiar with it. It was the look of someone who expected to be taken down a pint any minute.

"Please. I promise you will never need to be scared of me. I won't drink from you. You smell delicious, of course"—Penny smiled and I wanted to pinch her for stirring the pot—"but I just couldn't do that to you."

Jenny had started murmuring the Lord's Prayer at that smell comment.

"If I have to shake you like a tambourine to get you to calm down and listen to your sister, I will." I said it quietly but Jenny got the message.

"Uh, okay. Talk." She looked from me to Penny.

"Vampires, like Glory and me, are immortal. We live forever unless some wise guy manages to stake us." Penny paused when Jenny's eyes darted around the room. "Looking for a stake? Trust me, you couldn't do it. Not only aren't you strong enough to take me out, but"—Penny reached out and gripped Jenny's arm—"I don't think you really want to kill me, do you?"

"N-n-no." Jenny's eyes filled with tears. "But this is bizarre."

"I know. I still wake up from my death sleep and think it can't be true." Penny shook her head. "Can you believe it?

I'll look like this forever. Nineteen. Exactly this size." Penny frowned down at her admittedly chubby figure. "That part's a bitch."

"Seriously? You can't diet or exercise to get rid of that roll?" Jenny actually reached out and lifted Penny's jacket to snag the bulge at her waist. The immortality thing seemed to have gone right over her head.

"No, but I've invested in a lot of Spanx. Now hear me, Jen. You have a perfect figure. Are young and beautiful. If you want to stay like that forever . . . Well, I can arrange to have you turned."

"Turned." Jenny snatched her hand back. "Vampire? May God have mercy on us both. You would do that? Condemn me to hell along with you?"

"Now just a damned minute. Penny is a good person. The same good person she was before a deranged vampire made her a vamp against her will. She is not going to hell. Get that into your pretty, empty head, missy." I jumped to my feet and got in her face. I also let her see my impressive four-hundred-year-old fangs. That sight was enough to make her fall back into the corner of the couch, pale and shaking.

"N-no offense, Glory. Seriously. I just thought . . ."

"No, you didn't. You judged us based on comic books and movies. You don't know who we really are." I sat back down. "Penny, this is a bad idea. The council will never go for it."

"You don't know that. I could ask Damian first. Explain the circumstances. He has a sister in the program."

"Program?" Jenny's voice went up three octaves. "This is a program?" She shoved Penny away from her. "I've been thinking. I haven't seen you during the day for months, have I, Pen? I bet you can't go out in the daylight."

"No, I can't." Penny frowned as Jenny sat up.

"And our donut and coffee runs are history now. Can you even eat real food?"

"No again. We drink blood, that's all. But we have good synthetics like Glory said. I can get you set up with that."

Jenny dug into her purse. "I'm thinking the movies aren't

all a crock." She pulled out her compact then swept me with a disdainful glance. "Glory, you fall onto your blush brush tonight? Obviously you people can't see yourselves in a mirror." She checked her reflection, wiped lipstick off her front tooth then passed it to Penny.

"That would be a no." Penny passed it back without pretending to glance at it.

"And you expect me to buy into this?" Jenny thrust the compact into her Dooney & Bourke tote. "You're nuts. How would I go to cheer practice? Attend class? Organize the pledge breakfast? I could go on and on. Things you two wouldn't understand but are important to me." Jenny gave me a superior look. "While I realize Glory knows some interesting people . . ." She grabbed Penny's thigh, suddenly not so high and mighty. "Oh. My. God. Are you telling me Israel Caine is a vampire?"

"Not telling you anything. I just happen to know him." I got up and sent Penny a mental message to let this go for tonight.

"Now listen to me, Jenny. Penny made the offer. We get it. You're not interested. Fine. But you will not tell anyone else about your sister, vampires, any of it. Understand?" I looked her in the eyes. "If you do there will be bad consequences. To you and your family."

"My family?" Jenny turned to Penny. "You wouldn't let them hurt Mom and Dad, would you?"

Penny understood even if her sister didn't. "Our survival depends on staying under the radar. I couldn't stop the vampire council if they decided you were a danger to vampires in Austin. They might come after you, or just start with Grammy and Grandpa. To make a statement."

"Oh, God save us all. What have you gotten us into, Pen?"

"Penny didn't get you into anything, Jenny. She was dragged kicking and screaming into this paranormal world but she's making the best of it. You really should be proud of how she's adapted after a major trauma. But you're too self-involved. Obviously." I gripped Jenny's elbow and got her to her feet. I could tell that she didn't like my hand on her. "Now I bet you have to get back to the sorority house. And we crash at dawn."

"Oh, right." Jenny glanced at her watch. "Look at the time. I don't know how long I sat there. And then that demon—Lord above watch over me!—told me you had moved out, Penny. You should have told me!" She glared at her sister.

"It was recent. And you don't usually drop by." Penny kept apologizing until Jenny shook her head.

"Never mind. I, uh, love you no matter what you are but I need some time. And my lips are sealed." She put up her hand and shook her head again when Penny tried to hug her.

"They'd better be. Vampires are everywhere, Jenny. We will know if you let our secret slip. Believe me." I was aggravated that Jenny still wouldn't touch Penny when she so obviously needed reassurance.

"Okay. I get it. I said I'll keep quiet. You tell that to your nasty council. No one needs to get hurt to make me keep my mouth shut." She grabbed her purse and made it to the door on wobbly heels.

"Jenny." Penny was tearing up. "I'm sorry. About that demon. She really scared you, didn't she?"

"I'll say. Look." Jenny held out her shaking hands and we could see that she'd bitten her cuticles until they were red and bleeding. The smell of that blood made Penny and me sigh. "You know how I worked to break that habit. One bad night and I'm ruined again."

"I'm sorry. Best get home and put some cream on them then." Penny practically shoved her twin out the door. "Good night."

We looked at each other as soon as Jenny was out of sight. "Synthetic." A trip to the fridge for both of us and then Penny had to hurry to Trey's before the sun caught her. I was ready to hit the sheets. It had been a long night.

First I looked in a mirror. Yep, Lucifer had taken away that gift. No surprise there. So I grabbed my computer monitor that had a webcam I used like a mirror. Ian's tranquilizer that he'd obviously slipped into my synthetic had given me a case of ruddy cheeks that would have made a Highland sheepherder look pale. I wasted a few minutes rubbing in moisturizer I knew wouldn't help then fell into bed. I didn't want to think about what came next.

"There is no way in hell you're going to meet the Storm God without me beside you." Jerry had arrived soon after sunset and he figured I was recovered enough to get into this.

"Relax, Jer. I'm not eager to have a confrontation with the guy. If I do decide to have a face-to-face, I'm sure I'll want you there at my back." But did I really? Whatever we heard from Achelous was probably going to either break Jerry's heart, send him screaming into the night or make him want to kill someone. Hopefully that someone wouldn't be me. But if he decided to attack a god? I had to keep Jerry calm or he'd end up a mere charred stain on the ground once the Storm God got through with him.

I might not have memories of our ancient history, but my recent showdown with his high and mightiness was a vivid and horrifically clear picture in my mind. Achelous loved to toss lightning bolts for one thing. My hair had been fried, my nerves sizzled by power surges and I hadn't been able to hear for a week after our thunderous encounter.

"No, I'm in no hurry to see the Storm God again."

"Glad to hear it. If Aggie is right, the man rejected you. You have no reason to think he'd want to see you again." Jerry played with my hair which was now clean and untangled, thanks to a nice hot shower and shampoo.

He'd wanted to join me in that shower, but I'd reminded him that Laurie still occupied my spare bedroom. She must have arrived some time after dawn. And, while my death sleep had cured any lasting effects of my meltdown other than rosy red cheeks, I couldn't deny I was more than a little depressed and not exactly in the mood for a wild romp in the bathtub.

"I do have questions for Achelous but I wonder if I'll like the answers." I leaned against Jerry as he moved his finger down to trace the vein in my neck. Maybe I wasn't as depressed as I'd thought. "Anyway, I promised to go shoe shopping with Flo and Aggie tonight. I'm not about to tell Florence any of this. Just that we got rid of Alesa." I heard a thump from Penny's old room. Laurie was packing her things after doing yet another cleansing ritual. I was all for whatever magic she performed. I couldn't seem to get the stench of demon out of my nostrils.

"Shoe shopping?" Jerry dropped a kiss on top of my head. "That sounds refreshingly normal after the week you've had. I say have at it. Buy some shoes on me." He dug for his wallet.

I stopped him before he could pull out a platinum card. Stupid maybe, but I wasn't accepting charity and I was determined to fight any Siren tendencies. One of those avaricious creatures would have gladly maxed out Jerry's card and come back for another one.

"That's okay. I've got this. I'm not really in the mood for an orgy of retail therapy anyway. I'm planning to cut this outing short if I get the chance." I laughed when Jerry frowned, laid his hand on my forehead and peered into my eyes.

"Are you ill? You look flushed. I swear if MacDonald slipped you one of his potions . . ."

I was keeping that latest dose to myself. I was definitely piling on some concealer as soon as I could get to my makeup bag.

"I'm fine, Jer. Now I need to get ready. Later. When we come back from the mall. Be here. You're paying Laurie off tonight, aren't you?"

"Yes, a nice severance package. I had no idea we'd wrap things up so quickly." He released my hands and pulled me into his lap. "We will actually be alone here. Finally. I can chase you naked through the entire apartment."

"Chase? Am I supposed to run?" I leaned forward and bit his ear, drawing blood and sucking it away greedily. Oh, yes, this was my man. I felt the hard length of his arousal press-ing against my hip. To hell with shoe shopping. I'd feign a headache. Send Flo and Aggie off together and . . .

"Excuse me, you two." Laurie cleared her throat. "I'm ready to go."

I reluctantly gave her my attention. It was a shame I'd never seen her tiger. I bet it was awesome. Then again, if she had to shift into that, we'd be in a hell of a mess, wouldn't we? Of course she blocked her thoughts. I decided to test my powers and concentrated. Could I blast through that block? It felt like I was shoving against a rock wall. Powerful entity. And she'd held her own against Alesa.

"Give it up, Glory. I'm more than I seem." She threw a hand up toward the ceiling and around her body. The air shimmered in an arc, encasing her in what looked like glit-tering crystal.

"Wow. Guess so." I blinked as I felt her punch through my own block to flip through my thoughts like they were yesterday's newspaper. Her grin said she'd picked up on how I'd just wiggled against Jerry's erection to torment him. "Hey, I was practicing. Aggie told me about a few of the powers I'd had as a Siren. I'm seeing what might be hanging around."

"Powers. Yeah, give them a try." Laurie nodded. "You can never have too many weapons. So if they're there, keep them sharp."

"What the hell are you two talking about?" Jerry looked pained as he eased me off his lap. "That statue thing you did, Gloriana? I'd say you have a fifty/fifty chance of getting that from either the demon or a Siren."

"I doubt Alesa would have left Glory with anything more than a headache." Laurie nodded. "Face it, Jerry. Glory's got a Siren thing going on." She didn't look particularly both-ered by the idea. "Now I need to head out. I got half my pay from Rafe. He said you'd give me the rest, Jerry." Laurie had on her usual dull outfit of plain T-shirt and khakis. I never had gotten a chance to give her that makeover I'd wanted to try. With her coloring she'd look fabulous in green or a bronze silk.

"Are you sticking around town for a while?" Jerry pulled out his checkbook. I thought about looking at the number he was writing but spared myself the guilt. I knew it was probably more than I could ever afford.

"Yeah. I'm exploring a few options. I got word the council might have some work for me. Even Ian, who I despise, is short a bodyguard. I'd have to be desperate to take that gig, though." Laurie smiled wryly. "You and I are on the same page about MacDonald, Jerry. Don't trust him."

"See, Gloriana. Someone agrees with me." Jerry ripped out the check. "I have instincts about people."

I decided to ignore the Ian bashing. "My friend Israel Caine might need someone else to work for him. He keeps guards around because of rabid fans. Let me give him a call for you, Laurie." I was back to thinking about shopping. Might as well get it over with and the women were set to be here soon anyway.

"The rock star? I could go for that." Laurie grinned. "Yeah, hook me up." She reached out and took the check Jerry handed her then shook his hand. "Thanks. Nice doing business with you. Let me know if you need me again, Jerry. Now I'm getting a hotel room, then heading over to N-V for a drink. Locking horns with a demon always leaves me dry." She winked at me. "You need me, Glory, without involving this guy, you've got my numbers. I left them by the phone next to your bed. Special rate for independent women. I figure we should stick together."

"Hey, why didn't I get that special deal?" Jerry glanced at what had to be the huge check he'd just given her.

"You hired me, not her. I set my own rates and can pick and choose who I work for. Sorry, but I believe you got your money's worth." Laurie picked up her duffel and slung the strap over her shoulder. Did she even own a purse?

"Yes, of course. Gloriana told me how you had Alesa afraid to even sleep in the bedroom. Brilliant." Jerry walked her to the door and opened it. "You were worth every penny. You need a recommendation, use my name."

"Will do. Thanks. Now see ya around. Call me about the Caine gig, Glory. Sounds like my kind of setup." Laurie stepped into the hall. "I swear I still smell that demon's stench in your apartment. If you need another cleansing, call me about that too. No charge."

"Thanks. It does still smell like burned cookies in here, doesn't it?" I leaned against the doorjamb not about to share that Alesa had paid an extra visit here last night to leave her "surprise." "I'll dial Ray when I get back from the mall. And thanks for making me feel safe, Laurie. I didn't think anyone could handle Alesa, but you sure did. You can add my name to the recommendation list."

"I let you down when Lucifer got there last night." Laurie shrugged. "But you stood up to him." She popped me on the arm. "Way to go, Glo." She nodded to where Jerry had moved into the kitchen, pulled out his cell phone and was checking his messages. She lowered her voice. "Blade's a stand-up guy, shelling out the bucks like that. You got a keeper there."

"What about you? You seeing anyone?" I couldn't resist. She was heading to N-V, wasn't she?

"Not yet. But I'm keeping my eyes open." She waved her hand. "I'll be seeing you." She sauntered off down the hall, suddenly putting a feminine hip thrust into her stride. Maybe Rafe would like her after all. And I had no business feeling jealous about it.

"I've got to go home, make some calls. I need some figures that I've got in my office there." Jerry pulled me against him.

"Go. The girls will be here any minute." I turned in his arms and kissed him on the lips. "I'll call you when I get back."

"Can't wait." He patted me on the bottom and strode away.

I sighed and leaned against the closed door. I really didn't want to lose him but this knot of dread about what Achelous might say just wouldn't go away. It stayed with me even after Aggie and Flo arrived and we headed for the mall.

"Glory, what's the matter with you?" Flo had just decided on her third pair of shoes and was making a salesclerk very happy. "You should be laughing and taking advantage of these great sales. You said that demon is gone for good. Isn't she?"

"Yes, she's gone. Lucifer too. We are totally rid of all demons." I glanced at Aggie, who was in front of a mirror on the other side of the store, admiring her feet in a pair of chocolate brown suede pumps.

"Then why the gloomy face?" Flo glanced at Aggie. "Is it her? She *is* irritating, but she does know her shoes. She's not so bad to shop with."

"I'm fine, Flo. I'm just sad that you're leaving." I gave her a hug. "Who will I have to hang out with?"

"If you didn't have your business, you could come with us. It will be great fun. CiCi is coming, so are Freddy and Derek. We will shop till we drop in those great Paris boutiques that I love." Flo sighed. "Now I am sad. Call me. We will share all the gossip on the phone."

"Of course." I forced myself to try on a pair of boots. They fit, were on sale and the right color. I couldn't get excited about them but I decided to buy them anyway. "I'll take these," I told the salesman when he approached.

"Good. Now everyone has bought something. What say we head over to N-V for drinks to cap off the evening?" Aggie had whipped out her gold card and handed it to the salesman.

"*Perfetto.* I'll call Ricardo to meet us." Flo began to dig out her phone.

"No, just the girls." Aggie put her hand over Flo's. "Or is that forbidden since you got married?"

"What? You think I am controlled by my husband?" Flo's dark eyes flashed.

"Of course not. But maybe you've lost your taste for a little adventure. Become one of those homebodies who likes to just stay in front of the TV in your jammies with the old man."

Aggie smiled as if she knew exactly what she was doing.

"Aggie, cool it. I'm tired and Jerry's coming over later." I handed the salesman my own credit card when he came up to have Aggie and Flo sign their sales slips.

"Oh, so now you're also a dull stick-in-the-mud." Aggie pulled out a new shrug she'd picked up at a little shop farther down the mall and ripped off the tags. It was a shiny gold Lurex knit and, when she slipped it on over her blue silk minidress, made her look ready to party.

"We are not dull sticks." Flo threw her card in her purse and the receipt at the startled salesman. "We go to N-V and without the men."

"Flo, seriously. I'm not in the mood." I grabbed my card and signed the receipt, standing when I got my shopping bag.

"Want to tell your bestie why you're not in your happy place? Why Glory the dancing fool can't work up the energy tonight?" Aggie had a malicious smile that made me want to smack her.

"Shut the hell up, Aggie." I jerked her arm as I pulled her out into the mallway. "Flo, I don't know why Aggie is trying to start something but I just want to go home."

"No, she's trying to push you to tell me something." Flo was right on my heels as I headed toward the exit to the parking lot. "What is it, Glory? What has you so upset? You think I can't see that you're worried, *mia amica*? Why do you hide things from me and tell them to this, this sea creature?" Flo's Italian gesture made Aggie hiss.

"You want to start something with me, little vampire?" Aggie seemed to swell, growing about six inches taller as we hurried across the parking lot. The lights above us blew out with loud pops and plunged us into darkness.

"Aggie, stop it!" I halted and faced her, grabbing her arm. "Leave Flo out of this. What do you want from me? A night of dancing? A pledge to be your best friend while she's gone?"

I threw my hair back behind my shoulders in an imitation of the Siren and bared my fangs. I didn't care who saw me. That was what the whammy was for. "Damn it, leave my friend out of your little games. You want to be my 'sister' then say so. We'll bond over Siren memories if that's what you want. But I'll be damned if I'm ever going to love you like I do Flo here. She is kind and good-hearted, something you have no idea how to be." I shoved Aggie away from me.

"Glory! Explain to me what is happening? Why are you and Aggie having this fight? What is she to you? Sister?" Flo pushed between us when Aggie lunged for my throat with her nails. "Don't you dare!" She glared at Aggie, who actually stopped in her tracks. "Stay here. Glory, behave! I have to make these mortals forget they saw your fangs. Now put them away. Please! Aggie, you want friends, put down your hands. Now."

I saw tears in Flo's eyes and quickly ordered my fangs up and out of the way. Aggie said a few words that consigned me to a watery grave after some inventive tortures but she did lower her claws. Yes, she was furious. Tough shit. She'd started this and she'd needed to hear the truth. It would be easy enough for her to read my thoughts anyway. I remembered how horribly she'd treated Ray and me when we'd first met her, constantly threatening to drown me and give Ray to a vindictive goddess. It gave me perspective. Sisters? No way in hell.

Eleven

"Get in the car." I pointed to my convertible, hit the remote to unlock it and would have laughed at Aggie's expression if I wasn't so pissed. She hated my small car, especially since she'd been crammed in the backseat. She'd griped about it all the way to the mall. My tiny trunk barely held our packages as I tossed them inside none too gently. I'd kept the top up since Flo hadn't wanted her hair windblown so even headroom was an issue that Aggie had complained about. Of course her knees were practically under her chin too as we'd heard at least five times. Like I cared.

"Watch who you're issuing orders to." Aggie nevertheless squeezed into the backseat again.

"I want to know what is going on between you two." Flo dropped into the passenger-side bucket seat then grabbed my arm before I could start the car. "Now, Glory. Why is Aggie being so mean? What is this sister thing?"

I leaned back. I really didn't want to get Flo involved, especially now when she was set to leave town. I turned to glare at Aggie. "Why did you start this? I thought we had an agreement."

"Because the Storm God knows all and sees all when it

comes to one of his herd. He called me on the carpet today, while you were enjoying your peaceful death sleep. God, I hate vampires. No offense, Flo." Aggie showed her perfect white teeth in a mocking smile.

"No offense?" Flo's gesture made it clear that she was certainly offended. "You insult me and Glory. But what is this about the Storm God?"

"Oh, yeah, he called me in. It was a special time. He raked me over the coals for my cooperation with Ian. But now that the cat's out of the bag, so to speak, he wants to meet with his pretty kitty." She hissed again. "Namely you, Gloriana."

"Gee, can you trot out any more clichés?" I took a steadying breath, ignoring Flo's gasp.

"What is this? The Storm God? Glory? What is this cat thing? Are you in trouble with another god?" Flo kept her grip on my arm until I looked pointedly to where her silver-painted nails were digging in and leaving marks.

"Tell her, Glory. Tell her how the blood test you took showed what you really were before you got kicked to the curb a few centuries ago. And, yeah, score another cliché for *moi*. I love 'em." Aggie yawned. Like this was the most boring subject ever. "Achy may decide to make the end of your relationship permanent this time. How sad. Say good-bye, Flo. By the time you get back from gay Paree, you may be in the market for a new best friend. I'm available. I can overlook fangs when the girl has great taste and a fine wardrobe." This time Aggie's smile had an angelic quality. Give the girl an Oscar.

"I could never be your friend, Siren. Every word out of your mouth is spiteful, mean. Look at the way you make Glory sad. She is shaking." Flo had her hand on my shoulder now. "What does she mean, *amica*? Tell me, *favore*."

"Ian's blood test showed that *I* was a Siren before Jerry met me. The Storm God obviously made me mortal after he tossed me out of his harem." I sent Aggie a mental message that made her raise her perfect eyebrows.

"You want to say that to me again? In the parking lot

where I can get at you, bitch?" Aggie grabbed a hank of my hair and jerked, bringing tears to my eyes.

"Stop it!" Flo snatched a handful of Aggie's new sweater. "Let go of Glory's hair or I rip a hole in this sweater too big to be repaired. It was expensive, right?"

"Gang up on me, why don't you?" Aggie released my hair while muttering ugly words that would have been at home on any cell block.

"What time, Aggie? What time and where are we to meet the high and mighty Storm God?" I grabbed Flo's hand when I saw that she wasn't through with Aggie. "Let go, Flo. My car isn't the place for this."

"Hah! Lucky for *questa femmina* that I have respect for fine leather." Flo released the sweater and faced front.

"Thanks." My car was new and I wanted the upholstery to stay rip free. If those two got into it between the seats, I didn't want to think about the damage. As it was, I sent a mental message to my best friend thanking her again for the quick save. My scalp still felt like I'd been dragged through the parking lot by my hair. "Aggie? Details?"

"Midnight. And you'd better adjust your attitude, missy, before you see him or you won't last five seconds." Aggie was examining her sweater. "We go to the same terrace where you met him before. Behind the burned-out shell of Israel Caine's rental. The house was torn down and it's just a vacant lot now, surrounded by a stone fence. It's for sale and deserted. A good place for a showdown. Brace yourself. The meet will probably feature a thunderstorm, lightning bolts and, oh yeah, maybe a typhoon." Aggie smirked at Flo. "Better drop the little one off first. She won't be able to handle it."

"I can handle anything for my best friend." Flo looked daggers at Aggie. "You don't have to go, Glory. Ignore this sea cow and her handler."

Aggie laughed out loud. "Take a look at your friend there, Flo. Achy made sure Glory is the cow. Check out her butt. Did you use Google yet, Glory?"

"Drop it, Aggie." I frowned. Of course I had. And gotten all kinds of weird sites, most claiming Sirens were half bird.

"Tell Flo what you found." Aggie leaned forward. "It's a crock, of course, but you look just like the pictures on the Net." Aggie chuckled and slapped me on the shoulder. "Bird butt. Isn't that just perfect?"

"Shut the hell up." I gave her a look that should have warned her off. "I really don't want to get into this now."

"She's right, Aggie. Calling her silly names isn't helping. And what does a bird have to do with a Siren anyway?" Flo stared at Aggie until she settled into the backseat again. "You swim. I thought you turned into mermaids."

"Do I look like a Disney cartoon to you?" Aggie's smile would make sharks flinch.

"Then what?" Flo frowned, not happy to be kept in the dark about anything. Actually neither was I.

"We can be whatever we want. We do a lot of things in the water. What we shift into is up to us." Aggie obviously wasn't going to spill any details, not to Flo anyway. "Now look. We have some time before we have to meet Achelous. Why not go to N-V, get a few drinks—you guys can get that blood with alcohol there—and then go with Glory to face the music? I've got to show up anyway and maybe Glo *would* like her best friend along to help pick up the pieces afterward."

I wanted to scream, curse, maybe sob a little. Why tonight? When I was still trying to come to terms with this? Of course that was why. Gods always wanted the upper hand. Not that he thought I was a worthy opponent on any level.

"I *do* have to go, Flo. I have questions that need answers and Achelous is the only one who has them. But, Flo, you shouldn't—"

"No, now Aggie is making some sense. Of course I would want to be with you if you have to face this Storm God." Flo squeezed my shoulder gently. "What happens if she just doesn't show up, water witch?"

Aggie's laugh this time made my skin crawl. "Ignore a

summons? Well, I sure wouldn't want Achy to come looking for *me*."

"Then we go. And I could use a drink. But you really believe this, Glory? That you could have been *una Sirena*?" She gestured at Aggie. "You are nothing like this one. Pah! Such a bitch! More like a slimy creature that would crawl out of a cesspool. Eh?"

Aggie spat something in Italian and looked ready to reach between the seats again and continue their catfight.

"Stop. I can't take one more upset tonight. Not with the Storm God on the agenda later. I say bring on the blood with alcohol. And loud music to drown out my thoughts." Did I want to call Jerry to go with me to this midnight meet? No. He might get hurt. Rafe too. If I could ditch Flo, even better. I'd get Aggie to help me with that even though the idea of asking her for anything made my hands tighten on the steering wheel.

"Whatever you wish, *amica*. This is your night." Flo touched my hand. "Start the car. Take us to N-V. Tell me more about the Storm God, Aggie. I have never met a man I couldn't wrap around my little finger. Right, Glory?"

I nodded, hoping Flo wouldn't have a chance to try her skills on Achelous. Whatever womanly wiles Flo had, and she had plenty, I was sure Achy would be more than happy to let her practice them on him. Then he'd destroy her. And if he did let her go after this night was over? What would her sojourn with the Storm God do to her marriage?

No, I wasn't about to let Flo anywhere near that monster. He'd use her whether she wanted him or not. How did I know that? The bone-deep surety I felt made me want to stop the car and puke on the side of the road. My life before Jerry must have been a horror beyond my imagination.

I caught a glimpse of Aggie in my rearview mirror and realized I felt sorry for her. No wonder she had an edge. Who wouldn't, living at the beck and call of a sadistic monster with an insatiable sexual appetite? She caught my eye and I almost swerved into the oncoming lane at the hatred I saw there. Of course she despised me. I'd escaped. She had no chance of it. Clearly I had to watch my back when I was around her. And this was the woman who'd called me "sister"?

I almost didn't recognize the first person I saw when we walked into Rafe's club. Laurie leaned against the bar talking to the hunky bartender. She wore a lime green satin tank top that showed off a surprisingly impressive cleavage and tight black skinny jeans with high platform heels that put her at six inches over six feet. Since the shifter serving up drinks was a big guy, her height didn't seem to bother him, especially as he had a nice view down her top when she leaned over to whisper something to him.

"Well, look who's here. Your guard kitty." Aggie sauntered up next to Laurie. "Can't believe you actually own decent clothes. I figured you spent your off days close to nature so you could enjoy some deer sushi"—she glanced down the bar at the mortals crowded nearby—"between shifts."

"Buzz off." Laurie threw back a tequila shot then stepped away from her. "Glory, haven't you got better things to do than hang out with tuna breath here? I met her at Ian's. He made sure I got the 411 on their sex life." She flicked Aggie with a glance that should have drawn blood. "He never did discriminate when he could get it cheap and easy."

I could see a bar fight brewing and figured Rafe wouldn't thank me for letting it happen. Risking my own life, I stepped between the two women.

"Can we dial it down? I know you don't care who Ian's involved with now, Laurie. And you remember my friend Florence."

"Ah, Glory told me you handled Alesa like a charm. I will remember that if, God forbid, we have visitors of that sort again in the future." Flo smiled and nodded.

I signaled the bartender and ordered my favorite flavor of blood, with alcohol. I was glad to see that Laurie had taken my point and decided to ignore Aggie as she slipped Flo a business card. Networking. Why not? I wasn't so sure the Siren was on the same page. Then the bartender, obviously used to deflecting volatile situations, grabbed the Siren's attention with a question about her drink order. Aggie cast one more evil look at Laurie's back then decided to ignore her too.

Flo put in her own order. "This round is on me. I'm avoiding the alcohol. We have a meeting later and I need my head clear. Glory? I think she wants oblivion." She leaned closer to Laurie. "If you are free at midnight, we could use you. I will pay."

"No, Flo. I don't want to drag any more innocent bystanders into this or tap your bank account. And I'll go easy on the alcohol. I can't afford to be oblivious." Though it would be nice to be toasted during what was sure to come. As for Laurie? What in the heck could a were-tiger do against the Storm God anyway? He could make anyone into a statue with a glance.

"Storm God?" Laurie looked meaningfully at the nearby mortals. Of course she'd read my thoughts and wasn't about to turn down a chance at a paying gig. "There somewhere we can meet privately? I might know a thing or two that could help you, Glory."

"Give me a freakin' break. What's a tiger gonna know about Achelous?" Aggie had asked for a dirty martini and now gulped it down. She signaled for a refill. She obviously didn't care that we were surrounded by strangers who'd begun to stare at us curiously.

"There's a break room. Come on." I grabbed Aggie's arm. "Shut up. You really are determined to make me hurt you, aren't you?" I hustled her toward the employee break room. Luckily the club was busy and there wasn't anyone inside. Laurie and Flo followed us in.

"Just try it, Gloriana." Aggie jerked her arm out of my grasp as soon as we were inside with the door closed. "We are so going to settle this as soon as Achy is through with you."

"Yeah, I look forward to it." I had no idea how I'd come

out in a fight with Aggie, but suddenly itched to try to take her. My scalp still screamed where she'd pulled my hair.

"Stop it! Glory, you need your energy for what's coming. Fighting with this *creatura* doesn't help. *Sí?*" Flo waited for my reluctant nod, then touched Laurie's arm. "Do you know about Glory's news? That Ian discovered she used to be a Siren?"

"Yes." Laurie shook her head. "Nasty business. Glory had to be carried out of Ian's office after hearing the test results."

"Oh, *amica*! I wish I had been there for you." Flo hugged me. "Of course you would be horrified to think . . ." She released me, her eyes awash with tears. "You know."

"It's okay, Flo." I was feeling pretty watery myself.

Laurie glanced at Aggie. "Don't blame you for taking that hard. Sirens. Bitches of the deep. *I* sure wouldn't want any part of that pack of she-devils. But it's better than being related to Alesa, I have to say."

"Swell. You put me one step above a demon from hell." Aggie actually worked up a tear. "What's with you people? Sirens are not all bad. We cleared out a lot of the pirates that used to plague the ships in the Mediterranean. And our songs are beautiful. Some say Aphrodite was once one of us, you know. Men worship us. Will do anything for a Siren."

"Men can be fools. I think we can all agree on that." Laurie looked around the room.

Even Flo nodded. "*Sí.* It is the brain in their *pantaloni* that does their thinking. It works to my advantage, I tell you. Has for centuries." Flo stayed solemn, like she was imparting the wisdom of the ages. And in a way she was. "A smart woman learns early how to use a man's desperation to get under her skirts."

"Okay, let's agree we can manipulate men with sex. But I doubt the Storm God is so vulnerable. After all, he has a stable of women he's kept corralled for thousands of years." I looked at Aggie. "You said he knows all and sees all. You think we need to worry that he might be tuned in to this conversation right now?"

"Not likely. This is his usual playtime. He's out with a couple of the sisters having a conjugal visit." Aggie wrinkled her nose. "At least it wasn't my turn in the rotation. He likes us to pair up, two on one if you get my drift. Of course he gets into the mix too. I've got plenty of libido but it's the same old same old, century after century. And it takes forever for him to—"

"Please." I held up my hand. "You've answered the question. Now answer another one. Is there any way we can get the best of him? Make sure I come out of this alive?" I tried to read her thoughts and hit a hard impenetrable wall. She stalled just long enough to drive me crazy, feigning boredom as she studied a minute hangnail. I wanted to grab her, throw her against the wall and pound her until she answered me. Finally, she glanced up and fake smiled.

"Seriously? I figure you're golden, Gloriana." The way she drawled my name made it sound like an insult. "If Achy wanted you dead, honey, he'd have done the deed centuries ago." Aggie's face went hard again. Jealousy. That was her emotion of choice now. "But maybe he's changed his mind. Does the Storm God have vulnerabilities? Beautiful women, of course. Charm him if he gets out his death ray. That's your best bet."

"Death ray?" I sank down on the sofa where I knew employees sometimes napped. "What the hell?"

"That's what the sisters call it. It's when the big guy is so mad he shoots lightning out of his eyeballs. Scary as hell." Aggie shivered. "You really, really don't want him to go there." She smirked at Laurie. "Tiger, you have anything you can pull out of your furry ass that could beat that? Got to warn you, he'll see a bite or a scratch as foreplay."

"You'll just have to wait and see, now won't you?" Laurie's growl meant business and certainly convinced me she might have a surprise or two left to show us. I sure hoped so. "When's this meeting?" Laurie glanced at her narrow platinum watch. Tonight everything about her was feminine. Even her earrings were delicate dangles and I swear she'd used a curling iron on her tiger-striped hair. The Storm God would be all over her if she didn't have a way to shut him down.

"Midnight." I studied the large clock on the wall above the door while my stomach hopscotched up to my throat. "We have two hours."

"Not much prep time, but I may have a thought or two. Tell me the location and I'll meet you there." She grabbed a pad off the employee dining table and wrote down the directions Aggie gave her.

Flo sidled up to me. "It's no use. I don't like this. We can charter a plane and be on our way to Paris before midnight. What do you say?"

"Tempting. But I can't afford—"

"I afford. For my best friend. Let this god throw his lightning bolts at Aggie. She needs a shot of electricity up her butt. I don't think she even wears panties. Slut. Trying to hurt you . . ."

I swallowed a giggle at the fierce look on Flo's face. But the urge died quickly. I knew I couldn't run, as tempting as that sounded.

"Thanks, pal. That is the most amazing offer I've had in my entire life. But I've got to do this. Just in case . . . Hell, maybe Jerry's right and this is all a scam—something Aggie and Ian cooked up together."

Flo grabbed me. "Is it possible? To torture you like this. Oh, *il mio dio*! I will kill her."

"No, she's mine." I patted Flo's narrow back as I hugged her, tears making the room blur. When I looked up, Laurie had slipped out of the room and Aggie was giving us a disgusted stare.

"Achy would get off to seeing you two in a clench like that. Try not to give in to the urge around him unless you think it will get you off his hit list." She pulled open the door. "Great band tonight. I'm going out there and find a man to dance with. Come on, ladies. This may be Glory's farewell fling."

She shook her hips to the music and disappeared into a group of students headed toward the dance floor.

"Oh, but I hate that creature." Flo sniffed and stepped away from me.

"Me too. But we might as well go out and at least finish our drinks. I'm hoping we get to this meeting and Achelous doesn't show. Then we'll have our answer—I was never a Siren and this was all a hoax." I grabbed a tissue off the table and went to the mirror to repair my makeup. Except when I stared into the glass there was no Glory. Oops, forgot. I sighed as Flo came up behind me.

"Your reflection is gone!" Flo tried to look sad but failed. "Sorry, but that makes me feel better about you, Glory. Though I did notice you are heavy into the concealer tonight. Your cheeks look almost sunburned." She used my tissue to smooth under my eyes.

"Don't tell Jerry, but I think Ian slipped me another drug, a tranquilizer, and the red cheeks are the result. You know I can't take something like a normal vamp could."

"Poor Glory." Flo gave me a hug. "Ian shouldn't have done that. But obviously you were beside yourself. Who wouldn't need a tranquilizer after hearing such horrible news? But at least the demons are finally finished with you. Hah!" She gestured down at the floor. "Stay in hell, burn forever, *bastardo* Lucifer, *puttana* Alesa!"

"Uh, Flo, don't think I'd taunt them if I were you. You never know when the demons might think we deserve one last torment." I thought about telling her the Jenny story, but tonight was already too full of angst to add another layer. Instead, I gave one last glance at the mirror, sighed, then headed for the door.

"Ack! You are right. Out of here, quick. I guess Rafael would object if I dragged one of his customers in here for a"—Flo showed the tips of her fangs—"real drink."

"Don't you dare." I held on to her arm. "He welcomes us here as long as we behave. Go finish your synthetic. Then—"

"Stop! I read your mind." Flo gave me a stern look as she

threw open the door. "I know you think to make me stay out of this meeting but you can forget it, my friend. I am going with you. And that is that." She flounced down the hall and toward the bar.

"What meeting is this?"

I jumped and turned. "Rafe. Where did you come from?"

"Stockroom." He juggled a case of premium vodka like it weighed nothing. Which it did to him. "Good thing since I just heard something very interesting. What's going on, Glory? Who are you meeting?" He pulled me back into the break room and set the case on the table.

"Forget that. We went shoe shopping. Look at my new boots." I held out a foot.

"Give it up. Those are your old boots. You wore them yesterday." Rafe pushed me down on the sofa. "Now spit it out. You look guilty as hell. Where are you and Flo going? And did I see Aggie with you at the bar earlier?"

"Yes. My sister Siren is a pain in the ass. I tried but I will never, positively never, bond with her. Sirens are evil, Rafe. Do you think I was like that before Achelous kicked me out of the sea? Or could it be possible Jerry's right and Ian and Aggie cooked this up between them and it's all a lie?"

"I suppose it's possible. Though Ian did have all those test results." Rafe studied me from head to toe. "Then I look at you and can't imagine . . . You're right. You're nothing like Aggie. I used to think Blade was paranoid about MacDonald but maybe in this case he's right. It's easy enough to fake papers like those Ian showed you."

"But then there's other evidence. My reactions to Ian's drugs. And what I saw when I was with Aggie. The statue trick I can do." I took a shaky breath. "I feel it's true. I know it. Here." I rested my hand between my breasts. My snug red V-neck sweater didn't leave much to the imagination and I saw Rafe take in the view where the knit clung to my nipples even through my industrial-strength bra. Yes, he was a man, proof positive that sex was always on the agenda no matter how serious the conversation. Well, I didn't care what he was staring at or why he reached for me to settle his hands on my shoulders. It was my message that was important here.

"Aggie showed me real memories of my time as a Siren. It was intense but I saw myself actually lure men onto the rocks. I made them, um, serve me and then I just cast them into the sea." I dropped my hand. "It was all at Achelous's bidding."

"Real memories? You sure?" His hands were warm as he drew me closer. "I'm sure Aggie could show you *Gone with the Wind* on the wide screen of your memory if she put her mind to it. Don't trust her, Glo. Things like that can be faked. And what's this about Achelous? Is that who you're meeting with? The Storm God?" Rafe's hands bit into my shoulders.

"Yes. Aggie says he wants to see me. It's a command performance." I sighed. "Which blows apart the conspiracy theory, doesn't it? If this is a MacDonald trick, then Achelous certainly wouldn't lower himself to play along, now would he?"

"You never know what amuses these creeps. Look at what Lucifer did for Alesa." Rafe pulled me into his arms. "You can't go to this meeting. I remember that bastard. He's violent, unpredictable and throws around lightning bolts for fun. Those electrical charges can kill you where you stand."

"Don't I know it." I shuddered and leaned against him. "But I have to go, Rafe. If he shows up, I can ask . . ." I glanced up at Rafe. "Oh, God. I can't stand the thought that I could have been one of those evil Sirens."

He brushed my hair back from my face. "You are nothing like Aggie. Hold *that* thought."

"Yeah, well, you are definitely prejudiced. Which I thank you for. But no matter what, I have to *know*. It's like I have amnesia. Wouldn't you want to know what was missing if you had a hole where your memories should be?"

"What does Blade say about this meeting? Where is he?" Rafe looked around. "In the men's room? He'd better not be drinking his dinner from one of my customers in a bathroom stall."

"No, he's not here. He doesn't know about this. It just came up." I frowned. "And I'm not telling him, Rafe. If the Storm God does show, Jerry would end up getting himself killed trying to protect me. I won't have it."

"That's not your call, Glory. The man deserves to make that decision. After all the years he's got invested in you?" Rafe grabbed my shoulders again. "Look, you know how I feel about you and Blade being together, but I respect the man and what he's done for you. He's proved time and again that he'll do anything, anything to keep you safe. Under some kind of Siren's spell or not, that earns him the right to be there if you do confront Achelous."

"What do you think the Storm God is going to do if I drag my lover in front of him? Just smile and say hello?" I jerked away and was across the room in a flash. "I'm sorry, Rafe, but you're wrong about this. No man needs to be anywhere near this meeting if it happens." I took a steadying breath.

"You're going to meet him with just Aggie and Flo as backup? I'm betting Florence didn't tell Richard about this either." Rafe waited for my answer, his stare making me look away.

"I've begged Flo not to come." I grabbed a tissue and wiped away a stupid tear and saw concealer come with it. "She's insisting. She's such a good friend. Is even paying Laurie to show up. The tiger says she has some tricks that may help us."

"Yeah, great. But you've got another good friend standing right here. You know I'd go to the mat for you too if you'd let me." Rafe frowned when I shook my head and blew my nose.

"Damned stubborn female. Will you at least kiss me good-bye? A real kiss, not some lame peck on the cheek. Hell, I have a feeling this might be the last time we'll be together." He pulled me into his arms. "Glory, see reason. Don't do this."

I touched his cheek. "We need to say good-bye whether I survive this night or not and you know it." I wound my arms around his neck. I shouldn't have kissed him but I didn't have the heart to deny him. He took my mouth as if he wanted to drink in every bit of Glory while he had the chance. I did love Rafe. He would always be a special friend. But when his arms tightened and I felt his hunger move toward something primitive and wild, I pushed him away.

"I'm sorry, Rafe, but thanks for listening." I gave him the best smile I could manufacture—I knew it wasn't much— and walked out of the room. I found Flo sitting on a bar stool, my untouched drink on a napkin next to her. I quickly drained it, the alcoholic kick welcome, and glanced at my watch. It would take a while to get to the isolated spot where Ray had lived before his house had burned to the ground. Arriving early wasn't bad strategy and maybe Laurie would be there with some good news.

"Look at that *puttana* dancing. No grace or style." Flo nodded toward where Aggie flailed her arms and jerked her hips awkwardly to the music.

"She looks like Rafe did when he got Tasered out at the EV compound." My laugh was probably three parts hysteria, one part amusement. "Guess Sirens aren't so great when they hit the dirt. Luckily, when I lost my swimming skills, I picked up some dry-land coordination. Come on, let's get out of here." I stalked over and rescued Aggie's partner from further embarrassment. She grumbled until I warned her we might be late. Apparently the idea of keeping the Storm God waiting terrified her enough to get her hustling.

"Glory, we could shape-shift out to this place. It would be quicker," Flo said as we forced Aggie into the backseat of my car again. "What about you, fish girl?"

"Quit calling me that! And, no, while there are stupid myths that we were once half bird, I don't shift except to look human then back to my best form for swimming. Ow!" Aggie bumped her head on the convertible top. "Put the roof down on this stupid ridiculously tiny car. When we are in front of Achy, he'll probably work up a Cat 5 hurricane anyway. Trust me, your hair will never be the same. And Flo's hair started out looking like she styled it with a pitchfork." She kicked off her shoes and wedged her bare feet between the seats. "You at least need new hair spray, midget. I can give you the name of my brand."

"Right. Like I take advice from a woman who wears starfish for a hair accessory." Flo shoved Aggie's feet away. "Eww. You have been dancing, sweating, and now you smell like rotting fish."

"You Italian runt! Keep tossing the insults and I'll rip your frizzy hair from your head." Aggie crammed her feet into the back again. "And, by the way, that's your best friend you're insulting too, you know. She used to be just like me, smell like me, dance like me. Screw the men and toss them into the sea to die like I do too."

"That's enough, Aggie." My stomach rolled as I started the car. I didn't put it in gear yet, though. I pushed the button to lower the top then looked at Flo's pale face under the light from the streetlamp. "You okay, Flo?"

"I'm sorry. I didn't mean . . . You are nothing like this creature." She hissed when Aggie reached through to adjust the rearview mirror so she could reapply her lipstick. "I have only known the vampire Gloriana, my dear friend. The one who dances like an angel and has ancient vampire blood, not blood that reeks of seaweed and clams. You are nothing like *her*, Glory."

"Gag me. What next? A flurry of Facebook posts about how much you love your BFF? Or maybe you should tweet about it. Just spare me listening to this crap." Aggie tossed her lipstick into her purse. "Get going. If we're late, we'll all be sorry."

"You want to get out, Flo? I wouldn't blame you. In fact, I hope you'll stay here. Aggie's aggravation is nothing compared to what the Storm God will pull out of his bag of tricks." I touched Flo's clenched fist. "Please. I don't want you to get hurt because of me." I gave Aggie a "Go to hell" look when she broke into "O Solo Mio."

"No. We go. We fight. We win." She hit Aggie's hand

when the Siren reached for the rearview mirror again. "Sit back. Now that the top is down, your smell will blow away in the wind. And know this, Aggie. My best friend is nothing like you. You should pay attention to how she treats people. You say you want friends of your own? Then watch her and learn." Flo opened her own purse and put on fresh lipstick by feel then handed the tube to me. "This is a new color, Firecracker. We will blow this god out of the water. He will worship at *our* feet. Eh?"

I sighed. "Wait, honey. Maybe we should stop and pick up nuns' habits. Do you really want to charm a guy who has a harem?"

"Pah. I only know one way to deal with a man. I use it." She nodded at the lipstick. "He didn't kill you when he had the chance, *amica*. I say go with your best look."

"You have a point." I shook my head and applied the color with the expertise of years of practice. Leave it to Flo to make this into a battle she would fight with her best weapons. I turned and glanced at Aggie. I knew where all this hostility was coming from. I'd had centuries of freedom, well away from Achelous's obviously abusive reign of terror. I could afford to cut the Siren some slack.

"Relax, Ag. I really don't want to be your enemy. You've obviously had a tough life. If Achelous asks? I'll say you've been singing his praises. Almost making me sorry I ever lost my spot on a rock." Of course if he reads my mind . . .

"Glory, you can't say that. You might end up back in an ocean somewhere." Flo grabbed my hand before I could shift into drive.

"She's right. I'll speak for myself. But I appreciate the thought. Best to just let Achy do the talking. He will anyway." Aggie shuddered. "I don't mind telling you I'm creeped out. Any meeting with Achy is a crapshoot. I have no idea how this could play out. So let's just get this over with."

"Yeah. One way or another, I want some answers." But would I be able to live with them? And why did I have the feeling that getting out of this meeting alive wasn't exactly a sure thing? I put the car in gear and had to force my foot to hit the accelerator. When I had to stop at a red light, I looked up into a clear night sky. Not a sign that a storm was coming. If only I could count on that.

Twelve

Laurie was waiting for us when we walked onto the stone terrace that faced the lake. We'd had to leave the car in the driveway and pick our way around the debris from the ruined house to the meeting place. It was a shame that a confrontation with a sicko vampire hunter had led to the house going up in flames. It had been a rental, fully insured, but the depressed real estate market had apparently kept the owner from rebuilding. Too bad. The view from the terrace was spectacular with stone steps leading down to a charred boat dock and one of Austin's many lakes gleaming in the moonlight.

"No sign of him yet." Laurie hadn't changed out of her pretty outfit. I guess she figured looking good might come in handy as a weapon in this case or at least a distraction.

"We *are* a little early." Aggie stared out at the lake. "I wonder if I have time for a swim." She laid her sweater on the stone wall and reached back as if she was about to unzip her blue silk dress.

"Spare us." I grabbed her arm. "We really don't want to watch you strip down."

"Speak for yourself." The booming voice was accompanied

by a sizzle of lightning that popped and snapped nearby. A small bush went up in flames and we all froze. The man shimmering into view was tall, athletic and garbed in a Roman look, from the laurel wreath crowning his golden blond hair to the snow white toga draping his perfect body.

Aggie bowed before him, her forehead almost touching her knees. She gestured like the rest of us should do the same, but I decided that just wasn't happening. Flo and Laurie took their cues from me. I felt sick that apparently at least some of what Aggie had been telling me was true. And Ian's report. Siren blood. God. I had to struggle to keep from running screaming back to the car.

"Achelous. You summoned me?" At least I could still speak and actually move. I could shift the hell out of there. No, this had to be faced. Flo nervously fussed with the hem of her top and bit her lip, signs he'd left her free too. Laurie eased nearer the low stone wall. He must not have thought much of my allies to allow them their mobility. Of course the god could make any of us statues on a whim.

"Yes, Gloriana. Aglaophonos informed me that you now know your true identity and that you have questions for me." Achelous's smile, a dazzling show of perfect white teeth, reminded me of Lucifer's. Both of them were cold, self-centered men who didn't have a lot of respect for women. "I thought I was done with you centuries ago. But obviously somehow you managed to avoid the fate I intended. Amazing, really. Imagine my surprise when I saw you here the first time. And a blood sucker at that." He swept his gaze over me in a way that made me want to cover my breasts. "Come closer, my dear."

"I'd rather not. I had a taste of your temper when we met here before. Down at the boat dock and not that long ago." I glanced at Aggie. "Can she get up now?"

"Aglaophonos? Of course. Child? Quit prostrating yourself. Feeling guilty? You should. It is your carelessness that brought Gloriana and me together again. I thought myself well rid of her." Achelous waved his hand and wind whipped across the clearing, stirring up trash and bending tree branches.

"I-I'm sorry, sire. I didn't know that my blood—" Aggie blanched when he placed his hand on her shoulder.

"You gave your blood to a vampire. Not just to test, but you let him drink from you, shared his bed. Is that not so?" Thunder shook the stones under our feet as Achy glared at the Siren. Flo and I exchanged glances. So Ian drank from Aggie during their bed play. No surprise there.

"Is it forbidden? Mentioned in the archives? I didn't know." Aggie's voice trembled and she sank to her knees. "What is my punishment to be?" You could tell that her choices were bad and worse.

"Get up, out of my sight. I will think about it. It should be common sense that we don't share our blood with lesser beings." He thrust her away with his foot and she scurried off into the darkness. We heard a splash and I figured she'd jumped into the lake, clothes and all.

"Did you learn anything from that, Gloriana?" Achelous approached me and I tried not to cringe when he stopped just inches away.

"That you think vampires are beneath you?" I kept my chin up. "I figure a god would of course hold himself above all others." I didn't share that I was having a hard time swallowing the idea that Aggie was better than me.

"I see that you have pride in what you are now. Of course you do. You were always full of yourself. Thought you were above my rules." Achy flung out an arm and dark clouds roiled and roared. Okay, so I did cringe that time. The noise was horrific.

I noticed that Laurie had eased behind him and she wasn't a bit disturbed by the racket. If she went tiger, could she take him down? I knew there was no way that she'd live through a move like that. I shook my head slightly when Achelous looked up to admire a particularly brilliant lightning display.

"What rules? You erased my memories so I have no idea what I did to piss you off. Then apparently you tossed me out of the sea. Want to tell me about it? Why I lost my place in what Aggie calls a sisterhood?" I wondered if I really wanted to know. I'd obviously served this man once just as Aggie still did. Done things . . . I pressed my trembling hands to my queasy stomach. It had been a lucky escape from what I could tell.

"How old am I?" The question popped out of me.

Achy laughed. "Interesting question. And one only a woman would concern herself with when her life is hanging by a thread." He walked around me, examining me. "You served me for a little more than a millennia. Add the several odd centuries you've been vampire to that and you have your age."

"You're fourteen hundred years old!" Flo gasped. "Glory, you're even older than I am."

"Thanks a lot, Flo." I let that fact whirl around in my mind for a moment. "Now will you tell me exactly why you banished me?"

"First, I must solve a little problem." Achy suddenly disappeared, just vanished. I peered into the darkness surrounding us.

"Where'd he go?" I figured Laurie would have the best idea.

"He's rounding up some visitors." She made a face. "We should have known they wouldn't stay away."

"What do you mean?"

"Look, Glory." Flo squeezed my arm and pointed to the edge of the clearing where the house had once stood. Sure enough Achelous was striding behind two men. You couldn't miss the procession because of the ring of lightning bolts forming bars around them, like a moving jail cell holding prisoners. Apparently Rafe and Jerry had decided to join the party.

"Oh, no." I started toward them.

"Don't even think about it, Gloriana. You'll get the shock of your undead life. And you might not survive it." Jerry's voice was hard. "He's got us penned in."

"Obviously we're not going to be able to do you much

good. Sorry about that." Rafe glared at Achelous as he brought
the men to a halt a few yards away from me.

"Behold your honor guard." The god laughed. "Still have
that power, don't you, Gloriana?" The lightning disappeared
but when Jerry reached for a knife he was turned to stone,
Rafe too. Neither of them could move other than to blink
their eyes.

"What power?" I prayed Achelous didn't mean what I
thought he meant. If he did, then my relationships with
Jerry, with Rafe, hell, even with Ray were totally bogus.

"You know exactly what power, Gloriana. I made you
mortal but it seems even I couldn't strip away your ability to
draw men to you. A Siren is born to seduce. She can always
get a man to worship her. You have the gift of enchantment,
even at this very moment. Luckily, I'm immune to it, though
you are still a tempting armful if I ignore those disgusting
fangs in your mouth." Achelous put his arm around me,
something I didn't dare shrug away from.

"I don't believe you." But I was very afraid Jerry and Rafe
did. Though their faces were frozen, there was no mistaking
the emotion blazing in their eyes. Fury. Impotent rage. At
me? I didn't dare analyze it. I prayed it was at this bastard.
The weight of his arm felt like a chain holding me and I could
smell the ozone surrounding him like a nasty aftershave.

"Face it, gentlemen. You would never have been able to
resist this woman. She's still a Siren where it counts and lured
you like dogs to a juicy steak." Achelous chuckled. "Aggie
told me one of you actually played the panting dog for a
while. How appropriate."

"Stop it." I wanted to cover my ears. "I don't believe you."

"Of course you do. Didn't you ever wonder, Gloriana,
why your men were so steadfast? One of them for centuries!" Achelous tugged on my hair. "Couldn't get rid of your
admirers, could you? But of course you didn't try. And you,
gentlemen. You never could seem to forget her, could you?
Especially you, vampire. How many hundreds of years have
you danced to her tune?" Achelous laughed again and swept

his hand toward the sky, a clap of thunder shaking the terrace. "My Sirens know how to hold a man until the day he dies! Of course usually that's not but an hour after he knows her." Achelous stepped away from me. "I have to say well done, Gloriana."

"You're lying!" I desperately blinked back tears even though he was saying exactly what I'd been terrified was true. "You're just trying to ruin my life now. This doesn't make sense."

"What doesn't make sense is that you're still alive!" Achelous stomped away from me, each step another thunderclap. "Zeus's toenails, but this infuriates me. How is it possible? I intended for you to have a short and mortal life. I planted memories of a disapproving family for you and watched you bewitch your first human, a poor actor. Oh, but you were ridiculous, learning to sew to help earn bread after he died." He glared at me. "I assumed you would live out your ordinary little life in the gutter and that would be that. In a blink of an eye you would be gone forever."

"But I didn't have an ordinary life. I met Jeremiah Campbell." I squeezed my hands together and begged Jerry with my eyes to forgive me.

"A fucking vampire!" Achelous threw up his hands and the clouds unleashed a torrent, dumping icy rain on us, everyone except him of course. There was no shelter anywhere and we had to just stand there and take it, the cold hard rain drenching us in seconds. "Conniving bitch. You persuaded him to make you immortal. You were supposed to die! I had no idea. Had quit watching you or—" He ground his teeth and sparks flew. "Hindsight."

As quickly as the rain had started, it stopped. The clouds rolled away and the moon appeared, a brilliant white circle in the night sky. Stars twinkled above us in a breathtaking display.

"Gloriana didn't die because I wouldn't allow it." The lilting voice seemed to issue from Heaven itself but instead came from a tiny woman who appeared at Laurie's side.

"Circe!" Achelous stopped in his tracks. "What do you have to do with this?"

"I was sick of the way you treated your women, Achelous. Your handling of this problem with Gloriana was the last in a long line of intolerable acts. I could not stand by and let you get away with abusing this poor girl." Circe, a goddess in her own right, had also stuck to the Roman look. I guess it was the norm up on Olympus.

She walked up to Achelous and, though she only came up to the middle of his chest, her regal air gave her an imposing presence. She had a breathtaking beauty, with mesmerizing vivid green eyes and her raven hair flowing down her back. But that wasn't what made her formidable. It was the power that shimmered around her. I sure wouldn't want to cross her.

"And how is that your business?" Achelous looked down his nose at her, obviously not intimidated.

"As a woman, I decided to make it my business." She poked his broad chest with a pearl white fingernail. "You cast Gloriana out without proper resources."

"Of course I did. She never appreciated the gold and jewels she had as one of my women. I wanted her to lose *everything*." Achelous spat the last word.

"I couldn't allow you to reduce her to such dire straits. She was close to starving. She had no way to earn a living." Circe smiled and held out her hand, compelling me to come closer until I faced Achelous too. "Except whoring. And she was too proud for that, weren't you, my dear?"

"I couldn't—" I did remember *those* days. After my husband had died, I'd been tossed out of our lodgings. I'd begged Shakespeare to let me do the odd sewing and cleaning jobs around the theater. Those had barely paid for food but at least he'd let me sleep in the dressing rooms.

"Too good to be a whore?" Achelous laughed. "Why? What do you think a Siren is?"

The crack of my hand hitting Achelous's cheek was as loud as a gunshot. And it felt good. That bastard had it coming. For what he did constantly to Aggie and the other sisters. And what he'd done to me.

"You are truly dead now, you bitch." Achelous's eyes flamed and he raised his hands, static electricity crackling from his fingertips.

"No, she is not." Circe thrust herself between us. "You must be stopped, Achelous. I proved I could thwart you when I took this man"—she pointed to Jerry and my heart sank—"and sent him into her path. He, of course, fell in love with her and made her vampire. I ensured she would have immortality and all the years you would have stolen from her, you pompous ass."

"You dare talk to me this way?" Achelous unleashed clouds, rain and wind that almost blew us off the terrace. Flo and I clung to each other and even Laurie had to crouch down next to the stone wall or be thrown into the lake.

"You owed me this." Circe stood toe-to-toe with him, raising her own hands to stop the deluge instantly.

"How is that?" He looked her over with what started as a sneer. While the rest of us were basically drowned rats, Circe's hair dried instantly into beautiful curls. Her toga clung to her perfect figure in all the right places and Achy showed a typical male appreciation for it before he remembered he was furious with her. His face hardened. "I owe you nothing."

"You didn't keep your word to me about a certain matter." She placed her hand on his chest and whatever she did must have hurt, because the god actually winced and jerked her hand away to hold it.

"This is not something to discuss in front of inferiors. Are you saying you deliberately used this vampire so that Gloriana would live forever?" Achelous turned to hit Jerry with a shot of lightning and I screamed his name when I saw him shudder with pain.

"Stop! She just said he was her victim." Oh, God. All those years of Jerry's devotion, protection, love. They had been because two gods had been playing games with us as pawns. Was anything in my life real?

"Deliberate or not, the result is the same, Gloriana. You are still here." Achelous started to hit me with a bolt, I was sure of it, but Circe reached out to stop him.

"Tell her why you cast her out.' She deserves to know." Circe gave me a pitying look. Flo had her arm around me because I'd started crying. Who wouldn't? But I shoved her away, out of the line of fire, when it looked like I might be getting hit.

"I already know. I'm not a killer or not much of one, am I? Move, Flo. If he's going to zap me into oblivion, I don't want you to be collateral damage." I wiped my eyes. "Yeah, Achelous. Be a sport. Tell everyone what I did to get kicked out of the Siren sisterhood. For some reason I'm not ashamed to be your castoff." My legs went weak but I managed to stay upright as I braced myself for the god's worst.

Circe gave Achelous a look that made me think there was some serious mental messaging going on. "You have quite an attitude, Gloriana, and remind me . . ." Circe shook her head. "Speak, Achelous. Explain your actions to the girl."

"Why not? Gloriana, yes, you were a failure as a Siren. And since Circe is so down on men, let me get a female witness up here. Someone she'll believe." Achy walked over to the stone wall, shoving Laurie out of the way. "What in the hell is a tiger doing here?"

"She's one of mine and fetched me. Touch her again and you'll regret it." Circe watched him closely.

"Whatever. Aglaophonos, get your ass back here!" He leaned against the wall near where Laurie watched him with narrowed eyes. "Let me see it. Change into your tiger. Should be amusing. Though your human form is not bad." He was checking her out. Her soaked tank top would have made her a winner in any wet T-shirt contest.

"Not on your life." Laurie raked him with a disgusted look then stalked over to stand next to me. "I'm not a circus sideshow."

"Could have fooled me." Achy had obviously gotten another mental message from Circe. "You women are really on a roll tonight. Don't think I'll forget this, Circe. When we get to Olympus, we're going to the top about this."

"Sure, Achy. Let's do that." Circe didn't look concerned.

"Yes, sire. What do you wish?" Aggie climbed out over the stone wall, her wet dress clinging to her body. I'm sure Jerry and Rafe appreciated the view; Achelous certainly did.

"Tell the group here how many kills you have. Since you became Siren." Achy stroked Aggie's wet shoulder in a familiar way that made me shudder.

"One million, seven hundred fifty thousand, five hundred six." Aggie smiled apologetically. "It would be more but GPS and other things—"

"Okay, we get it." Achy looked proud while I felt like throwing up. Over a million people killed? And she'd smiled, with no regrets except that she'd posted what she seemed to think was a low number. "Now I know you've been snooping in the archives about Gloriana here. Right?"

"Yes. Is it forbidden?" She blanched when he tugged on her wet hair.

"Yes, but I'll let it go this time. Tell the crowd how many kills she had before I tossed her out on her fat ass." He gave me an evil smile. "I made you wide on purpose when I tossed you, by the way. Bet that bothers you, doesn't it, Gloriana? Look at this Siren next to me." He ran his hand down Aggie's hip. "Her body is perfect. I wasn't about to let you have the same." He frowned at me and I braced myself. "Go ahead, Aglaophonos, spit it out. Gloriana's kill number."

"It was an embarrassment to you, sire. A mere one hundred and thirty-three thousand, four hundred sixty-one. And she'd worked for you for over a thousand years!" Aggie gave me a censorious look. "She was a disgrace to the sisterhood."

I hit the ground. Yep, my legs just could not hold me up. I'd killed over a hundred thousand men. And no telling how many more I'd seduced and let go. Thunder roared, lightning flashed and, for me, darkness fell.

• • •

"Glory! Wake up!" I felt hands on my back and groaned. Obviously Achelous had given me a parting shot of lightning as a going-away present. I sat up carefully, my feet and head Pain Central. I wasn't surprised to see my boots were charred on the soles.

"Are you all right?" Flo brushed back my wet hair and stared at me anxiously. "That bastard. He hit you with such a jolt. I was afraid you were done for."

"Yeah. He and Circe just disappeared after that. Aggie too." Laurie paced around us. "What a nightmare. I'm pissed that I couldn't do anything for you."

"Are you kidding? Laurie, you brought Circe here. She saved me." I reached down and unzipped one of my ruined boots, tossing it aside. The effort made my head throb but my feet were much worse. I hurriedly got rid of the other boot. Healing sleep would take care of my feet eventually but I dreaded the walk back to the car.

"Yes, well. You're right. I guess I did earn that paycheck, Flo." Laurie grinned then gasped when she saw my blackened feet. "Damn, but he got you good, didn't he?"

"You're going to need help." Rafe stood behind Flo. "Let me carry you."

"No, I'll do it. I may be under a damned spell, but I still want to take care of Gloriana." Jerry squatted down next to me.

"Jerry." I reached out to touch his cheek. "What you heard . . ."

"I know we were both manipulated, Gloriana." He carefully slipped his arms under my hips and lifted me. "I'll carry you to your car. Florence can drive you home."

"Can you ever forgive me?" I whispered this against his chest as he strode across the rough terrain to where we'd left my car.

"Forgive *you*?" He stopped and looked up at the sky instead

of down at me. "What have *you* done?" He started walking
again, stopping beside my car and waiting while a silent Flo
opened the passenger door.

"Oh, your beautiful car!" She began pushing water out of
the seat with her hands.

I glanced down. Right. I'd left the top down and Achelous had made it rain buckets. Swell. One more thing the
god had ruined tonight.

"Flo, relax. Gloriana can have it dried out professionally.
I'm sure insurance will cover it." Jerry shifted me in his arms,
like he was anxious to get rid of me. I didn't blame him. "You
are both already wet and I don't think the engine has come to
any harm. The keys are in it. See if it will start." Jerry spoke
calmly as he set me in the passenger seat and secured my seat
belt. Flo scurried around to the other side and soon had the
engine purring, all the while muttering in fierce Italian and
English about Sirens and gods who threw rain and lightning
around.

"Jerry, are you, I mean, will you come over? To talk about
what just happened?" I leaned back in the seat. Had I ever
been this wet or this miserable before? Even the pain in my
burned feet was minor compared to the terror I felt about my
relationship with Jerry. And Rafe? He stood behind Jerry, his
gaze questioning.

"Not tonight, Gloriana. Let your friends take care of you.
I need some time. To think. Surely you understand." He
closed the car door. "I'll call you."

"Glory!" Rafe moved up to take Jerry's place next to the
door. "If you need me, call." He reached through the open
window and cupped my cheek. "For blood to help you heal.
For anything. What you heard tonight . . . I know it's not
what you wanted to hear. But it makes no difference to me.
I don't need time to think." He leaned down and kissed my
forehead then slapped the hood as Flo began to slowly back
the car down the driveway.

I saw Laurie standing by her own car, just observing the

scene. She stopped Rafe when he turned away and I saw them talk to each other. Jerry had disappeared. He'd probably shifted to get here and was already flying home.

"How are you, really?" Flo asked as soon as we were on the open road.

"Horrible." I looked at her. She was soaked, her outfit ruined, her hair plastered to her head. "How are you going to explain this to Richard?"

"I'm going to have to confess everything. He will be furious, of course, that I went to see the Storm God with you and didn't tell him . . . Hah! As if I would have wanted him there." Flo's eyes glistened with tears. "That Achelous. *Ché bastardo!* I hate him."

"I think we can agree on that." I patted her hand on the steering wheel. "I'm glad you weren't hurt but that won't help soothe Richard."

"No, but I'll let him get me into the shower since I am so upset, you see. That will make everything all right." Flo winked at me. "Or at least help him forget I was in danger." She squeezed my hand. "But I wasn't. Not really. I was scared for *you*, *amica*. That god was so angry. He wanted to kill you."

"Lucky for us, Circe is for women's rights." I managed a smile. "And Laurie. She really did come through for me."

"*Sì.* I'll meet her tomorrow night to pay her." Flo held up her hand when she saw I was going to object, offer to pay. "I am glad to do it. She saved our butts. No?"

"Yes, she did. Who knew she had connections on Olympus?" I leaned back and closed my eyes. "At least I had on my old boots."

"Yes, and I checked the trunk. Our new shoes are still dry. Somehow Aggie got hers already or I would have thrown them into the lake. So many men she killed! I cannot like that."

"I killed—"

Flo reached over and clapped her hand over my mouth. "We will never speak of that again. I will not tell Ricardo that part either. You were a different person then, Glory. A different, how you say, species, I guess. So you cannot be held to blame. Move on. It is what I do when I have done something I am not so proud of. And I have plenty, I tell you, in my past that I would rather not think of again." She took her hand away. "Is it a deal?"

"Deal." I wasn't going to cry. No, that had to be water from my wet hair dripping into my eyes. But could I have a better friend? I certainly hated to see her head to Paris. My phone bill was obviously going to be astronomical because who else could I talk to about girl stuff?

When we got to my apartment, Flo fussed about how I was going to get up the stairs on my blistered feet. Obviously Rafe had figured things out because he showed up next to the car, shifting out of bird form just as Flo was about to call Richard for help.

"I snapped to the fact that you weren't going to be able to make the stairs." He eased me from the seat and lifted me into his arms. "This okay?"

I snuggled against him. We were both wet but I could feel his shifter's heat through our clothes. "More than okay. You're a godsend. No, scratch that. Not mentioning gods. Or at least—"

"Don't try to make sense now, Glory. Just close your eyes and let me carry you to your bed." Rafe's deep voice made his chest vibrate under my cheek. I sighed and relaxed, letting him take over.

Flo ran ahead, taking care of security codes and opening doors. "You've got to get out of those wet clothes but I don't want you to have to stand on your feet. If you lay on your bed . . ."

"Let Rafe take over, Flo." I waved her off when she began to pluck at my wet jeans. "Honestly, I'm beyond being embarrassed and you need to get home to Richard. He's bound to be worried about you. It's late and we were only supposed to go shopping. The mall closed hours ago."

Flo dug into her purse, which fortunately we'd stuck in the trunk of my car before we'd headed to that terrace. "Yes, he's called and left messages. I think it's better if I just go home."

"Yes, you're right." I held out my hand. "I'll never forget how you were there for me tonight. *Mi amica.* That's what you call *me*. You're the best."

"You will not make me cry." Flo sniffled then gave Rafe an assessing look. "You will be a gentleman, eh? She has been through too much. Help her get clean and dry and put to bed. Give her some of your blood if she wants. That's all. *Capite?*"

"I get it, Flo." Rafe kissed the top of my head. "No hanky-panky. I'm not the asshole Achelous was. Glory's beat. Traumatized. I'm not about to make some stupid move on her now."

"Hey, I'm here you know. And if I want him to climb into my bed for more than a snooze, that's on me." I winked at Flo, though I knew that was the last complication I needed right now. "Good night, Flo."

"I'll call you tomorrow night. If you want me to cancel my trip to Paris, say the word." She also sent me a mental message not to do anything foolish with Rafe.

"No, take your trip. And quit worrying about me. I'm going to survive. I've managed things so far. Maybe I can get Laurie to give me Circe's phone number. Find out how I can get rid of this Siren whammy."

"Not sure I'd do that, Glory." Rafe smiled down at me. "It's come in handy for you over the years. Bought you protection at least."

"I'm leaving. This isn't something for her to talk about now, Rafael. Get her in the shower, dry her off, feed her. Now, good night." Flo stalked out of the apartment and closed the door.

"We have our orders." Rafe carried me into the bathroom. He carefully set me on the closed toilet and pulled my ruined red sweater off over my head. Then he reached back and turned on the water in the tub since it took a while to heat up.

"I'm not sure these jeans will come off. They were snug when they were dry." I got the button open and the zipper down. "That damned Achelous. To deliberately give me wide hips. How mean can you get?"

"They aren't wide. They're perfect." Rafe lifted one hip and managed to slide the jeans and my panties down then did the same with the other. He was very careful when he had to pull them off over my wounded feet. Still, I hissed when the stiff fabric rubbed against them.

"Thanks, Rafe." I reached behind me to unclasp my bra. He was being very clinical about undressing me, for which I was grateful. I knew he still wanted me; I could see the bulge in his own wet jeans.

"Wait." He wrapped a towel around me. "I'm thinking you can't get in this tub with your feet like this. It will be agony."

I glanced at the filling tub then down at my feet. "God, you're right. The very thought of that hot water touching them . . ."

"I'm carrying you to bed and feeding you first." He turned off the water then started to lift me in his arms again.

"Wait. Take off your shirt. It's soaked and you can dry off. I've got one of your old T-shirts in my dresser drawer."

"Right." He jerked off the shirt then picked me up and carried me to bed. He laid me down gently then disappeared into the bathroom again. When he came out he was wearing only a towel around his lean hips. "Give me another minute and I'll throw my jeans into the dryer."

"Good idea." I lay back and closed my eyes, so exhausted I couldn't have put logical thoughts together if I'd tried.

"I'm back. Did you doze off?"

"Guess so." I felt the bed sag as Rafe sat beside me.

"Drink from me, Glory. You've got to get those feet healed. You also have bruises on your shoulders."

"I've got a killer headache too." Killer. Oh, God. I looked away from Rafe.

"Stop. You are not that person. Not like Aggie." Rafe gently turned my chin so that I faced him. "That bastard really did a number on you, in more ways than one."

"Understatement. The way he and Circe manipulated all of us. Like Jerry said." Rafe's mouth tightened at the mention of Jerry's name. I reached up to trace those lines. "I'm sorry. You're also one of my victims. Do you hate that?"

"Never." He leaned down and kissed me carefully on the lips. "Drink from me. At least heal before you try to reason any of this out." He pulled my arms around his neck and offered his throat.

I was powerless to resist as I slid my lips along his jaw to the sweet spot where I could hear his blood pumping and smell the richness calling to me. Rafe was right. I had to feed and he had just what I needed.

"Thanks, Rafe. You know I love you, don't you?" I didn't give him time to answer before I took his vein. Sank into him with a sigh. It was bliss and I felt the power surge instantly. I knew my feet were healing and strength flowed into me as my headache evaporated. Rafe's blood had that special something, his own shifter essence that made me want to drink forever but I knew I was going to have to pull away soon.

"Well, I see I needn't have worried, Gloriana."

I jerked away from Rafe, his arm steady around me as I grabbed at my slipping towel.

"Jerry! You came back." I didn't stop Rafe as he stood, his own towel not doing much to disguise the fact that our closeness hadn't left him unmoved.

"Like a fool." Jerry stood in the bedroom doorway, his fists clenched. He'd changed clothes and was nice and dry. It almost made me mad to realize that had been his first priority.

"What do you mean?" I sat up and grabbed the sheet to better cover myself with. "Rafe was feeding me. You saw my feet. I needed blood to heal. Are you standing there jumping to conclusions or will you listen to the facts?"

"What difference does it make, Gloriana? I am powerless to resist you. Whatever you tell me, whatever you do, I will come back to you. Always." He ran his hands through his hair. "I don't know how to take what we just heard out there by the lake. I tried to stay away from here just now. But I kept seeing you lying there on that terrace, hurt." He swept his eyes over Rafe. "I should have known one of your other victims would be here for you."

"That's enough, Blade." Rafe stepped forward.

"No, let him get this off his chest." I wiggled my toes and realized my feet were healed enough for me to get up. I dragged the sheet around me and stood next to Rafe. "You're both my victims, I get that and I hate it. Whatever you need to do, Jerry. Do it. I won't hold it against you." Even though my heart was breaking at the look on his face.

"I need time. And space. To think about this tale the Storm God told us. I'm going home." Jerry stared at me, searching my face. For what? Signs that I wanted him to stay? I kept my face carefully neutral, refusing to work any womanly wiles on him.

"Home? And where would that be? You've been a nomad for the last few decades." My energy for bravado leached out of me and I dropped to the edge of the bed.

"Castle Campbell. My roots, you could say. Leave me alone for a while, Gloriana, and I'll see if I can do the same for you."

"Dramatic much, Blade?" Rafe shook his head. "Give the woman a break. Clearly none of this is her fault. You sound like you're punishing her."

"Bugger off, Valdez. You're so eager to be her lapdog, have at it." Jerry stepped into the room and grabbed me by my shoulders. He jerked me to my feet and kissed me. It was an angry kiss, a seeking kiss and a farewell kiss all in one. I didn't fight it, just leaned into it. Even tried to hold on to him and send him mental messages not to go, that we could work it out. But too soon he thrust me at Rafe and stormed out of the room.

"I'm sorry, Glory. Sorry the man is such a hardheaded Scot." Rafe caught me as I staggered.

"Hardheaded? Yes. But also hurt, disappointed. I . . ." I

had nothing else to say. And neither did Rafe as he settled me in bed again. He tenderly covered me with my floral comforter.

"Are you going to be all right?"

"I have no idea, Rafe. No idea at all." I closed my eyes and wished it was time for my death sleep. Death. A nice solution to what seemed like insurmountable problems and, yes, so deliciously permanent.

Thirteen

A couple of weeks went by. My life was actually getting back to normal. Hah! As if I knew what normal looked like. I couldn't get a handle on my new identity for one thing. Gloriana the Siren turned vampire had to be careful even waiting on a male customer. I felt like I should wear a surgical mask so I wouldn't spread my fatal attraction. It would have helped with my red cheeks too. I laid foundation and cover stick on with a trowel and still looked like I'd spent too long under a sunlamp.

Rafe, of course, wanted to be there for me. I had to gently remind him of his promise to move on with his life. He didn't take it well. Which meant I tried to avoid him. No N-V for me. Translation: no social life. Fine. I wasn't up for fun anyway. Even a cell phone commercial about dropped calls could make me weepy.

I decided my best move was to throw myself into my business. Flo had headed to Paris on schedule with Richard mad at me again. Seems I was the one who always got his wife in danger. I couldn't blame him for his attitude and wouldn't be surprised if he kept them over there on one pretext or another for months.

I missed having a best friend around and Penny was a poor substitute. She never had been all that interested in fashion and even let me pick out her wardrobe—something Flo would never have allowed. That shopping spree was fun for about five minutes then I had nothing else to do in my spare time. Jenny might have been a good companion for shopping and had even started hanging around the shop. But she watched me like she wanted to catch me with my fangs down. Her endless questions about the vampire lifestyle were getting on my last nerve. I was very afraid she was thinking about a pair of fangs as a college graduation present.

I rattled around in my empty apartment, rearranging furniture and overdosing on reruns of *Buffy the Vampire Slayer*. I think Jenny would have been on board with joining me but her football games and sorority mixers were a conflict during Buffy.

I missed Jerry and seriously intended giving him the time he thought he needed. But it was almost impossible. I'd go from being sad and crying into my pillow to ashamed that I'd been part of this scam that had hooked him in the first place. It was a short drive from there to furious at the world, Achelous, and Jerry himself for giving up on us so easily. Finally I worked and reworked my checkbook, trying to figure out if there was any way I could get my butt to Scotland.

It was no use. Even though I knew Erin and Lacy could handle the shop for me—they were urging me to get my gloomy face out of town—I just couldn't afford the trip. The shop did okay and the rocky economy helped my kind of store. Vintage clothing was cheaper than the brand-new mall variety unless it was designer. Unfortunately, I didn't find the really quality stuff that often. And my overhead was steep. Prime locations like mine on Sixth Street cost plenty and I paid my help well, especially the day crew. It was critical that I trust them not to drop the ball while I was dead to the world.

So the reality was that flying overseas was an expensive proposition and not in my budget. My friends who'd flown to Paris had shared a chartered flight. Jerry had probably shifted and taken off on his own wings—the man had no fear. Me? I had to screw up my courage to shift and fly across town. So I would have to drive or catch a plane to either Dallas or Houston for a transatlantic flight that would cross during the night and still arrive in London or Edinburgh before dawn, a scheduling nightmare.

I had a horror of falling into my death sleep on a commercial flight. Yeah, picture a puzzled flight attendant trying to deal with my "body" when we arrived at Heathrow Airport. See? Logistics were almost impossible. Not to mention I'd be paying off the credit card bills for years afterward. And what if Jerry just slammed the castle doors in my face when I got there? Oh, how pathetic could I get, chasing after a man who didn't want me? Or at least didn't want to want me.

Erin poked her head into the back room. "Glory? You've got company up front. She's, uh, vampire and says you know her, but she's got some serious bodyguards. You want to slide out the back door and I'll tell her you must have already left?"

I almost welcomed the distraction from my discouraging math. I threw down my calculator. "Did she give you a name?" A woman with bodyguards. And Erin hadn't recognized her. Must be someone from my past.

"No. She wants to surprise you. Which kind of worries me. She has a hard edge to her even though she's wearing the most fabulous suit. And then she's put a few high-dollar items in a stack on the counter, obviously to buy. So I didn't dare alienate her." Erin glanced back over her shoulder. "Guess I talk too much. Here she comes."

"Glory!" A perfectly manicured hand shoved Erin out of the way and the door banged open wide. "When I heard someone in Austin was asking about me, I just had to come check it out personally."

I backed up and grabbed for the nearest thing that could pass for a weapon. The calculator was a cheapie from China so it wouldn't incite fear unless the woman had a math phobia.

I knew this one actually loved everything to do with numbers as long as they had dollar signs in front of them.

"Lucky, what are you doing here? *I* sure didn't ask about you." But I knew who had. Ian had stuck his Scottish nose into her business when he'd been investigating my blood. "You can go back to Europe now. In fact, didn't your daddy forbid you to ever darken my door again?" He had. Luciana Carvarelli aka Lucky Carver had worked for her father's loan-sharking business as a debt collector. After she'd been turned vampire in my back alley, just a few feet from where I stood now, she'd managed to alienate most of Austin's paranormal community. Papa Carvarelli, who did good business with paranormals, had banished her to Eastern Europe as punishment.

"Daddy died a few months ago. Heart attack." Lucky sighed, then pasted on a bright smile. So much for mourning. "I'm in charge of the business now. I can go where I damn well please. I'm at the headquarters in New York again. But I thought a little visit to my sire would be a nice vacation."

"Vacation?" I put down the calculator. Yes, I was her sire. Not my proudest moment, though I *had* saved her life. Hindsight, I'd have been doing the world and especially Ray a favor if I'd let her bleed out when I'd found her behind my shop.

"I liked Austin when I was here." Lucky looked around and pounced on a vintage designer scarf I hadn't priced yet. She flipped her hair which was a rich deep mahogany this season behind her back and secured it into a low ponytail with the scarf. "Nice piece. Add it to my tab."

"It'll be expensive."

She waved her hand. "As if I care. Good to see you're still here. So many small businesses are going under these days." She gave me the once-over then frowned. "You could do with a fashion intervention. What's up with the black? Somebody die?"

"End-of-month laundry crisis. Not that it's any of your concern." I gritted my teeth. Of course she was another of those great-looking women with a perfect figure. I seemed to be surrounded by them.

Tonight's awful outfit had been a result of my don't-give-a-damn attitude lately. Maybe I should check with Ian about vampire Prozac. Right. And I'd probably break out in hives or grow a third boob. Damn that Siren blood.

"Glory, where is your brain tonight? Pay attention. You need to treat yourself. You've got some great stock just a few feet away." Lucky inspected a shelf of sweaters intended for a sale table. "I obviously should have come back sooner. I like your little shop."

"I'm not that desperate for business, Lucky."

She whirled around and glared at me, a coral cashmere sweater in her hand. "Are you saying I can't shop here?"

"Do you have amnesia or something? Your time in Austin was a train wreck. You created chaos. And I'll never forgive you for what you did to Israel Caine." I stalked to the back door, unlocked it and threw it open. "Take a hike."

"Now, Glory. Settle down. I admit I could have handled things a little more diplomatically when I was here before." She dropped the sweater back on the shelf. "But I was a new vampire. The whole dying and waking up with fangs thing did a number on me. I was crazed."

"Should have remembered that before you passed on the experience. And I'm not buying that excuse. Most of your bad behavior was you being you, Lucky. Don't bother to deny it." I wasn't budging. I wanted her out of there. What she'd done to Ray was unforgivable.

"I had things I had to work out. As my sire you were supposed to help me deal with my new condition. I realize now I shoulda let you." She smiled and held out her hands. "My bad judgment. I know that now. But I'm here to fix that. You owe me a certain amount of guidance, you know. To keep me from making more mistakes. I've asked around to other vamps I've met since then. You and me, we have a bond, a blood tie. I have some questions for you now and you owe me answers." Lucky turned and spoke to the twin hulks who'd been on high alert standing in the doorway to the shop. "Shut the door and wait outside. I'll be okay."

I wanted to deny it but didn't bother as the door closed. I had a few things I wanted to say. "I gave you immortality, Lucky. Something you made damned sure I regretted. If I wanted to take that away from you, I have the power. I'm not the same woman you left here with a naked rock star in her bed." I was snarling I was so furious.

"Yeah, I can see that. I like you better for it." Lucky actually grinned and it was all I could do not to knock her against the wall. Why was I hesitating? I could certainly turn her into a statue and do whatever I wanted to her. But did I want to show her my power? No.

"Don't like me, just leave." I counted to ten, deciding letting her goad me was just playing into her hands.

"Not till I get what I want. Now calm down and talk to me like a sire should." She walked over and brushed the seat of my lone chair. She had on a cream wool pantsuit that looked straight from Milan. The buttoned jacket was cut to showcase her figure and she obviously wore nothing underneath it except a slim gold chain that dipped into her cleavage. That scarf she'd added couldn't have been more perfect. It had a cream, gold and red design that made her pale skin and hazel eyes glow.

"You think I'm going to dish with you? Like we're girlfriends or something?" I finally shut the back door and paced in front of her, feeling dowdier by the minute. She set a red leather purse I'd have killed for on the floor and pulled out a small electronic tablet. She clicked it on. Right. She was planning to write down my words of wisdom.

"You owe me. You made me a vampire. We share the same blood." She smiled serenely, showing the tips of her fangs. "And I've discovered, with the help of an old crone in the Trans area, that our blood is something special. At the time I blew it off, figuring it was a fairy tale—the woman owed me money. Then I get to New York and a doctor looks me up asking about my blood too. So I'm thinking maybe there's something to it and I should go to the source." She pointed at me. "What's up, Glory?"

"Why should I tell you anything? Lucky, you killed a man I care about. Ruined his life. Ray and I are close now." I jerked that damned tablet out of her hand, then tossed it on the table behind me. "He's been suicidal since you left. And no wonder. He was a sun worshiper and you made him lose daylight!"

"I know that!" She widened her eyes. "That's why making him vampire was the perfect payback for what he did to me. He broke my heart." She wasn't smiling now and her fangs were long and lethal. She jumped to her feet. "You expect me to feel sorry for that asshole just because you're probably banging him now? No fucking way."

"Ray and I aren't . . ." I decided my exact relationship with Ray was not something I needed to clear up. "Guess that's my answer to you when you want info from me. Forget it." I shoved her back down in her chair.

"Let's leave the rock star out of this, okay?" She waited and I decided she wanted me to nod or something.

"That's a little hard to do, Lucky. You dropped him in my lap, remember? I may be your sire, but you're *his*. Funny, but he's not exactly looking to you for a bonding moment, is he? At least not without a stake in his hand." I crossed my arms over my chest. I'd consider that fair warning. Bodyguards or not, Lucky was going to have to watch her back while she was in Austin. Once Ray found out she was here . . . ? I didn't want to imagine the confrontation between those two.

"Yeah, well, I knew you'd take good care of him. Who could miss the pile of Israel Caine memorabilia you had in your place? What did you call it? The shrine? I knew you'd be thrilled to play vamp mommy to that bad boy. Was I right?" She actually grinned at me.

"Oh, sure. I got to be his savior while he figured out he'd never see the sun again. You remember how you felt waking up with fangs? It was much, much worse for Ray. He didn't even know vampires existed until he became one." I grabbed her by the lapels of a suit that cost more than the sum total of my clothing budget for the year. "Get this straight, Lucky. It was hell pulling Ray through his transition. And he's still not 100 percent into being a vampire. You RUINED. HIS. LIFE."

"Tough. Shit." She jerked my hands off her jacket and examined the cloth with a frown. "I gifted you with the man of your dreams, Glory, and don't bother to deny it. Where's the gratitude?"

I just shook my head. Obviously I was wasting my time trying to find this woman's compassion.

"Just listen to my proposition. I'm not asking you to toss me a freebie. I learned at my father's knee that you don't get anything without paying for it." Lucky was breathing hard so I guess I had gotten to her a little. Rookie. She didn't remember that lung action wasn't necessary for us.

I knew I should throw her out on her perfect ass right then and there. Instead, she must have noticed my hesitation and plowed ahead.

"Yes, I'll pay. I remember that you were always hard up for cash. I'm sure if nothing else you'd like to update your wardrobe. That Transylvanian said I should get in touch with my sire. That you had a message for me. She was very specific. Psychic mumbo jumbo but I've learned to listen to it." She put a fingernail in the middle of my stomach and shoved. "Back up before I call in my boys."

"You're serious about listening to a Transylvanian witch? They're kooks, Lucky." I did step back and threw her tablet at her. Interesting that this crone had obviously picked up on Lucky's Siren blood. "Here's a message: Get lost."

"No. Pay attention, Glory. The really ancient Trans witches are powerful and have valuable knowledge that I paid to get." She arched a brow at me. "Like I said, I'm willing to throw money around when I want something and I went over there needing to find out more about this vampire business." She sighed and studied her nails. "Without a sire to guide me, what else could I do?"

"They obviously saw a sucker coming." I grinned. "You just wasted a trip. And know this." I got sober in a hurry. "If you pulled a stunt like turning Ray vamp today, the vampire council we've got now would terminate you."

"They're playing hardball? Radical." Lucky didn't look concerned. "Especially for Austin, home of the proudly weird."

"It's not an empty threat. They offed a vampire recently who turned a college student." I sat on the table again.

"I stand warned. Now listen up. I bet, in spite of all this 'poor Ray' crap, I can get you interested in my little proposition." Lucky smiled, sure of herself on this turf. "I *am* my father's daughter. A verbal contract will do. You clue me in with stuff I need to know. About our blood. I called this doctor, Ian MacDonald, when I got here. He won't tell me jack now except that he would like a sample of my blood. For some kind of experiment. Now you know I'm not just handing over something without an explanation." Lucky shook her head. "But he just kept mum. Said any details would have to come from you. So here I am. I'll give you fifty large to tell me what you *should* tell me for free, *sire*. Deal?"

"Fifty large. Is that fifty thousand?" I swallowed, the amount more than adequate to get me to Scotland. Damn her for tempting me.

"Yeah, Glory. American dollars, in case you didn't know that part. Not euros or dinars. Is it a deal?" She held out her hand.

I thought about it. Hard. Could I be a sellout? But that money would buy all the plane tickets I needed to get overseas. Maybe I should give Jerry time, but with this much in my bank account I'd have options. Maybe I *should* tell her about the blood. Ian swore it might be addictive. It was what any sire owed a vampire they'd made.

"I have conditions. First, you stay the hell away from Ray."

"No problem. I figure I got my licks in. But if he comes after me . . . ? My boys don't let anyone get near me with a stake. They don't care who he is or how many Grammys he's won. You might pass that word to your lover man."

"He's not—" I closed my eyes against the temptation her outstretched hand represented. This was wrong. I should let Jerry have the next century or so to lick his wounds, or maybe I could—

"Clock's ticking, Glory. Don't you owe me a little guidance? Why not make a chunk of change and do your duty at the same time?" Lucky dug into her purse again and pulled out a designer checkbook. "A thousand bucks to get this party started." She filled out the check and signed it with a flourish then dropped it in my lap before settling back in her chair with a satisfied smile. "Come on, Glo, spill."

I bit my lip as Lucky obviously tried to read my thoughts. Not gonna happen. If Lucky stayed in town and began loaning money or collecting debts, she was bound to pick up gossip. Aggie didn't believe in keeping secrets and we hadn't exactly bonded.

"One more condition. You leave town again. I don't want you hanging around here where Ray can run into you."

"Aw, gee. Thanks for the warm, fuzzy feelings." Lucky showed her fangs. "Give me two weeks. I do have some business here. And I want specifics, not some generic story you make up to get rid of me. Ways to verify the facts. First, what's up with our blood? What's special about it? That check is a down payment. Are we doing this deal or not?"

Two weeks. An eternity or a mere blip when you live forever. I swallowed my guilt and held out my hand.

"Deal. You'd better not make me regret this, Lucky." I sat on the table and crossed my legs. I hated to admit it, but Lucky had been right about my clothes. My long black skirt and saggy black sweater had suited my mood when I'd gotten dressed but they both needed to hit the charity gift bag sooner rather than later. I kicked at the table with my new black boots, the only stylish things I wore. Even my bra was old and comfy, stretched out and gray from too many washings and spins in a hot dryer.

"Great." Lucky had her tablet in hand again, ready to write.

"Okay. About our blood. I started out life as a Siren. My blood is Siren blood and, even though Jerry made me a vampire, I still seem to have some Siren attributes." I almost laughed at the look on Lucky's face. "You're not typing. Don't you believe me?"

"If you're going to make this into a joke, don't expect to keep my money." She tossed her things into that fabulous designer bag and jumped to her feet. I grabbed her arm before she could snatch that check.

"I wish it was a joke, Lucky. Read my mind. I'll let you in this time. Or ask Dr. MacDonald. You can tell him to call me and I'll give him permission to share the blood test results." I sighed. "I recently had a horrific meeting with the Storm God, Achelous, and he confirmed the whole thing. Before I met Jerry and he turned me vampire, I was a Siren. One of those creatures who lure sailors and their ships onto the rocks with their song. I killed over a hundred thousand men before Achelous kicked me out of his harem for being too soft on my victims."

"You're serious." Lucky looked me in the eyes. She was obviously reading my thoughts and checking my facts. "That is freaking awesome."

I sagged back on the table. I should have known that Lucky would be impressed rather than repulsed. After all, look at her idea of revenge on an old boyfriend.

"Awesome? Are you kidding me? I have to live with the fact that my relationships with men aren't because they truly love me but because I have this power over them." I jumped when she moved closer and put her hands on my knees. "And the doctor claims my blood may even be addictive. He wants to market it as a drug, to enhance power and libido." I really needed to shut up. Lucky looked like I'd handed her the keys to the kingdom.

"Are you listening to yourself?" She was intensity personified. "Glory, do you think you still have this fantastic power over men?"

I forced myself to shrug like this was no big deal, like it hadn't caused my life to crash and burn.

"Apparently. I lost my memory of sitting on a rock, but seem to have kept some of the powers. Not sure exactly what yet. It's all new to me."

"Well, it's the coolest thing I've ever heard. You can make men fall in love with you. Girlfriend, that is freaking amazing." Lucky stepped back and sank onto her chair. "Could I have possibly inherited that Siren thing from you when you gave me your blood? This old woman in the Trans told me she could tell by the smell that a nonhuman had made me. I laughed it off, called her crazy. I mean vamps aren't human, but used to be. Aw, shit, you know what I'm trying to say." She closed her eyes and pressed her fingertips to her forehead. "Let me think."

"About what?" But I was thinking too. Could this Siren power be hereditary? I'd had to give Lucky my blood to turn her. But I'd given my blood to Jerry during sex how many hundreds of times? And to Ray whenever he'd overdosed on alcohol. Even Rafe had needed to drink my blood once when he'd been wounded. Surely my Siren magic couldn't be passed on so easily. Ian had discounted the possibility.

I rubbed my own forehead. This wasn't making much sense. But then we were talking paranormals. Freaks. Logic rarely had much to do with our world, even if Ian was always trying to make a case for it.

"I'm trying to remember how I attracted the men I had relationships with in Europe. If I had to put any effort into it." Lucky opened her eyes and smiled. "Of course I'd had work done before I was turned and was in the best shape of my life, thanks be to God. So I had plenty of success. Men were after me all the time. But I thought, okay, it's the vampire thing. It's sexy to flash your fangs. And we have that great libido." She winked. "Of course men go for a woman who wants it often and likes to get her kink on. I know my way around a bedroom too. I certainly never had any complaints in that department before or after I got my fangs."

"TMI, Lucky. But I get what you mean." She didn't look close to her real age which I knew was pushing fifty. She'd had a top-tier plastic surgeon on speed dial when she'd been mortal so her "work" had been flawless. Now she'd forever look like a midthirties woman in her prime.

Yes, no wonder they called her Lucky. But the fact was our history made me hate being in the same room with her. Ray was going to go ballistic when I told him I was cooperating with her. And I had to get to him fast, before he heard it somewhere else. Two weeks. Was there any way to speed her on her way out of town faster?

"I think my numbers were up in Europe. So the Siren thing could have been working for me." She adjusted her jacket so that it showed even more cleavage. "But I never stick with one guy for long. My experience with Ray ruined me for long-term relationships. I have trust issues."

"Oh, please. You know he was forced to break up with you back then. Your father's goons threatened him." I would never forget the story of how Ray had almost been castrated by Mr. Carvarelli's men. Her father had decided the unknown singer wasn't good enough for his daughter. That incident had convinced Ray to break up with Lucky and leave town without a word of explanation to her. This had been way before Ray had become famous.

"I know that now. I didn't know it when I was young and in love!" Lucky jerked the scarf off her hair and stuffed it into her purse. "I've been trying to get over my issues. Europe was good for me. In the man department anyway. I had my pick and played the field. But I can't really say I was *that* much more successful." She shrugged. "Could have just been the vamp thing. So I'm not sure I'm buying your Siren story."

"Buy it or not, it's true. About me anyway. Go by Ian MacDonald's house. He has a lab there. He can test your blood and see if it matches mine. I have no idea whether you inherited the man magnetism or not. I don't control stuff like that." I sighed. "Look. I held up our side of the deal and

I need to get out of here. We're done. I'll take the rest of the money now."

"Oh, no. We're not done. There have to be powers that go with the blood thing. We're meeting again. After I get Mac-Donald's confirmation." She handed me a business card. "I know where you live. I expect to hear from you soon. And don't think you're getting any more money yet. That little tidbit wasn't worth even the first grand. I want to hear more about this Siren business. *Capite?*"

The Italian word made my eyes mist as I thought about my buddy Flo, so far away. I could really use her wise advice right now.

Lucky wasn't finished. "I want your best sire effort for fifty large. And we have a contract. So I don't want to hear any more about it. You don't like dealing with me? Tough."

I stalked over and threw open the door into the shop. "I'll tell you what's next, fledgling. As your sire, I call the shots. Now get the hell out. Don't call me, I'll call you."

"Hah! Look who grew a pair. I like the way you're stand-ing up to me, girlfriend." Lucky patted me on the shoulder and sauntered toward the cash register. "Ring me up, sales girl."

"Erin, that scarf Ms. Carver has in her purse is one fifty. Add it to her bill." I smiled as Lucky narrowed her eyes. "That's one hundred and fifty dollars, not large at all. And I am not your girlfriend." I walked into the back room and closed the door. Then I leaned against it. Lucky Carver. God, I hated that woman. She'd called me "girlfriend" and patted my shoulder with Erin as a witness. If Ray heard about that he'd feel so betrayed. I had to get to him. But there would be no way to diffuse the rage he'd feel when he realized she was here, close enough to kill.

I dug my cell out of my purse and dialed his number. We exchanged pleasantries then I got down to business. Could he see me tonight?

"Glory, babe, of course, come on over. Or do you want to

meet me at N-V for a drink and dancing?" He sounded sober and happy to hear from me.

"That would be fun another time but I have something serious to talk to you about." I cleared my throat when nerves seemed to close it. "I'll be out there as soon as I can."

"Is it about your meeting with the Storm God? You know I hired your old bodyguard Laurie. She didn't give me details, of course. She's discreet. But she did say you had a rough night when I asked her about it."

"Yeah, I did. I'll tell you all when I get there." I ended the call and walked out the back door to my car parked in the alley. No need to get Ray stirred up about Lucky before I had a chance to tell him face-to-face. I dreaded this. But somehow I had to calm him down and get him to accept the fact that I wasn't betraying him by working with her. Hah! Now if I could just convince myself of that, it would be all good.

Fourteen

When I stopped my car in front of Ray's house on a cliff overlooking one of Austin's lakes, I realized I'd forgotten something important. I still wore those awful black clothes. I started to turn around and head home to change when he threw open his front door. He was barefoot, looking too delicious in low-riding jeans and a snug T-shirt that would have brought big bucks on the vintage-band rack in my shop.

"Are you coming in or not?" He grinned and loped over to my car. "What's the matter? Did you want to put on lipstick first?"

"It wouldn't be a bad move." When he opened the car door, I took his hand and let him pull me out. Ray loping. It was just novel enough that I grabbed him and kissed his smile. "You are looking really, really good."

"Well, thanks. Can't say I can return the compliment." He checked me out from head to toe. "What's up with the outfit? You look like a bag lady. And I know you like the top down but I have a feeling you didn't bother much with your hair tonight before the ride out here. Your cheeks are red too."

"Wow. Way to make a girl feel special, Ray." But since he was right, I just stepped away from him and spoke to Laurie who was hovering near his front door. After he shut it with her still on the outside, I turned to him. "I'm glad you hired Laurie. She's amazing. You sleep with her yet?" I figured if he could be blunt, so could I.

"I don't sleep with my bodyguards." He slung his arm around me. "And I'm sorry if I hurt your feelings, babe. Just hate that you're obviously bummed about something. Come in the living room and tell Ray all about it."

I leaned against him. "Yeah, I'm bummed. Let me unload on you. You won't believe what the Storm God told me." I sank down on his leather couch so that I had a view of the lake. I knew far down below us there was probably a boat tied up at the dock; Ray always had one—a real go-fast. Lights twinkled in the distance along the edges of the large expanse of water and it was a dreamy setting. I turned to Ray as he settled beside me and I gave him a dramatic version of the whole tale.

"Sounds like you're well out of that Siren scene. Not surprised Aggie's killed that many men. She's exactly what I thought she was—a stone-cold bitch."

"Yeah, well, I sort of feel sorry for her now. She's got to keep serving that guy. And has been at his beck and call for over a thousand years. Imagine, Ray." I sighed as he rubbed the back of my neck where my muscles were tied in knots.

"Rather not." He turned me so he could work the kinks out. "Relax, babe. You are so stressed. And no wonder. What did Blade think of this? And Valdez?"

"I'll get to them in a minute." I gave him a blow-by-blow of Achy tossing around lightning bolts and Circe's appearance, along with the bombshell she'd dropped about Jerry and how we'd met.

Ray's magic hands had relaxed me to the point that I'd gone along when he'd coaxed me into lying on my stomach. Now his hands stilled and he pressed a kiss on the back of my neck. "You're shittin' me. She set Blade up?"

"Yeah." My voice wobbled but I sucked up the urge to cry.

"Guess he didn't take it well." Ray's hands started moving over my body again.

"You could say that." I sighed as his hands eased aches I hadn't realized I had. "Jerry's gone to Castle Campbell in Scotland. Enough said."

"I'm sorry, sweet thing." Ray's deep voice was close and he nuzzled my ear with his lips before he continued easing every taut muscle in my back.

"Thanks." I rested my heavy head on my hands, getting more relaxed by the moment. "Mmm. You know you could get a job doing this." I actually yawned.

"Record sales tank, I'll keep it in mind." Ray's fingers wandered to new territory that I knew was more erogenous zone than tight muscle. "What are you going to do about it? About Blade?"

"Can we change the subject?" I started to steer his hand away from the naughty direction it was taking but it felt too good. "I'm sick of my own drama. Tell me what you've been up to."

"Staying sober, though it hasn't been easy. But I have to admit I got scared straight." Now both his hands were getting a little too bold. Sue me, but they felt good enough that I swallowed any objections and let Ray have his way.

"What do you mean? That fall from the concert stage do it? You seemed to laugh that off at the time." So much for relaxation. I'd been there, watching Ray trying to entertain thousands even though he was staggering drunk. Unfortunately he'd lost his balance and taken a header into the audience. I shuddered as I remembered him lying unconscious on the concrete. Ray rolled me over to face him.

"No, Glory girl. You'd think that night would have done it, humiliating myself in front of my fans. But it took something even worse to get my head on straight." Ray ran his hands down my legs then up, my skirt sliding up too. "I really played the dumbass this time. You know how I love my daylight drug."

"Yes, sure." I tried to sit up but he pushed me down with

a gentle hand on my shoulder. "What the hell did you do, Ray?"

"Please relax. I never should have started this story." He smoothed his hands up from my ankles. "Poor baby, your calf muscles are really tight. Work in the shop tonight? On your feet a lot?"

"Some." Ray's fingers were firm yet gentle as they eased ever higher and my eyes started to drift closed even though I really wanted to know . . .

"Did you watch a sunrise?" My eyes fluttered open when Ray's hands reached my thighs and I put my hand over his. "You didn't stay outside too long, did you, Ray?"

"I'm getting to that part." He laid my hand back on my stomach then lifted one of my legs and bent it at the knee, still gently massaging. At least I'd shaved my legs the night before. "I sat there, drinking the blood with alcohol—sorry, but it's a poor substitute for Jack—and thought I'd take another hit of the daylight drug. I figured what could it hurt? Stay out a little longer. You know?"

"You were under cover, weren't you? Or inside, looking out a window?" I couldn't just lie there when he was obviously building up to something. When he abandoned my skirt to reach for my waist, I grabbed his hands again. "You're scaring me, Ray."

His smile was rueful. "Damn. Am I killing the mood here?" Our waistline tug-of-war had moved under my sweater. I couldn't deny I loved his hands on me and I was really regretting that raggedy bra I'd worn.

"Forget the mood for a moment. What happened, Ray?" I touched his cheek and he pressed a kiss to my palm then scraped it with his fangs. "Wait. Don't tell me. Show me. This is a Siren trick that Aggie used on me. Let me see if I can do it."

"What is it?" Ray looked puzzled when I grabbed both of his hands again.

"Just remember what happened. The scene, exactly as it was. It will be like I'm watching a movie if this works. Will you do that for me?" I wasn't really sure I wanted to do this, but had to try. Ray and his daylight. The man was such an addict. Though he didn't want to hear that.

"Fine." He gripped my hands and closed his eyes.

I closed mine and suddenly I could see Ray leaning against the cool glass of the French doors when the sky started to glow on the horizon. He had a full drink in his hand and I could actually smell the alcohol in the blood, taste it as he took a deep swallow. God, but he loved this time of day. The way the sun began to streak across the water. It was cold and clear and he could just glimpse the bow of his boat down at the dock.

He felt the death sleep pulling at him. No. Shit. He wasn't going to give in. He reached in his pocket and pulled out the packet to take another hit. There. That should give him a half hour. The sky was actually pink now. He wanted to smell it, feel it on his skin. The wind would be laying off now, not a bit of breeze, and the quiet would be peaceful, like God was taking it all in. The beauty of his creation.

Damn it, his glass was empty. He snagged a fresh bottle out of the minifridge and didn't bother with the glass, just chugged it. What the fuck. He was going for it. The sunlight was starting to shimmer on the water which was smooth as glass. He had to be there. Take the boat out. If he fried, who the hell would miss him? And it wouldn't be a bad way to go.

He opened the door, stepped outside and felt the burn start. One inhale, that's all he got, when strong arms wrestled him back inside. Damn it, who paid these people? They worked for him. If he wanted to go for a boat ride, they could just step aside, let him go up in flames, by God.

But they just ignored him, knocking him down on his own fucking rug when he tried to get past them. He was firing every one of them. See if he didn't. Except he couldn't focus enough to see who the hell had him now. Who dropped him on his king-size bed and stripped him down to his boxers.

Death sleep. Shit. Missed another day.

"Ian had always warned me not to mix the daylight drug

with alcohol but I didn't listen." Ray's voice was husky as he stretched out next to me, his hip bumping into mine. His breath stirred my hair and his scent surrounded me.

"I almost lost you, Ray. I can't believe you did that." I stared into his eyes. They were kind, intent and, yes, beautiful. I wanted to drown in them. They were like crystal lakes that the Siren in me would have floated in, reveling in the sheer beauty of the clear water that reflected the perfect blue of a summer sky. I couldn't cry, actually wanted to shake him, hit him, wake him up to his value.

"The sun, Glory. You know how I am about the sun. I just had to feel it on my skin. I wanted it so damned bad." Ray brushed my hair back from my face, his fingers sliding gently over my forehead.

I looked away, sick at how close I'd come to losing him. I focused on one of his dark curls caught in the neck of his black T-shirt to keep from crying. He needed some tough love, not me begging him to live. "Lucky for you someone saved your sorry ass."

"Yeah, seems Nate had given the guards orders. They're my babysitters too." Ray nuzzled my forehead with his chin. "You mad at me?"

"Not if you learned your lesson." I shuddered and slid my hands up to his shoulders. "Promise me you won't ever do that again, Ray. Mix daylight and alcohol." Oh, shit, I was afraid I was going to cry after all.

"I swear it. I was a damned fool. I'm off the alcohol. If I have to choose between them, seeing the sunrise beats the hell out of the pitiful buzz that high-octane blood gives me." Ray gathered me in his arms and rocked me against his hard chest. "Admit it, Glory, all your men are stupid bastards. You deserve better." He held me tight as I finally let loose and cried against his soft cotton shirt.

I grabbed fistfuls of the cotton and held on then threw one leg over his. I felt Ray's desire behind the zipper in his dark-wash jeans. Had all his kindness just been foreplay? With Ray, it didn't take much to get his motor running. And of course he was another one of my Siren victims. This bitter thought just made my tears flow faster. He ran his bare toes up and down my calf in a gesture of comfort. Surprisingly it did make me feel better, that and his strong arms surrounding me. I held on to him as I realized that and rubbed my cheek against his firm bicep.

"You're just as enchanted by the damned Siren thing as Jerry and Rafe are, Ray. You don't have a snowball's chance of getting out from under my spell." I sniffed and leaned back to look up at him. To my surprise he grinned.

"You are so very wrong, sweet thing. But aren't you adorable for trying to talk me out of making this move?" He wiped my eyes with his palm then leaned down and kissed me. It was one of his soul-taking, give-me-all-that-you've-got kisses.

I'm no fool. I sank into him and let it happen. He tasted great and knew how to work with what he had, which was quite a lot. His hand came down to my backside to press me against him and I moaned into his mouth. Now who was weaving a spell? I gasped and pushed back.

"No, this isn't right."

"It is and way overdue. Listen to me." Ray brushed my wild hair back behind my ears. "Your blood is in me, courtesy of that bitch Lucky Carver."

I looked away, not about to let him see how much I didn't want her name brought up right now. My news about her would end what was proving to be a welcome distraction from all the angst I'd been feeling lately.

"Yes, she has my blood. And I guess it probably has some Siren characteristics." I closed my eyes again when Ray slid his hand under my skirt and squeezed my hip. My eyes popped open. Panties. What the hell kind of panties had I put on this evening? Black thong. Okay. Not so bad.

"Possibly. I let Ian check my blood when he was doing all his tests. Seems my blood is very similar to yours. So if you have Siren blood, then so do I." He nibbled on my earlobe then grazed my skin with his fangs, clearly on a path to my jugular. "If anyone can resist your call, lady, it would be me." He kissed my pulsing vein for a breathless moment. "And I hate to burst your bubble, sweet thing, but, when I was in L.A., I hardly gave you a thought."

"Really, Ray?" I shoved my hands into his hair and tugged until he looked me in the eyes. "I want to read your mind. Will you trust me enough to let me?"

"Yeah. If I'm lyin', I'm dyin'." He grinned and opened those laser blues wide.

I sought the answers I wanted and found them. Seriously. I saw him with a leggy blonde, a vampire who'd showed him how getting his fangs involved made sex hotter than hot. He'd called it popping his vamp cherry. I felt the heat rise in my cheeks and swatted his shoulder. Then there were a variety of groupies, fans who always hung around the band and would do anything to say they'd scored with a famous rock star. Those scenes made me curl my lip, especially when I saw he'd used them for a taste of human blood then wiped their minds clean after the fact. Had I been anywhere in his thoughts in L.A.? I shoved him off the couch.

"Fine. You're a dog and not the tail-wagging kind— obviously not one of my victims." I sighed, then realized how ridiculous that sounded. I offered him my hand, matching his unrepentant grin with a smile.

"Keep looking, babe. There's something else in my head for you to see besides my sheet action." Ray was solemn now and didn't that make me shiver.

"You serious?"

"As a heart attack." He settled half on top of me, his body fitting in a way I wanted to arch into. I resisted, still not convinced this was a good idea. "Look into my mind." He stared down, intense, his thoughts very open now.

I did see more there. I saw the Ray who had woken up lost and confused, the man who totally understood what I was going through now. Who got that suddenly not knowing who or what you were shook your world until you weren't sure if you could even live there anymore.

At least he'd been lucky. He'd had an angel by his side after he got over the initial shock, someone he could count on to guide him through this new life that he had to live in the dark. It wasn't a magic spell or even gratitude that made him want to hold me and comfort me. No, he just wanted to be there for me, like I'd been there for him. Yeah, he was new to this vampire gig, but he'd love a chance to be *my* anchor for a change. Did I trust him enough to let him try?

"Thanks, Ray. Yeah, I trust you." I pulled his mouth down to mine again. Our kiss was something special. I let him know that it meant a lot to me that he wanted to help me. That we were both survivors and maybe it was right that we were here together tonight. And if I *was* a Siren, then there was one surefire way a Siren knew to celebrate life.

Ray pulled back and grinned. "You don't have to tell me twice, Glory girl." He drew my sweater up and off to toss it across the room.

"Fancy underwear." He laughed when he saw my bra and I hit him.

"I didn't plan to let anyone else see it when I got dressed this evening." I tried to cover what even Goodwill would have rejected.

"Then we'd better get it off fast." He quickly unhooked the back and ripped it off me, then turned and aimed for a small trash can. It hit with a clang, falling half out of it like a sad flag of surrender. "You will let it stay there, won't you?"

"Absolutely." I reached for him again, shivering as he kissed a path from one nipple to the other. He traced an erotic journey with his fangs then drew on each peak until I shuddered and almost tore his shirt off in my eagerness to get his chest bare to my touch.

"You're not going to stop me this time, are you, babe?" He had his hand on the waistband of my skirt, ready to send it to my feet.

I knew as well as he did that we'd been to this point before and I'd called a halt. It wasn't fair or kind to keep doing this. I did a gut check. Jerry was gone, abandoning me without a thought to how I was dealing with the news of what I was. He'd just taken off and never looked back. Was that love? I'd told Rafe to move on and I'd meant it. I didn't want to ruin his life by holding him with a spell. What did that leave for Glory? An empty apartment and a hot guy who wanted her.

Ray understood what I was feeling too. That peek into his mind had resonated like nothing else could. We'd both had our very foundations rocked. He'd turned to alcohol and a search for oblivion. Was I turning to meaningless sex? I met his gaze and knew nothing with this man could ever be meaningless to me. We had a soul-deep connection that included friendship and a binding of our blood that would help us get through this together. I pushed my horrible skirt and thong down, kicking them away until all I wore were my boots.

"All systems go, captain. Let's blast off." I shoved him off the couch and onto the floor where I landed on top of him with a throaty laugh. After a long kiss that left us both breathless, I unbuttoned and unzipped his jeans and opened them wide.

Oh, wow, did I remember this. Ray had always liked to strut his stuff in front of me when we'd pretended to be engaged a few months ago. I'd seen the piercing before and now it glittered with a diamond that just begged to be kissed. It jutted boldly from that open zipper and I leaned down to tease it with my tongue.

"Glory." Ray groaned and reached for me.

"Not here. With the windows uncovered? I bet Laurie does a regular walk around the perimeter. I don't want her for an audience." I glanced at that spectacular view outside then down to the one below me. I let my hair brush his erection and saw Ray shudder. Nice.

"She won't. But if we're playing spaceship or *Star Trek*, I have some, um, toys." Ray grinned up at me. "I have this fantasy . . ."

"Hmm. I know. Yes, I saw a little of that when I was doing the mind sweep." I grabbed the hems of his jeans and jerked them off to fling them across the room. Then I stood and put my hands on my hips. When had I lost all my inhibitions? Sure I had figure flaws, but a handsome, man-of-my-dreams rock star wanted me. Lucky had gotten one thing right. The new vampire she'd had dropped into my bed had been my fantasy man for a long while. Time to make that fantasy a reality. No tricks, no long-term complications. I'd think about those other short-term issues later. For now, I was more than ready to have fun.

"Game on. What about my boots?"

"They look good. Keep 'em on, definitely. The launch pad is down the hall." Ray jumped to his feet and pulled me after him as he ran toward what I assumed was his bedroom. I laughed as I imagined what was in store for me. Ray did have a reputation. But, honey, when I saw what was in that room . . . The tabloids didn't have a clue.

"What *is* this room?" I stared around in wonder.

"My playroom. I've been collecting since I was a kid. Nate and I have an agreement not to bid on the same things or we end up jacking prices against each other online." Ray didn't seem to have any qualms about strolling around naked as he showed off his collection of comic books, *Star Wars* figures and everything to do with superheroes. I had a hard time concentrating on his toys when he was the main attraction as far as I was concerned.

"Is this Captain Kirk's chair?" I didn't dare sit in it naked but recognized it instantly.

"Are you a Trekkie?" Ray grinned. "Reproduction. Sit. It's okay. No, wait. Let me go first." He dropped into the chair then pulled me into his lap. "Now that's what I'm talking about."

I snuggled my bottom against his eager erection. "Hmm. Seems like there could be a better way for me to sit than this."

"Oh, yeah. But not yet." He eased me off his lap. "We've got to take full advantage. Stand in the middle of the room."

Suddenly I was self-conscious and grabbed what looked like one of Luke Skywalker's jackets and slipped it on. Ray hit a switch and the lights dimmed. I looked up and gasped. We were in an alternate universe with stars above us in a night sky projected on the ceiling.

"This is awesome." I loved the way the mysterious blue glow made everything seem more beautiful. Though Ray's body didn't need the help, it would definitely make it easier for me when I had to drop that robe.

"Wait for it." He hit another switch and soaring music filled the air. "It's a special remix Nate and I have been working and reworking since we were teenagers. You'll definitely recognize some of the tunes."

I was still caught up in the magic of the stars and sound when Ray slapped a lightsaber into my hand. He'd donned a Darth Vader mask.

"What? Are we fighting?"

"Why not? Want to see if you can score against me?" Ray lightly tapped me on the hip, then used the saber to open that jacket. "Nude fighting is more fun. Getting shy on me?"

"A little. And I'd like to see your face. Those creepy breathing sounds coming from your mask aren't sexy." I got in a few hits with my saber on his arm and hip.

"Then I lose it." He carefully laid it on a shelf, then turned back. We did a few minutes of fake swordplay until he managed to knock my saber across the room. "Gotcha." He moved in and slid his hands under my jacket. "Mmm. I get a reward for that."

"What kind of reward?"

"This." He leaned in and kissed me breathless, shoving my jacket off at the same time. He finally eased back and looked me over. "Did I ever tell you how much I love your breasts?" He nuzzled each one of them, his thumbs pressing against my nipples. "The real deal. Man, I love the real deal."

I sighed, very grateful that I pleased him. Then I walked him back until he was sitting in that captain's chair. I'd worked up a fantasy of my own.

"Now I wonder, Captain. Will you let me take over the controls?" I ran my hands down his chest, my mouth following.

"If you promise not to let us crash and burn." He leaned back, his legs spread. "But listen first. Glory, you have got to know that this Siren shit is stupid. You are quite a woman all on your own." He moaned when I licked my way up and down his cock. I stopped at the diamond ring piercing. Some devil made me grab that ring with my teeth and tug.

"God, yes, Glory." He slid his hands through my hair, eager to keep that going, but I released him and scooted out of reach and across the room.

I was very aware of his eyes on me. Ray made me feel sexy like . . . Wonder Woman? No, too obvious. So many of these superheroes were men. And *Star Trek* had featured very few women. There was a rack of their tiny minidresses in various colors but none of them were close to my size. Princess Leia. Ah. A sexy harem costume she'd worn in one of the Star Wars movies. Seemed appropriate since I'd escaped from a harem myself. But her tiny bra top was designed for hills, not my mountains. I finally settled on her headband and wore it like a crown.

Then I picked up a small whip with leather thongs a character from a comic must have used and hit it against my hand. I turned to face Ray and strutted toward him, stroking that whip lightly up and down my body. I figured it was a good distraction from my figure flaws.

"Tell me, Captain, are you certain you will allow me to control the ship and, um, you?" I ran the whip down Ray's chest, teasing his nipples.

"For you, Leia? Of course." He grinned. "Come closer and I'll be happy to do whatever you wish or I'm afraid I'll suffer the consequences." He nodded at the whip. I saw him swallow when I brushed the thongs across my breasts.

"Then you must obey my commands. Now kiss my breasts, only my breasts, and nothing else. And you will stop when I tell you to. Understand?" I walked around him, the whip brushing his ear and my nipples grazing his biceps.

"Yes." The word came out hoarse and I gave an evil laugh of triumph.

"Now begin." I sat on his lap and presented one breast to his mouth. Ray attacked it like it was his only birthday gift. Oh, yeah. I braced a hand on his shoulder and tried not to moan as I felt the pull of his mouth all the way to my toes. I smacked his arm with my whip. "No hands. I did not say you could use your hands." He gripped the armrests like he was about to launch off the chair. I would have laughed but I was about to leap into the air myself.

So I finally scrambled away, gathering my dignity and trying not to show how he'd affected me. I stalked around the room, hitting my thigh with the whip until I changed directions. "The other breast now. Take care of it," I ordered, sitting in his lap again.

Who was I torturing? He latched on and I squeaked when he pierced me with his fangs. It was heavenly hell. His hand crept to my hip and I hit him again. "Bad boy. I said no hands." He actually obeyed me. We were really into this but I wasn't sure how much more I could take. His erection was rock hard against my hip, the diamond scratching me. I smelled fresh blood. Mine. I shoved his face away from my breast.

"Glory," he groaned as he looked up at me, my blood smeared on his cheek.

"Quiet. I am almost ready for liftoff, Captain." I wiped away the blood and stuck my finger in his mouth. He closed his eyes as he licked it clean. I slid off his knees and stood.

"Now. Our destination is Orgasmis. Have you been there before?" I eyed his cock when it jerked against his stomach.

"Yes, but not with such a skilled crew. I'm thinking it will be a short journey this time." He still held the arms of the chair as if afraid to let go.

I strode to the center of the room where I turned to face him. "I'm sorry to hear that. I like long, slow trips with lots of sightseeing when I travel, Captain. I hope you will not disappoint me by rushing this. I want the scenic route." I reached between my thighs, slowly sliding the whip handle between them.

Ray watched my every move and I saw him swallow again.

Was he finally going to give in and jump out of that chair? No, he stayed put but I could see the muscles in his arms quivering. I made a show of examining the damp handle.

"Why, I believe I am almost ready for departure." I sauntered up to Ray and waved the handle a few inches from his nose. "What do you think, Captain? Are all systems go?" His nostrils flared. "Shall I come on board?"

"God, Glory. Let me taste you." His eyes narrowed on my hips hungrily.

"Perhaps next trip. If this journey is to my liking." I tossed the whip aside, more eager for that ride than I wanted to let on. Surrounded by the scent of our arousal, I quivered with wanting him. I reached for his cock, desperate to feel it inside me. Games. I looked up into his eyes and grinned. Why not?

"It will be to your liking, woman, or I will die trying." His voice was little more than a growl as I leaned closer and slid my knees alongside his. My breasts pressed against his chest and I gave him an openmouthed kiss that seemed to go on for decades. Finally, I leaned back.

"Then I'm glad we're immortal." I picked up his hands and slid them around my waist. "Prepare for boarding, Captain." Before I could say another word, he lifted me, giving me just enough time to grab the back of the chair and spread my legs to accommodate him before he settled me onto his lap. When I felt his cock finally glide into me, I couldn't bite back my moan of pleasure.

Oh, God, but it felt good. I spared a moment to wonder about that diamond but it only added another level of excitement, a new thrill that I savored as he filled me. My knees settled onto the leather seat on either side of his narrow hips.

"Don't. Move." Ray put his hands on my face and stared into my eyes. "Look at me and listen. You are an incredible, amazing woman, Gloriana St. Clair. And I want you to know that I have never brought another woman here, to my playroom. Do you believe me?"

I stared back, for a moment utterly speechless. From Ray,

this was about as serious as it got. I was in the inner sanctum. And speaking of . . . I could feel him throbbing inside me, the pleasure intense but not nearly there yet. I wanted to move, to scream, to . . .

"Uh, yes, and thanks, Ray. Now, please, kiss me?" I grabbed his hair and held on as I fit my mouth to his. Oh, but I loved him. Ray was so much more than a man with a golden voice that could melt me. He was caring and charismatic and larger than life. He made me feel beautiful and worthy and, oh God, he began to move. I squeezed my inner muscles, holding him tight. He groaned and held my head to kiss me deeper, surer, as if he couldn't get enough of me. The chair creaked and I wondered if it would be able to handle what we were about to do in it. I grabbed the leather back again.

"Preparing for liftoff." Ray grinned and held my hips as he pounded into me. "Accelerating." He must have seen my eyes glazing over and my face flushing as an orgasm shivered and shuddered through me. "Destination in sight."

"Ray, oh, please." I leaned down and took his vein. Just couldn't help myself. It was part of the action and he obviously expected it. The music soared along with Ray's rhythm, bringing me closer and closer to a climax that was pulling me apart and yet putting me back together again. His hands tightened and I felt such a screaming wonderful wildness inside me that I never wanted it to stop.

With a clash of cymbals, pounding of drums and a trumpet's blast, Ray shouted my name and drove into me a final time. He held the back of my head while I drank greedily. When I finally licked away the fang marks, he plucked the crown from my head and tossed it away.

"I believe we have arrived safely, Princess." He ran his hand down my back. "Are you satisfied with the captain's performance?"

"Mmm. Yes. This time." I sat up. My body quivered around him, and I had to steady myself as I clasped Ray between my knees. I looked up at the galaxies on display above our heads. I had a new respect for that chair and would certainly never hear the theme from *Star Wars* again without getting a new kind of thrill. Of course, as a vampire, Ray could keep doing this all night long and was already stirring inside me.

"This time? Are you saying you would like another trip?" Ray dropped a kiss on the tip of each breast and I shivered.

"Hmm. It's entirely possible. I may require more demonstrations to be sure that you are competent in all maneuvers when handling"—I walked my fingers down his chest—"space travel."

"I will be more than happy to let you try out all my various techniques." Ray jumped to his feet and carried me down the hall. "But first you need to see how we welcome guests to Orgasmis. My shower is a double and equipped with showerheads designed to add pleasure to your bathing experience. Conquering other galaxies can be sweaty work. What do you think?"

I relaxed against him. "I think you're amazing. Thanks, Ray. You definitely took my mind off my troubles."

He stopped in the doorway of a massive master suite. "You're more than welcome." He kissed me, a sweet, subtly erotic kiss. "How many times have you brought me back from the brink of something ugly? I'm happy to help. And you know it wasn't exactly a sacrifice."

"Yeah, I'm another notch on that famous bedpost." I nodded toward the king-size bed facing a pair of French doors with another great lake view.

"Never, ever think you are on that list." Ray slid me to my feet. "Damn it, Glory. You're special to me. Don't you dare put yourself down like that. I'd kill anyone else who tried to say such things about you."

I saw that he meant it and bit my lip. "Yeah, I get that. Sorry. Give me some time to get used to this. Okay?"

"Babe, you can have all the time you need. Just don't run home and start spouting nonsense about how this was all a big mistake. I won't have it. You hear me?" Ray took my elbow and marched me into the bathroom. "Now I don't know about you, but I need a shower. I've got shower gel and fancy shampoos in whatever flavor and scent strikes your fancy. Knock yourself out. I'm going to run give Laurie her orders for the rest of the night before I join you. Are we cool?" Ray stared at me, waiting.

"Yes, we're cool and very, very hot." I touched his cheek and kissed his lips. "Go, I'll be fine." I sat down to take off my boots while he stepped into a pair of running shorts. My thoughts were in a whirl. He had said exactly what I'd been thinking even though I'd been careful to block my thoughts.

Relax, Glory. I was still quivering from a world-class orgasm and I'd be damned if I'd ruin this night with worry. My favorite fantasy was becoming reality. Ray had rocked my world. I owed it to myself and to him to savor every moment.

Fifteen

I was rinsing off my hair when Ray joined me in that fabulous shower stall. The glass tiles were the color of the sea. Seemed like since I'd found out about my Siren connection I was seeing water everywhere. Were latent memories coming back or was it my imagination? Aggie and I needed to talk. But so did Ray and I. Of course talk wasn't on the agenda when he slid his arms around me. Ray's idea of a shower was less about getting clean and more about seeing how many ways he could take me in that stall. Finally, as I collapsed against the tile for the fourth time, I called a halt.

"Siren or not. I feel the dawn coming and the urge for a dry bed."

Ray glanced at his waterproof watch. "Plenty of time left before the sun comes up. Or we could take some daylight drug and watch it rise. What do you say?"

"Not tonight." I smiled at the thought of a sunrise in his arms. "Can we slow down a little, rock star?"

"Fine. I won't say no to moving this to my king-size bed." Ray handed me a tiny towel that couldn't possibly go around me.

I wrapped it around my hair and grabbed a bath sheet to tie around my body. "You're insatiable."

"Maybe it's our Siren blood." Ray ran a comb through his wet hair. After blotting a towel over his body, he hadn't bothered to cover it. Which was fine by me. He turned to me and slipped open the knot between my breasts. "I have a theory about this Siren stuff. I think we really are all that when it comes to sex."

I brushed a strand of wet hair back from his beautiful face. "Vampires are sensual creatures too, Ray. At least every vamp I've met is highly charged sexually. Well, except for a few Energy Vampires. They seem to get off to power more than sex." I probably should tell him what Ian had said about my blood, *our* blood.

"I think what we have is more than the vamp thing. We've got to get with Aggie, much as I hate her, and see what she's got to say about Sirens. There are bound to be powers there too. Things we can use to our advantage." He got the towel away from me and pulled me against him. What can I say? He felt damned good and I felt damned easy.

"Well, I can turn people to statues. That's one. And Alesa hinted that I might be able to blast through mental blocks." I hated sharing that one but my defenses were down, especially with Ray doing interesting things with his hands. Reading thoughts . . . If Ray could blast through mine . . . No, not thinking about Lucky now. Sex. Fabulous sex in his bed just a few feet away. Thinking about that.

"Excellent. We'll have to explore that. Later." Ray dropped to his knees in front of me.

"Ray?"

"Relax, Glory. Put yourself in my hands." He nudged my legs apart.

Well, what woman would say no to that?

I woke up to music. I stretched and realized I was naked in Ray's king-size bed. It wasn't a recording I was listening to but Ray at his piano singing a new song. I liked it. It was optimistic and upbeat, the kind of music he hadn't written for a long time. I found my sweater and skirt on the foot of the bed. No underwear. Oh, well. I pulled them on, used a new toothbrush and toothpaste I found in the bathroom and attempted some order with my hair, then padded out to the living room.

Ray sat at the grand piano. I knew my time was up. I was going to have to tell him about Lucky and my deal with her. I was really, really dreading it. I wanted to run, throw up, something. Instead, I firmed my resolve even though my knees were so watery I had to hold on to the piano when I got there.

"Come. Sit. Tell me what you think." Ray grinned and patted the piano bench next to him. He wore silk boxers and nothing else, the rest of his beautiful body a great distraction. Guess lots of hot sex will do that to you. Make you crave more. For a moment it actually took my mind off what was coming.

"The song? What I've heard so far is fantastic. Very catchy chorus. I can imagine dancing to it in a club." I sat and listened while he pounded out a rock beat and sang in the voice that had made me fall for him long before I'd ever met the man behind it. Seeing him full of joy, belting out a tune that he ended with a grin and a flourish made me lean against him, tears burning my eyes. I knew what my news would do to that great mood.

"Still needs some work. The end isn't right yet." He wrote something on the sheet music in front of him.

"Sounded perfect to me." I sniffled, couldn't help it.

"Thanks, babe. Lucky for me you've always been a fan." He took my face into his hands and gave me a sweet kiss, the kind that could melt your bones.

"Ray—"

"Wait. I've got something to say. This Siren thing. It's really bugging me. Come sit beside me on the couch." He pulled me up and led me there, catching me when I stumbled. He looked uncharacteristically serious.

"What is it? I know Aggie's a bitch but I hope I won't

suddenly start acting like her now just because I know . . ."
I sat and he settled beside me.

"No, nothing like that. You were once a Siren, Glory. You
had a song, a beautiful captivating voice. You could lure men
to their deaths with its beauty." Ray's eyes became a little
unfocused and I could see that the artist in him was trying to
imagine it. He shook his head. "And that bastard Storm God
ripped it out of you." He pulled me into his arms and rested
his cheek on my hair. "God, baby, it's a fucking tragedy."

"Ray." I patted his back, comforting him. "Thank you.
But I really don't remember any of it. And, seriously? Who
would want the kind of song that made men willing to die
for you?"

"That's a misuse of talent. It wouldn't have to be that
way." Ray held me tight.

"I guess. But don't worry about me. I listen to your voice
and it moves me. Music and your kind of talent means
the world to me. But I simply can't imagine having it inside
myself."

Ray pulled back, his eyes actually shimmering, like the
emotions were getting to him. "Babe, that's what's so crimi-
nal about this. You were robbed." He smoothed back my hair.
"And taken from the sea too. I've seen Aggie swim, savoring
the water on her like she was born to be there. Which I guess
she was. You lost all that too."

"Yes. Now, when I'm in that lake out there, I choke, terrified of what might grab me and pull me under." I finally
got it and anger shook loose inside me until I wanted to
pound something. Not that it would do me any good. Ancient history. "Damn Achelous to hell!"

"There you go. Get good and mad." Ray held me again
and whispered in my ear. "I wish there was something I
could do to help you."

"Promise me something." My stomach knotted. The time
had come and I knew I couldn't put this off.

"Sure, anything." He leaned back. "Music lessons?"

"No, that ship has sailed." I rubbed his cheek with my

thumb. I hate, hate, hated what I was about to say. "Just listen and don't go off on me. Please?"

"Now you've got me worried." He captured my hand. "What's on your mind?"

"Last night was great but—"

"Don't start." Ray frowned, dropped my hand and jumped to his feet. "Here we go. I knew you were going to pull this. Forget Blade and Rafe and all the crap that you always drag out as reasons why you and I can't work. I'm not proposing marriage. Can't we just enjoy ourselves for a while? No strings?"

"That's not it, though I'm tangled up in a bunch of strings you don't know about, Ray." I spied my boots next to the coffee table and began to pull them on. I couldn't believe he thought I regretted last night. As if any woman could.

"So we'll cut through them, together. Tell me what they are." Ray sat beside me again.

"I have something to tell you, Ray. Something I should have spit out when I first got here. But then things got going between us and it was great. Really. Better than great. I'm not sorry it happened, not at all. But when you hear what I have to say . . ." I zipped up the last boot to stall for time then pressed my fists to my rolling stomach. If I got through this without throwing up it would be a freaking miracle.

"How bad can it be?" Ray was smiling again, his hand on my shoulder. "Come on, babe. Just get it out."

"Lucky Carver is in town." There, I'd said it. And Ray reacted as predicted.

"The hell you say. What is that bitch doing here?" He jumped to his feet and stalked over to the French doors. He flung one open. "Laurie, come here!"

"Yes, boss?" She was there on the run.

"Pass the word to the other guards. There's an old enemy of mine in town." Ray glanced at me. "What color is her hair now?"

"I call it mahogany. It's a dark red. Laurie, she's of Italian descent, about my height, size six and looks midthirties but is a decade older. A loan shark named Lucky Carver. I told her to stay away from you, Ray." I locked eyes with Laurie. "I want to get with you sometime. To talk to you about what went down at the meeting with Circe and Achelous. When is your night off?"

"Tomorrow. N-V? Ten?" She looked from me to Ray and back again.

"Make it my place, say at eight?" I glanced at Ray. He was pacing the living room, about to freak because obviously I'd had a conversation with Lucky and had been reluctant to tell him about it.

"Sure, we can do that." Laurie nodded. "See you then. Anything else, boss?"

"I'm not afraid of that woman. Far from it. But if she shows up here, she's not to get past the gate." Ray waved Laurie off then turned to me. "So you've talked to Lucky. When were you going to tell me about it? Oh, wait. Guess that would have ruined the mood for sex. Smart move, Siren." He faced me, an angry man.

"I didn't come here for sex, Ray. That was your idea. You were the one who started all the touching with the massage routine." Hey, I could get mad too. I jumped up, hands on my hips. "Don't keep throwing that Siren crap in my face. Lucky came to see me in the shop. I wanted to toss her out on her ass. I hate that freak."

"You and me both. So did you? Toss her out after warning her to stay away from me?" Ray grabbed my elbow.

I'll be damned if he wasn't trying to read my mind. Then I felt him trying to blast through my block. Siren wannabe. No way in hell.

"Stop it! You aren't a damned Siren. Quit trying to play mind games with me. I talked to her. I'm her sire. Which she tried to use to get to me. I had her tossed out of Austin before without any guidance."

"Because of what she did to me, Glory!" Ray shook my

arm, then realized he was on the verge of violence and took
a step back. "Sorry. I don't hurt women. Not that it stops
them from hurting me. Case in point—Lucky Carver."

"I know, Ray. I made it clear to her that what she did was
unforgivable. That the council would put her down if she
did something like that now." Oh, God, was there any way I
could make this deal with Lucky sound like something other
than disloyalty?

"Damn right they would." Ray ran a hand through his
hair. It was the same gesture Jerry made when he was agi-
tated. No, couldn't think about *him* now.

"She was contacted by Ian about our blood. Since I sired
her, she really does have my Siren blood. Some crone in Tran-
sylvania took one whiff and told her it's special. Then Ian let
her know there's something hinky going on with her blood
too. She's desperate to get the goods on it." I reached for
Ray but he stepped back. "I feel like maybe I owe her an
explanation."

"Seriously? You owe that bitch something? I owe her too.
A stake through her black heart." Ray walked over to the
piano and slammed the lid shut, the noise making me jump.
"Damn it, Glory, if you help that woman, I will take it as a
personal betrayal." He wouldn't look at me but stared out at
the lake where a speedboat roared across the dark water.

"Ray." I fought back the urge to cry. He was right. I
couldn't make any kind of deal with Lucky. I was tearing up
her check. Letting her know I wasn't honoring her stupid
contract. What could she do about it? Do to *me*? Yes, she had
thugs, but I wasn't about to be intimidated into anything.
I had powers now. And I'd go to the vampire council for
help if I had to. They didn't like loan sharks hanging out in
Austin.

"So are you? Going to help Lucky?" Ray finally turned
around and walked over to look me right in the eye.

"No. I can't do that to you, Ray. I wish now I'd had a
stake in my hands when she came to see me. She caught me
off guard or I'd never . . ." I slid my arms around him and

held on. "I'm so sorry. That I was tempted for even a moment to take her money."

He shoved me away and stared at me. "She offered you money? Why? To be her mentor?"

"Something like that." I wanted to cut off my own unruly tongue. Why had I said that?

"Why do you need money? Is the shop in trouble?" Ray kept his distance.

"No. It's doing okay." I wanted to be honest with him. I owed Ray that much. "I was, uh, thinking about going to Scotland."

"Well, shit. Of course. To chase after Blade." Ray's bitter laugh pierced my heart. "Why the hell not? You afraid the Siren whammy isn't strong enough to pull him back across an ocean and half a continent, Glory girl?" He stalked across the room and pulled out a bottle of synthetic blood from the small fridge in the bar. He drained it, then threw the bottle against the wall where it shattered. "Fuck. When will I ever learn?"

"That was before last night, Ray. I would never do that now. Not after we—"

"I get it. Now you've got the guilts. Can't go crawling to Blade with me on your conscience." Ray picked up his cell phone from the coffee table and hit speed dial. "I need a delivery. The special blend. Yeah, I'm sure. Don't give me a speech, just do it." He hung up and tossed the phone onto a cushioned chair. "Now, where were we?"

"What did you just do, Ray?" I ran over and grabbed his phone. I hit redial. "Who is this?"

"It's Damian. Who is this?"

"Glory, Damian. What did Ray just order?" I knew Damian supplied many vampires with high-end synthetic blood, not the cheap stuff I ordered on the Internet.

"The blood with alcohol, Glory. I tried to talk him out of it." Damian sighed. "I know his history. My sister asked me not to fill his orders again. But I am a businessman. You should understand."

"Yes, I do. Go ahead. I'm not his mother." I ended the call then threw the phone against the same wall the bottle had crashed against. "You fucking idiot! Is that language you understand?"

"Why, Glory, I believe that's the first time I've heard you use that word." Ray just grinned and sat on the couch like he didn't care that he'd just shattered my heart along with that bottle. "Bet it won't be the last. And, no, you're not my mother. As last night proved, in spades."

"Bastard. Fool. What do I have to do to get you to treat yourself right?" I sat beside him and buried my face in my skirt. His hand landed on my back.

"I don't know. Kill Lucky for me?"

I jerked as if he'd taken a stake to me. I knew he wasn't kidding. I sat up and faced him. "I don't kill people. Not now."

"Neither do I. Or I didn't until now. But I wouldn't shed a tear if Lucky fell on a stake." Ray leaned back and stared at me, his eyes hard now with no sign of the lover in them. "Seriously, something needs to be done. Justice, that's what I'm after. She can't get away with what she did to me."

"Yes, we could call it murder. She killed you, then brought you back to this life you hate so much." I put my hand on his bare knee. At least he didn't slap it away. "I told her that. Let her know I despised her for it."

"Well, I'm sure that broke her heart." Ray put his hand over mine and gripped it. "Damn it, Glory, you know she's been gloating about it since then. That she stole my daylight. She knew exactly how important that part of my life was to me, even back then. We spent hours at the beach the summer I thought I was in love with her." He shook his head. "I can use the excuse that I was young, a kid. But hooking up with Lucky Carver was the biggest mistake of my life."

"You sure paid for it." I hated for Ray to relive that mess with Lucky. And it was just the kind of trigger to get him back on the alcohol. Even one drink could start him on a spiral that could quickly get out of control. His buddy Nate and I had both done our best to watch him when he went on one of his benders before. But he was right—I wasn't his mother. And Nate wasn't his father.

Ray had to decide for himself that life was worth living. But with the alcohol in his system, he had no judgment. I kept imagining him staggering outside again when the sun came up. I squeezed his hand and let him see how terrified I was for him.

"You really don't want me to get into the alcohol again, do you?" Ray pinned me with a sharp gaze.

"No, you can't control it. You know as well as I do that you're an addict. Sorry if that sounds harsh, but it's the truth as I see it." I wasn't about to break eye contact and was glad to see that he was really listening, not already thinking about the drink coming his way. Of course I read his mind, there was a lot riding on the next few moments. "You're healthier and happier when you're off the sauce. That song you've been working on? No way could you have produced genius like that under the influence."

He closed his eyes, thinking I hoped. I cut him a break and left him to his thoughts. When he finally opened his eyes again I saw resignation and I put my hand on his leg again.

"Ray?"

"If I cancel that order, it's because I want to, not because you told me to." His mouth quirked, like he was trying not to smile. "You broke my phone."

"You can borrow mine." I grabbed my purse off the coffee table and dug my cell out. "Damian's number is in there." My hand shook as I held it out to him.

"How about a reward?" Ray glanced at the phone then at me, his eyes taking a leisurely path down my body. "For taking your advice?"

"That could be arranged." I slid my hand up his bare leg and inside the hem of those shorts. I ran a fingertip along his firming interest in my proposition.

"Don't suppose you'd play first?" His hand was now under my skirt where he discovered my lack of underwear.

"No way." I hit speed dial for Damian. When he answered, I handed the phone to Ray.

"Cancel my order. Glory's talked me out of it." Ray grinned as he eased a finger inside me. "Yeah, she can be pretty persuasive." He ended the call, tossed the phone aside and then covered my mouth with his.

I didn't bother to think about what we were doing or whether this was right or wrong or consequences. With Ray I was all about wonderful feelings and the excitement of surprises. This time it was a slow sensual hum of my senses as Ray sang his way from one end of my body to the other.

I'd lost my own song. I hadn't had time to really think about that. I'd once been able to sing as wonderfully as Aggie did. When she sang everyone stopped to listen and felt compelled to follow her. Like that old fairy tale where the mice trailed along behind the Pied Piper. As I listened to Ray's hum of satisfaction while he played my body like a master, I tried to sing along in my mind. It was hopeless. I had no music in me. The miracle was that I still had any Siren magic at all. It made me wonder how that was possible. I needed to talk to Aggie. Sooner rather than later.

I almost quit thinking as Ray plucked the strings of my heart and love vibrated through me. It occurred to me that he wasn't pressuring me to drink my blood. What did that mean? Ian said my blood was addictive, that it gave men a boost. Was Ray immune because he had enough of mine in him already?

I abandoned the puzzle as he moved over me with a grin. This man was so special. And he'd even forgiven me for consorting with his enemy. But Lucky was still out there to be dealt with. My last thought before I lost my mind completely was that I hoped I never saw her again.

Sixteen

Of course Lucky was waiting for me when I got home. Too much to hope that she wouldn't be. She posted her bodyguards outside my door before turning to me with a knowing smirk.

"Geez. Look at you. Still in last night's clothes and reeking of sex. Blade? Or Israel Caine?" She plopped into a chair. "Caine, of course. You had to go running over there to warn him that the big bad bitch is back, didn't you?"

"He was hot to stake you, but I talked him down. Only because I didn't want him to have a hassle with the vampire council here. They might not like him staking another vamp, even one who *really* deserves to die." I headed into my bedroom and slammed my door. I was determined to change clothes, sick of feeling inferior in the fashion department around Lucky. I stripped off, pulling out fresh underwear and slipping into it in record time. Next I found my most expensive designer sweater, secondhand of course, and a flattering pair of black pants. When I felt ready I opened the door and walked back into the living room.

"That was quite a speech. Bottom line, Caine's not coming

after me?" Lucky gave me a good, long look. "Decent, though skinny jeans would have been better."

"I hate skinny jeans." Because I couldn't get them up past my thighs without a struggle. "Besides, my fashion choices are not on the agenda. Let's get this over with. Did you go see Ian?" I headed to the kitchen for a bottle of synthetic.

"Yes, he's testing my blood. Hot guy. He'll know tomorrow night if we're a match. I don't see why we wouldn't be." She sighed and nodded toward my bottle. "You going to offer me one of those?"

"Not hardly." I showed her the label.

She wrinkled her nose. "Gah. I only drink premium brands anyway. Now tell me more about this Siren thing. Any powers go along with the blood?"

"Don't know. Wouldn't tell you if I did."

"Talking to Ray really got a bug up your butt, didn't it?" Lucky sniffed.

I just sipped my drink and decided to test one of my so-called powers. I reached out with my mind. Of course Lucky's thoughts were blocked. I tried to punch through that block and bam! I made it. I saw her startled look as I read that she was bored in Austin and needed to get back to New York. Ian had made a pass and she'd played it coy. Now she was aggravated and confused. Siren magic or Lucky as usual?

"What the hell did you just do?" She aimed a shaky finger at me.

"Pushed through your mental block. How'd you like it?" I grinned and set my bottle on the coffee table. "Ta da! Siren power."

"I don't believe you. What was I thinking?" She grabbed her tablet out of her purse and turned it on.

"For one thing, when Ian made a pass at you, you didn't know if it was the Siren thing or if he was really attracted to you. It pissed you off." I crossed my legs like this was no big deal.

"I'll be damned." Lucky tapped in notes.

"Maybe it's from my Siren blood. Or it could be a holdover from when I had a demon inside me. My life's been a nonstop party since you've been gone, Lucky."

She crossed herself. "A demon? I hope you got rid of it."

"Let's get down to business, Lucky." I stood and loomed over her, clearly startling her. "Yes, you probably have Siren blood and I don't give a damn if you do. Because I swore to Ray that I would not, under any circumstances, help you. And I will definitely not take money from you. *Capite?*"

"What did you just say to me?" Lucky jumped to her feet.

"The deal is off." I pulled her check out of my purse and ripped it in half. "Forget it. I won't mentor you. Not for any amount of money. Ray's friendship means too much to me."

"We have a contract." Her face turned red and she fisted her hands. Was she actually going to get violent about this? I zipped across the room in a vamp move as I read her thoughts. No, she wasn't, but her "boys" were about to.

"You know what you can do with your contract and it won't do you any good to call in the troops. I have a weapon now that will make them useless." I smiled and leaned against the wall next to the kitchen.

"Oh, yeah? I'd like to see that." Lucky stalked over to jerk open the door. "Get in here. We've got a deadbeat. Show her how we deal with those."

"You got it, boss." Bodyguard number one, who could have been a poster boy for steroid use and a bench press championship, ambled toward me. I had him frozen in place before he'd taken two steps.

"What the—" Lucky glanced at her second guy. "Get her."

The second bodyguard nudged his partner then, obviously puzzled by his lack of response, shrugged one massive shoulder and started toward me. I let him get pretty close, playing with him, before I turned him to stone.

"How'd you like that demo, Lucky? Impressive, isn't it?" I dusted off my hands, like I'd just finished a messy piece of work. I strolled around the men to admire what I'd done. "When I thaw them, I want you to take them and get the hell out of here."

"Hold it. That statue trick. Is that because of the Siren blood? You think I could do it?" Lucky grabbed her purse, going for that damned tablet again.

"Maybe, though it could have come from the demon." I grinned when Lucky dropped her purse and crossed herself again. "I've even had personal business with Lucifer. Seems he took a shine to me." I glanced at my wooden floor. "Maybe the Siren allure works on the Devil too."

"Blasphemy! I won't listen to this. But turning people into statues. I just bet a Siren can do it. I want to know how." Lucky picked up her purse again.

"Then you'll have to work with another Siren because I'm not telling you a damned thing." I pointed at her men. "I'm counting to three then thawing these fireplugs. Take them and get out. Or do you want to become part of my decorating scheme too?"

"You wouldn't." Lucky narrowed her eyes.

"Wouldn't I? Imagine being stuck where you stand, not able to even blink. I've been paralyzed like that more than once and it's hell. Once I was on a boat and almost fell overboard." Her eyes widened. "Yeah. Imagine going under water and you can't do anything to save yourself." I shivered, remembering. "How would you like a long walk off a short pier, Lucky?"

"We're going. But this isn't over. No one welches on a deal with Lucky Carver and gets away with it." She threw her purse strap over her shoulder and opened the door. "Thaw 'em. I'm out of here."

"Good. Just remember that I'm stronger than you are, Lucky. As your sire my blood is way more potent. You might think you can do what I can do, but I doubt it." I thawed her men and she ordered them out to the hall when they cursed and started toward me like they were planning to take me apart.

"We'll just see about that, won't we?" Lucky huffed and puffed then strutted out the door and down the stairs.

I slammed the door and leaned against it. Trying to out-bitch a bitch had plain worn me out. When there was a knock almost immediately, I admit I jumped.

"Glory, it's Laurie. I waited until your company left. Are you okay in there?"

I threw open the door. "Yes, fine. But am I glad to see you." I sagged against the door frame. "A few minutes ago I might have asked you to shift into your tiger. God, I hate that woman who just left. That was the infamous Lucky Carver."

"Ray's enemy. Glad I got a look at her." Laurie looked thoughtful. "He told me you sired her. But the way she stomped out of here, I'd say there's no love lost between you two."

"Ray probably also shared how she turned him vampire against his will, then dumped him on me." I paced the room, finally collapsing on the couch. "Sit. Can I get you any-thing?"

"I'd ask if you have any meat left but I know you don't." Laurie grinned. "I cleaned you out when I left."

"You were welcome to it." I sighed. "This Lucky thing. It's a war now. She wanted me to act like her sire and teach her about Sirens. But I promised Ray I wouldn't do it." I put my feet on the coffee table, something I usually forbid any-one to do. At this point I could care less about my furniture. "Anyway, Lucky and I had a contract and I just broke it. To Lucky a contract is sacred so now she's out for my blood." I grimaced. "Well, you know what I mean."

"Sure I do. Her type can't stand to lose anything. She has to think she put something over on you." Laurie got up and wandered into the kitchen. She came out with a pint of Chunky Monkey ice cream and a spoon. "May I?"

"Go ahead. I can't eat it. Rafe's not coming over now, so it's up for grabs." I rubbed my forehead. "When you left Ray was he still okay? Not rethinking that order for alcohol was he?"

"No, he was working on a new song, though this one

wasn't upbeat like what he had been playing. You learn quickly in that job to gauge Ray's mood by the tunes that come out of there. This stuff you two are going through has brought him down. I won't pretend he's not struggling. The guards are all talking about it." Laurie swallowed a spoonful of ice cream. "To change the subject—since you're keeping away from Rafe, I guess that means he's fair game."

"Sure. But will it do any good? If he's under a Siren's spell, can he actually break free of it?" I was up again, collecting my empty bottle and going back for a new one. I glanced at Laurie. So she was going to make a run at Rafe. Why not? Like I'd noticed before, they'd be good together. And I had no right to be jealous. No right. "I need to talk to Aggie. Get some details. Of course the men she traps with her song never have an opportunity to pull free, they're doomed."

"Aggie would say each man dies with a smile on his face." Laurie sighed. "Sirens are a different breed, Glory. You can ask Aggie for help, but I'm not sure what she'll offer. They don't have much heart." She smiled. "Not like you. I got to know you well enough to see that Achelous had a good reason to toss you out of their club. You're way too humane for that gang."

"Well, thanks." I smiled back. It was a relief to hear from someone objective.

"As for Rafe." She took another bite of ice cream. "Time will tell, I guess."

And time for a subject change. "What's up with you and Circe, Laurie? That was quite a trick you pulled, bringing her to the meeting the other night. How'd you manage it?"

"I have my ways." The were-tiger played with her spoon. "Circe and I have a connection. I knew she had some old issues with Achelous so when you told me what was going down, I called her, told her the deal. She was eager to get into it with us."

"Obviously I was just a pawn in her little game with him." I twisted off the top of my fresh bottle. It was some of my expensive stash that I hadn't wanted to bring out in front of Lucky. "It's great that she cared about his Sirens, but he's still treating them like his personal slaves. I don't know how Aggie stands it century after century." I took a swallow and savored the smooth slide of the rich liquid down my throat. "I realize now how lucky I was to escape, even if I did lose my song and love of the water."

"Those are big losses. But when he wiped your memory, Achelous actually did you a huge favor. Think how horrible you would have felt all these years, wanting what you couldn't have." Laurie and I were quiet for a few moments, each thinking deep thoughts.

Finally, I spoke my thoughts out loud. "But why did he leave me with any powers at all? I obviously can still draw men to me, can freeze people in their tracks and burst through mind blocks. Maybe I can do even more. I'll have to talk to Aggie about that. The bottom line is that I have plenty of good stuff inside me that Achelous didn't take."

Laurie moved over to sit beside me. She put her hand on my shoulder and stared into my eyes. "Seriously? I think Achelous did all he could do to you, Glory. He couldn't reach any deeper. And that, my friend, is news that Aggie and the sisterhood really should hear. You might hold the key to their freedom."

We smiled at each other. Yes, Achelous was a bastard and I'd like nothing more than to pay him back for what he'd done to me. Free the Sirens? Suddenly I had a plan.

It was a beautiful night, not a cloud in the sky, but I still shivered. Maybe because I was on the shore next to a lake again. Too many memories haunted me as I stared out at the calm water. That boat ride when Ray and I had met Aggie in the first place. Achelous's temper tantrum on a terrace not far from here. I could go on. But tonight I'd called Aggie and arranged a meeting. Without telling Ray about it. He wouldn't like it when he heard, but this was *my* business. I'd give him a report later if there was anything he needed to know.

A quiet splash signaled that my date had arrived. Aggie emerged from the lake, for once bothering with a bathing suit. I knew she didn't usually hide her assets when she was out trolling for victims. How, I didn't know. Instinct I guess. Had she killed someone tonight?

"Quit staring at me like I'm some evil creature from a horror flick." Aggie wrung out her wet hair, blinked and she was dry and dressed in a pair of skinny jeans and a snug red T-shirt. Her hair was dry too and it was beautiful, with golden waves down her back.

"Neat trick. Why didn't you use it the other night when we were with Achelous?"

"I was going for his sympathy. Not that I got any." She frowned. "And I hoped the wet look would take his mind off my misdeeds."

"Snooping for my records in the archives?" I sat down on the blanket I'd brought along. "You've got to know the kill numbers you trotted out blew my mind." I stared down at my hands. "God, so many." I looked at her again. "How can you deny you're evil, Aggie?"

"You used to kill too. Though your numbers were puny." Aggie sat across from me. She materialized a leather bag and pulled out a compact and lipstick. "Guess we're both evil. Deal with it."

"I'm trying to." Not that I was making any progress. Killing for sport? I just couldn't imagine being part of that. I swallowed a nausea that had been with me ever since I'd found out I'd been like her once, able to kill and then just . . . powder my nose before looking for my next victim. God. I tried not to let her see how much all this was getting to me and lifted my chin. "Achelous is a piece of work. You really have to debase yourself like that every time you meet with him?"

Aggie closed the compact with a snap. "I pander to his

ego. It's a game the Sirens play, to keep the peace. I don't appreciate your attitude."

"Sorry if I'm upsetting you." Of course it had humiliated her that we'd seen her cowed by that god. The Aggie who strutted around Austin in her designer duds took no prisoners.

"Like you could." She tossed her hair, determined to play the tough girl.

"Yeah, well, humor me. I have questions about myself. And maybe an answer for you. We could exchange information—if you care to share." I put my hand on her arm. This was important, and I knew she could tell me to just stuff it and take off at any moment.

"I came here, didn't I? I've actually felt kind of sorry for you, Gloriana. The sisters and I talked about you. We realize Achy did you dirty. All of us have had bad seasons when our numbers were down. The idea that he could toss any one of us out and wipe our memories? Hon, it's sickening." Aggie shuddered then carefully put away her lipstick and compact. "So I'll cut you some slack. What do you want to know?"

"First, about my blood. I've made a vampire, then she turned Ray, Israel Caine. They have Siren blood now. Will that give them any Siren powers?"

"Don't they wish. But we don't get our power from the blood, it comes through the mind and the body." Aggie ran her hands down her own perfect shape. "Which is one reason I was so freaked when Circe cursed me that time and took my beauty away. Bitch. But I have to admit she came through for us the other night. Women should stick together. Tell Ray and that other vamp they get nada, zip, from their Siren blood." Aggie grinned. "Except maybe a little status. It's a rare thing, don't you know."

"Of course." I hit her hand when she offered it for a high five. Why not? She was right. But it made me wonder about Ian's claims. Clarity. If nothing came from blood, then how could he make a drug from it? I'd have to think about that later. Right now I had Aggie here and more questions.

"We'll have to experiment to see what powers you've got now. This vampire change is bound to have done a number on your abilities." Aggie frowned at me.

"Well, I've still got my body and my mind, even if my memory's shot. I've figured out that I can turn people to statues, just like you can. Alesa the demon showed me that one. And blast through mind blocks, though anyone more powerful than I am seems to be able to stand up to me on that score." I made an attempt to read Aggie's mind and hit a wall.

"You'd better believe I can resist your little foray into Aggieland, sweetie. But you can resist me too, when I come at you. Firm your wall. Not even I can read past your block if you're really determined to keep me out. Try it." She focused on my face.

I threw up the Great Wall of China then thought about Ray and how we'd made love. I saw Aggie frown as she concentrated and actually felt her shoving at the barrier.

"Nice job, Glo. I think you've got it." She turned to look at the lake. "Still scared of the water?"

"Terrified. Achelous must have planted that idea in my head." I looked out at the reflection of a moon on the shimmering surface but didn't see beauty, only danger hidden beneath the water. "I don't suppose we can do anything about that."

"Doubt it. He's a real son of a bitch." Aggie sighed. "And he took your song. That's a killer. But surely . . ." She stared at me for a moment. "Try to sing. Right now. I want to hear what you've got." Aggie leaned back on her elbows.

"Seriously, you don't. I can't carry a tune. It's pathetic." I shook my head but she just kept her eyes on me, daring me. "Okay, you asked for it." I raised my chin and belted out one of Ray's love songs. I knew every word and had sung along to his CDs in the privacy of my car and in the shower. But I knew my efforts were painful to listen to. I didn't even make it to the chorus before Aggie stopped me.

"Please!" Aggie had covered her ears. "You make it hard to believe you were ever a Siren. Girl, this is the worst. Achy should go to hell for what he did to you."

"It's odd, but I don't miss singing. Ray's about to go into a deep depression over it. As an artist, he says it's 'tragic.'"

"Ray's right. It is." Aggie wiped at a tear and cursed fluently in several languages. "Wait till I tell the sisters. This is unforgivable. We each have our own special song and it *defines* us. It's our signature, I guess you could say. Damn it. Achelous took your identity, Gloriana."

I felt tears pop into my own eyes but blinked them back. Wait a minute. I didn't need a song to know who I was, did I? I'd managed to create a life, make friends, develop a personality and all without singing a single note.

"It's okay, Aggie. I've coped, but it wasn't always easy. Luckily, I did have help along the way. Not sisters, of course. Like you do." I couldn't believe it when Aggie actually patted my hand.

"They're my family, Glo. It's a shame Achy cast you out without one." She sniffed, then pulled out her compact again.

"How does the sisterhood work? Aren't you scattered all over the world?" I leaned back on the blanket.

"We communicate telepathically." She tapped her head. "Though we can get together in a blink of an eye. Doubt you can teleport. It takes a pretty powerful psychic connection to each other to get us into a group. And an emergency. We're too vulnerable when we're, um, clustered." Aggie appraised me. "I feel funny sharing Siren secrets with you, Gloriana. You're one of us, but you're not. Swear to me right now that this stuff stays with us. Or I'll hunt you down, girl. And you know I can make your life a living hell."

I held out my hand. "Aggie, I never had a sister that I remember. And a group of murdering Sirens isn't exactly what I had in mind. But I won't betray you. I'm here to help you. Other than the powers I've already showed people, what we say here, stays here." We shook hands and I let Aggie read my mind to reassure her.

"Okay then. What else do you want to know?" She seemed to finally relax.

"This one is really serious. Do you think I'm still drawing men to me? Achelous claimed I was. Putting them under my Siren's spell." I looked out over the water until I got the urge to cry under control. "I think that Jerry, Rafe, and even Ray only love me because I've enchanted them."

"Achelous is a freaking liar, Glo." Aggie sat up straight and grabbed my hand. "Listen to me and listen good. A Siren draws men to her with her song. Since you lost yours when Achy threw you away, you have never, since that day, been able to enchant anyone. Got it?"

I shook my head. "Are you sure? I mean how does that explain . . . ?"

"I know my business, Gloriana. I've been doing it for over a thousand years. I can walk the streets anywhere and men might look twice because, honey, I *am* hot. But they are not enchanted by any stretch. Not until I sing my song. Got it?" She squeezed my hand then let it go.

"I, I don't know. I have evidence. Jerry's stayed with me for *centuries*. And Rafe. He won't give up on me, even though I begged him to take off and find someone else."

Aggie looked me up and down. "Men are funny creatures. Sometimes I even hesitate to kill them." She waved a hand. "Oh, I get over it and do my duty, but honestly, Glo, you must have something special that they love." She shuddered. "Hate that word."

"You don't ever love anyone?" I focused on her, not trying to read her mind, but her emotions. I realized there was a deep core of sadness inside that shell of bravado and kick-ass Aglaophonos.

"No point. The guy's gonna bite it. Can't get attached. Tried it a time or two and it didn't end well. You remember when you met me?" Aggie gave me a lopsided grin. "Circe had cursed me, made me look like a monster. And it was over a man, Glo. Lesson learned. I won't go through that again.

Fun and games only for me from now on. Unless I'm working of course."

"Okay, I get it. And I'm sorry." I really was, even though for myself I was struggling not to laugh and dance along the shore I was so relieved. I hadn't whammied my guys! How about that?

Aggie picked up a rock and tossed it into the water, staring at the ripples it made. "Are we done now?"

"No, not yet." I waited until I had her complete attention. "You and the sisters have served Achelous all these years because you're afraid of him. Right?"

Aggie plucked at a loose string in the blanket. "I guess you could say that. We needed a leader and he's it. He offers us protection."

"From what, Aggie? You look pretty self-sufficient to me." I saw I'd hit a nerve.

"You don't remember how it is on Olympus, Gloriana. Sirens . . . We aren't part of your world. We're . . ." Aggie shook her head. "Never mind. You can't come back to us. He did make you mortal somehow and now you're vampire. There are some things I can't share with you."

"Olympus stuff?"

"Maybe." Aggie stared out at the lake, like she was about to leave me where I sat.

"Just listen for a minute. Achelous's protection seems to come at too high a price. I'm a prime example of how he treats women who don't fall in line with his policies." I waited until she looked at me again. "You want to chance losing your song and your love of the sea?"

"No, hell no." Aggie's face told the story. She was appalled.

"Then you need to get away from him. Instead of being in his harem, where you have to do God knows what when he calls for you, why not defect? I bet Circe wouldn't mind being in charge of the Sirens. If you really feel like you need a god or goddess to protect you."

"What a radical thought. Circe shares the man-hater thing so our mission statements align. But she has her own issues— remember me as a sea monster? Still, another woman . . . Yeah, I like it." Aggie jumped to her feet. "If Achelous got wind of a plot like this though? I can't imagine . . ."

"If you band together, all of you, what can he do? Destroy the sisterhood? Surely he wouldn't do that. How would that play on Olympus?"

"Not too well. We have something of a reputation up there. And ties to some pretty important people. The sisters have always spread our favors around where it counts if you know what I mean." Aggie winked at me. "It's just good politics. But if Achy's listening in right now . . ." Aggie bowed her head, obviously doing some listening of her own. "No, he's still up there with Circe in front of Zeus. I heard they've got a battle royal going. But he'll be back soon." She grinned at me. "Clever girl. Now I've got a going-away present for you. One more power for you to try from your Siren arsenal. Let's see if your vampire body can manage this one. It's what they call mind over matter."

"Seriously? What is it?" I was up and ready for anything.

"You ever dematerialize?" Aggie said just before she disappeared.

"No. You mean I could?" I jumped when Aggie suddenly appeared behind me.

"Possibly. Achy brainwashed you. I'm pretty sure, with a good shrink, you could actually get back some memories. Like your love of the sea and your song." Aggie's hand landed on my back. "Go see Ian. He's a genius at that kind of thing. We didn't just have pillow talk. He's a brilliant psychiatrist."

"Good to know. But I think Ian has been lying to me about something big." Did I want my song back? No way in hell. I glanced at the water a few feet away and felt a sudden longing. It would be wonderful to be able to swim again, to cut through the water and feel the sea claim me as one of her own. "Now about this dematerializing thing. Tell me how.

And I wouldn't mind being able to create outfits and dry hair either."

"That, my sister, I'm afraid might be beyond you." But Aggie did share secrets and they were remarkably simple. Then she took off, obviously eager to discuss her thoughts on rebellion with her sisters. I sat back on the blanket and stared at the lake. So the men in my life were there because they chose to be. I knew what I needed to do next. I gathered up the blanket and skipped to my car. I'd love to sing my joy but knew better. And that was okay.

I could hear the music as soon as I drove up to Ray's front door. Laurie was on duty and took my keys from me.

"I'll put it in the garage if you're staying the day." She grinned at me.

"No, leave it out front. I'm not sure how this is going to go." I leaned against the trunk. "I met with Aggie. Ray's going to be disappointed by what I found out. He's not getting anything from his Siren blood."

"I don't think that matters. He's got a connection to you anyway, Glory." Laurie tossed my keys back to me. "He's been singing about you all evening. Or at least that's what it sounds like to me."

I cocked my head and listened. Ray's song was about a woman who couldn't make music. It was a ballad with a refrain that made you want to cry into your Bloody Mary. I hoped I could cheer him up and out of that mood.

"That won't do. Too much of that angst and he'll be ordering alcohol again." I tucked my keys into my purse. "Any sign of trouble tonight?"

"No more than usual. A paparazzo climbed up from the lake and got a picture of Ray strutting around the living room in his black silk boxers. I had fun smashing that guy's camera and tossing him in the water. Then a couple of thirtysomething housewives tried to climb the fence for an autograph.

Ray came out and obliged before we ran them off." Laurie's smile was tigerish.

"You look like you're enjoying this job." I headed for the front door.

"I am. And it doesn't hurt my feelings that Ray does parade around in a little bit of nothing most of the time." She fanned her face. "The man has quite a body. But I don't need to tell you that."

"No, you don't." I was grinning as I walked in the house and dropped my purse on the entry table. Ray kept playing though I knew he saw me enter the living room. The drapes were closed for a change. Probably because of that incident with the photographer.

"Nice tune." I settled on the couch. "But I'm not feeling it."

He stopped playing. "You have news for me?" He jumped up and strode to the couch. He'd put on jeans, probably when he'd made the housewives' night. Now he sat beside me and pulled me in for a quick kiss.

"Maybe, but you'll have to do better than that to worm it out of me." I brushed my thumb across his lips.

"I can handle that." He lowered his head and took my mouth in a leisurely way that curled my toes. Before I knew it I was stretched out on that long leather sofa and he was on top of me.

"Mmm. Ray, I think I'm ready to talk." I ran my hands over his bare back, savoring the ripple of muscle there. He'd worked out before he'd been turned and it showed.

"Forget it. Talk can wait." He pushed up my sweater and smiled when he saw my leopard print bra. "I like this. You came ready to play."

"Maybe." I sighed when he licked the edges of the demicups then nosed them down to circle my aching nipples. "You are very good at this. I'm happy to tell you that it's not the Siren blood that's doing it's magic. You can take total credit in the seduction department."

"Really?" Ray didn't even bother to look up, too intent on unfastening my jeans and easing them down. I had worn a scrap of black lace that made him growl. "Been talking to Aggie without me?"

"Yeah, woman to woman. Oh, Ray." He'd kissed his way down to delve into my navel, then slipped my panties down along with my jeans. They got hung up on my thighs. Ray didn't push them farther, just used them to hold me while he kissed and licked me with a master's expertise.

"So my Siren blood doesn't count for anything?" He rolled me from side to side until he could get those jeans down enough to part my legs even farther. "There's what I'm after." He bent his head and used his hands to open me to his mouth.

"It, um, counts to, oh, make you, ee, unique." I gasped and trembled on the verge of climax. "There are so few of— oh my God!—you."

"Just me and Lucky." Ray sat up and tore off his clothes. My jeans and sweater were the next to go. "And you, of course. What does your blood do, Gloriana?" He pulled me to my feet and to the middle of the enormous room. What did he have in mind? The piano bench? The hot tub bubbling on the terrace? That one made me shudder. Or was he going to drag me down to the black and white rug and finish this there? For a moment we just faced each other, both of us naked. He was perfect. Me? Not even close.

"Nothing. I can't draw men to me, Ray. Only my song can and I don't have it. Isn't that great news?" I waited, not sure for what, and rested my hands on his shoulders.

"So what I'm feeling for you is real?" He ran a fingertip from my shoulder to my breast to my hip.

I shivered and ran my fingertip down the same path on his body. "I'm not sure exactly what you feel for me, Ray, but it's not some kind of Siren magic. It's just me, Gloriana, here. Chubby thighs and all." I flushed and realized that was a damned stupid thing to say. Now, of course, he'd look at them,

judge them and compare them to the model-slim thighs he'd
seen and screwed in Hollywood and all over the world.

He dropped to his knees in front of me. "I love your thighs.
They're strong and grip me hard when I'm between them."
He ran a row of kisses along each one. "And I love you.
Damned if I don't." He pulled me down to the rug and on top
of him. "Make love with me, Glory girl. I need you."

"Ray." My voice shook as I dropped down in front of him
and kissed him with my heart in it. "I love you."

"I know that this may be the last time we're together like
this." He lay back and pulled me on top of him. "I'm not an
idiot."

"The last . . ." I stretched until my toes tangled with his,
my body savoring the feel of his against every inch. His hard
shaft nudged me and I opened my legs. But he didn't try to
take me yet.

"Blade, Glory. I know you still want to see him. To clear
things up with him." Ray pushed his fingers into my hair.
"He left here thinking you trapped him, didn't he?"

"Yes." I kept my eyes on Ray's, not about to deny that.
"His pride was terribly hurt."

"I'm gonna hurt too, when you're gone." He pulled my
head down to kiss me deeply then rolled us until he was on
top, looking down at me.

"Where am I going, Ray?" I wrapped my legs around his
hips and moaned as he pushed inside me. I wanted him,
couldn't wait for that glorious movement that would take us
out of ourselves and into that special place where nothing
mattered but pleasure. Why did he have to bring up such
serious matters now?

"Scotland, of course. It's necessary." Ray began to move,
thrusting deep so that I felt every inch of him. "But if he's
idiot enough to refuse to take you back?" His pace quickened
and he lifted my hips so I could feel just how strong and
right we were together. "Baby, you *will* come back to me.
Got it?"

I trembled, feeling the waves of pleasure crash on my shore

as he leaned down to take my vein. I raked his back with my nails and smelled his blood, similar to mine but with a salty difference that was as erotic as it was irresistible. I wanted that pull of his mouth on my neck, needed that pressure of his cock deep inside me and loved the words he whispered in my mind as the world disappeared and we held each other. Ray. He was sending me to Scotland.

Seventeen

I had to tell Rafe the good news too. That he wasn't one of my victims. But I couldn't do it while I was reeking of sex with Ray. I'd stayed and played and spent the day sacked out in Ray's arms. Then he'd arranged a chartered jet to Scotland for me. Got to love a man who'd do something like that when he knew I was going to see his rival. I admit I was misty-eyed as I kissed Ray good-bye, fully intending for it to be the last time before my trip.

I stopped at the apartment first and washed from head to toe to get every trace of Ray off of me. Rafe had a shifter's nose and I wasn't going to make this news any more challenging for him. When I walked into N-V, I didn't want to throw out any lures but a woman has her pride. My usual black pants were snug enough to be interesting and my red and black tunic top roomy enough to hide the tummy bulge that was finally almost gone. The red cheeks? At least the lighting at N-V was dim. I was really going to have to talk to Ian about that. And his lies about my blood.

I sidled up to the bartender and ordered some of the blood with alcohol. "Is Rafe around?"

"Sure is. Hang here and he'll be out in a minute. I called

him about a customer giving me some grief." Skip, the bartender, nodded down the long and crowded bar. Oh, I should have known. Who was parked on a bar stool, her thugs behind her, but Lucky? She was knocking back the high-octane blood and arguing with my friend Diana Marchand, the owner of Mugs and Muffins. Interesting that one of the thugs was a new guy, not a thick-necked shifter but a tall, dark and handsome vampire whose power could be felt even from where I stood, yards away. Can't say I liked that development.

"Let me guess. Trying to collect a debt?" I gestured toward Lucky. Other customers were easing away, trying to give the pair some space.

"You got it and the loud one wouldn't take it outside. Believe me, I tried." Skip grimaced and wiped down the bar. "Here comes the boss now."

Rafe smiled at me then looked down the bar and did a double take. "You've got to be kidding me. When did Lucky Carver hit town?"

"A few days ago. Still the same Lucky we love to hate." I knew that when Lucky saw me, she'd shift her attention. Diana would be grateful, but things might get ugly. "Can I talk to you in your office?"

"Not yet. I want her out of here." Rafe looked like he meant business, obviously excited by the prospect of tossing Lucky out on her ass.

"Be careful, Rafe. Her goons take their jobs seriously." I put a cautionary hand on his shoulder.

"I can handle this. Lucky. I'll be damned." Rafe squeezed my hand. "Be right back. Hang tight."

I followed him with some idea of offering backup. He stepped between Diana and Lucky and both women paused in their argument to scope him out appreciatively. He wore his usual uniform for work, one of those black T-shirts with the red N-V logo slashed across the front. Of course it fit like a well-worn glove. So did his jeans. Several other women at the bar were giving him the eye too. Diana used his arrival as a distraction and tried to slip away.

"Not so fast, lady. There's the matter of the money you owe me." Lucky latched onto Diana's arm and signaled her "boys." They moved in, blocking Diana's escape route. Lucky's new vampire put his hand on her back and she got a deer-in-headlights look. "You aren't leaving until I get something on account."

"I told you—" Diana obviously didn't have the money and glanced down like maybe a bag of cash with her name on it would magically appear at her feet.

"Hey, this isn't going to happen here." Rafe pried Diana's arm from Lucky's grip but kept a hand on Lucky. "Take it outside, Lucky."

"You know who I am?" Lucky smiled with lips expertly colored and lined with a bold coral. "How?" She shook her head when the guards made threatening rumbles and stared pointedly at Rafe's hold on their boss.

"I'm Valdez. I was there when you first arrived in town." Rafe's frown made it clear it wasn't a fond memory as he glanced at nearby mortals.

"My, oh, my. You shucked off the fur coat." Lucky caught my eye. "Nice."

Rafe gently pulled both women off their bar stools and to their feet. "Diana?"

"Can I go to the ladies' first?" She aimed a panicked look across the room.

Lucky firmed her lips. "Not unless one of my boys goes with you." She aimed a painted nail at Diana, who was already inching toward the exit. "She'd be out the back door if I let her go."

"I wouldn't—" But Diana wasn't a great liar.

"Okay, we keep it here but we keep it down." Rafe signaled the bartender, who picked up a phone. Within moments, the band announced a new set. That got the bar emptied as eager patrons hit the dance floor. "Diana, you owe Lucky money?"

Diana drained her glass then avoided Lucky's glare as she talked to Rafe. "Yes, stupid of me, but I did take out a loan when business got bad last summer." Diana glared at Lucky.

"This woman passed out cards before she left town last time, courting my business. When no bank would give me a loan, naturally I called her." Diana held on to her black clutch like it was a lifeline. "The terms are just horrid, Rafe, but what was I to do? I figured business would pick up and it did, but . . ." Diana was from the South and her drawl was becoming more obvious along with her distress.

Lucky held up her hand to cut her off. "Do I care why? No. Payment's three months overdue. So pay now or I take possession of your collateral." Lucky's smile was pure predator. No wonder they called them loan sharks. "I wouldn't mind owning a little coffee shop next to Glory's store." She glanced down the bar and gestured at me. "Don't hang back. Come join us, Glory. We could be neighbors. What do you think?"

I stepped to Rafe's side. "I think I'd help Diana sell her soul first."

Diana's gasp and Rafe's incredulous look let me know I'd just stepped in it. I guess my history with Lucifer and the demons was still too fresh to even joke about hell. Diana actually crossed herself. Lucky's new bodyguard cracked a smile and wasn't that interesting? The way he was studying me, though, was getting on my last nerve. Mr. Intensity might laugh at my jokes, but I didn't doubt he was ready to do whatever he had to for Lucky's protection. I ignored him.

"Hey, kidding! I'm just here to see Rafe. You really should go outside like he asked you." I smiled at Diana. "Sorry about your troubles. Why don't you call Damian? I'm sure he'd bail you out."

"I'm not asking him for money." Diana looked down at the floor again. I hated myself but read her mind anyway. She'd always believed that only whores asked their lovers for money. She'd tried to avoid that in her long, long life and she wasn't about to sink that low now. "He's such a great businessman and I . . . Well, I'm just not good with money. I tried to save but there always seemed to be an emergency."

"Sure, like a shoe sale at Nordstrom's." Lucky eyed Rafe

then got down to business. "I've done some digging, Diana. Don't give me any sob stories. If we wore the same size, I'd be taking those Prada slingbacks right off your pretty feet as a down payment." Lucky nodded and we all looked down.

Diana had on this season's suede peep toes and I knew they'd cost her several hundred dollars even on sale. I sure couldn't afford them. Hmm.

"You wouldn't—" Diana's cheeks were pink.

"Sure I would but, like I said, wrong size." Lucky winked at me. "Sounds like I'm getting that spot next to you, after all, Glory. I'll hire a decent manager, then, when I'm in town, we can hang out here together." She actually gave Rafe a hip bump. "Valdez, I like your little club."

Rafe dug into his back pocket. "Diana, how much do you need? For this first payment?"

Diana whispered to him and my eyes popped. She glanced at me. "The interest is terrible but I have bad credit. I told you, I don't handle my finances very well." She mumbled something about a shopping addiction.

"I'm not judging. You know I used to have a gambling problem. Totally blew my credit rating. There are twelve-step programs . . ." I caught Rafe's look. "Well, I highly recommend them. I know I had to reach bottom before I got that though." I couldn't believe that Rafe was writing out a check. Did he have that kind of cash to spare? I glanced around the club. It was doing well and had really caught on with the college crowd. Vampires too liked to have a place to hang out and I saw several at tables on the balcony with glasses of blood, probably with alcohol, in front of them.

"There, now get out, Lucky. Diana, you and I will talk later. This is a loan. With interest. Though not as high as what Lucky obviously charged you." Rafe began pulling Lucky toward the front door. The bodyguards stayed out of it when Lucky waved them off again.

"Rafe, wait!" Diana threw her arms around him. "Thank you!" She kissed his cheek. "I can't believe you did this for me."

"Not for you, Diana." Rafe stared at me. "I don't want Lucky planted next to Glory, or to have any reason to stay in town. Understand?"

"Oh, sure. I remember their history." Diana gave me a sympathetic smile. "Glory, I promise I'll pay back every penny. Like Rafe said, with interest."

"Can you stop a minute?" Lucky jerked her arm out of Rafe's grip. "Quit with the bum's rush. Maybe I want to hang out for a while. Drink and dance. Isn't my money good here?" She fluttered her eyelashes at Rafe.

"No way in hell." He looked grim. "Glory, what do you say?"

"Hit the road, Lucky." I turned toward the bar and picked up my drink, ignoring her squeal of outrage.

"You owe me, bitch. Don't think I'm letting this slide."

"Ms. Carver, you want we should handle this?" One of her guards, the thick-necked shifter, put his shoulder close to mine.

I heard Rafe growl before I turned to send Lucky a mental message. It would cause all kinds of problems, but I could make those boys of hers into statues here and now then take care of the fallout later. If she wanted to save face, she'd better move along. She got it.

"No, this is getting to be a bore. I have a date later anyway. Let's go." She twitched her hips and waited while the shifter rushed to open the door. Then she headed out into the night. Her vampire guard stopped and glanced back at me, catching my gaze. I read something dark and determined there that made me shiver before he disappeared into the night.

"What the hell is she doing in town?" Rafe took my arm and steered me toward his office.

"Ian contacted her. About her blood. She wanted to know what it meant." I waited until we were inside with the door closed. "I talked to Aggie. Seems unlikely it means anything. It's not the Siren blood that's important."

"Well, if you talked to Aggie, does that mean you found

out whether I'm under your spell?" Rafe moved close and slid his arms around my waist.

"Seems Sirens draw men to them with their song. I lost mine thanks to Achelous." I sighed and gently took his hands off of me. "So any feelings you have for me, Rafe, are purely your own."

"Never doubted it. But what about yours for me or any of the men orbiting planet Glory?" He frowned and sat on the edge of his messy desk. A few papers fell to the floor but he ignored them. "You say you love me. You love Blade. Hell, I've even heard you say you love the rock star. What does that mean to you, Glory? Seems to me you throw the word around a little too easily. Hell, you even love your new boots."

"You making fun of me? You have to know this whole Siren thing has put me through the wringer." Was I looking for sympathy? I could see by Rafe's expression that I wasn't getting any here. "And, for the record, I don't love my new boots. I just bought them because they were on sale."

"You know what I mean. Don't try to deflect. This Siren thing is just the latest wrinkle in the Glory-go-round." Rafe kicked a paper across the room. "Under a spell or not, I don't like hanging around waiting to see how your love life falls out." He crossed his arms over his chest. "Maybe I'm finally ready to jump off the ride."

"Rafe." I wished there was something I could say to get our old friendship back where it belonged. But Rafe had his pride and I'd hurt it. Damn. "I hope that loan to Diana wasn't just for my sake. To keep Lucky from moving in next to me." I wanted to touch him, say something to ease the tension he was clearly feeling. "I can handle Lucky and her goons."

"So I should just let you try?" Rafe moved closer. "Sorry, but I can't stand back and wait to see if you really can handle her. The Glory I know and love isn't exactly known for kicking butt." He smiled wryly. "So much for jumping off the ride. Obviously I'm still yours whether you want me or not."

I looked up into eyes that knew me too well, cared for me more than I deserved. I didn't want to lead him on.

"I appreciate everything you do, have done for me, Rafe. But you have to stop it. If I have problems, they're *my* problems and I have to deal with them. If I fail, then the fallout is on me, no one else." I laid my hand on his arm. His skin was hot, shifter hot. God, but I felt weak where he was concerned, wanting to lean on him and let him take care of me. Even now, it was all I could do not to rest my head against his broad chest.

"Maybe I'm finally getting the message, Glory. You keep pushing me away, telling me to move on." He stared at the ceiling, his jaw tight, then looked at me again. "I get pissed and feel like saying to hell with you. No woman is worth what you put me through. But then I see you and all those good intentions evaporate. Damn it, I keep thinking I'm right for you, that we make a great team. And someday you'll realize that and decide my time will come again."

"Rafe, I can't—I won't—" I shut up, not sure what to say to him. He was the best friend I'd ever had. He'd taken care of me, guarded me, risked his life for me. I did love him. And he was right. He wasn't the only man I loved. The Siren in me didn't seem to be built for monogamy.

"You are really blocking your thoughts. Maybe I don't want to know what you're thinking." Rafe scrubbed his hands over his face.

"Maybe you don't. I can't make any sense out of this anymore." I pulled his hands away to run my fingers over his jaw, so strong and masculine. "I'm a mess right now, Rafe. And one thing I need to do is straighten things out with Jerry. I'm going to Scotland. To let him know that he's not under that Siren's spell. I don't know if that will make a difference to him, but it's something I have to do."

"Blade. He's always first with you, isn't he?" Rafe pulled me to him and, being weak, I allowed it. "I saw it up close for five years, Glory. I don't like it, but I know you love him, really love him, and it's not the new-boot kind of love."

"Yes. Maybe I'm the one under a spell. Could Circe have done that?" I shook my head. "No, not blaming some goddess for my own feelings. He saved me, Rafe. When I was about to starve. And he's been my hero more than once. Just like you've been." I kissed his cheek, the kind of kiss I would have given a brother.

"So we're friends now." Rafe hugged me and breathed against my hair. "I'll take it and try to learn to live with it."

"Thanks." I sighed and pushed back. "Now what about that check for Diana? Where did that money come from?"

"It tore a hole in my savings. But I wasn't about to let Lucky have a reason to come back to Austin. She's nothing but trouble. Why is she here anyway? What about her father and his rules?"

"He died and she took over the family business. Apparently she's doing a good job if that demo with Diana is any indication. She did get her payment." I stepped away from him. "And you'll get your money back. Diana and I will have a little chat. As her friend maybe I can help her get her financial house in order, get into a twelve-step program if this is an addiction to shopping. Shoe sales?" Of course I had new boots myself and then had come up short when I was scrambling for plane fare. Lucky for me I seemed to always have a man handy when I needed bailing out. Diana had too much pride for that. Why didn't I? It was something for me to think about. And I got a queasy feeling that it was a conversation with myself that was long overdue.

"We can both help her." Rafe smiled. "She has no idea what she's in for now that I hold her note. I'm going to be looking at her books, making sure she pays off the rest of Lucky's loan ASAP. The sooner all ties with that bitch are broken, the better."

"Good." I glanced at a clock on his wall. "I need to go. I'm heading over to see Ian now."

"Why?" Rafe opened the office door and the loud music after the quiet in the well-insulated office was a shock. But the steady beat made me want to dance. At least Achelous hadn't managed to kill my love for music.

"I want to get a few things off my chest. Yes, he helped

me find out what I was. But he also lied to me about a few things." I walked toward the front door, Rafe by my side.

"Be careful. How are you getting to Scotland?"

"Ray's chartering a plane for me. Can you believe it?" I said it like it was no big deal but Diana's words were haunting me. *Only whores asked their lovers for money.* I hadn't asked. But what was the difference, really? I'd accepted quickly enough when it had been offered. Like I usually did. Money, favors, bodyguards. Rafe was staring at me, probing my thoughts and coming up empty. I kept a carefree smile on my face though it was becoming harder and harder to do.

Rafe shook his head. "Are you sure you don't have us all under some kind of spell, Glory? I swear the things you get men to do for you boggles my mind."

"Yeah. It's nuts, isn't it? But Ray insisted. He hopes, I think, that Blade will slam the castle door in my face. And it might happen." I managed a shrug, like my entire future happiness didn't hang in the balance.

Rafe leaned against the door frame. He cocked an eyebrow. "A charter flight is a little steep for a 'friend' to pay for. Or is there more going on now?"

"Never mind." My face was hot. "Got to go."

"No, you don't." Rafe examined me closely. "Shit, you did it. Finally slept with him, didn't you?"

"Can you blame me? The guy's like my fantasy man, Rafe!" Yes, I sounded defensive.

"The surprise was that it took you so long." Rafe had a rueful grin. "Come on, Glory. The guy pursued you hard and fast. I knew how you felt about him. You were a fangirl. A total groupie."

"Oh, yeah." I flushed again. "I'm sorry." I squeezed his arm, hating the way he looked so serious standing there. "Guess I'd better go. Bye." He didn't say another word as I hurried out the door.

When I got outside, I stopped and took a minute. Rafe. I would never have a better friend and I hoped he could find someone to make him happy so I didn't feel so guilty . . .

"Get over here before my guy drags you by your hair." The voice came out of the dark alley next to the club.

"I thought you had a date." I strolled over to where Lucky and her two henchmen waited. "Aren't you going to be late?"

"I believe in making a man wait for me. It gives me an edge." Lucky raised a coral-painted nail. "Now let me tell you something, Miss Thing. You think you're all that with your statue trick but I'm serving notice. I've had feelers out to find a way around that. I'm taking you down. You hear me? No one messes with Lucky Carver and gets away with it."

"I'm shaking." I raised my hands and did mocking jazz hands.

"You should be." Lucky jabbed her fingernail into my chest before I saw it coming. "Bitch. You owe me. We had a contract and I want it honored."

I was all set to vanish out of there, when I felt an arm around my neck. Damn, her vampire bodyguard had been too quick for me. Aggie had warned me that you couldn't dematerialize if someone anchored you in place with a touch.

"You really don't want to do that, *chica*." He growled it in my ear, his voice low and slightly accented. Hispanic. Probably one of the vamps who'd immigrated here from Mexico. That explained his dark good looks.

"Yes, I do." I focused on Lucky. I could still turn her into a statue.

"Freeze her and I'll tear your pretty head off. Can't heal from that, can you?" He chuckled then tightened his grip until I heard a bone crack in my neck.

"How do you like that, Glory?" Lucky strutted around me in a victory lap, her glee adding a bounce to her step. "Miguel, you are even better than advertised." She slid a fingernail down his bicep.

"Touch me again, Miss Lucky, and I'll let her go. You would make a fine statue, I think." Miguel's deep voice sent shivers through me and stopped Lucky in her tracks.

"Well, I guess I understand our relationship now." She jerked her hand back. "Kill her? Or not? Hmm." She tapped her fingernail against her fangs, brought down by her excitement. "Consequences would be a bitch."

"Damn right. There's the council here for one. They'd hunt you down and terminate you for ordering the hit." My voice came out hoarse as I tried to find some wiggle room, but Miguel wasn't about to ease his grip on me. "And, Miguel, you'd be toast too. Burned and crispy in the morning sun."

"Doubt it. I wouldn't be here." His cheek brushed my hair.

He smelled masculine with a spicy scent that I would remember if I met it in the dark again. I could feel his hard body pressed against mine and figured he was a good ten inches taller than I was and solid muscle. I might be able to outwit him but he obviously had skills. I'd been so proud of my new Siren status, but a clever vamp could still take me down if I wasn't careful. I was truly trapped, my only option to think healing thoughts for my throat.

"Yes, I guess you would disappear, Miguel, you were hard enough to track down." Lucky frowned. "I'm well-known, my business easy to find. It's a nuisance looking over my shoulder all the time."

"And it would be a shame to close this territory for you, Miss Lucky." Nice that he didn't seem too worried about taking me out. Guess it was true—I had no Siren magic working my wiles on men.

"True enough. And then there's Glory's fan club. All those men she's enthralled with her Siren ways. They'd be after me for revenge too, I'm afraid. What a nuisance. Not that you couldn't handle them, Miguel." Lucky sighed. "But let this be a lesson for you, Glory. Your new power isn't a match for a strong and fast vampire who knows what you can do and is prepared to deal with it." She smiled at Miguel. "And I can afford to hire the best."

"I'm releasing you now, *chica*. Will you behave? I must warn you, this freeze thing of yours—I know how to take it off your victims. So don't bother doing it to Miss Lucky. And I will stay behind you, I think. As a precaution. *Entiendes?*"

Miguel slowly eased the pressure off my throat and I coughed, then reached up to rub my neck. Unfortunately Miguel kept his hand on my shoulder like the bastard knew I would disappear if he let me go entirely.

"Yes, I get it. Score one for you, Lucky." Oh, how I wanted to put Lucky in her place. Her gloating was getting to me and I felt my temper rise. Miguel squeezed my shoulder.

"Don't."

"Miguel can read through any mind blocking too, Glory. Just like you can. Isn't that a bitch?" Lucky laughed then and turned her back on me.

"Wait!" I shrugged off Miguel's hand, surprised when he let me. "I want you out of Austin, Lucky. Forget that so-called contract. You got your down payment back in a timely manner. Our deal is null and void. How do you like that legalese? Why not go back to New York and your homies, where people appreciate your style? Here? We don't like you and we don't want to do business with you. That scene with Rafe should have convinced you of that."

Lucky stopped and turned around. "You are one straight-up bitch, you know that?" She smoothed down her black cocktail dress, a little much for Sixth Street but mouth watering, and actually smiled. "I swear we could be friends if I didn't hate you so damned much. I admire a woman who can stand up to me."

"Yeah, well, you know why I won't ever be your friend."

"I know. And I'm getting really tired of Texas, if you want to know the truth. So as soon as I get with the handsome Scottish doctor, I'm ditching this place. Maybe I'll leave Miguel here as my rep. I still have loans out that need collecting and he seems to have a natural talent for intimidation. A wonderful skill, don't you agree?" Lucky smiled and nodded at him. Yes, he was still way too close at my back.

"Of course, Miss Lucky. I would be happy to be of service." Miguel had a cadence to his speech that was almost charming. Too bad his power surrounded me and I wanted to run from him as fast as I could manage.

"Intimidation. Yeah, he has that, in spades. *Adiós*, Lucky. If I never see you again, it will be too soon. And here's a parting gift. Your Siren blood isn't worth shit. If Ian tells you otherwise? He's lying to you just to get in your pants. But then he wouldn't have to do that, would he? You're much too easy for him to bother." I rubbed my sore neck again, even though I was sure it was already healing courtesy of the synthetic blood I'd just downed at Rafe's club.

"Now who's the liar? What do you say, Miguel? Is she telling the truth or not?" Lucky stalked up to me like she was about to slap me silly. I hoped she tried.

"No lies, Miss Lucky. This one has powers, you do not." Miguel didn't sound sorry about it either.

"Well." Lucky just stood there, obviously frustrated. "At least I can afford to buy good help. Good-bye, Glory." Lucky turned on her Louboutin pumps that I would love to own. Did she travel with a hairdresser? The way her dark red hair tumbled to her shoulders was too perfectly artless. I grinned at the thought of her shifter wielding a round brush and a blow dryer. Why not? I knew better than to stereotype.

"Oh, Lucky?" She stopped and looked over her shoulder. I realized Miguel had vanished, the empty space behind me a welcome relief. "News flash. Your Siren blood? Also not worth a damn for attracting men. Sorry about that." And with a finger wave I concentrated and vanished, sure that I'd left her with a gaping mouth. Hah! I waited until I was a block down in another alley before I rematerialized and went to check on the shop. I'd got what I wanted—Lucky was leaving town. Things were running smoothly at Vintage Vamp's so I just walked through to get my car from the alley.

Oh, she did not do this. But I had a feeling she did. I should have known Lucky would find a way to make me pay for slipping out of our contract. My tires were slashed and as flat as Diana's wallet. I really hated to call in another insurance claim but four new tires . . . I loved my sassy new car but even the tires were expensive. I walked around the vehicle three times inspecting for other damage. If Lucky had keyed it or broken so much as a taillight, I'd find a way to freeze that bitch into a Lucky-cicle until New Year's.

But apparently Lucky had some respect for a fine Italian sports car and had contented herself with ruining the rubber. I decided to let the tires go for tonight and called Erin, asking her to leave a message for the day crew to get the tires taken care of tomorrow. I kicked at one, hurt my toe, then shifted to fly out to Ian's. This was not how I'd wanted to arrive.

He let me in with a smile. I was part of an experiment to him now and Ian loved his experiments.

"So, Glory, what have you found out about Sirens? Aggie won't tell me anything. Claims it's a sisterhood thing. Not for men to know, if you can believe that." Ian was in a good mood as he led me into his expansive living room.

"She's right. It *is* a sisterhood and apparently I made a lucky escape when Achelous kicked me out." I settled into a comfy chair with a view of one of Austin's lakes. There was no way I was accepting the glass of premium synthetic he offered me.

"But he left you ignorant. Unforgivable not to know you were a Siren. What about the blood? Did you find out if it carries any powers?" Ian picked up an electronic tablet off of a glass coffee table, then settled on the couch.

"Not a speck." I jumped to my feet. "And, Ian, I don't appreciate the lies you told me. Clarity? Here's some for you. That b.s. about drinking my blood and getting off to it was obviously a ploy. A way to drive a wedge between me and Jerry, wasn't it?"

"Glory, how can you say that? I told you. The feud is ancient history. And Penny took the drug. She gave you her statement." Ian looked like he wanted to smile.

"Get her in here. I want to interview her about that little experiment." I sat again. Lying bastard. "Damn it, Ian, if you laugh at me, I'll show you a power that will make you very uncomfortable." I entertained myself with visions of Ian as a garden gnome. "And look at my face! You slipped me another drug and now I'm wearing a permanent flush."

"Calm down, Gloriana. That night you were overwrought. I thought I was doing the right thing. And I might have a cure for your residual redness. If you're willing to take another drug." Ian got serious. "Forgive me. As a doctor, I always turn to medicine as a cure."

I settled back in my chair. "No more drugs. Now call Penny in here. I know she was supposed to work tonight."

"Yes, she's here." Ian's finger hovered over his tablet. "But first won't you tell me what powers you got as a former Siren?"

"Did you hear me? I'm furious with you. You drugged me. Lied to me. I do have some of the powers the Sirens have, but I'm sure not sharing anything with you."

Ian tapped the tablet. "Fine. I'll get Penny." He walked over to an intercom and buzzed another room, asking for her to join us.

"What's up, Glory?" Penny smiled at me as she walked into the room. She wore a white lab coat over her jeans and T-shirt, looking cute and very professional.

"I want to show Ian that I'm on to him. You remember when he let you have that dose of Clarity? Supposedly made from my blood?" I frowned at Ian. "Experimenting on Penny. So not cool."

"Don't be ridiculous. Penny is a scientist. She was a willing subject, weren't you, my dear?" Ian put his hand on her shoulder.

Penny jerked away from Ian when I nodded. "What do you mean 'supposedly'? What did you do, Ian?"

"I told you, I made a drug from Gloriana's blood. She's here making wild accusations, just because she and Campbell apparently broke up." Ian smiled. "Not my fault, Gloriana. The man is a hothead."

"We'll see." I couldn't resist. I froze Ian with a look. He stood there, his eyes burning and not able to move a muscle.

"How do you like that Siren power, Ian?" I turned to Penny. "Now remind me exactly how you felt after you took Clarity."

"I had hyper vision, hearing and an enhanced libido." Penny flushed. "It was really cool and a breakthrough drug." She glanced at Ian. "You shouldn't have done that, Glory. I can tell Ian's furious. When he thaws, he can call in his guards and you'll be outnumbered."

"No worries. I have more tricks I can play. And he can't be mad at you. I'm the villain here." I tapped Ian on his chest. I read his thoughts. Wow. He was steamed. Being helpless was like his worst nightmare. He and Jerry were more alike than they'd ever admit.

"Now I want you to drink some of my blood. Straight from the source, Penny." I held out my wrist. "Just enough to be sure you have a good sampling. Then we'll see what effects it has on you, won't we, Ian?"

"You sure? It was kind of embarrassing the first time. I was so horny." Penny looked at her feet. "Well, let's just say I shifted over to N-V and dragged Trey into a supply closet. He was thrilled but I was mortified."

I laughed. "No worries. I have a feeling none of that will happen this time. What do you say, Ian? Oh, I forgot, you can't talk." I concentrated and thawed just his head. "Now you can comment."

"Gloriana, you will regret this. Thaw me out this instant." I swear spittle came out of his mouth Ian was so enraged.

"I'd rather not. Come on, Penny." I sat on the couch and held out my wrist then patted the seat next to me. "Have at it."

"Penny, ignore her. She is trying to make you look fool-ish." Ian made this sound like an order.

"It's an experiment, boss. I think I should do it. In the interest of science, don't you know." Penny sat and took my hand. "Here goes." She bit into my wrist delicately, like she was afraid she'd hurt me. "Mmm." She sent me a mental message that I tasted great.

I timed her then pushed her away and told her to lick the punctures closed. "Okay, how do you feel?"

Penny looked around the room. "Sight's normal. Say something, Glory. No, let me listen and see if I can hear the guards outside. Last time, I could hear conversations from a block away." She screwed up her face, concentrating. "Nope. No luck." Then she sat back on the couch and looked Ian over. Uh-oh.

"Penny, if you value your job . . ." Ian growled.

"Sorry, boss, but you're not my type. I'm in love with my shifter and I am not in the throes of lust like I was after I took Clarity, whatever that was." Penny turned to me. "Glory, you're right. It wasn't made with your blood. You've got rich, delicious vampire blood, but it's not an aphrodisiac."

"Good to know." I got up and felt her get up beside me. "Ian obviously has created a new drug that he can market but it's nothing to do with me. Right, Ian?"

"Obviously." He lifted his chin. "Penny, don't you have work to do in the lab?"

"No, I don't think I do." She pulled off her lab coat. "I can't work here anymore. Not when I'm used to deceive my friends."

Ian's face was a thundercloud. "You won't find another job like this one."

"I hope not." She took my arm. "Let's get out of here, Glory."

I was proud of my fledgling but worried that Ian would retaliate in some way. "Hold up a minute. Ian, you will give Penny a good recommendation, won't you? I don't think the council would like to hear about your deceptive practices here."

"I never sold Clarity, Glory. It was just a little experiment." Ian frowned at both of us. "But she is an excellent scientist. Don't be impulsive, Penny. We can surely work something out."

"No thanks. I have some money saved and some time to

think about options. Maybe I'll just hang out with Glory in her shop for a while." Penny smiled at me, pretty relaxed for someone who'd just given up her dream job.

"Actually, I'm heading to Scotland."

"Scotland?" Penny wasn't in any hurry to leave. "What's up?"

Ian seemed interested in the answer too.

"Jerry's gone home to the family castle. Since he left, I found out that only a Siren's song can enthrall a man and, when we met, I didn't have one, thanks to Achelous. I need to tell Jer that. To relieve his mind."

"You could do that with a simple telephone call." Ian smirked. "Even the primitive Campbells have cell phone service."

"Yes, well, we didn't part on good terms. Thanks to your interference." I hated Ian's amused expression, like he was above my little love drama. "I feel the need for a face-to-face."

Ian made a noise. Was he *laughing*? That brought my chin up.

"Fine. Maybe I'll beg for his forgiveness. Though what *I* did, I have no idea." I sighed and let my shoulders slump. "Obviously I have no pride where Jerry's concerned."

"Aw, Glory, I'm sorry." Penny put her arms around me. "It's okay to go after the man you love. If Blade's got any sense, he'll be hoping you do that very thing."

I sighed. "Circe put him in my path, but I had no song to bind him. He fell in love with me on his own."

"There you go. You're irresistible." Penny glanced at Ian, obviously thinking he didn't need in on this conversation.

"Thanks, Penny." I patted her back. "I hope you're right."

"You have a safe trip." She stood and walked toward the labs. "I've got to get my stuff together." She stopped in the doorway. "How are you getting there anyway? I can't imagine it's easy for a vampire to negotiate such a long distance with the time differences and the death sleep."

"Ray's chartered a flight for me." I couldn't look at Ian this time.

He laughed loudly. "Oh, there you go. That will cap it off for Campbell. He'll figure out what you had to do to get a plane from Caine and wash his hands of you, my girl. See if he doesn't." He wore jeans and a knit shirt tonight but I could imagine him in a kilt, attacking the Campbell fortress. "You may well get that castle door slammed in your pretty face, Gloriana. And if you've ever turned the man into a statue like you've done to me, it's a certainty."

"Thanks a heap, Ian. Ray and I are friends. He's chartering the flight for me as a favor. I hope Jerry can understand that."

"Just friends, Glory?" Ray stood in the doorway. "You can tell Ian the truth. We're more than friends and you didn't think I was going to let you get on that plane by yourself, did you?"

Eighteen

Ray turned to me as soon as Penny made her excuses and hurried out of the room. "I can't believe you froze Ian. You have a death wish, Glory?"

I glanced at Ian. "I had some things I needed to say. Now I guess I'd better thaw him."

"Yes, it's past time." Ian looked like he was going for my throat as soon as I did.

Ray was on his cell phone. I saw why as soon as his bodyguard, Will Kilpatrick, came into the room. He was a Scot Ray had hired who happened to be from a clan near Jerry's. He was also brother to the mother of Jerry's child, but I liked him anyway.

"What's this now?" Will grinned at me. "Rumors are flying among the guards. Did you do this, Gloriana?" He came over to kiss my cheek. "Ah, lassie, 'tis a fine skill."

"Yes, but now what?" I smiled at Ray. "Thanks for the backup, Ray."

"Ian, I'm a valuable customer. Glory is leaving town for a while. And you know the council won't stand for you hurting her. Neither will I. Can she thaw you now without reprisals?"

Ray motioned to Will and he stood beside me, stake at the ready.

"No need for violence. Glory proved a point. I had a little fun at her expense. It's over now and we're done. I want nothing more to do with her." Ian's eyes flashed. "Just get me the fuck out of this, Gloriana. Now!"

"I didn't really hear an apology." I felt Ray squeeze my hand. Okay, so Ian had a dozen guards he could call in. "Fine." I thawed him then braced myself.

Ian just strode around the room, obviously testing his freedom, then stopped to write something in his tablet.

"Son of a bitch but I hated that! Wish I could do it myself though." He glared at me like it was my fault that I couldn't transfer the power.

"Did she tell you she can also blast through your mental blocks when you're trying to hide your thoughts?" Ray threw himself into a chair. "That one's a real pisser."

Ian blanched and frowned at me. I gave him a finger wave with a smile, not even pretending I hadn't poked around in his brain.

Ray gestured at his bodyguard. "Will, you can go back outside now. Disaster averted."

"I hope so. MacDonald, is he right?" Will waited until Ian nodded. "Too bad. While you were standing there frozen, I had a chance with my stake. But it wasn't to be." He ignored Ian's growl. "Glory, good to see you. Glad you and Ray here finally hooked up. Though I'm sure Blade wouldn't agree." He winked at me. "Don't see anyone's ring on your finger, though, do I, lass?"

"Will, aren't you supposed to be outside sharpening that stake or something?" I really didn't need to hear Jerry's name right now.

"Sure. Guard duty. I'm on it. Just one more thing." Will stopped in the doorway. "MacDonald, Blade sent ye a message from the homeland." He said something in Gaelic that Ian obviously took exception to. Will grinned and saluted before taking off.

"Might be time to let that slacker go." Ray grumbled.

"Couldn't agree more." Ian threw down his tablet. "I assume you're here for the daylight drug, Ray. I'll go get your order." He left the room after sending a last angry look my way. An effort to read his thoughts just got me a bunch of indecipherable Gaelic. Ian had obviously switched languages, my hopelessness with any languages other than English no secret.

"I wonder what Will said."

"Doesn't matter. I won't fire him. He's a hell of an Xbox player and we have a tournament going. He's on my team against Nate and one of the other guards." Ray smiled ruefully at me. "No comment on the plane trip?"

"Let's wait until we're out of here for that discussion." I sat on the arm of his chair. Before I could stop him, he'd pulled me into his lap. "I'm sorry, Ray, that you walked into the middle of that. But have to say I wasn't sure how it was going to play out." I didn't let him know I could have vanished out of there.

"Glad to help. Ian was certainly pissed. Please don't do that to me. Not sure I could take it." He pulled me close, my head snug against his chest. I inhaled, savoring his nearness and realizing again how much he meant to me.

What was wrong with me that I could have such strong feelings for three different men? And be willing to use them so shamelessly? Because I had to talk Ray out of going with me on that plane yet it seemed like I was going to let him foot the bill. If I could pay him back somehow . . . Oh, sure. How many thousands of dollars did a charter flight cost? I'd end up like Diana, drowning in debt.

But I'd let Jerry pay for bodyguards for hundreds of years. Obviously using men was Siren behavior, I just hadn't known that's where it had come from. It was past time I let it go. I didn't want to be that person anymore, always taking.

"My, oh my. Look at the cozy couple."

"Get up, Glory," Ray growled in my ear.

"No. Ignore her, Ray. Lucky, go away." I noticed she hadn't brought her bodyguards in with her.

"Are you kidding? Ian's expecting me. We have a date." She tossed her hair then smiled. "Hey, Ray. How's immortality treating you?"

"Glory, I'm about to dump you on your pretty behind." Ray stood and dropped me on the chair. "Lucky, I figure you don't give a shit about me and my immortality."

"But I do. Didn't Glory tell you? I'm sorry, Ray. I've had time to think since I did the deed. Maybe I was hasty, turning you like that." Lucky was smart enough to keep the couch between her and Ray, especially when Ray stepped closer to her.

"*Maybe?* You hadn't seen me in what?—decades—and you rip out my throat and make me vampire on a fuckin' *whim?*" Ray stalked her, fangs down, following her when she backed away from him. "Now 'Sorry' is supposed to clear the air? Some things are unforgivable, Lucky. You with me on that, Glory?"

"Ray, settle down. It can't be undone so there's no point in—" I stood behind him, trying to find the magic words to calm him down. He kept his eyes narrowed on Lucky like he was ready to spring.

"In what? Taking revenge? But it would feel so damned good." Ray jerked a stake out of his back pocket and Lucky and I both gasped.

"What the hell are you doing? Vampires don't—" Lucky's eyes were saucers and she'd backed up until she hit a wall. A painting that had hung there fell to the floor with a crash. I figured the only reason that Ian hadn't come running was because he was somewhere enjoying the show.

"Don't stake each other? You wish. I figure sending you to hell would be a public service, Lucky." Ray's hand was steady as he aimed the stake at Lucky's heart. There was still a leather chair between them but I knew it would be an easy leap for him to be on her.

"Ray, the council won't stand for this. You know the penalty for taking out another vampire." I kept my hand on his back, willing him to listen to me.

"Let them try to find me." His smile was wry. "I have the resources to live wherever the hell I please."

"I won't run with you." I squeezed his shoulder.

"I'll miss you like hell, sweet thing, but that threat won't stop me. And I'm warning you, Glory. If you freeze me now, I'll never forgive you. You hear me?" Ray's voice was cold and I believed him.

"I won't do that to you, Ray. This is your decision. But she's just not worth it. You've made a decent life here. I can't bear the thought of you bringing it down over this worthless bitch." I leaned my face against his shirt, too sick and terrified to cry.

"Freeze *him*, Glory. I know you can do it." Lucky's voice wobbled and I realized she was actually scared.

"No." I rubbed his back, absorbing his pain, hurt and fury. If I were still a killer, a real Siren, I'd take her out for him. Obviously I was damned anyway. No wonder Lucifer had been drawn to me, wanted me for himself. I swallowed nausea at the thought.

But I knew Ray wasn't the cold-blooded killer he thought he could be and regret would haunt him later. I held on to him, feeling the thrum of his tension in the set of his shoulders. How could I help him?

"She's all yours, Ray. Make your choice." I raked her with my eyes and pinned her where she stood.

"You froze her." Ray turned and faced me. "I can stake her now and she can't get away from me."

"Right. So make a decision. Do it and ruin everything. Or let her go. Lucky's promised to leave town. I don't think she'll be interested in coming back." I sucked in a breath. It took everything in me not to fall to my knees and beg him to do the right thing.

I'd left Lucky's eyes mobile and she blinked frantically as

if to say she was more than ready to get out of Austin. Ray glanced at her then back to me again.

"She doesn't deserve to live, Glory." His voice was low as he leaned his forehead against mine. "I've dreamed of doing this ever since . . ."

"I know, Ray. I do." I slid my hands up to his face, running my thumbs over the stubble of his evening beard. "Look at me. Please." He leaned back and it took me a moment to collect my thoughts. "I love you, Ray. Enough to step back and let you take her out if that's what you need to do. But please let Lucky go." I felt his jaw tighten under my fingertips.

"Glory . . ."

"Don't do it for me, Ray, do it for yourself. You're vampire. Done deal. We can't turn back the clock."

"That's the problem, babe." He looked down at the stake, the sharp point too close to his own lean stomach in its dark T-shirt. "What she did . . . I can't be mortal again. God knows I've done everything in my power to try to figure out a way . . ." He met my gaze again. "Sorry, but you know how I feel about losing daylight. If I'd had a choice, like you did . . . Shit. But I didn't." He gritted his teeth. "She took the choice out of my hands and that's what I just can't accept."

"Well, accept this, Israel Caine." I gripped his hand that held that stake. "You're stuck. Get over it." I sighed and kissed his cheek. "I'd hoped you'd become used to this life enough by now to realize how much it's brought you— immortality, strength, enhanced senses. Damn it, love the night, Ray, and quit fighting against it. Find the beauty and stop mourning what you can't freakin' have."

"Shit." One arm went around me and he took a breath as he held me for a long moment. Finally he looked at me again. "Guess I have turned into a whiny SOB, haven't I?" Ray's mouth worked until he managed a slight smile. "But I want to kill her so damned bad."

"I know. She's done horrible, unforgivable things. But I've got to believe that somewhere down the line she'll get what she deserves. Divine justice. What goes around, comes around. Karma. Whatever you want to call it I'm pretty sure Lucky will get hers in the end. Can't we leave it at that?" I took the stake from his fingers, surprised when he let me. "You're a good man, Ray. That's just one reason I love you, whines and all. What say we let her go now and then get the hell out of here?"

"Yeah. I want to hold you, be with you, before you leave. And, no, I'm not going with you. There's nothing for me in Scotland. But I'll send Will with you. How's that?" He kissed me sweetly, then hungrily. "Damn, Glory. I can't believe I let you talk me out of this."

"Neither can I." Ian walked into the room with a small package. "Daylight drug. Now go stand by the terrace doors, then release Ms. Carver, Gloriana. I'll deal with the fallout." Ian nodded toward Lucky. "I've got a note here for Campbell. An answer to the message passed by Kilpatrick. Will you take it for me?" He held out a small sealed envelope.

"It's not going to aggravate the feud, is it? I don't trust you." I stared down at it. I was too anxious about Ray right now to get into Ian's thoughts. I was pretty sure they were still in that indecipherable Gaelic anyway, the note too. I awkwardly held that stake, not about to hand it to Ian, though I was desperate to be rid of it.

"It shouldn't if Campbell is reasonable." Ian smiled like he doubted that. "Good luck." He nodded at Ray. "I'll see you another night. Enjoy your daylight."

"I always do. Now if you get the urge to poison that bitch"—Ray glanced at Lucky—"go with it. No great loss."

"I'm beginning to see that some people think so. Please just take off. Gloriana?" Ian raised an eyebrow.

"She's thawed." I stuck the note in my bra then ran out the door behind Ray. We shifted, only stopping long enough to get Will from the front lawn where I handed him the stake. Then we headed toward Ray's house.

When we got there it was quiet and Ray pulled me into the dark living room.

"I have a question for you," I said before he could drag me down the hall to either the playroom or the bedroom.

"Shoot." Ray faced me, not even trying to evade the showdown.

"What in the hell were you doing carrying a stake?" I paced the length of the room.

"I started the night you told me Lucky was in town." He sat at the piano and stared down at the keys. "What did you expect? I hate her. The fact that she was here and I could run into her was eating me alive, Glory. I figured she was still gloating about what she did to me. I had to do something about it."

"She told you she regretted it, Ray. She isn't gloating and I believe her." I sat next to him. "You have any idea how dangerous it is to have a stake on you? You're still a relatively new vampire. What if someone had overpowered you? Or frozen you, like I can do? They could take that stake and use it against you, Ray." I bumped against his shoulder. "Please promise me you won't do that again."

"No worries." He played a bar or two of scary music. "I'll let Will handle it from now on. That's what I pay him for." He smiled.

"Thank God." I laid my hands on top of his.

He turned his hands over and gripped mine then stared into my eyes. "You sure you need to go to Scotland? I think we've got a good thing going right here. You really came through for me back there. I could feel the love." He pulled me to him, holding me almost too tight. "Damn, girl, I seriously felt all that emotion from you just lift me right out of my anger."

"I was hoping . . ." I held on to him and rubbed my face against his shoulder. "I couldn't bear it if you self-destructed, Ray. But, like I said, don't do anything for me, do it for yourself. You're worth it. Believe that if you believe nothing else."

"Shit. This sounds like a good-bye speech." He leaned back and smiled sadly. "You leaving now? Tonight? Without . . ."

I put my fingers over his lips. "I can't take your plane. It's not fair. And I'm not taking Will either. I'll get to Scotland on my own somehow. Don't worry about it."

"No plane. Then how . . . ?" Ray brushed my hair back. "No, I don't want to know. Just promise me you won't shape-shift and try to fly yourself over the Atlantic as a bird or bat or something. That's too much for anyone but one of those macho types like Blade. And I bet even he has pit stops."

"No, I won't try to do that. A girl's got to have luggage, you know." I leaned against him again. I knew I had made the right decision.

"Okay. You're smart. You'll figure it out. You need cash—" He didn't get to finish that offer with my hand over his mouth.

"I'm through with what I've figured out is Siren behavior, Ray." I stopped and shook my head. "No, that's an excuse. I'm through being a user. Especially men. Jerry, Rafe, now you. No money, bodyguards, plane rides." This was like stepping off a cliff, no safety net, no bottom in sight. But I pasted on a confident smile, glad Ray couldn't blast through *my* mental blocks.

"For God's sake, be careful." He pulled me close. "And to hell with this independence shit. If you get in real trouble, call me. Promise." He looked deadly serious and waited until I nodded.

"Okay, I promise. But it'll have to be a dire emergency." I smiled at his palpable relief.

"Quit beating yourself up about this so-called Siren behavior, Glory." Ray frowned. "Men like me, the Scot, and, yeah, even your faithful hound, *want* to do things for you. Because we love you. You're not like Aggie, not by any stretch. She's obviously out for whatever she can get." He rubbed my arms as he kept his eyes on mine. "You have a generous heart, a spirit that makes you a great friend." He finally smiled. "And a helluva lover."

"Ray." My voice cracked. "I wish . . ."

"Don't say it. I know you have to go do your thing with Blade. I'd like to blame it on the sire/fledgling connection but I sure don't have that with Lucky." Ray smiled sadly. "So kiss me good-bye and make it a good one." Ray leaned down and took my mouth.

Ray made sure he left his mark on me, his mouth a master class in seduction that tempted me to pull him down the hall for a last romp on his satin sheets. Instead, I slipped from his arms and walked out to his terrace.

"Ray, you won't—"

"Go back to the booze?" He smiled and shook his head. "Don't think so. I've got the itch to write a song. Pretty gloomy stuff but, hey, that's my mood, you know?" He rubbed my shoulder then frowned. "You've got a bruise on your neck, what's that about?"

"Nothing. A little accident earlier. It's healing." I was afraid if I told Ray about Lucky's new bodyguard he'd feel compelled to go after him and even the score. I didn't want them to go to war over me, especially if Miguel was going to stay in town and take over Lucky's "territory." "I'll expect your new song to be finished when I get back. Just don't go all *The Phantom of the Opera* on me."

He laughed, loud and long, hugging me until I gasped. "Oh, babe, you so have me pegged. I figured I'd go skulking around the lake in a black satin cape. Not sure about the mask."

I grinned and traced his smile with a fingertip. "No, a mask would be a crime. You're too pretty for that."

"But not pretty enough to keep you here?" He nipped my finger with a fang.

"I've got to do this, Ray."

"Will you come back?" He leaned against the railing, back to the lake. "What if Blade wants you to stay there with him?"

"I have a shop here. A life. I'll be back." I turned to look out at the lake. "And Jerry's parents live at the castle." I shuddered. "We aren't exactly best buds."

"Their loss." Ray leaned over and kissed my cheek. "Take care, Glory girl. Promise?"

"Sure. You do the same." I watched him head inside then heard the piano. It *was* a sad melody, but beautiful. I walked down to his boat dock just as Ray started to sing. He'd be in his own world now, writing down the melody, adjusting the lyrics. I envied him that creative ability.

I stopped to stare out at the lake. I'd miss this, even if the water did still terrify. When the water rippled and a head emerged, I wasn't even surprised.

"Glory, you've got to come with me. To the other side of this lake." Aggie pulled herself up onto the dock. She was naked and didn't bother to cover herself. If I'd had her perfect body, I'd have flaunted it too.

"Why?" I stepped back when she reached for me with a wet hand. Aggie actually looked desperate as she flung her hair behind her back. Too much of a good thing if you know what I mean. I looked away to peer at the dark lake.

"Achelous is meeting all the Siren sisters and Circe at Ray's old house in a few minutes. Please. This is our chance for freedom and it was your idea. You have to be there to help us."

"Are you kidding? He'll kill me." I backed away from her.

"I'm not giving you a choice." And with that she grabbed me and jerked me into the water.

Nineteen

I'm sure they heard my scream on every side of the lake. That is before water rushed into my mouth. After that I just concentrated on keeping my head up. Aggie had morphed into her half-fish form, what mortals called a mermaid. She was cutting through the water at warp speed and dragging me by one arm. Obviously she didn't care how I fared as I hit the waves behind her.

I sent her a mental message to bleepin' slow down. That earned me a laugh and a leap into the air that made me gasp and swallow a half gallon of lake when we hit the water again. My curses were drowned out when she did a deep dive that reminded me I didn't have to breathe at all. Oh, yeah, we were having a great time.

When we surfaced again I could see the burned-out shell of Ray's old dock in the distance. Thank the goddess. Geez, now I was even thinking like Aggie. Just as well since I was about to meet the sisters. I shuddered to imagine a whole gaggle of Sirens. If I lived through this picnic, I was shifting and flying home. Good idea. I tried to shift right then and felt a burning sensation that meant my circuits were down.

Weird and totally a new feeling that made me want to throw up all that lake water.

"Okay, put down your feet. You can walk in from here." Aggie stopped and gave herself legs again.

To my relief I could touch down, though the bodysurfing adventure had me staggering. I looked back but couldn't even see the shore or the lights from Ray's house. I hoped he hadn't heard my shriek and jumped into his cigarette boat thinking to rescue me. No way did I want him to meet Achelous. But if Laurie showed up and went tiger . . . Well, it was a nice fantasy anyway.

I made an ungraceful landing on the rocky shore, scraped my knee and tore a hole in my favorite black pants. I'd lost my slingbacks in the lake and the rocks bit into the soles of my feet as I staggered behind Aggie. At least it looked like we were the first to arrive. I wrung out my hair as I collapsed on a nearby boulder.

"What a wimp." Aggie dragged my top down where it had ridden up to expose my tummy. "I wish you could do that thing where you make yourself dry clothes. You look horrible." She, of course, had already put herself into a fresh outfit and had dried and fluffed her hair.

"As if I care." I did close my eyes and give the transformation thing a shot. Dry hair, a new pair of designer jeans like Aggie wore and a sweater to match my eyes would be swell. I looked down. No go. Screw it. "I don't want to look appealing for the Storm God anyway." I wiped my face with my hands and saw black mascara on them.

Aggie just shook her head. "You're right. Stick with the pitiful look. You've got raccoon eyes, no lipstick and could be a drowned reject from *The Biggest Loser*. Achy won't give you a second glance."

"Thanks. Oh, hello, looks like we have company." Ghostly figures began to materialize around us. The sisters, I assumed. As I watched they solidified into beautiful women, perfect in every way. They were all different heights and color combos, but their figures were poster worthy. Thank

God they hadn't arrived naked since I didn't think I could take so much blatant beauty on full display. Instead, they were dressed fit to kill—oops, bad analogy. But obviously these get-togethers were an excuse to try to outdress each other. The clothing budgets they had boggled my mind as they greeted each other with hugs, then gathered around me.

"Gloriana." They breathed my name then poked and prodded me as if to test for doneness. I just let it go. If I'd once looked like a member of this club, no wonder they were having a hard time believing their eyes. One of them burst into noisy sobs.

"Ariane, please. Nothing can be done now. Forget about it." Several of the sisters clustered around her.

"But we were best friends and she doesn't even know me." Ariane, the one who could cry and her eyes and nose didn't even turn pink, approached me. She rocked a turquoise silk wrap dress and peep-toe lizard pumps as she picked her way across the beach. "Gloriana, you really don't recognize me?" She held out her hand. "Please, take my hand. I want to show you something."

"Sorry, but as far as I can remember, we've never met." I did like her smile. She seemed friendly with her pretty dark eyes and deep dimples. She was a brunette and petite, about Flo's size. In fact, she reminded me of Flo and I think my best bud had that same dress in yellow. Which gave me the heebie-jeebies. I took a chance and let her hold my hand.

Suddenly pictures formed in my mind. This girl and I laughed on a beach and then dove into the waves. We weren't shy and both swam naked, which seemed to be the Siren preference. I guess we did it so we could sprout our fish tails when we felt like it. But I seemed to have the same perfect body she had. My hip issues were another reason to hate Achelous.

Like switching channels, we were suddenly in another scene, in a palace at the bottom of the sea. We were at a banquet and sat, down the table from Achelous. He gestured to us and we went to him together. We laughed behind his back but were happy to serve him. This time we wore sheer togas that left nothing to the imagination. Our jewelry was heavy and worth a fortune. Hmm. For dessert we did things to and with Achy and each other . . . I flushed and jerked my hand from hers.

"Did you see? How close we were, Gloriana?" Ariane's eyes shimmered.

"Yes, I'm sorry. I really don't remember any of my Siren past. I hope you found another friend." I stiffened when she threw her arms around me and hugged me.

"Up to your old tricks, I see, Gloriana. Keep your hands off my women." Achelous roared the order and the heavens shook with his displeasure.

"Sire, she did not willingly touch me. We were just . . ." Ariane bowed and scurried back to join her sisters clustered on the other side of the clearing.

"I had tricks? Didn't know. But then you did erase my memories." I knew I should keep my mouth shut but I hated the way the sisters quaked at the sound of his voice. Even now he froze Ariane where she stood before he stalked over to place a proprietary hand on her shoulder.

"Yes. And I can do it to any one of you females here. Do you doubt me?" Achelous actually spoke softly this time and it was even scarier than his thunder. Of course the crack of a lightning bolt helped punctuate his threat.

"I think they've suffered enough at your hands, Achelous." Circe shimmered into view with her usual display of clear skies and twinkling stars.

"What business is it of yours how I treat my Sirens? Why are you here?" Achelous looked ready to start storming.

"Your Sirens begged me to intervene. They've asked for my help." Circe's smile was obviously meant to goad Achelous and it did the job. He whirled and pinned me with a gaze of pure hatred.

"I know where this is coming from. Gloriana, have you been meddling? Inciting my Sirens to rebellion? I thought I heard whispers when I was at play." He jerked Aggie to his side with a harsh word. "Confess. Has Gloriana been filling your head with seditious plots?"

"Don't blame Gloriana, Achelous. You are high-handed. Ill suited to rule a group of women like the sisterhood of Sirens. Your methods are abusive." Circe opened her arms. "Come to me, ladies, and I will see that you are well treated."

"What? You think to steal them from me?" Achelous's face turned red. "Take one step, you ungrateful bunch of females, and I will strip the song from each of you." This stopped the women in their expensive tracks and they sank to their knees in the dirt. I gasped. Designer clothes deserved better. But of course he'd pull out that trump card.

"You will not." Circe waved her arms and a golden band of twinkling stars shimmered around the ladies. What? Were we in a Disney movie? But obviously this was a power move because Achelous looked ready to spit sparks.

"The Sirens are under my protection until we get this settled. Don't think I won't go to Zeus about this, Achelous. The very fact that the Sirens asked me to take them on will displease him. He's already unhappy that you and I need him to mediate our disputes."

"This is way more than a dispute, Circe. You are interfering in my territory." Flames did shoot out of his eyes as he stared at her. "Woman, I will never forget this, no matter what Zeus decides." Achy stomped his sandaled foot and thunder and lightning filled the night. He pointed at me and electricity made my hair swirl around my head. "I lay this entire debacle on your head, Gloriana. My ladies were perfectly content until Aglaophonos began consorting with you."

"Content? How could they be?" I studied the women who still looked terrified. "You send them out to kill and then reward them by demanding they satisfy your every appetite." I tried to stand but gave up the effort, my legs still rubbery.

"Mouthy bitch. You will regret this, Gloriana." Achelous raised his hand and a lightning bolt tore through my pants and pinned my leg to the rock where I sat.

Dear God but I'd never felt such pain. The world dark-
ened and I smelled burned flesh and my own blood welling
from the hole in my leg. I reached shaking hands to pull out
the pulsing light shard but realized it wasn't solid, but a
high-voltage missile that I couldn't grab no matter how hard
I tried.

"Stop!" Circe commanded.

Achelous ignored her, making the stones beneath us shake
with his fury before opening the skies to a freezing rain. I
screamed when he tossed another bolt at me, this time
through my other leg. I couldn't have moved even if I hadn't
felt like I was being electrocuted from the thighs up. My
nails shredded as I dug for purchase on the hard rock and
tried to keep from falling back and ripping the lightning
down the length of my legs.

For the first time, I wished Achelous had turned me into
a statue. I bit my lip, damned if I'd give him the satisfaction
of tears or pleas for mercy. I kept my chin up and my eyes
fixed on him.

"Having fun?"

"You mock me?" Achelous looked like he was winding up
for another round.

I had some things I wanted to say before he put me down
even if the pain was making it hard for me to think straight.
I glanced at the sisters now clustered behind Circe. They
were safe, at least, behind their twinkling barricade. I noticed that not even Achelous's rain could penetrate that circle
of stars and they were dry and pretty as they stared at me in
horror. Aggie was still a statue, trapped behind Achelous.

"You'd like to blame me for the Sirens' defection but
blame yourself, your high and mightiness. They saw what
you did to me and decided they couldn't take a chance that
one day you'd have performance issues or whatever and give
one of them the same treatment. These women are too smart
to just wait for the ax to fall." I licked my lips, tasting the
rain and wishing it was something stronger. I needed to heal

and fast. The lightning in my thighs pulsed hot and I leaned back to try to ease the pressure. No such luck.

"Smart?" Achelous snorted. "Sirens aren't valued for their brains, Gloriana. Or their clever conversation." That got a reaction from the ladies but he ignored it. He looked me over. "There are uses for a Siren's mouth and talking isn't one of them."

"You really are a Neanderthal." It was getting harder for me to form words. God, but I wanted to leap across the clearing and show him how a vampire's mouth could go to work. I'd rip out his throat then . . . When he aimed for me again with a furious glare, I was sure it was going to be the death blow, through my heart, but another roar, not thunder, stopped him. A beautiful Bengal tiger leaped in front of Achelous. It was enough of a surprise to make him pause.

"What's this? Gloriana, is she here at your bidding or Circe's?"

"What does it matter, Achelous?" Circe smiled as she held a weeping Ariane against her. "Give up and let the sisters go. You have such a low opinion of them, why don't you pick up whores somewhere else to satisfy your appetites?" The sisters flanked her now and there were angry mutters. Apparently the "whore" comment wasn't sitting well. Of course Achelous had insulted them first and he got his share of angry glares. Circe silenced them with a gesture. "If you think you're being wronged, let's go to Olympus right now and take this up with Zeus."

"Not so fast." Achelous watched Laurie pace protectively in front of me. "The tiger wants to make a fight of it. I'd like to test her powers."

"Leave her alone, Achelous." I looked down, shocked to realize the lightning bolts had vanished and he'd released me. I was still bleeding and felt weak as the tiger slipped close enough to bump against me. I reached for her and pressed my hand on her back, taking strength from her warm fur as I staggered to my feet.

"Why should I? She seems to be the only one here with enough power to make this night interesting." Achelous laughed with his head thrown back, his white teeth gleaming. "I took you down with one lightning bolt, didn't I? And my Sirens? Easily cowed, hiding behind Circe's skirts." He flicked a dismissive look at the women still close enough to the goddess to touch her toga. "If I decide I want them back, I will get them. Zeus and I will have a talk, man-to-man. He won't deny me."

I could see their terror. My sisters. Somewhere inside me I did remember and I found the courage to stand straighter.

"You want a fight? Come at me again. Burn me to a crisp but let the tiger and the sisters go. What kind of man lets women do his work for him anyway? If you want to kill, gather an army of men and go to war. That's how real men fight." Laurie's warm fur rippled beneath my fingers. A warning? Yes, I was talking tough. But I hated his macho act and I kept getting flashbacks of things he'd forced me to do, degrading things that made me feel sick and filthy.

"You think I'm not a real man?" Achelous moved closer to us and the tiger growled low in her throat. I, for one, thought it was one of the scariest sounds I'd ever heard. "You want some memories to remind you of how much of a man I was with you, Gloriana?"

"Having sex with unwilling women doesn't make you a man. It's called rape." That earned me gasps from the sisters. Oh, yeah, I was on a roll. I had no idea if I was being brave or stupid.

"I don't have to rape women, they want me." He reached up to unpin the shoulder of his toga and let it drop to the ground. Of course he was built. Does the term Greek god ring a bell? But looks aren't everything. This guy was as hollow as a chocolate Easter bunny. Achelous didn't even register on my lust-o-meter.

"I don't know." I turned to the gathered sisters who were practically gripping Circe's skirt, all except Aggie, who was still stuck behind Achelous like a piece of garden statuary.

I'd have to do something about that. "Show of hands. Who really wants or likes to do it with Achelous?" Hmm. Every one of the Sirens stared down at her designer shoes, her perfectly manicured hands clutched in front of her.

"Damn them." Achy looked back at Aggie. "What if I make them all hate water like I did you, Gloriana? How does that feel? I saw Aglaophonos dragging you across the lake. Sirens live to be in the sea."

"It was mean, the kind of dirty trick only a man who needs to prove his power would do." I smiled. "Having power issues, Achy?" I almost missed the tiny sign that I had hit a nerve.

"You must have a death wish, woman." Achelous gave me a long look and the wind picked up, blowing cold against my wet clothes. Laurie pressed against me with another growl.

"You thought to kill me once." I figured he would kill me now and waited for the end, calm and surprisingly accepting. This was probably for the best. Jerry would find a woman better for him—please let it not be Mara. Ray would write songs and find a lover who would give him her whole heart. And Rafe. I gripped Laurie's fur. I hoped she would look after him. They would be good together.

"And yet you still live." Achelous released Aggie and she ran to join the rest of the sisters. "To hell with this tug-of-war. I'll give the women to you on one condition, Circe."

"It seems that I already have them. But I'll humor you. I'd like to keep this out of Zeus's court if we could." Circe patted Aggie's shoulder as she slipped into place. "What are your terms?"

"I want a few moments alone with Gloriana." Achelous stared at me and I stared back. What fresh hell did he have in store for me? Laurie paced, obviously against the idea.

"Why?" Circe didn't mince words and I could hear the sisters murmuring. I caught enough to realize they were all for throwing me to the wolf. Anything to get them away from the big bad.

"What do you care?" Achelous picked up his toga and pinned it on again. "She is merely a vampire, after all."

"You're right." Circe nodded. "The tiger will leave as well."

That earned a growl but Laurie was obviously under orders. She disappeared along with the group of women and I was suddenly alone with Achelous. Merely a vampire. Guess that made me bottom of the food chain.

The rain had stopped and there was only a distant rumble of thunder and the drip of water from the surrounding trees to remind me of the storms his temper had unleashed. I looked down and saw that my wounds were almost healed. I thought about shifting out of there, but I doubted Achelous would let me get very far.

"Well, you've got me alone. Are you trying to decide how to kill me?" I made it back to my boulder and sat, well and truly drained from what I'd been through.

"If only I could." Achelous strode over to sit on the rock closest to mine as if ready to chat. "Don't even think about taking off. I could easily find you now that I know you are still on this planet and not dust."

"Good to know." I looked up at the night sky. My last night? Well then. "Wait a minute. You can't kill me? Why not? Seems like you did the next best thing, kicking me out of the harem like that. If it wasn't for Jerry, I'd have been dead centuries ago."

"Yes, but not by my hand. It was my clever way of getting rid of you without actually doing the deed directly, you see." Achelous glanced up at the sky too. Looking for eavesdroppers? "Not clever enough. Because here you are, damn you."

"Get to the point, Achy. Why can't you kill me?" Was I crazy? I should just be glad someone had put limits on this megalomaniac and figure out a way to disappear while I had the chance.

"Did you ever wonder where Sirens come from, Gloriana?" He said the words conversationally.

"Uh, no. I guess I figured they were like all creatures that go bump in the night. They just are. No one tries to explain Olympus or the kind of action you just put me through. Hell, even vampires are the stuff of nightmares and fairy tales."

Achelous laughed. "Nightmares indeed. Gods, I couldn't believe it when you showed up with Aglaophonos after centuries. It was like a cruel joke."

"Yeah, it was really funny how you left me in the mortal world with no memories or resources." I really hated the man's arrogance.

"Without resources?" Before I could stop him, he grabbed my hand. His fingers were warm, almost hot. I guess from tossing around lightning bolts. Was he revving up for more torture? I snatched my hand back and saw sparks fly but he let me get away with it. I did try to read his mind but hit a stone wall.

"If I had any resources, I sure don't remember them."

"Gloriana, I left you your Siren's beauty and body, though I couldn't resist adding a little extra in a few places." He laughed when I looked down at my hips. "A god's got to have some fun. I planted memories for you of a mortal family too, religious zealots. How did you like that?"

"Glad you could amuse yourself." Bastard. I sent this mental message but he just grinned.

"Before I'd been away from you for more than a human fortnight you had a man taking care of you, in love with you." Achelous quit smiling. "Mortal fool."

"My husband." I remembered the young actor who'd taken me off the streets and adored me. But he'd died so soon and of a freak accident. Or had it been an accident? My heart seemed to roll over in my chest and I felt sick. "Did you kill him?"

"Naturally. You were supposed to suffer, Gloriana." Achelous's eyes were cold as they swept over me.

How easily he spoke of taking an innocent man's life. I

felt chilled and wanted to slap his face. I came to my senses but couldn't hold my tongue. "All this because I didn't have the stomach for the killing? Is that the acid test for you?"

"Of course!" He jumped up. "As soon as I was satisfied that you were alone and starving I really did leave you to your fate. I had no idea Circe took a hand in things after that and sent you a vampire to make you immortal." He looked down at me and shook his head. "I couldn't believe my eyes when I saw you here, by this lake, still alive hundreds of years later. Meddling bitch."

"I'm glad Circe got the better of you. She saved me and now she's taking your Sirens away from you. What you did to me proves you're not fit to have them, Achelous." I felt his power wash over me as he frowned down at me. The hairs on my arms stood on end and the wind began to howl. "You going to strike me down for telling it like it is?" I braced myself.

"I probably could kill you now and get away with it. The Siren part of you has been polluted by your years as a blood sucker. God, you even have fangs." He stepped back and raked me with a look that should have incinerated me. But he was holding back for some reason.

"Polluted? Thanks a heap. Yes, I'm vampire. I won't apologize for that. And you're a god who can manipulate people as you wish. What you did to me . . ." I turned to look out over the lake. "Do you know I can't bear to even stick my toe in that water without fear?" I looked at him. "And I can't sing a simple song and stay in tune." I sighed. "You already killed some of the best parts of me, Achelous."

Achelous threw out his hand and shot lightning at the nearest tree. It broke in two and burst into flames. He towered over me and for a minute I wondered if he was about to finish the job. I gritted my teeth, fangs down, thinking that I'd sink them into his neck and make him bleed before I'd stand here and just take it.

"Zeus's armpit, but you've turned into a disgusting hag.

I blame it on your living in the mortal world for so long. Remember this." Achelous rested his hands on my shoulders and I felt electricity sizzle through my body in an excruciating arc. Smoke actually came out of my toes and I could smell my hair burning. "You are a daughter of Olympus. That and only that has bought you your life tonight."

My teeth clicked together and it was a moment before I could speak. When I finally managed a breath, I tried to jerk away from him.

"What do you mean?" The sky was full of roiling clouds and I shivered in the chill wind.

Achelous suddenly shoved me away, his own legs firmly planted in the sand. He was the picture of strong male and utterly merciless. "I've said enough. Get the hell out of here before I decide to take my chances and end you now, Gloriana."

I scrambled to put more distance between us. "Okay then. And thanks. For kicking me to the curb." Before he could decide to fry me with another lightning bolt, I pulled together what little strength I had left and shifted into bird form. Then I flew out of there as fast as my wings could carry me.

I kept expecting to be shot out of the sky, well-done before I hit the ground. Instead, I actually made it across the lake and landed not far from Ray's house in the woods near the shore. I spotted my tiger friend prowling the grounds.

"You okay?" Laurie shifted and stood beside me while I got back to human form. It took me a while because I was at pretty low tide on the energy scale.

"Okay? Um, let me check. In one piece. Yes. Still sizzling. Kind of. Achy did a number on me but he let me live. All in all it was pretty intense." I smiled at her. "Thanks for coming to the rescue." I felt my hair and came away with some pieces that were toasted. I was obviously going to need a trim before I traveled anywhere.

"You handled it pretty well on your own. And, I'm sorry I abandoned you, but I was under orders I had to obey. I felt hor-

rible leaving you there." She clapped me on the back so hard I
staggered. "Let me make it up to you. Ray says you're headed
out of town. Need backup?"

"No, I'm good. Did he send you? Across the lake?"

"No, he never heard a thing. Too into his music. Circe
called me. I left Will in charge of Ray and took off." Laurie
shrugged. "Guess you must have figured out that I'm hers to
command. I don't exactly advertise that fact so keep it to
yourself."

"Sure. We all have secrets. Keep an eye on Ray while I'm
gone, will you?" I sighed, the idea of flying back to my apartment absolutely exhausting.

"Glad to. And if you want a ride tonight, I've got a car
parked a block away." She grinned. "Yes, I read your thoughts.
Come on."

When we were in the car, Laurie glanced over at me. "You
look terrible and you lost a lot of blood. I never saw anything
like what Achelous did to you, Glory. Stabbed with lightning. Ouch."

"Yeah. It wasn't exactly a walk in the park." I sighed and
leaned back in the seat.

"You're drained." She held out her wrist. "Here. Help
yourself."

"Are you kidding me?" I had to admit my fangs had been
down since I'd landed next to her. Hot shifter blood.

"I can take it. Got to warn you, my stuff is high-octane."
Laurie grinned. "It'll rev your engine."

"Then I'm not saying no." I picked up her wrist and took
a whiff. Hello. "Promise to pull me off if I get carried away."

"You got it." Laurie didn't even blink when I sank my
fangs into her vein.

Oh, sweet Heaven but she'd been right. High-octane and
I could feel the power flowing into me with each swallow. It
was a matter of will to ease away from that fountain and lick
the punctures closed. Were-tiger. And plugged into Olympus. Oh, yeah, there was something extra here.

"Thanks." I sighed with contentment as Laurie started her car and headed to Sixth Street.

"No problem. You really let Achelous have it tonight. Watching you two go at it, I admired your guts." She laughed. "Or figured you were suicidal."

"I was just really, really steamed. I kept having these flashbacks, seeing the things I'd had to do with him, for him, horrible things." I shuddered. "No woman should have to live like that. The Sirens were abused for too long."

Laurie nodded. "Circe says there's a Siren treasure. You did work for Achelous for a thousand years and change. Seems like that should have earned you a little compensation. Not promising anything, those gods and goddesses do like their gold, but you might have something coming to you later. The wheels of justice will turn slowly and Zeus will have to pry it out of Achy's hands, you know. But Circe says she's going to try to get you a little severance pay."

"No kidding? Thank her for me."

"She owes you, Glory. You don't think she took the Sirens on because of girl power, do you?" Laurie smiled wryly. "It was all about the gold."

"Wow. So Achelous . . . ?"

"He'll be after some of it as reparation. The Olympus CPAs will be very busy over this whole deal."

"Interesting." I sighed. "Well, if a little of it comes my way, I'll be thrilled but obviously I won't hold my breath. Thanks for letting me know. And thanks for the backup." I hugged Laurie when she let me out at the apartment building. When I got upstairs I had a visitor waiting.

Aggie sat on the top step. "Girlfriend, that was some tough talk you pulled out of your ass tonight." She jumped up and threw her arms around me. "The sisters sent me to tell you we're in your debt."

"Hey, glad I could help. I had some things to get off my chest anyway." I unlocked the apartment door. "Come in. You think Circe will be okay as a fearless leader?"

"I guess. Remains to be seen. I'm not putting a whole lot of trust in anyone who hangs their hat in Olympus, you know what I'm sayin'?" Aggie shrugged. "We're all more than a little freaked-out now that we know we can lose our song and the sea, like you did. As a punishment, it's a living death, you know?"

"I don't know. That's the only thing Achy did right, wiping my memory. I can't mourn what I didn't realize I had." I settled on the couch, still jazzed from Laurie's donation but itching with the need for a shower.

"You going to share what the private convo with Achy was about? We're dying to know." Aggie made herself comfortable in the chair across from me.

"No big deal. He just wanted a couple of last words. Like he said. He popped me a few times with lightning too. Just to make sure I knew who was a god and who was a lowly vampire." I wasn't about to get into this with Aggie. Not tonight. A daughter of Olympus. Did that mean I had a mother somewhere? A goddess? The very idea made my head hurt.

"Well, you look like the last words were 'Die, bitch.'" Aggie got up and patted my shoulder. "I'll leave you to shower and do whatever vampires do to recover. Jump a mortal in an alley or whatever."

"I have synthetic blood if I need it." I walked her to the door. "I'm heading to Scotland soon. Going to tell Jerry he's not my victim and see what happens. Wish me luck."

"Sure. Go get your man." Aggie grinned. "Me? There's lots of fish in the sea. Speaking of . . . If you ever want to get over that water phobia, look me up. I'll start you off in the shallow end of a pool. Sorry about that rough trip across the lake before. I was a little, um, nervous about the confab with Achelous and Circe."

"I get it. But I won't forget it." I was wet and felt like I had lake creatures in my bra as I said good-bye to Aggie. One thing I did pull out was Ian's note to Jerry. I tossed it on my dresser. Maybe it was for the best if it arrived illegible. I didn't really trust Ian to pass a love note to the Campbells.

I was getting undressed and examining my various wounds when I heard the familiar chime that meant I had a text. Alesa giving me an update:

Beelzebub and LuLu born 12pm Sat. C.U. Mama A.

Two more demons in hell. I wondered how they celebrated. Had Alesa enjoyed a baby shower? Was there a maternity ward in hell's hospital? I knew I couldn't worry about the two little ones and that "C.U.," which must mean "See you." Waste of energy. Demons were unpredictable and uncontrollable.

I jumped into the shower. If tonight had done nothing else, it had taught me that I was tougher than I'd ever imagined. Hey, I'd taken on the Storm God and survived, by damn. If I could do that, I could certainly handle a little trip by myself to a foreign country. Because I was going. On my own with no help from anyone. Of course, what I'd find when I got there was anyone's guess.

Maybe it was the were-tiger blood I'd downed that made me feel pumped and ready to take on anything. Or maybe it was the idea that I was a daughter of Olympus, whatever the hell that meant. But Glory St. Clair was on her way to Scotland. The guys in kilts had better watch out.

Dear Reader,

I had such fun revisiting some favorite characters in *Real Vampires Hate Skinny Jeans*. To read more about Lucky Carver and the night she turned Israel Caine into a vampire, you can check out *Real Vampires Get Lucky*. And then there's Aggie, the Siren, who really got Ray and Glory into trouble in *Real Vampires Don't Diet*.

I hope you enjoyed this chapter in Glory's life and will hang in there with me for her next exciting adventure as she journeys to Scotland. You didn't think she was going to give up on Jerry, did you? Keep reading to find the first chapter of book nine in the Real Vampires series. I hope you enjoy it.

To keep up with Glory and for sneak peeks at future releases, go to my Web site at www.gerrybartlett.com and sign up for my newsletter. You can also follow me on Twitter or go to my author page on Facebook. I hope to see you there! Thanks for jumping into the world of Real Vampires.

Sincerely,
Gerry Bartlett

Read on for a special preview of
Gerry Bartlett's next novel

Real Vampires Know Hips Happen

Available March 2013 from Berkley Books!

I couldn't get out of the car. Ridiculous. I was a badass vampire. I knew this place, had been here a hundred times or more. Sure, not all of them had been good times, but at least I'd had Jerry by my side. Now Castle Campbell in all its ruined beauty was just yards away, and I felt the determination that had carried me across an ocean and several countries drain right out of me.

I had to smile, though, when I noticed the laird had let the National Trust open the place to tourists at five pounds a pop. Not that the family of vampires cared what happened during the day in the stone fortress above their heads. The family would sleep like the dead in the luxurious quarters they'd built centuries ago belowground. It was dark now and the tourists were long gone, the tea and gift shop in the tower closed.

"Get out of the freaking car." I hit the plastic steering wheel. Talking to myself. Trying to screw up my courage. Because I wasn't supposed to be here. Jerry had asked for time. To think about our relationship. And had I given it to him? Of course not. Glory St. Clair worked on her own timetable. And right now I needed, desperately, to see my man and explain some things to him. But actually sitting here, staring at the castle where centuries ago his mother had treated me like a whore her son had dragged home, had brought me crashing back to reality.

Maybe Jerry would be better off without me. I was a freak. Not who or what he'd thought he'd fallen for all those years ago. He deserved better. For once, his mother and I agreed. I sagged against the car window. What had I been *thinking*?

A knock on the glass next to me made me jump. My vamp instincts sucked if I could be surprised like that. I rolled down the window. El cheapo rental car didn't even have power windows.

"Aren't you coming in?" Jeremy Blade, Jeremiah Campbell III, my sire, whatever you wanted to call him, smiled at me.

"Do you want me to?"

His answer was to jerk open the door and haul me into his arms. "How can you ask that? Do you have any idea how much I've missed you?" He buried his face in my neck and just inhaled. In vamp terms that was the equivalent of the "Hallelujah" chorus.

"I was supposed to give you some thinking time." I murmured this against the soft wool of his plaid, carelessly thrown over a cotton shirt. I inhaled him too, soaking in the dear, achingly familiar scent of male and Jerry that I craved with everything in me.

"I shouldn't have taken off like that. You needed me." He leaned back and looked into my eyes. "God, but I'm sorry." He kissed me then, making sure I knew just how much he cared. Tears pricked my eyelids, but I wasn't about to let them fall and ruin this moment. My gamble had paid off. And things would only get better once Jerry knew the truth about how we'd met and fallen in love.

I smiled as he pulled back. "I have so much to tell you."

"No kidding. Like how you managed to cross the Atlantic." He glanced at my rental car and dismissed it as unworthy. "I would have sent a plane for you, Gloriana."

"The details about my trip can wait. I have big news for you, Jer." I held on to him, so glad to finally be with him, because the trip had been harrowing and not the lighthearted adventure I'd paint for him when I got around to sharing. I'm always on a budget and the death sleep makes travel complicated. Enough said.

"Come inside, lass. Mara had just arrived when the servants spotted you on the security cameras. She claims to have big news too." Jerry tugged me toward the family quarters and the heavy wooden and iron door hidden behind clever landscaping.

"Mara." Not my favorite person. She'd always wanted Jerry for herself.

"You can be nice to her for five minutes. Then we can be alone." Jerry gave me such a brilliant smile I had to stop him in the doorway and kiss him again.

"Are you sure we can't slip away into the pasture for a real reunion instead? I remember a time or two . . ."

My lover laughed. "Or twenty. Not yet. Da is inside and eager to greet you. He always did love you, you know. My mother is in Paris, so you can relax on that score. And we'll make sure Mara is sent on her way quickly." Jerry slid one hand around my waist and the other up to investigate my plunging neckline. "Very quickly."

"See that you do." I sighed as he kissed me again, lingering over it as his hands explored me. I'd stopped in the village of Dollar down the hill from the castle and booked a room so I could freshen up before I came here. I wore a low-cut sweater in his favorite blue with a skirt that showed off my legs and distracted from my hips. I pulled back and glanced around. "Where are the security cameras? Are we giving some worker a thrill?"

Jerry nodded toward a dark corner of the doorway. "Afraid so. Da's outfitted the entire area with cameras, sensors. He's big on security, and you know how the clan is about the feud with the MacDonalds."

"Don't start." I held up my hand. "Let's get this deal with Mara over with. Then we can be alone."

"I'm with you there." He pulled me into the large living area, where his father sat talking with Mara, the widow of Jerry's best friend.

"Well, now, it *was* Gloriana. Welcome to the castle, lass. Mara, look who's here." The laird, Angus Jeremiah Campbell II, got up to hug me, then led me to the couch to face Mara. We exchanged wintry smiles. As usual, she was dressed expensively to show off her slim figure. She had the dark red hair, pale skin and altogether perfect looks of a true Scottish lass. I was the epitome of a blond, blue-eyed Englishwoman. Or I'd always thought of myself that way. It had marked me an outsider when I'd first arrived on Jerry's arm.

Angus asked me questions about my trip, and I answered in a general way. Apparently Jerry hadn't told his father about the problems between us that had sent him home this time. I sure wasn't going to bring them up.

"Well, Mara. Jerry says you have big news." I wanted to move things along.

"I do." She smiled shyly and glanced at Jerry, then held out her left hand. The huge diamond on her ring finger should have given us all a clue. "I'm getting married."

"Wow. Just wow. Who's the lucky guy?" I sat down on a love seat, happy when Jerry sat next to me, his hard thigh snug against mine.

"Davy McLeod. You know him, Jeremiah. He says you two used to race horses together at Newmarket." Mara stared down at her ring and actually looked happy.

"Sure. Davy's a good man." Jerry picked up my hand. I had a feeling he was thinking that I'd never accepted a ring from him.

"A fine clan, the McLeods. Allies in times of war. Not like those backstabbing MacDonalds." The laird got up and kissed Mara's cheek. "Well done, lass. Well done. I wish you happy."

"And you, Jeremiah. Do you wish me happy?" Mara stood and the gentleman in him got Jerry to his feet instantly.

"Of course. If you want this and love the man, have at it." Jerry put his hands on her shoulders. "But if you need money or feel pressured for any other reason . . . Well, you are my daughter's mother. I will always make sure you are cared for."

"How thoughtful." Mara stared up at him, and for a moment I saw the bitter twist to her mouth that told the true story. She'd always wanted Jerry for herself. But she realized now that she couldn't make him love her and had apparently decided to cut her losses. This McLeod obviously had the bucks and was a decent guy if the laird approved of him. Knowing Mara, she'd already run him through his paces in the sack as well. I kept my mouth shut. I knew anything I had to say would be unwelcome at this point.

"You know you and I . . ." Jerry glanced back at me, then shook his head. He leaned down to kiss Mara's cheek. "Be happy."

"Of course. Will you walk me to the door? Help me with my cloak?" She smiled and smoothed her designer skirt.

"Certainly." Jerry proffered his arm in the courtly manner of centuries past.

I couldn't sit still. Something about this whole show seemed off to me. Mara was being docile, almost robotic. Where was the fiery woman who would have at least made a cutting remark to me? Instead, she'd treated me like I was invisible. Which was an improvement but so not like her. She should have been gloating, bragging about the rich, handsome husband she'd captured. Even waved that rock under my nose. I was steps behind the pair as they reached the door to the outside.

"I shifted here and will shift away again. I'll be all right. Davy's waiting for me in the village." Mara let Jerry help her with her long cloak. The Kilpatrick plaid, of course. Once she married, she'd start wearing the McLeod colors. She'd gone back to her original clan when she'd been made a widow. Everyone in this country seemed to wear their plaids like a badge. Jerry had on his kilt and looked a treat. Even the laird was lounging in his plaid in front of his big-screen TV, which he'd just turned on. *CSI* was starting. The man loved blood any way he could find it.

"Be careful." Jerry settled Mara's long cape over her shoulders and fastened it at her neck.

"Always." Suddenly a knife appeared in her hand. "Too late for you." She plunged it into his chest.

"Jerry, my God! Angus! Help!" I lunged toward her as Mara lifted the knife again. Jerry had grabbed her arm, but she'd obviously wounded him seriously with the first blow because he dragged her down to the floor with him, then slumped, seemingly unresponsive.

I jumped on Mara and wrestled the knife out of her hands to toss it away. Then I pulled her off of him and shoved her to the stone floor, where she struggled like a madwoman, scratching and hitting at me.

"Stop it! What the hell are you doing?" I slapped her face and her eyes widened, like she was coming out of a daze.

"What? Get off of me!" She looked over to where Jerry lay in a pool of his own blood. "Jeremiah? Who did this to you? Gloriana! Did you hurt him?"

"No, you stupid bitch. You stabbed him. How can you deny it?" I climbed off of her and thrust her into Angus's arms, then dropped to my knees next to Jerry. "Jerry, can you hear me?"

When he didn't answer me, I got frantic, searching him for other injuries. There was only the one wound, though, and it was relatively minor, for a vampire, and had already stopped bleeding. I pressed my hand to his heart and felt the slow, steady thump. Of course, he was alive, but why wasn't he stirring? I felt my own heart in my throat as the hall filled with men and noise.

"What happened here?" Angus held on to Mara. "Lass, what's this about?"

She sobbed and leaned against him. "I don't know. I don't know. There was a knife. I only remember the knife. Someone gave me a knife. Outside."

"Witchcraft. You were spelled." Angus gestured at the men who'd gathered when he had sounded the alarm. A few murmured questions and hard looks at Mara confirmed my version of what happened. Obviously the security cameras had caught the whole attack. "Outside, search the grounds. Who gave you the knife? What did this person look like?"

"I don't know." Mara shook her head. "A woman. Old, I think, not sure. Face covered. Stayed in the dark. I—I couldn't help myself." She collapsed on the floor next to Jerry. "What have I done?"

"Well, you haven't killed him. Lucky for you, or I'd put that knife into your heart and rip it out of your skinny body." I cradled Jerry's head in my lap. "Come on, Jerry, please wake up." Why had he lost consciousness? The knife had gone in between two ribs but hadn't hit his heart.

Yes, he'd bled a lot and would need to feed, but I'd be more than happy to take care of that. Jerry was strong and healthy. This kind of stab wound shouldn't even have dropped him. I heard Mara blubbering and wanted to slap her silent. Witchcraft? Not sure I was buying it, but something was off about this.

"Careful with that knife. It may have poison on it." That was the only explanation I could come up with for Jerry's condition. The servant who'd been about to pick up the weapon jumped away from it.

"Poison." Angus stared at Mara. "Are you sure you don't remember who gave it to you?" He shook her, not too hard, but as if he wanted to make sure she was truly aware of her surroundings. "Speak up, girl. You just stabbed my son. No lies now. Why did you try to kill Jeremiah?"

"I don't know, Laird. I feel like . . ." She rubbed her forehead. "I need Davy. Can you call him for me? I only remember a woman, all in black. She gave me the knife and told me what to do. I didn't want to do it. But I couldn't seem to help myself. Like you said. I was bewitched." She stared up at Angus with her bright green eyes, almost feverish now. "He's not going to die, is he?"

"He'd better not." I couldn't look at her as I ran my hand over Jerry's strong jaw and the slight roughness of his beard, there no matter how often he shaved. To my relief he moaned and his eyes fluttered open. He stared up at me for a moment, then glanced around the hallway before focusing on me again.

"Jerry, are you all right? How do you feel?" I leaned closer, willing him to say something.

"Like I took a knife in my gut. But if you're offering to feed me back to health, lass, then I reckon I'll be up and about in no time." He grinned and slid a hand to the back of my head to draw my neck down to his mouth. I saw his fangs descend.

"Here? On this cold stone floor? Let's get you cleaned up and moved to your bed." I tried to pry his fingers off of me, but he wasn't ready to let go. "Come on, Jer. This is ridiculous. I'll feed you. But not here." I glanced at his father and Mara, who kept staring at us.

"Tell her, Da. The lass seems reluctant. But you paid her well, didn't you? I need to feed, so I can go after whatever bastard stuck me." Jerry jerked me close again.

"Wait!" I put my hands on his chest and shoved. "Look at me." I bit my lip, terribly afraid that I knew what was wrong. "Jeremiah Campbell, just who do you think I am?"

"Your name? No notion. But you're comely enough and your blood smells like fine wine, damned if it doesn't." He sniffed the air, but his smile faltered when he pressed a hand to his chest. "Bloody hell, but that hurts. Let's get on with it, lass. Quit playing coy and do your duty." He struggled as he tried to sit up, then looked at his father. "Da, was it the MacDonalds again? Tell William to saddle Thunder and

we'll ride out as soon as I've healed. We'll teach them to attack us inside our own home."

Angus didn't answer, just nodded at me to allow his son
to drink. As if I'd deny him. So I let Jerry pull me close until
his fangs pierced my neck. He drew deep and I closed my eyes
before I slipped my hands up to cling to his silky hair. I sat
on the cold stone floor in his father's castle, the man drinking
my blood holding me as if we were strangers. Jerry, my sire,
the love of my life, didn't know me. What was I going to do?